For my families -

The one I was lucky enough to be born into
and the one I was lucky enough to be chosen by

In the Footsteps of Shadows

Prologue

The man ran blindly down the dark alley, rubbing furiously at his eyes as the sweat poured down his face and blurred his vision. The blood pounded in his ears as fear and adrenalin spurred him on, desperately hoping he had managed to lose them in the maze of streets.

He pressed himself up against the wall as he reached the end of the alleyway, forcing himself to stop and calm his breathing before he peered cautiously out into the square. No movement that he could see, hopefully a good thing. He summoned his courage and stepped out into the shadows, hugging the walls as he crept on, his eyes darting about as groups of drunk tourists appeared from smoky bars along his way.

Not much further now, he allowed himself to think as the road where he had left her appeared before him. Just a couple of hundred feet more and they...

His blood ran cold as he spotted the car and he broke into a run. Please, God, let her just be hidden, he thought as he got closer. Maybe she had realised what was going on and gone into one of the bars? He reached the car and stared into it, searching the seats front and back before running his hands through his hair in a panic, spinning around in the street as he tried to work out where she would go.

Suddenly he heard a muffled cry from across the street and moved towards it cautiously, his heart in his throat. He peered down the dark passage and moved forward quickly, holding his hands out in front of him to show the heavyset man holding a gun to his wife's head that he was no threat.

"Please," he said, willing his voice not to crack. "Let her go. I have money. I'm reaching for my wallet."

"I don't want your money, cabron," the gunman said, pushing the muzzle tighter against her head with a cruel smile. "Where's the book?"

"What book? Here, look," he said, opening up his wallet. "There's...three hundred dollars in here. Just take it and let her go."

He sucked in a breath as a sharp object was pushed into the small of his back and he felt hot breath on his ear. "It would be unwise to lie to us at this juncture I think," a soft voice said as he was forced further along the passage. "You and your wife have no need to die in a filthy place such as this. Just give us the book."

"Don't do it," his wife said quickly before her captor slapped his hand over her mouth, smacking the butt of his gun into her temple.

"You son of a bitch!" he swore, lurching towards them before his legs were kicked out and he landed painfully on his knees, a knife pressing into the soft flesh of his throat.

"Your wife is as stubborn as you are, I see," the soft voice said again.

He turned as best he could to look up and see who he was dealing with. The man was nothing much to look at, medium height, short black hair, olive skin, the same runner's build that he had himself. He could probably take him if it came to that, but there was something about his eyes...

"You are thinking you have a chance of fighting your way out of this," he chuckled as he knelt down in front of him, the knife held loosely in his hand. "Maybe you have. Maybe your wife will catch my friend over there off guard and take his gun. Maybe the two of you will kill us and escape. But I ask you, is it really worth it when you could just give us the book?"

"You're damn right it would be worth it," he spat, locking eyes with his wife. "But I don't have this book you're so interested in so get the fuck out of my way and let us go."

"You are really willing to give up your life for this," the man sighed as he stood up and put away his knife. "What about your daughter's life?"

"What?" he whispered, his heart almost stopping in his chest.

"I am bored," he said suddenly. "Now, we both know that you do have it, just tell me where it is and we can be on our way. Your daughter can carry on with her life and everything will be fine. Or, you can continue to lie about it, I will kill you, then your wife," he pulled his gun out quickly and pointed it behind him. "And then I will give the order for my associates in New York to take your daughter and do...hmm, whatever they feel appropriate. Is this what you want?"

He sat down heavily and ran his hands through his hair. What choice did he have? The man could be lying but what if he wasn't? Could he really take that risk? He looked up at his wife and saw the answer reflected back in her eyes.

"Alright," he said in defeat. "I'll take you to it."

Chapter 1

Maya stepped off the boat and turned her eyes to the hills rising above the town, her fingers pulling gently on the worn pendant around her neck. In the fading light, she could just about make out the aged ramparts of Fortín Solano and she allowed herself a brief moment to believe that tomorrow she would find what she had come here for. Moving carefully through the throng of tourists crowding the harbour, she made her way towards the old town, a small smile dancing on her lips. Of course it wouldn't be that easy - where would be the fun in that?

She pulled the crumpled piece of paper out of her pocket and adjusted the pack on her back as she re-read the directions Claudia had sent her earlier. It felt good to be back out on the road at last, putting her research to the test and walking through the places she'd been reading about for weeks. This was the place Claudia had picked for them to meet, though really - Café de la Música? Not exactly what she had in mind. Still, it served alcohol, she was in Venezuela - how bad could it be?

She got her answer ten minutes later when she pushed through the door, her senses immediately assaulted by the sound and vision of a blonde chick with a diamante headband flailing about on a stage and absolutely murdering a Heart song. Maya literally stopped in her tracks halfway into the building as the 'notes' the woman was producing rang in her ears, causing her eye to twitch as her brain tried to process what was happening.

"Every second of the night…" she screeched. "I live another life…"

"Jesus, Claudia," she muttered as she scanned the bar for her friend, murder on her mind in more ways than one. Squaring her shoulders and silently praying to be stricken with a temporary hearing disorder, she let the door close behind her and crossed the dusty floor in only a few steps to get to the bar.

"Hola," Maya shouted over the 'music' to the grimacing bartender. "Tequila, por favor, y una cerveza."

He nodded and moved about the bar, glancing up at the stage occasionally and muttering to himself with a shake of his head. Maya dropped her pack on the floor and took another look around the place. It was small, kind of rustic, and made the most of the available space. The decor was predominantly dark and wooden, brightened by strands of twinkling lights hanging from the ceiling, reminding her of her loft back home, although with an infinitely worse soundtrack. There were only a few people in the bar, none of whom were Claudia: the demented blonde on stage, a small group who were obviously with her, judging by their raucous applause and laughter, and an oblivious local, passed out on his stool at the bar. Maya idly wondered if his comatose state was booze-related, or if it had been induced by a sheer desperation to be free of this cacophony.

"Gracias," she murmured to the bartender when he returned with her drinks. She immediately raised the shot to her lips and knocked it back gratefully before picking up her beer with a glare at the stage. The bartender chuckled and poured himself a shot, holding the glass towards her with a smile and another shake of his head. She clinked his glass and chuckled as he knocked the drink back.

"Diabla," he muttered towards the stage, shuffling away.

Maya smirked at his assessment and pulled out her phone, cursing Claudia's name under her breath as she did so. Sure enough, there was the message informing her that her friend was running late. Of course.

"Hi there!"

Maya glanced up at the blonde leaning on the bar next to her, waving enthusiastically at the bartender.

"Could I get another two beers, two margaritas and a Coke please?"

She was wearing a bright turquoise sundress and large round sunglasses, and she was cute, in a Reese Witherspoon sort of way, and Maya was absolutely not drunk enough to deal with her overtly cheerful manner. She was also obviously with the banshee onstage, which was frankly not a point in her favour. She turned to look at Maya and flashed her a dazzling smile before tilting her head slightly, scrunching her eyes up in a curious, searching expression.

"Hi," she said. "Have we met?"

"No entiendo. No habla inglés," Maya muttered with a dismissive shake of her head, snapping her eyes back down to her phone as someone else stepped up next to the blonde

"Oh my God!" the newcomer hissed. "I thought we agreed not to let her sing!"

Maya risked a glance up at this piece of information. Another woman, this one shorter, brunette, gorgeous in an off-beat sort of way, was looking between the annoyed bartender and the stage with an expression of flustered anger.

"I'm sorry!" Reese Witherspoon answered quickly. "The minute you went to the restroom, she just jumped up there! I tried to stop her, but she wouldn't listen, and you know how the guys just encourage her…"

"God," the brunette said tersely, pressing a hand to her forehead. "I love Vanessa, but honestly, her voice is like blasphemy."

Maya bit back a laugh as she reached for her drink, carefully observing the newcomer in the dusty mirror behind the bar. She looked stricken by the actions of her friend and the way she kept covering her mouth with her hand in embarrassment only served to draw attention to her expensive manicure and the discreetly tasteful bling that graced her hand and wrist. Over privileged American girls were not something that usually caught her attention, but there was something different about this one…

"Lo siento, señor, mi amiga es mala," the brunette said to the bartender, placing a hand on her heart in a universal gesture of apology.

"Sí," he replied, placing their margaritas on the bar with a nod. "A veces lloro de lo mal que canta."

Maya almost choked on her drink at the exchange, coughing into her hand in a less than successful attempt to control her laughter and almost slipping off her chair as she turned away. When she had recovered herself enough to look back up the bartender winked conspiratorially at her and she grinned at him as he finished pouring the beers, placing them on the bar with a flourish before taking the brunette's money and walking off to ring up the round. Maya picked up her beer and took a sip of it, glancing to her left as she felt eyes on her. Reese Witherspoon was walking back towards her table with half the drinks but the other woman was staring at her curiously, so Maya cocked an eyebrow at her challengingly, surprised when she simply leaned on the bar and carried on staring, the corner of her mouth lifting in a small smirk.

"Gracias," the bartender said gruffly as he returned with her change, drawing the woman's attention so that Maya could thankfully return to her drink and the difficult task of ignoring the music.

"Lo siento," the brunette said again, nodding to the man as she picked up her drinks and walked away.

Thankfully, the song came to an end and the new-fallen silence in the bar was positively blissful. Maya let out a sigh of relief and finished her drink in peace, glancing out into the street in the hope that Claudia would appear before anyone else started singing.

After ordering another beer she looked up at the mirror to observe the small bar, filling up a little now that the evening was wearing on. Her gaze landed on the table by the stage, her fingers moving automatically to her pendant. They were all laughing and drinking, just a happy little group of tourists on vacation, enjoying a night out on the town. Everything she was not. She pulled her phone out again to check for news of Claudia and huffed in annoyance as she dialled her number and pressed the phone to her ear, her fingers tapping on the bar whilst she waited for her friend to pick up.

"Claudia," she hissed as the voicemail kicked in. "Get your ass here right now. I am not even joking. If you are not here in three and a half minutes, I swear to God I will take you out into the middle of the closest forest - which, by the way, is very close - and leave you tied to a tree. Fuck." She went to stab at the 'end' button and swore again when she missed.

"I thought you didn't speak English," said an amused voice from beside her. She looked up quickly, and saw the brunette standing beside her, waving at the bartender to get his attention.

"What can I say? I'm a fast learner," Maya muttered, stuffing the phone back into her pocket and staring out into the street. Still no sign of Claudia and she was starting to feel the effects of her long day of travelling. She stretched her arms out behind her and cracked her neck to shift some of the stiffness in her limbs, stifling a yawn as she leaned back on the bar.

"So, you here on vacation?" the woman asked her.

"Ah, yeah...something like that," she replied.

"Something like that? What does that mean? Work or play?"

"Can't it be both?" Maya replied with a smirk.

"Depends on the person, I guess," she said quietly, definitely catching Maya's attention now.

"And what about you?"

"What about me?"

"Are you here for work?" Maya asked, turning slightly to face her as she decided to see where this was going. "Or play?"

The woman dropped her elbow on the bar and turned towards her, her other hand resting on her hip. "What do you think?"

"I'm not sure," she admitted, narrowing her eyes as she tried to figure out what this chick's angle was.

"But I bet you'd love to find out," she laughed as she turned to collect her drinks from the bartender. "Gracias."

Maya's eyes flicked back up to the mirror to watch as the brunette headed back to her table. What the hell was that? Suddenly the door was thrown open by a group of wildly drunk guys in gaudy shirts, baggy shorts and flip flops. One in particular looked like he had been doused in lard and given a lounger three feet from the actual sun, and Maya would have felt sorry for him if he hadn't immediately fallen into her and knocked her drink to the floor.

"I'm sorry señorita…" he slurred in her general direction before his eyes focussed on her and went comically wide. "Wow, okay, really not sorry! You are all kinds of hot! Let me buy you another drink."

"Que te jodan," Maya snapped as she jumped away from her spilled drink and wiped the fluid from the front of her top.

"Was that a yes? I think that was a yes." Lobster man winked at his buddies as he raised his hand for a high five. "How about you and me get a bottle to go?" he leered at her as he sidled in closer.

"Ah, don't worry about that, she has a fresh drink over here," a voice spoke up as cool hand wrapped itself around her own. "Come on, we're just talking about the boat trip."

Maya felt her face melt from rage into confusion as she was led away from the bar, and the drunken letch she'd been about to do serious dental reconfiguration on, to be pushed gently down into a chair. She turned her head to shoot daggers at the asshole at the bar, fighting down an almost overwhelming urge to attack him with a real bladed weapon when she saw the lewd moves he was now performing for his friends, before her attention was fully captured by the hand still holding hers and the woman it belonged to.

"You alright?" she asked, her deep brown eyes scanning Maya's face, her smirk still in place.

"Better than he would have been if you hadn't pulled me out of there," she spat glaring back at the bar again. "Thanks, by the way."

"You're welcome," the brunette shrugged. "I kind of like this place and I didn't much feel like leaving so they could clean his guts off the floor."

"I don't think I would have actually eviscerated him," Maya scowled as she watched him argue with the bartender before being escorted out by his friends. "Maybe just broken his nose, a few ribs."

"I have no doubt," she laughed, reaching her perfectly manicured hand across the table. "I'm Rebecca, by the way."

"Maya," she smiled, shaking her hand quickly and leaning back in her chair as she searched for something to say. "So, you're going on a boat trip?"

"No."

"Oh," she frowned. "I thought…"

"Just an excuse to get you out of there," Rebecca smiled as she folded her arms on the table and leaned towards her. "But obviously I was right."

"Right about what?" Maya couldn't help asking.

"That you would love to find out what I'm here for," she replied with a wicked grin.

Maya fought to keep the smile off her face. No way was she letting this woman beat her at this game. She sat forward in her chair, mirroring the other woman's position and resting her elbows on the table. "Maybe I was just making polite conversation?"

"You don't exactly strike me as the type to make polite conversation," she chuckled softly, her voice barely above a whisper so that Maya found herself leaning closer to hear. Sneaky.

"Oh?" Maya asked, running her thumbnail lightly over her bottom lip and smirking slightly as Rebecca's eyes followed the movement. "And why is that?"

"Because the way you look you don't need to."

"Maya!" Claudia's breathless voice cut through the bar, breaking the atmosphere that had been building between them. "I'm ever so sorry. My flight was delayed and the bus I got took forever to get through, something about...well, you know my Spanish isn't that great."

Maya looked round to see her friend approaching, her shirt wrinkled from travel, her long, red hair dishevelled, her green eyes drooping with tiredness and her pale skin flushed with the heat. "About time you showed up," she muttered as she stood up to hug her. "You can't imagine the fun I've been having."

"I'm sure I can," she muttered back, shooting a glance at Rebecca. "But I swear to you, it wasn't my fault this time. Don't give me that look, Maya! It really wasn't." She started rooting through her bag, apparently having finished with her apologies, and wandered over to the bar, now thankfully devoid of drunkards. "Scusi? Hi? Un beer, por please? Two? Er, dos?"

Maya scrunched her face up in embarrassment as her friend effortlessly mangled her language without even a hint of an accent other than her own soft English one. How could they have been friends for so long and 'dos' was as good as it got? She smiled apologetically at Rebecca as she sat back down.

"So I guess you don't have to tie her to any trees now?" Rebecca asked, amusement twinkling in her eyes.

"Were you listening to my entire conversation?" Maya asked, eyes narrowing slightly.

"Sorry," she laughed, holding her hands up in admission. "Old habits."

"Oh really?" she said, raising an eyebrow as she rested her arm on the table and leaned forward again, totally intrigued by this woman now and deciding to play a little. "Let me guess. Spy?"

"Well, you know what they say. I could tell you…" Rebecca brushed her hair over her shoulder and stood up. "Anyway, now that the danger of you murdering drunk perverts has passed I suppose I should return to my friends and leave you to yours."

"Ah, yeah, sure." Maya replied, feeling a slight sense of disappointment. "Uh, thanks again. For you know, saving me and all."

"Something tells me you can handle yourself," she winked as she raised a hand in goodbye and walked back to rejoin her table.

With a sigh of irritation, Maya wandered over to her seat at the bar, 'accidentally' kicking her friend in the leg as she drew her feet back up onto the footrest.

"Ow!" Claudia cried.

"Sorry," she smirked, her mouth curling up into a proper smile when she spotted Rebecca glancing back at her in the mirror.

"What was that?" Claudia asked as she turned and placed a beer in front of her.

"What was what?" Maya shot back innocently as she picked up the drink.

"Don't play the innocent with me, Rodriguez. You are totally flirting with her."

"I flirt with everybody," she shrugged. "What of it?"

"Oh my God," Claudia chuckled. "You don't recognise her, do you?"

"What?" Maya narrowed her eyes at her friend before glancing discreetly back at the brunette. "Recognise her? Should I?"

"How much tequila did you have? That's Rebecca Bronstein."

"Who the fuck is Rebecca Bronstein?"

"God, Maya," Claudia rolled her eyes and gestured at the bartender. "When it gets to the stage you hate so many people you can't remember them all you need to have a word with yourself. Or start writing them down."

"Claudia…" she said, voice dangerously low.

"Alright, alright. Remember that couple? The ones who were always in the trade papers, then kept getting picked up by the national press? The 'Celebrity Tomb Raiders'?"

"God, I hate those guys." Maya scoffed, shaking her head as she did so. "They barely even found anything worthwhile and they just kept focussing attention on us when we could really do without it. God, and their daughter who was like some goody two shoes Ivy League wannabe but still found time to...no shit!" she swore, her eyes widening in alarm as she swivelled round in her chair so fast she almost fell off. "That's her? Oh my God, isn't she like sixteen?" she whispered, shooting a worried glance at her friend and feeling slightly ill.

"Um, no." Claudia laughed. "She was, when you decided you hated them all, but that was about eight years ago."

"Really? Wow." Maya scrunched up her nose and turned back to her drink. "Maybe I should keep a list. So where are the parents?"

"Are you serious? Do you read the newspaper? Like ever?"

"Why would I? Anything worth hearing you tell me," she shrugged.

"Ugh, you are exhausting." Claudia spat as she turned back to her drink. "They disappeared. About six months ago. They were out on an expedition and they just vanished. Rumour has it the daughter is trying to find them."

"Oh, God," Maya shook her head and stared down at her beer. "Well let's hope that's not what she's here for. The last thing we need is search parties scouting the area looking for her when she gets lost. I swear, people like them make it so much harder than it should be."

"But they also bring in more money."

"It's not about the money!" Maya slammed her drink down and turned to her friend. "It's about finding answers. It's about learning from the past to make a better future."

"Alright, okay. Indoor voice." Claudia said quietly, earning her a glare. "I know that, Maya, I do, and I agree with you. But you have to admit, a little money does make things easier."

"Yeah, well it depends on who provides the money, who uses it, and what their intentions are," she grumbled into her beer. "How many ancient sites have to be completely destroyed by these glory hunters before people learn that?"

"Okay, well, I think it's time we got some rest, don't you?" Claudia announced suddenly, throwing some money on the bar and waving at the old man as she pulled Maya up by her elbow and shoved her towards the door.

"What? But I'm not finished my beer!" Maya cried, spinning back to grab it from the bar and catching sight of Rebecca striding towards them. She turned back to her friend, eyes narrowed. "What's the matter with you?" she hissed. "Do you honestly think I'm going to pick a fight with her in the middle of the bar?"

"Honestly? Yes. Remember Ca.."

"If you say Cabo I will slap you." Maya held a finger up in warning. "That was a totally different situation, Claudia, don't you dare bring that up again."

"Going so soon?" Rebecca's voice rang out from behind her. "I was going to ask the two of you to join us for a drink."

"Oh, I don't think that would be such a good idea." Claudia smiled sweetly at her over Maya's shoulder. "Early start tomorrow, you know? Lots of sights to...see."

"Oh. Well okay then. Hopefully we'll see you around? It was nice to meet you...I'm sorry, I didn't get your name?" Rebecca reached around Maya and extended her hand.

"Claudia," Claudia smiled as she shook it. "And you are?"

"Rebecca," she said with an amused smile, looking at Claudia appraisingly before turning to Maya. "Nice talking to you, Maya, is it? Hopefully we'll meet again."

"Likewise," Maya smiled tightly. "You never did tell me why you're here?"

"That's right, I didn't," Rebecca replied, folding her arms and fixing her with a challenging look. "And neither did you."

"Well then I guess it will remain a mystery," she shot back, mimicking her stance.

"I guess it will."

Maya stood her ground, unsure how to play the next move. Now that she knew who this woman was the balance between them had shifted and she couldn't get a hold on exactly how. She knew why she was acting like this, but why was Rebecca? She didn't seem to be remotely confused by this abrupt change and it intrigued her, caught her interest in ways she didn't want to think about.

"Right," Claudia said abruptly. "On that note I think we'll be leaving. Maya?"

"Yeah?" she asked, her eyes still locked on Rebecca's.

"Shall we go?"

"Sure."

A small smile tugged at the corner of Rebecca's mouth. It was infuriating. She didn't know whether she wanted to slap or kiss it off her face but she was saved from either course of action by an exasperated Claudia picking up her bag with a sigh and dragging her out the door.

"Bye Rebecca." Claudia called over her shoulder as they went.

"Bye!" she called after them, laughter lacing her voice. "Stay safe you two!"

Chapter 2

Maya awoke the next morning to the sunlight streaming in through the open window and sending a pleasant warmth up her dangling arm. She lifted her head from the pillow and opened her eyes as slowly as possible. She could hear Claudia banging about in the tiny kitchen and knew it wouldn't be long before she would have to get up but for now she was content to lie here and let the sun do its work.

The apartment they had rented to be their base was simple but perfectly located, far enough from the centre of the town to be quiet but close to any amenities they would need, and the view was breathtaking. Located high enough up in the hills to look over the town out across the sea, it was still low enough to see Fortín Solano casting its watchful eye down over the port it had once defended.

Maya rolled onto her side and gazed up at the structure thoughtfully. If all went well they would return here tonight with its secrets uncovered and in their possession. Their task was risky, and theft was not something she enjoyed, much as Claudia would argue otherwise. But the possessions of a man captured and killed two hundred years ago had not been made public, at least not the parts that she needed, and Maya was certain that the answers she was looking for lay among them.

The man in question was Antonio Zuazola, a Spanish Commander who had been defeated by Simón Bolivar's forces in 1813 and swiftly executed. In the years before that he had gained a reputation for mutilating prisoners in the east of the country, and this unpleasant pastime was what had sparked Maya's interest. Bolivar had been building an army of people from all over South America in an effort to overthrow the royalists, and many of these fighters had travelled up from their homelands in Peru, Brazil and what was now Bolivia through the east of Venezuela to join the patriots in the Admirable campaign. These were the prisoners that Zuazola had been focusing on, those of any other origin were simply imprisoned or executed, and according to information Maya had recently uncovered, the man had kept extensive journals. So where were they? And what was it that had made Zuazola leave his secure position in the east and take up residency right in the path of the advancing army?

Maya let the thoughts and questions roam around her head as she lay on the bed in the sun, toying idly with the worn pendant around her neck. It was a little silver monkey her father had given her on her eighth birthday, the chain long since snapped and discarded, the piece of leather that currently held it the latest in a long line of guardians. Her father had been the one who had sparked her interest in history, telling her stories about ancient cultures and mythological creatures in place of bedtime stories as a small child, and moving onto European explorers and how they had come to shape the world she grew up in as she got older. To a relatively poor kid from Puerto Rico, her father's stories had made the world seem huge and exciting, so much to see and learn, and she knew then that that was what she wanted to do with her life. Losing him so early only cemented that desire and she had worked hard to get herself to this point, her natural curiosity and tenacity serving her well on the way.

An all too familiar heavy sadness fell over her as she thought of him and she wondered what he would think of her now. She hoped he would be proud. Sometimes she imagined sitting with him after one of her trips and discussing the places she had been, the things she had done, but the realisation that she never could just depressed the hell out of her so mostly she tried not to. She sighed as she sat up and stretched, letting the sun bathe her face for a moment longer before swinging her legs out of the bed and making her way into the kitchen.

"Ah, you're awake!" Claudia smiled as she entered the room. "Coffee's hot and I was just about to make some eggs. You want?"

"Thanks, Claud," she mumbled as she grabbed herself a cup. In some ways she was grateful her best friend and travelling companion was a morning person because it meant coffee and breakfast, but must there be so many words?

"Okay, well why don't you grab a shower while I make them? Scrambled? Poached?"

"Yeah," she mumbled again before heading back out to shower.

As the water washed over her she tried to focus on the day ahead but her mind kept wandering back to the previous night. Rebecca Bronstein. She knew there was something about the girl the minute she laid eyes on her but she hadn't been able to put her finger on it. Now that she knew who she was she wondered if that was all there was to it, that she had subconsciously recognised her? That couldn't be it, though. She hated that family and everything they stood for so she would have been far more likely to insult her than flirt with her. She placed her hands on the wall and turned her face into the spray.

David and Daniella Bronstein - celebrity 'Tomb Raiders', wilfully playing up to the Hollywood version of the field they worked in, acting out an exciting, champagne lifestyle to attract endorsements. Such bullshit. Truthfully archaeology was a lot more boring than the brochure made out. Most of Maya's time was spent in musty old libraries and searching through ridiculous conspiracy theories on the internet in the hopes she would uncover some fragment of truth that would lead her to her goal, or freezing her ass off in some godforsaken dig site in the Faroe Islands carefully sifting through two millimetres of dirt at a time.

But these people made it seem like it was all glitz and glamour. The outfits, the gadgets, having documentary crews follow them everywhere, extensive photo shoots in exotic locations. And all the while their perfect, Yale bound baby watching from the sidelines, shuffling into shot every once in awhile with her megawatt smile and flawless complexion, droning on about how much she loved her parents and worried while they were away but, just as they supported her and believed in her academic ambition, she loved them and supported their dream of uncovering historical wonders for the world to treasure. Or some shit like that. It was enough to make Maya want to vomit.

She herself had never been one to smile for the cameras. She could, of course, if she wanted to. She was gorgeous and hilarious. She would own that shit. But the only soundbites she gave usually consisted of

"Fuck off" and little else. And yeah, she wanted these 'historical wonders' to be found, she wanted to know where they came from, what they could learn from past civilisations, but she wanted these things to be uncovered correctly, by people who knew what they were doing and who gave a damn, not by glory hunters who would leave a trail of tourists in their wake. Not by people who would destroy any beautiful and possibly incredibly important site they happened to stumble across in their quest for the money shot.

Maya sighed and turned the water off, her whole body tensed with irritation. If Rebecca Bronstein was here it could only mean one thing. She was looking for her parents and that could potentially spell trouble for her and Claudia.

"Thank God," Claudia said as she slid the eggs across the table to her. "I thought I was going to have to come in there and get you."

"Yeah, sure," she scoffed as she sat down and reached for the salt. "You just wanted to get a look at the good stuff."

"Please, you walk around in a state of undress so often seeing you fully clothed is the real challenge."

Maya took a bite of her food as she mulled this over, then shrugged in acknowledgement. Claudia poured them both coffee and sat down opposite her, watching her carefully for a few seconds.

"Something on your mind?"

"It's a big day," she shrugged again, eyes on her plate.

"Yes," Claudia said. "Places to see, historical documents to steal, a potential short, brunette spanner in the works…"

Maya glared at her and picked up her coffee. "It never even crossed my mind."

"Well it should have," she shot back. "Come on, Maya, she could really mess this up if she gets in the way."

"Look, we don't even know why she's here, and even if she is looking for her parents there is no reason to believe that her search would be taking her the same place we are going." Maya sighed and set down her fork. "Look, Claud, I'm not an idiot. I know that she could be an issue for us but there's no point in worrying about her until she actually becomes one."

"So she has been on your mind, then?" Claudia asked, hiding her smirk behind her cup.

"Why do I get the feeling you're not talking about the job anymore?" she muttered, picking up her plate and heading to the sink.

"I have no idea. What else would I be talking about?"

"I have no idea," Maya mimicked sarcastically, turning to face her friend with her hands on her hips. "What time is the tour?"

"One."

"Alright, perfect. Let's get out of here. I want to walk about a bit before we go in, see if I can spot anything useful."

"Or anyone..." Claudia smirked, placing her empty cup in the sink.

"Claudia, just drop it, okay?" Maya spat. "I am not interested in Rebecca Bronstein in any capacity other than if she gets in our way while we are doing this job, alright?"

"Sure," she nodded, hands clasped loosely in front of her. "Sorry. I won't mention it again."

"Good."

"Unless she becomes an issue. Then I reserve the right to say 'I told you so'."

"Fine. Go for it. Now can we leave?"

"Of course," Claudia smiled as she headed towards her room. "Let me grab the bags."

Maya shook her head as she quickly washed their breakfast things. Sometimes she questioned why she and Claudia were friends at all. The woman was infuriating. Of course, she was also almost always right.

Chapter 3

Maya pulled her hat down further to shield her eyes as they climbed higher on the track. It was only eleven a.m. but the sun was already beating down on them. She spared a brief thought for lobster man, maybe secretly hoping he was in a lot of pain, and thanked her parents once more for her complexion. She turned back to see how her red-headed, alabaster skinned friend was faring and was completely unsurprised that the answer was not too well. She stopped and pulled off her pack, opened it and grabbed a bottle of water for Claudia as she waited for her to catch up.

"You okay?" she asked as her friend yanked the bottle gratefully from her hand.

"I'm not going to lie, I've been better." Claudia muttered before downing half the bottle. "I'll be okay. It's just a bit of an adjustment after spending the last two weeks in Norway."

"Yeah, I know." Maya replied, taking in her bright red face and stooped posture. "Well just take it easy, alright? It's only day one and I don't want to have to carry your sweaty ass."

"Love you too, Maya." Claudia snarled at her, recapping the bottle and standing up straight. "Let's go."

"I know," she smiled sweetly. "It's not far now. Let me know if you need to stop."

"Yeah, right."

Maya smirked to herself as the girl stomped past her and pulled her pack back on as she follow her up the path. "How is Turid anyway?" she asked as she caught up. "I haven't spoken to her in a while."

"She's good," Claudia nodded. "Really good, actually. She got her funding so she's really excited to get started."

"That's great!" Maya smiled. "I'll have to get in touch."

"Yes," she replied with a smirk. "You should."

Maya's gaze drifted up to the fort a couple of miles in front of them and she thought back to her research. The rebels would have taken this route up from the town as they stormed the place. Details of the assault were sketchy and although their numbers were fairly significant she couldn't help wondering how they had managed to overpower a full, well trained Spanish garrison with an experienced leader. This was partly why she had wanted to get there early, to feel the place out, see if there was anything about the surrounding land that set off her spider sense.

Claudia soon began to slow again and Maya overtook her with what was meant to be an encouraging smile. The scowl she received in return suggested that maybe she had not quite achieved the look she was going for so she filed it in her 'reasons not to play nice' column and stalked off up the hill.

Twenty minutes later she reached the shade of the fort and removed her hat gratefully, waving it in front of her face as she began to move around the surrounding wall. She shot a look back at her friend and, once she had established the woman was not in danger of death, continued her search, running her hand along the cool wall as she went. After a few moments she came to a strange indentation in the grass, running at a right angle away from the building ten or so feet out to a boulder about the size of an armchair. Maya dropped to her knees and felt about where the line met the wall.

"Found something?" Claudia's voice called from behind her.

"I'm not sure," Maya mumbled as her friend's heavy steps moved closer. She stood back up and followed the line towards the boulder.

"Odd. Maybe some sort of drainage?"

"I guess," she conceded as she approached the end of the line. "It could be something that was put in much later but...oh, shit!"

"What?" Claudia yelled in alarm as Maya grabbed her arm and pulled her to the ground. "Ow! Maya!"

"Ssh!" Maya shot back as her eyes focussed in on the group wandering along the trail below. Five of them, all wearing back packs and carrying an assortment of gear.

"What the fuck?" the redhead hissed as she clambered into a kneeling position and peered over the rock to where Maya was pointing. "Oh, bollocks. Is that them?"

"Well, I think that answers our question," she answered as they passed close enough to be clearly identifiable as the group from the bar. Rebecca Bronstein led the way, her stride brisk and confident, the blistering heat not seeming to faze her at all.

"Yes. They are obviously not heading for the fort but that's a lot of equipment for a holiday. I wonder where they're going?"

"My guess?" Maya sighed, leaning back against the rock. "San Esteban maybe? Piedra del Indio? Her parents were looking into petroglyphs, right?"

"I thought you didn't know about their disappearance?" Claudia asked, eyeing her suspiciously.

"I may have read a bit about it last night in an attempt to ignore your Wagnerian snoring," she shrugged as she uncapped a fresh bottle of water.

"Right," her friend muttered as she sat down next to her. "So what's so interesting about the petroglyphs on this one?"

"Nothing as far as I know. They're just like all the others. Random carvings that we don't know enough about to fully understand."

"Have you seen it?"

"I've seen pictures," Maya said as she turned to peer back over the rock.

"And you don't think that maybe…" Claudia tailed off as her friend's dark eyes turned back to her sharply.

"What?"

"You don't think that maybe, um," she toyed nervously with a piece of grass as she searched for her next words. "Well, that maybe we should…go and have a look for ourselves."

"You mean do I think we should follow them and see if they know something we don't?" Maya muttered through gritted teeth.

"Well, I wouldn't put it exactly like that, but…"

"No, Claudia."

"But what if…"

"I said no, Claudia!" Maya snapped. "We don't even know what they are looking for but it's got nothing to do with what we're doing. We are here to pick up that book. That's it."

"And keep an eye out for a potential artefact in the area, remember?" Claudia pointed out.

"The articles I read on her parent's disappearance didn't say anything about what their ultimate goal was, just that they were looking into South American petroglyphs. For all we know they were just looking for a key to understanding them. There's nothing to suggest they were looking for an artefact. It's totally unconnected to what we're doing."

"As far as we know…"

"Claudia," she pinched the bridge of her nose in an effort to remain calm. "Look, I know you love a good plot twist, but this isn't one of your Rizzoli and Isles books. Do you really think that of all the things the Bronsteins could have been looking for, in all the world and from any period of history, that they would just so happen to have been researching something in the same vein as what we're doing? And then, after their sudden disappearance, their daughter takes up the cause and decides to set out looking for whatever they found on the same day as we attempt to retrieve Zuazola's journals, and that somehow it's going to all conveniently link up?"

"Okay, alright, when you put it like that it does sound relatively implausible," Claudia grumbled, peering over the rock again. "They're gone. What are we looking at here?"

"I don't know. Probably nothing. Let's keep moving," Maya snatched up her bag and continued her search.

An hour later they were standing in the middle of a group of tourists waiting for the tour of the fort to begin. Next to them a large family were loudly discussing the failings of their hotel (they only had Venezuelan tv, the pool wasn't as big as it looked in the brochure), their previous night's meal (no pizza on the menu) and generally making Maya want to beat them to death with a rock. Out of respect for her friend's delicate British sensibilities she settled for glaring at the back of their heads and silently cursing them with every debilitating disease she could name, and since a large portion of her degree concerned Anthropology, there were a lot of them. Claudia subtly positioned herself as a buffer and furiously fanned her overheated face with her hat, turning her back on Maya so as not to draw attention to the fact that they were together.

The plan was relatively simple; they would look around the fort with the rest of the group until they spotted the entrance to the areas that were not open to the public, then Claudia would create a distraction whilst Maya slipped out and found her way to the archive room. Strangely, they had been unsuccessful in finding an up to date plan of the place so all they really knew was that the room they were looking for was likely to be downstairs somewhere, as the rooms above were all relatively open to the elements.

Finally the tour was announced and the group began to shuffle through the doors into the courtyard. The tour guide jumped up onto a platform and waved her arms to gather them all in closer before welcoming them and beginning her speech about the origins of Fortín Solano and a brief summation of the events that had occurred there. Maya's eyes wandered about the place as the introduction continued, trying to get her own feel for it and the particular event she was concerned with. The surprise attack had happened on September 1st, 1813, and from what little information Maya had been able to gather it had been a short and bloody battle. Again, this seemed unusual to her. Even taken by surprise the group of well trained Spaniards should have been able to withstand an attack from the rebels. They were in the middle of a war and occupied a fortress. Something just didn't add up.

Eventually their guide began to lead them inside and Maya started to gear herself up to make her move. She dawdled at the back of the group as Claudia and the rest headed through the doors, wanting to keep as much space between the two of them as possible so no one would put them together when Claud did…whatever she was planning to do to create a diversion. Maya just hoped it was better than her attempt in Bilbao. That had just been embarrassing and not nearly as effective as expected. The group moved through the first exhibition room, many of them seeming more excited by the cool temperature of the room than by any of the exhibits. Maya looked up at the giant portrait of Bolivar taking up the majority of the far wall and rolled her eyes in irritation. She ran her fingers gently over a glass case next to her, barely paying attention to the ageing weapons it held as she scanned the walls for the door she needed. Nothing in this room. She looked at some of the other cases and stopped by an old manuscript which seemed to be a log of activity at the fort. Sadly it was opened at a date twenty odd years before where she needed it to be and she didn't want to risk jimmying the case for something most likely not that helpful.

After ten minutes or so the tour moved on and Maya followed the rest of the group through a tiny stone doorway into the next room. As she passed through she bumped up against a burly security guard and stumbled.

"Lo siento, señor," she muttered, an apologetic smile plastered on her face as he held her up, his hand lingering on her waist a fraction too long. She turned quickly away from his leer when he tucked his thumbs into his belt and dropped his gaze to her chest. She grimaced and pocketed his keys discreetly as she hurried to catch up with the tour.

"We are now standing in the old armory," their guide announced. "The weapons you see on display are identical to the ones they would have had during the Admirable Campaign, although of course these are replicas. Beneath us are the cells and they will be our next stop. Prepare yourselves to come face to face with the ghosts of the revolution!"

The group murmured in approval and followed the woman over to the stairs at the far end of the room. Maya stuck close to the back, her eyes scanning her surroundings for any sign of the archive room. She didn't know how long the tour would last but the fort wasn't a big place and she didn't know how much time she would have when she found the room, if she found it at all. God, she didn't even really know what she was looking for.

As she was halfway down the stairs there was a loud crash from the room below and she tried to peer over the heads of the people in front of her to see what was going. A siren started blaring and the group surged forward in a panic.

"Ladies and Gentlemen, please remain calm!" their guide shouted over the commotion, looking mildly irritated. "There is nothing to be concerned about, one of the exhibits has been knocked over. Please, just follow me."

Maya reached the bottom and saw Claudia sprawled on the floor next to a toppled pillar and a shattered glass case, its contents strewn behind her. Great diversionary tactic bringing the entire security staff down here, she thought. And where the hell was she supposed to go? She backed away from the group as the burly guard from before bustled past her and knelt down by her friend. Stumbling slightly she put a hand out to brace her fall and found herself leaning on a door with key card access. She pulled out the guard's keys and glanced back at the group as she swiped his card. The door buzzed open and she ducked through it quickly with a sigh of relief.

A dark corridor lay before her and she moved down it quietly, checking each door she passed for any signs of life, or access to the archive room. Just as she reached the end of the corridor she heard approaching footsteps and ducked into a room on the right hand side, thanking her lucky stars it was unlocked. She pressed her ear up to the door and listened as the footsteps moved rapidly on. She sucked in a deep breath and turned to look at the room she was in, a dark and musty place, the only source of light a tiny window high up on the wall. It looked like a junk room but there were rows of metal shelving off to the left hand side with packing boxes stacked on them so she moved over to them and scanned the labels on each one. Most were not very informative and there was a lot of water damage but when she pulled the lids off them she saw that they were full of old papers. She rifled through a few of them to try and work out if there was any order there, or if they would actually be of any use, and allowed herself a small smile when she came across a box dated 1815.

"Getting closer," she muttered as she replaced the lid and moved on to the next box. 1837. Dammit.

After she had scanned through around twenty five boxes she heard voices in the hallway outside and froze in place, her eyes locked on the door like she could keep it closed with her glare. When the voices stopped right outside she started to slowly back down the room towards the final row of shelves and had just managed to drop down into a crouch in the furthest, darkest corner when the door opened and one of what she assumed was the museum's curators entered carrying the broken artefacts from Claudia's 'fall'. The man was still in conversation with the other person in the corridor and barely looked into the room as he backed in and deposited the broken items on a table by the door.

Task completed he walked straight back out and shut the door behind him with a sharp click. Maya relaxed a little and went to push herself up, pausing as something caught her eye. She reached forward and moved a box out of the way to get to the one behind it, a slightly larger and more robust box which, although it was damp and the script was faded, she could just about make out 'azola' on the label. She pulled the lid off quickly and turned her face away as the smell of mould shot out of it. Using one hand to cover her face she reached into the box and lifted up a few inches of mulchy paper, grimacing as it came apart at her touch. As carefully as she could she reached down the side of the box and felt her heart jump in excitement as her fingers connected with something more sturdy. Placing her hand on the top of the damp paper she tipped the box up gently until its contents were upended on the shelf in front of her. There, right at the bottom, was a leather bound book with a tiny golden figure emblazoned on the spine. She picked it up gently and opened it. The pages were damp but the leather binding had offered a little protection so the contents were at least still legible. She flipped open the front cover and smiled broadly as she saw the words written there : Antonio Zuazola. Angostura. 1810.

"Score." she whispered to herself as she carefully closed the book and pulled a cloth out of her backpack to wrap it in. Quickly checking the boxes around the area in case there was anything else she moved back towards the front of the room and wondered how long she had been in there. If felt like about four hours, although she was sure that couldn't be true. Maybe half an hour? Either way, her tour group would be long gone by now and she didn't know how she was going to get out. In desperation she looked around the room for something to disguise herself with, maybe a lab coat or something?

"Great idea, Maya, if you were trying to escape from some kind of evil science lab," she muttered to herself as she looked up at the tiny window. No go. Even if she did manage to climb up there and sacrifice a limb there were bars on it. Looked like it would be through the front door then. She could do this. She could. Just one foot in front of the other and hope to God she didn't run into anyone. Solid plan, Maya. What could possibly go wrong?

Well, the curator could have locked the door for starters, she realised with an irritated sigh as she tried the handle. Quickly she pulled out the guard's keys and started trying each one in the lock, going through the bunch about four times before she eventually gave up. Shit. Now what? She looked around the room again, a sense of panic starting to creep in as once again she saw nothing of use. She walked over to the wall and looked up at the window again, willing to sell her soul to channel Eugene Tooms for the next ten minutes, when she heard a faint dripping sound. She held her breath and strained to find the source of the sound, dropping to a crouch and following the wall along, breaking only to skirt round a filing cabinet pushed up against it. When she pressed back up to the wall again she realised the sound was coming from behind her now and she turned back to look more closely at the metal object. She bent down next to it and ran her hand down the back. It was definitely colder down here than in the rest of the room so she pushed on the cabinet, putting all her strength behind her shoulders to shove it along the wall and reveal a semi circular hole in the wall with bars running down it at thirty centimetre intervals. Behind it lay a low, dark tunnel, probably some kind of sewer system.

"Great," Maya muttered, pulling uselessly at the bars in the hopes that one of them would give way and toppling backwards with a small squeal as one did. Huffing in annoyance she got back up and made a small effort to clean the dirt off herself before she realised she was probably about to crawl into an open sewer and therefore bound to get covered in much worse. Gingerly she maneuvered herself through the gap and reached into her pack for her flashlight, making a mental note to thank Claudia for her excessive Girl Scout packing skills later. She shone the light onto the thin stream of water running down the centre of the space and set off in the direction of its flow, bent double and her hand on the slimy wall for balance. The place gave her the shivers, and not in a good way. Unbidden, every horror film she had ever watched featuring a scene in a tunnel came screaming back through her brain so that by the time she came to the first junction she was completely freaking out and when she eventually saw the tiny crack of light breaking through up ahead she had gone into full on Buffy fight stance.

"Oh, thank God," she murmured, rushing towards the light before remembering where she was, and that she had no idea what was in front of her, and returning to her former cautious pace. Thankfully there were no sharp drops in her path and before too long she got to the end of the tunnel and found herself crawling out of a small overflow pipe and into the forest. She heaved a sigh of relief and put her torch away, pulling out her phone and letting out a string of Spanish curses when she saw it had no reception, curses that went above and beyond the call of duty and lasted until well after she had stuffed the offending article back in her bag and started looking around for signs of how to get back to the town. The water from the tunnel flowed down the hill into the river below so she figured she could follow it back to the port, or she could climb back up the hill to the fort and walk back that way. Maya was torn. She was tired and the hill was steep, also there could be people looking for her up there. Unlikely but she really didn't want to get arrested or anything, she was covered in shit, most likely literally, and really wanted a beer. On the other hand, Claudia could be waiting for her up there and she didn't know how far she would have to walk along the river, or if she would be able to follow it all the way. She took one last longing glance at the cool, clean water beneath her and turned to start the climb.

One hour, two skinned knees, five slips and three face plants later, Maya emerged victorious from the dense forest and staggered up the gentle slope towards the fort, eyes sweeping back and forth for her friend. If Claudia wasn't here now, so help her she would… The thought died in her brain as she saw a puff of smoke rising from behind the boulder they had hidden behind earlier. Maya would have broken out into a dramatic run if her legs had had anything left in them. As it was she staggered as quickly as she was able over to the rock and prayed that it was her friend smoking behind it and not some small animal spontaneously combusting. She rubbed at her face and wondered vaguely if she might be suffering from heatstroke, or dehydration, or a random attack of histrionics. Pushing the craziness from her head she rounded the boulder sharply and thrust out her hand.

"Cigarette," she croaked out in greeting.

"Oh, hey, you're back!" Claudia jumped up and went to pull her into a hug, stopping as she registered the state of her and the murderous glare on her face.

"Cigarette," Maya repeated, taking a slow step forward.

"Okay, alright. Here, have a new one. Have the pack," the redhead stuttered out, pulling out a fresh cigarette and hastily going to light it for her. Maya took a long drag on it and flopped down onto the grass. She closed her eyes as she exhaled loudly and allowed the sun to soothe her aching body.

"Here," Claudia said, gently pushing a bottle of water into her hand. "Are you okay? What happened?"

Maya snorted out a laugh. "I'm just peachy, Claud. Why would you think anything different?"

"Well, first off you look like you crawled out of the pit of hell…"

"That good, huh?" Maya chuckled as she sat up and opened the water.

"Yeah. And you also look…well, kind of crazy." Claudia said gently. "I mean, more so than usual. No offence."

"No off…? Whatever. Nice job on the distraction, by the way. Just throw yourself into a bunch of antiques. How did you spot that door?"

"Um, I didn't," she muttered, shifting uncomfortably.

"So how did you know to do it when you did?" Maya questioned, squinting up at her as she took a drink.

"I didn't. I fainted."

"What?!" she sputtered, spraying her friend with water. "Jesus, Claud, are you okay?"

"Yeah, I'm fine," she waved her hand dismissively. "It's just the stupid sun. I told you, I need to acclimatise after Norway."

"Fuck, I'm so sorry, I had no idea. I swear I would have helped you, I just thought it was part of the plan."

"I know. Did you find anything?"

"Well I fucking hope so after all we've been through today," Maya muttered, stubbing her cigarette out on the ground and standing to offer her hand to her friend. "Come on, let's get back to the apartment and check it out."

Claudia took her hand and pulled herself up, grabbing her bag and starting off down the hill towards town. She glanced up and down Maya's mud stained body a couple more times before trying again.

"Seriously though, what happened to you?"

"God, it's...I don't even know..." Maya laughed and shook her head. "I need beer, tequila and a shower. Then maybe I can talk about it. Maybe."

Claudia gave her a cautious glance and pulled her bag tighter on her shoulders. "Okay."

Chapter 4

Maya wrapped a towel around herself and wandered through to the kitchen, running her hand through her wet hair as she went. She headed straight to the fridge and pulled out a cold beer, popping the lid off and taking a long pull before before leaning back against the counter with a deep sigh. Claudia looked at her over the top of her glasses, lips pursed in distaste.

"Couldn't find an actual face cloth to wrap around ourselves, could we?" she muttered.

"What?" Maya asked in confusion before looking down at herself. Satisfied that the admittedly small towel was in fact covering all the important parts she rolled her eyes and took another drink. "It's not that short. Plus it's really hot in here and it's all I could find."

"It's really hot in here because you have been in the shower for the last forty five minutes with the temperature switched to what I can only assume is the 'molten lava' setting. With the amount of steam coming out of there I thought you were going to emerge dressed as Cher."

"Well excuse me for being thorough. Did you not see all that crap I was covered in? God knows what was in that sewer but I wanted to be sure I got it all off."

"And a good deal of skin as well, I imagine. I'm surprised your scales aren't showing." Claudia muttered.

"Okay," Maya sighed as she wandered over and sat opposite her friend at the table. "What's up?"

"Nothing!" she snapped, closing the journal and stomping over to the sink. "Is it too much to ask that your wear clothes in public like a normal person?"

"Since when have I ever done anything like a normal person?"

"God, you're infuriating."

"And you're talking to me like my mother," Maya snapped back. "Or worse, like I'm your mother."

Claudia stared out of the window and let out a long sigh. "I know. I'm sorry. I just have a really bad headache and I can't make head nor tail of that book."

"I'm not surprised, it's handwritten in outdated Spanish and heavily water damaged." Maya put down her drink and moved to pour a glass of water for her friend. "We both know your Spanish is awful, and, you know, you did collapse today."

"Don't remind me," she muttered, rubbing her forehead and accepting the water Maya held out to her gratefully. "So embarrassing."

"And expensive," Maya couldn't resist teasing, hip checking her gently before putting an arm around her shoulder. "I don't know how old that bowl was but I don't think it'll be back on display anytime ever."

"Maya!" Claudia squealed, shoving her away. "You know how I feel about breaking artefacts! Now I feel even worse." She stomped back to the table and sat down wearily.

"Ah, sorry, Claud, I'm only playing. It was like some gunpowder canister or something. It was fine. Maybe a little dented."

"You are terrible!" the redhead hissed at her. "Why would you do that to me?"

"Oh, come on, I had to! That thing went down with some force. Boom!" she laughed as she threw her arm out to demonstrate and drew it hastily back in when the action dislodged her towel. "Shit."

"Oh, for goodness sake." Claudia said, throwing her hands up in despair. "Just go and put some clothes on would you?"

"God, alright." Maya muttered, hastily trying to recover herself. "It's not like you've never seen me naked before…"

"And I am sure I will again, given your proclivity for nudity," she sighed and reopened the journal. "Between you flashing your boobs at me and Zuazola's penchant for sketching a stickman with what appears to be a three foot penis I feel like I'm in a porno directed by Artaud."

"Wait, what?"

"He was a French surrealist director who invented something called the Theatre of Cruelty. Actually, it's quite fitting for…"

"I'm not talking about that, idiot, where is this stickman?" Maya finished fastening her towel and moved around to Claudia's side of the table.

"Really?" Claudia gave her a strange look as she flipped open the book. "I wouldn't have thought that would be your thing…"

"Don't be ridiculous," she tutted. "I just need to make sure…"

Claudia turned to the relevant page and Maya grabbed the book from her hands, her mind going into overdrive at the sight of the sketch.

"You have got to be kidding me," she slammed the book back down and marched over to the counter to retrieve her bottle of tequila and two shot glasses.

"What is it? What's wrong? Do you recognise it?"

"Yes." Maya muttered pouring the two shots and sliding one over to Claudia.

"And? Where is it?" Claudia asked, putting her glasses back on and inspecting the page as Maya wandered off towards the bedroom. "Maya?"

"Piedra del Indio."

"Oh, you have got to be kidding me," Claudia chuckled before downing her shot, wincing as the action drew her attention back to her headache.

"So why are you so adamant there's nothing there?"

"Cause it's just a rock, Claud, a tourist trap. I saw a picture of it on Pinterest, that's how obvious it is," Maya sighed and rubbed her eyes. The journal lay open in front of her and she was desperate to find something in it, anything, that would point them away from Piedra del Indio. So far she had deciphered half of Zuazola's scrawl and the well endowed stickman was the only useful thing she had found. Tortured this guy from Chile, flayed this guy from Colombia, etc, etc. Nothing about anything that would bring him to Puerto Cabello except for the drawing, and the only thing to suggest why he had sketched it in the first place was a name - Vancho Huamán. That was it. No reference as to who he was or where he had come from, why, or even if, this Huamán had drawn the figure, or what it pertained to. Christ, Maya didn't even know if it was actually the one from Piedra del Indio, or if this symbol was present at other sites. She hadn't seen it anywhere else but then she was hardly the world's leading authority on petroglyphs.

Claudia studied her for a few seconds as if she was going to press the issue then turned back to her laptop with a sigh. Maya clasped her hands behind her and cracked her back before getting up to grab a couple more beers from the fridge. She opened them both and handed one to the redhead before retaking her seat and wearily going back to the book. The pair continued their research in silence for the next ten minutes, Maya squinting to make out water damaged passages in the vain hope of finding something useful, and Claudia tapping away at the keyboard looking for...whatever it was she was looking for.

"God, this is fucking useless!" Maya yelled, slamming the book down on the table after another half an hour. "All this guy talks about is what he did to them, what methods he used to extract information but he doesn't write any of what he got out of them down! Either they didn't give him anything or he was too fucking paranoid to record it. Fuck!"

"He doesn't say anything?"

"No! Aside from the stickman he mentions a lake a couple of times and the letter V keeps popping up, but that's it."

"Could V be the Van… Human guy?" Claudia asked, her nose wrinkling as she tried to remember his name.

"Vancho Huamán. And no, I don't think so," Maya reopened the journal and flicked back to the drawing. "I mean he shows up around January and the V thing starts showing up around April. If this guy was one of his prisoners he would just have killed him once he got what he needed."

"And there's no mention of who he was?"

"No, just a name."

"Can we get anything from the name?"

"Not much. Huamán is Quechuan and Vancho is kind of common in Peru so I would say that that was most likely where he was from, but what does that get us?" Maya closed her eyes and rubbed her neck.

"Okay, so if he was Peruvian then can we assume that Zuazola was looking for something in or from Peru? I mean, most of the people he tortured were from there?"

"Well, there and Brazil, Paraguay, Bolivia, or Upper Peru as it was then."

"Alright, so we suspect he was looking for something from the south. Why head north?"

"I don't fucking know, Claudia!" Maya snapped as she got up from the table and began pacing the room. "And if we had the first fucking clue then maybe I could get something more out of this semi-literate scrawl but we don't, and we need to find something quickly because we have to check in with her in…"

"Fifteen minutes," Claudia supplied at the agitated wave of the latina's hand.

"Fifteen minutes! This is just stupid." she sighed as she sat down again heavily. "She's given us some pretty slim leads before but this is just…" she dropped her head onto the table and groaned loudly.

Claudia clicked a couple of links on the laptop and folded her arms in front of her, clearing her throat before she began. "Okay, here is her email; 'Fortín Solano, Puerto Cabello, Venezuela. Access secure area and find information pertaining to Antonio Zuazola, specifically journals leading up to his death in 1813. Writings contained within should shed light on Zuazola's motives for torture of prisoners and sudden relocation. Suspect artefact in area, potentially of Inca origin.'"

"'Previously on Maya and Claudia's South American Tales…'" Maya muttered from her prone position.

"You said that Human is Quechuan, right?" Claudia continued, ignoring her friend's sarcastic quip. "That's the language the Inca used?"

"Huamán. And yes."

"So if Zuazola was looking for an Inca artefact then this drawing could be some sort of clue? Like a symbol, or part of a map?"

"No, the Inca didn't communicate like that, they used quipus for any form of measurement or counting, so any sort of map would have been based on that. It's thought that petroglyphs in South America were mainly used for Spiritual or Astrological markings, to symbolise something of cultural significance so potentially it could be an indicator of something happening nearby, but the Inca were never in Venezuela. Ecuador was as far as they got."

"And if the picture in the book is not the one from Piedra del Indio?"

"Well then maybe, but where is it?"

Claudia rested her elbows on the table and steepled her fingers in front of her mouth. "Okay. So what do we know about the Inca?"

"Oh, good God, Claudia, we don't have time to rehash our high school history," Maya sighed and got up to go to the fridge.

"I'd like to think we know a little more than we did in high school, Maya, and I know for a fact that you certainly do given you wrote several essays on the topic during our second year," Claudia chastised her before leaning back in her chair, her face scrunched in concentration. "Their empire extended around 2,500 miles along the west coast from Chile to Ecuador…"

"Thank you, Wikipedia."

"Maya," Claudia snapped, dropping her arms on the table. "Either help or be quiet."

Maya sighed and slid a beer across the table as she sat back down. "Okay, it lasted about 130 years, ending in 1533 when Pizarro executed Atahualpa and installed a puppet emperor. He rebelled and fled to Vilcabamba where the last Inca built a new base and fought back against the Spanish til 1572 when the conquistadors took the city and executed the last emperor, Túpac Amaru. The remaining Inca then fled to…somewhere else, and the Spanish claimed the land and wiped out all trace of their culture. Or tried to."

"So where did they go? Is it possible that the Inca from the north moved east? Into Colombia and Venezuela?"

"Well maybe, but I don't see why they would," Maya mused, picking at the label on her bottle. "I mean, the Spanish were fighting the nobility, the ones in the capital at Cusco. Why bother with the tail when you've cut off the head of the snake?"

"Well, there must have been some high ranking people in the north? How else would they have maintained control?"

"Fear, mostly. They had better weapons, horses, they had killed everyone of note," Maya sighed. "Quito was a power centre in the north, though. Atahualpa and his generals came from there, but the Spanish burned it to the ground and killed them all way before this. There would have been people in charge up there, but not necessarily Inca, they were a relatively small group of people, less than 100,000. The heart of the empire was Cusco. Once that was gone it pretty much fell apart." Maya opened the journal again and flicked through the next couple of pages with a sigh. "He doesn't mention the Inca once. Just 'V' and 'lago' and…" she stopped abruptly and flicked back a few pages, studying it closely before flicking back.

"What is it?"

"I'm not sure," Maya muttered, scrutinising the page before turning to the next one. "He mentions 'boca' a few times, at first I thought it was just…well, like a note as to where he wanted the focus of the torture to be…"

"Boca?" Claudia asked.

"Jeez, Claud, do you remember any Spanish?"

"I remember how to order tequila," she huffed, playing absently with the laptop.

"Barely. Boca means mouth, and now that I'm looking back he writes it a lot."

"And you think what? That it's linked to V? Or the lake? The mouth of the lake?"

"Maybe, although it doesn't really sit right," Maya turned another page. "Here it is again, but he says '¿Dónde está la boca?'"

"Ooh, I know this one! 'Where is the mouth?'"

Maya cut her eyes at her friend and carried on reading. She skimmed through a few more pages and squinted carefully at one before shaking her head and turning over. She held up her hands in surprise and turned the page back. "That's it!"

"What?" Claudia jumped up and started round the table.

"No, I mean that's it!" Maya slammed the book down. "End of discussion! Blank pages and some watermarks! Some kind of tetris on the back cover! Author dead!"

"Oh. Well that's disappointing."

"You think?"

"What did the last entry say?"

"Just more of the same," Maya sighed and cracked her neck. "Lago...V…"

Claudia reached over and grabbed the book, squinting down at it for a moment before smoothing out the page. "'Alto'. Is he singing?"

"No," Maya chuckled. "It means high. Or tall."

"He was high?"

"No!" Maya laughed again before gesturing for the book back. "At least I hope not. Or maybe I kind of do? Anyway, it says agua alta. High water."

"High water?"

"I guess he's talking about the lake again," she smoothed out the page and tried to make out the words. "There's something else here but it's really faded. 'La muerte llega con la marea alta, respuestas llegan con la baja.'"

"Aw, sounds beautiful!" Claudia smiled. "What does it mean?"

"'Death comes with the high tide, answers with the low.'"

"Oh," she wrinkled her nose. "Not so beautiful in English."

"No," Maya agreed, raising her beer to her mouth. "And not particularly helpful."

"Unless it refers to the mysterious lake V," Claudia muttered, turning back to her laptop.

Maya choked on her beer and slammed the bottle down on the table as she coughed. "Claudia, open the map!" she yelled as soon as she could speak.

"Why?"

"Quick! Look up San Esteban National Park!" she said as she moved quickly round to Claudia's side of the table and tapped expectantly on her shoulder.

"Okay, okay!" The page opened and she brought up the park pulling her hands up in submission as Maya reached over her to scroll down.

"There! I knew it!" Maya jabbed her finger at the screen and danced around the room in excitement.

"Lago de Valencia?" Claudia read, inspecting the large lake to the south of the park. "Do you think that's it?"

"Well, I think it's worth a shot, right?" Maya stopped her celebration and turned back to her. "I mean, it's the only lead we have. He tortures people, goes on about 'lake' and 'V' and 'mouth' and then moves out here?"

"Okay, but Maya 'V' could mean anything. Venezuela, vermin, vanguard, Vancho…"

"Oh, so now you remember his name…"

"And if it does refer to this lake, where's the mouth?"

"Well, where the river goes into it?" Maya said, hands on hips and sounding a little less sure.

"There are about 18 rivers feeding into it, none of them particularly large. Where do we start?"

"I don't know, at the top?" Maya threw her hands up and stomped over to her bag. "What else do we have to go on?"

"The stickman? Piedra del Indio?"

"No, Claudia," she grabbed her phone out of her bag and headed into the bedroom. "I'm going to make the call."

Ten minutes later Maya stomped back into the kitchen and grabbed the tequila bottle off the counter. She grabbed two glasses and poured them both a shot before sliding one across the table to Claudia. The redhead picked it up and studied her friend over the rim before raising it to her lips and knocking it back. She set the glass back on the table and waited a few moments.

"So," she began cautiously. "How did that go?"

"Hmm," Maya let out a dry laugh as she reached across the table to retrieve the glass. "Not great."

"Oh? How so?" Claudia asked as she picked up the fresh shot that came sliding her way.

"You got your wish," the latina smiled through gritted teeth before knocking back her shot. "We're going to Piedra del Indio."

Chapter 5

Maya stopped and readjusted her heavy backpack, rubbing her eyes under her dark glasses and silently cursing the bottle of tequila that was responsible for her head feeling like a washing machine on a heavy spin cycle.

"You okay?" Claudia called back cheerfully, clearly enjoying the role reversal since yesterday.

"Just peachy, Claud, thanks for asking," Maya forced a smile and continued her penitent march, her mind drifting back to the previous night and the phone call to their boss. Elaine was not the most pleasant of women at the best of times, even less so when she didn't hear the information she wanted.

"We found the diary but there's not much in it," Maya had begun cautiously, aware that this was not what the other woman wanted to hear. "He seems to have been paranoid about writing too much down."

"I'm not surprised, he was a paranoid man. Rightly so, as it turned out."

"Yeah. So, he mainly talks about a lake, the letter V, and a mouth. Claudia and I think he was referring to Lake Valencia, it's not far from here, and there's a phrase that he has written, 'La muerte llega con la marea alta, respuestas llegan con la baja.'"

"And you think he is referring to the levels of the tide in the lake?" the woman asked sceptically. "I don't think so, Maya. True, in the rainy season the level could rise substantially, maybe even enough to kill an unwary traveller, but that would mean the answer would be visible for the majority of the year. No, I think we need to look elsewhere. Was there nothing else?"

"Um, well, there was one other thing, but I'm not sure it's relevant."

"What is it?"

"It's a drawing," Maya began, her fingers pinching the bridge of her nose in irritation. "A drawing of a man with an object between his legs."

The woman on the other end of the phone was silent for a few moments. "An object? Like a phallus?"

"Maybe," Maya admitted grudgingly. "More likely some sort of weapon or staff, but either way it seems to depict a man of great power."

"Like El Dorado."

"Yeah, maybe, but I recognise the image, Elaine, and it's from a place near here that I don't believe can be connected to…"

"Piedra del Indio," the woman stated simply, though Maya could hear the shift in her tone and the change in background noise, like she had moved into a more private space.

"Well, yes," Maya admitted. "So I guess you know as well as I do that it's a tourist trap, if there was anything there it would already have been found and it's too far north to be anything to do with…"

"I want you to go there and check it out, Maya," Elaine said sharply. "It can't be a coincidence."

"Why not?"

"Because Zuazola wouldn't have come up this way if there wasn't a damn good reason for him to do so. This was his ticket out and he wouldn't have put himself in danger unless he was sure."

"Okay," Maya sat down on the bed, suddenly uneasy. "There's something else you should probably know."

"Go on."

"There's someone else out here, Rebecca Bronstein."

"David and Daniella Bronstein's daughter."

"Yeah."

"Interesting," Elaine was silent for a few moments and Maya could hear the distinctive rattle of ice cubes. "She's looking at the rock?"

"I think so."

"Have you spoken to her?"

"I...may have had a brief conversation with her, but not about her parents or what she's doing here."

"I'll bet," the woman muttered dryly. "Well, I assume you suspect she's there for the same reason I do so try and avoid her if you can but if it comes to it…"

"What?" Maya pressed after her boss had stayed silent a few seconds too long.

"Well, she may have information that we need," Elaine conceded. "All I'm saying is play nice, Maya. I know how you feel about glory hunters but all we know about this girl at the moment is that she is a concerned child looking for her parents."

"A concerned child with a privileged life and a boat load of cash…" Maya muttered.

"Maya.."

"Alright, okay. I'll play nice," she muttered. "But I get the distinct impression you're not telling me everything."

"Do I ever?" the woman replied. Maya could almost hear the smirk down the phone. "Do what you need to do, just...keep it professional, okay?"

"Come on, you make it sound like I have no self control!"

"Should I bring up Cabo?" Elaine asked pointedly. "Just call me in two days, alright?"

"Yeah, alright," she muttered.

"And Maya? Look after yourself, and Claud too."

"Always."

The rest of the evening had been spent on further research; Maya returning to Zuazola's journal to find any information she might have missed on stickman and secretly hoping to uncover anything that would lead them away from Piedra del Indio and the Bronsteins, Claudia plotting their route for the next day and looking into San Esteban and the petroglyphs in the surrounding area. She had been horrified to discover a similar carving of what appeared to be a woman with a key between her legs until she found out that the key was actually a child and the symbol referred to childbirth. This had caused her to launch into a 'fascinating' discussion on the 'advanced obstetric practices' of the people in the area compared to their counterparts in Europe in the 15th century. This had been the point of the evening where Maya had consumed the majority of the bottle of tequila and, consequently, why she held Claudia largely responsible for her raging hangover.

She struggled to shake off her lethargy and put an extra kick in her step to catch up with her friend. It was only 9 kilometres and on a normal day Maya would have been taking in the 'beautiful scenery' that Claudia wouldn't stop babbling about, but as it was they had reached the midway point, the mountains were climbing up in front of her, the sun was beating down, and all she could think about was her churning stomach, her pounding head and how she just really wanted to lie down. Still, she knew that she had no one to blame but herself and she sure as hell wasn't going to let Claudia know, so she just had to suck it up and get on with it.

"Tell me again why we brought all the stuff?" Maya muttered as they stopped for a break about fifteen minutes later.

"Because you said that we would most likely continue on from San Esteban to the lake when we didn't find anything, which I have to say is a very negative standpoint."

"Claud," Maya held her hand up to not so gently interrupt. "Rhetorical question. It's just heavy."

"Are you sure you are feeling alright?" Claudia asked as she put a hand on Maya's forehead that was quickly swatted away. "That was almost an admission of weakness."

"Fuck off," she growled, pulling her bag back on. "I'm just a bit tired."

"Hmm," her friend smirked as she gathered her own things. "Well, not long now, just the steep, twisty mountain path that climbs a thousand metres in under a mile…"

"You are just loving this, aren't you?"

"Whatever do you mean, Maya?" Claudia held her hand up to her chest, her face washed with hurt. "I am merely being my usual, supportive self and giving you a quick update on our route. Now come on, the sun is almost at its hottest and there's a lovely open plain that we have to walk across just at the top of this next really steep bit."

Maya shot daggers into her friend's back as she practically skipped off up the path in glee, then sighed and strapped her backpack on, her progress for the next few miles fuelled by pure rage.

By the time they reached the tiny village the heat and exertion had cleared most of the alcohol out of her system and she had long since moved ahead of Claudia on the path, somehow managing to restrain herself from doing any of the childish/evil things her brain was telling her to do. She looked about as she waited for her friend to catch up, her eyes drawn to the yellow and white mansion tucked into the trees on her left. It seemed at odds with the rest of the place, almost like it had been lifted out of Gone with the Wind and dropped in the middle of the forest. A sudden image of Vivien Leigh in a gingham dress and ruby slippers singing about rainbows popped into her head and she chuckled to herself as she pulled out a bottle of water.

"Has your hangover finally driven you mad?" Claudia panted as she caught up.

"I told you I was fine," Maya shrugged as she handed her friend a bottle. "Now let's go find this rock so we can get out of here."

Claudia rolled her eyes at her but headed off down a path leading out of the village and into the national park. The walk was a relatively short and Maya sighed in frustration at the small gaggle of tourists milling about the site as they approached. She put a hand out to stop her friend and pulled her further on down the trail.

"What are you doing? I thought you wanted to get this over with?"

"I do, but we're never going to get a proper look at it with all those people hanging about, and I'm not keen on having a cameo in a bunch of home movies."

"Please," Claudia rolled her eyes. "Like anyone would even notice. You're not exactly famous, Maya."

"Hey!" she huffed, genuinely insulted. "That wasn't what I was saying, but I'll have you know I am very noticeable."

"Well, you certainly make one hell of a first impression," a voice sounded from the edge of the path.

Maya wheeled around to see Rebecca Bronstein leaning against a tree with her arms folded and an amused smile dancing on her lips.

"Oh yeah?" she answered weakly, hands on her hips and a blush creeping up her neck. Jesus, she was normally so good at this! What was it about this woman that got her so flustered?

"Yeah," Rebecca laughed, pushing away from the tree and walking over to her. "It's good to see you again, Maya. I'm glad you managed to stay out of trouble."

"Yeah, well I…" Maya shook her head to try and clear it. Her throat was dry and she realised she had no idea what she had been about to say. She huffed out a breath and turned to face the other woman. "What are you doing here, Rebecca?"

"Oh, you know," she shrugged. "Touristy stuff. The museum, the swimming holes, the hiking…"

Maya took a step towards her, folding her arms and locking eyes with her. Two could play at that game. She waited for the smirk to leave her face before asking again. "What are you really doing here?"

"The same thing as you, I imagine," Rebecca answered after a beat. "Looking for answers."

"And why do you think I am looking for answers?"

"Because you're Maya Rodriguez," she smiled. "It's what you do."

"You know who I am?"

"Of course. Everyone knows who you are. Well, everyone who does what we do."

"So, that other night in the bar," Maya frowned down at her. "You were just playing me?"

"No, I was flirting with you."

"Why?"

"You flirted with me first," she shrugged.

"Yeah, well that's a matter of opinion. Besides, I flirt with everyone and I didn't know who you were, so…" Maya broke off and stared out into the forest, shifting her weight slightly awkwardly between her feet.

"Right. Good to know," the shorter woman replied tightly as she folded her arms. "And then your friend here told you that I was a fame hungry Bronstein and you decided I wasn't so fuckable anymore?"

Claudia gave an embarrassed cough from behind them, reminding Maya of her presence and giving her somewhere else to look rather than the bristling brunette in front of her.

"Well, I wouldn't put it exactly…" Maya turned to her friend for help but the redhead was steadfastly looking anywhere but at the two of them. She took a breath and turned back to Rebecca. "Look, I was just a bit shocked when I found out is all. When I'm working I don't expect to bump into other people in my field and when I do it usually means we're looking for the same thing and I…well, I don't really play well with others."

"Yeah, I heard."

"What?"

"People talk, Maya," Rebecca smirked again as she turned to walk back into the forest. "Maybe if you learned to 'play' better with others you'd know that. I'll see you around."

Maya stared after her in disbelief. What the fuck was that supposed to mean? She heard movement behind her as Claudia finally moved forward to join her.

"Well, that could have gone better."

"You think?" Maya spat, turning to stomp angrily up the path for a few moments before stopping abruptly and turning back to her friend. "People talk about me?"

"Um…." Claudia brought her hand up to her face and fiddled nervously with her lip.

"Claudia?"

"Well, you know, they don't really talk to me because they know I'm your friend and everything so…"

"What do they say about me?"

"Just, you know…"

"What?"

"Well, that you like to work alone," she said softly, eyes on the ground.

"And?"

"And that you're kind of a bitch."

"Right," Maya turned and walked on up the path, yanking her pack higher onto her shoulders. She heard Claudia sigh and start to follow her and they walked on in silence until they reached a clearing at the end of the path. Maya unclipped her backpack and dropped it on the floor, then lay down and rested her head on it, pulling her hat down over her face and closing her eyes. After a few moments she heard her friend settle a few feet away and start to pull things out of her bag.

"They just don't know you, Maya," Claudia said softly a few minutes later. "If they did they'd love you like I do. Even though you are a bitch."

Despite herself she felt her lip twitch up in a smile and some of the weight that had settled on her start to lift.

"Thanks, Claud," she said quietly.

As the sun was just beginning to set they made their way back to the rock, hoping that the impending darkness would have cleared the area of tourists. Thankfully it had and now that they had the place to themselves Maya set down her pack and wandered around as Claudia settled on the other side and started unpacking her equipment. As the redhead concentrated on the big rock Maya wandered over to the smaller and squatted down next to it to get a better look and try and work out what was going on.

The main figure on this one was a stickman with one arm up and the other bent with his hand on his hip. Forcing 'I'm a little teapot' out of her head Maya turned her attention to the other details, desperately hoping they would bring up more relevant associations. A carving that looked like a floating head sat just to his left above images resembling a pawnbroker's sign and a rocket. On his right was a snake, a symbol with a small circle in it and one that looked like a bird. As Maya tilted her head to try and work out what she was looking at she noticed that most of the carvings had similar sets of small circles near them and that, from this angle, some of the circles lined up. She straightened back up to look in closer detail at the ones which aligned; a squid like figure in the bottom right, the middle spot between the main figure's legs, one enclosed within his crooked arm, and the last linked to something that looked like an upside down question mark, or an old fashioned microphone. Above the final set was a something that looked like a tiny backpacker with a line extending in front of him, and she wondered if it was this association that was making her think of this as a map?

She shook her head to clear the thought and stood back up. The Inca didn't use drawings for direction, she knew that, so if this was a map it was unlikely to be what they were looking for. But then Elaine had only said that what Zuazola was looking for *may* be Inca and if it wasn't then...well, then they were no better informed either way. This was like searching for a needle in a sea of haystacks. With your hands tied behind your back. And a severe allergy to hay.

She sighed and looked over to see if her friend was faring any better. Claudia was working her way around the larger rock, taking photographs in the fading light and occasionally stopping to make notes on her pad, apparently oblivious to the futility of their task. Maya tried to shake off her despondency and looked back down at her own rock, trying desperately to get her brain to work. Okay, come on, Maya, start at the beginning. What is this rocket ship meant to be? And next to that… It looked like a dandelion clock. God, this was stupid. What was she even doing here? She sat down next to the rock and raised her eyes to the sky. The stars looked beautiful out here. She couldn't remember last time she had seen them properly, not much chance for stargazing in New York City.

Shit, of course! She scrambled back up and looked back at the drawings. The dandelion clock, the rocket, the floating faces with the circles around them…

"Claud, come over here a second," she called as she checked the pattern again.

"Find something?"

"I'm not sure," she drew a line through the air to show Claudia what she was considering. "See how the dots move round to a different position in each carving?"

"Yes?"

"So, you see these two down here?"

"The rocket?"

"Yeah, or maybe a crude drawing of a constellation?"

"A constellation?" Claudia raised the camera to her face and lined up the shot.

"Yeah, like they were marking its path through the sky?" Maya pointed out all the relevant markings as Claudia snapped pictures.

"Okay. But why? And what are all the other markings about? Why the snake?"

"Well that is…" Maya held her hand up dramatically. "I have no idea. And I have no idea what we're looking for."

"Come and look at this," Claudia tipped her head towards the larger rock and walked back over to it, leaning in to point as Maya joined her. "This one has all these things that I thought were paw prints, see? But they also seem to be plotting a path across the rock and see here? Another snake. And obviously you recognise our friend down here," she pointed out the stickman at the bottom.

"Okay," Maya nodded as she studied the carvings. "But what does it mean? And what were they following?"

"Well, when you said about the constellation I realised that the rocket ship and the paw print kind of looks like the Pleiades, right?"

"The Pleiades? As in the Seven Sisters? There's only five dots here though."

"Yeah, but there's more in this one, see?" Claudia pointed towards the middle of the rock.

"Still only six."

"Yes, but it's not like they had a damn telescope, Maya, and some of them shine considerably brighter than the others. And there are more than seven stars in the Pleiades anyway. And they're not sisters."

"Alright," she held her hands up. "Jeez, when did you get so sensitive about astronomy?"

"I'm not…" Claudia huffed and rolled her eyes as she turned back to the rock. "Look, there's also this guy down here. He seems to be on a boat, see? So maybe they were trying to use the stars for navigation?"

"Don't people usually use Polaris for navigation?"

"Well, yes, but…" Claudia sighed again and knelt down, flicking through the pictures she had taken on the camera. "God, this is stupid. Why can't it just be...what's that?"

"What?"

"In this last picture," she held the camera up so Maya could see it.

"What is it? Some kind of flare from the camera?"

"Maybe. Look, though, it's in this one too."

"Try taking another one."

Claudia held the camera up and took the shot. The light was much lower now than it had been even five minutes ago and the rock flared up under the light of the flash.

"Jesus! What is that?" Maya looked over at where Claudia was huddled over the screen.

"I don't know!"

"It's some kind of lichen," Rebecca's voice came from behind them.

"Oh, God," Maya groaned and walked away.

"Lichen?" Claudia asked. "But why is it flaring like that? Normally lichen reacts to water, not light, and it only appears to glow."

"It's phosphorescent, but not like any kind that I've come across before," Rebecca said as she approached, her eyes on Maya's retreating form.

"The closest I've seen is in the Appalachians, but even that behaves fairly typically."

"Is it natural? Did you test it?"

"It's organic and extremely old," she nodded. "But the placement of it is not random."

"Okay, how can you possibly know that?" Maya asked, curiosity bringing her back to the rock.

"We ran radiometric tests on the rock to determine the growth pattern and noted that the conditions present in the areas where the lichen had taken root were standard throughout the structure and therefore, excluding any redundant extraneous factors, the subject should display a consistent spread. However the conditions in the rock as a whole are not conducive to the growth of this particular genus so a manual influence must have been present at first exposure."

"What?" Maya asked, staring at her incredulously.

"She's saying that it shouldn't be here at all but if it was a natural occurrence it should be all over."

"Yes thank you, Claudia, I understood the big words the science lady used," she muttered, glaring at her friend before turning back to Rebecca. "What I was questioning was how the hell you ran radiometric tests on an ancient petroglyph site in the middle of a forest on such a scale that you have that much information?"

"We have some specialised equipment that allows us to carry out detailed testing in the field," Rebecca answered, squaring her shoulders slightly.

"From where? The Enterprise?"

"You're welcome to come and see the results for yourself if you'd like? Maybe share some ideas?" Rebecca offered, ignoring her question.

"Yeah, I don't think so."

"Of course not," she smiled and started to leave. "Okay, well, I guess I'll leave you to it then. Good luck with it."

"Maya!" Claudia hissed.

"What? You expect me just to fawn all over her cos she has all the fancy equipment and people think I'm a bitch?"

"Not at all," she said quietly. "I'm just suggesting that we maybe we don't piss her off quite so completely. She seems to know a lot about it and have an awful lot of resources. And we still don't know what she's looking for. God, we still don't know what we're looking for!"

Maya stared down at her for a couple of seconds before turning towards the path. "Hey, Rebecca."

The woman stopped and turned back.

"Thanks for the, uh, you know, help."

"You're welcome," she nodded. "We're just at the campsite where I saw you earlier if you change your mind."

"Thanks, but I think we'll take a look ourselves first. We don't even know what we're looking for yet," Maya admitted as she closed the gap between them. "You're actually camping?"

"Of course!" she laughed. "Why?"

"No reason, you just don't really strike me as the...outdoorsy type."

"Oh, I see," Rebecca linked her hands loosely in front of her and took a step towards her. "You figured the spoilt little rich girl would have rented the mansion for her stay in the woods?"

"Well, not exactly," she smiled. "Plus I think it's like a museum or something…"

Rebecca laughed lightly, her eyes sparkling in the fading light. A silence settled over them and Maya didn't really know what to do with it so she just nodded and gestured back to the rock.

"So I should…"

"Yeah, sure," Rebecca smiled and started to back away. "Well, you know where we are, even if you just want to share our campsite. Safety in numbers, you know?"

"Yeah, maybe," she smiled back. "Thanks."

"Great, then I'll see you later," she started to walk off before turning back once more. "Maybe."

Maya watched her make her way back up to the path before hurrying over to her bag and searching through it. When she found what she was looking for she headed back over as Claudia flashed the camera again and stared at the rock.

"It's incredible. It looks like it's in a pattern but it doesn't light up long enough to see it."

"Try this," Maya held out a small black light and moved it slowly over the rock.

"Bloody hell," Claudia breathed.

"You should get some pictures so we can try and work out what's going on."

Chapter 6

Maya stoked the campfire and waited patiently for Claudia to stop messing about with the laptop so they could check the footage. And by patiently she meant only shooting her a glare or throwing a stick at her once every couple of minutes rather than every thirty seconds. She was hungry and tired and wanted to get this over with so they could get out of here and away from Rebecca fucking Bronstein.

It wasn't so much that the woman somehow left her with the sexual repartee of a fifteen year old boy, or that she was a rich Yale graduate seemingly able to do anything she put her mind to, or even that her parents were everything she despised. No, it was more that Maya had the sneaking suspicion that Rebecca was trying to play her like a cheap fiddle, and that was something Maya would not allow to happen, ever again.

"Okay, I'm ready," Claudia huffed as she sat down next to her. "You can stop throwing things now."

"It's about damn time."

"Well, I'm very sorry, Maya, but it's extremely difficult to operate a laptop with frostbitten fingers."

"Don't be so dramatic, it's not that cold." Maya snarked, stoking the fire again quickly.

"It would have been a lot warmer at the actual campsite, I'm sure."

"Claudia…"

"I know, I know," she sighed and rubbed her hands together. "Alright, so I have tried to link all the pictures up into a collage so we can see the pattern. It's not quite perfect because someone kept throwing things at me," she shot Maya a filthy look before continuing. "But you get the general gist."

"Okay," Maya nodded as she looked at the pictures. "So it follows the paw print pattern like you said, but then the trail drops down to the guy in the boat and doubles back on the lower level, leading to our friend down here and ending with the snake."

"Yes. And then the second rock," she opened the second tab. "The trail circles around him and then moves through his arm to the snake."

"Right," Maya nodded, studying the picture. "So, we have the two series of pictures, two trails showing a pattern, and both patterns ending with a snake."

"Yes," Claudia smiled and pulled a bottle from her bag. "And we still don't have a bastard clue what it means. Cheers!"

Maya chuckled as her friend took a giant swig and grabbed the bottle out of her hand. "It's moments like these I remember why we're such good friends," she smirked as she took a drink and handed the bottle back. "Okay, so what are we missing?"

Claudia sighed and rubbed her eyes. "I don't know. There are two people in the first drawing, one in the second, not including the floating heads, correct?"

"Within the confines of the pattern, yes."

"Which would suggest…" Claudia spread her hands dramatically, then threw them up in the air when Maya merely widened her eyes and cocked her head slightly. "Maya! That was your cue to jump in with something!"

"Nothing, Claud!" Maya cried. "I have absolutely nothing!"

"Of course you do! That's what you always say right before you pull something amazing out of thin air and get the the best mark in the class, making the rest of us muppets who sat there all year taking copious notes whilst you slept off your latest hangover look like absolute idiots."

Claudia punctuated her sentence with another large swig before pulling out her cigarettes and lighting one angrily.

"Okay, I think that's a statement we'll be coming back to later," Maya said slowly, sliding the bottle out of reach and plucking a cigarette from Claudia's pack. "But for now, so, two people in this one, one of which is our friend stickman. Only one figure in this one, with three...objects between his legs."

"Hmm, not so well endowed as stickman," Claudia observed, grabbing the bottle back.

"Not really the focus I was looking for, Claud…"

"Still, probably for the best. Stickman looks to have collapsed from lack of blood to the head," she snickered before taking another drink.

"How can you possibly be drunk already?" Maya tutted, grabbing the bottle back. "Wait, a minute. Why is stickman lying down?"

"I already said, it's lack of blood to the…"

"Claudia, concentrate! The other two guys are standing up, the patterns are above them, or around them. See, even when it loops through this guys arm the trail breaks, like it's gone behind him, see?"

"Oh yes! But with stickman…"

"It goes right over him, like…"

"...like he's part of the trail, not the one who's being guided," Claudia finished, pulling the laptop back and zooming in on the prone figure.

"Yeah," Maya agreed, taking a drag on her cigarette and pulling absently on her pendant.

"Returning briefly to their genitals…" the redhead glared at her friend's snort and handed her the bottle. "Don't you think it's strange how they are so different? I mean, the man in the boat doesn't have any, the one on the small rock has three, and then stickman has this massive one that seems to be slightly detached from his body. I mean look at it. It's shooting off like a rocket."

"God, that brings some unpleasant images to mind," Maya wrinkled her nose and took a drink.

"But, speaking of rockets, Maya..." Claudia looked at her expectantly.

"Yeah?"

"Well, on the smaller rock. The constellation?"

"I can see you're trying to lead me somewhere, I'm just…" Maya shook her head and wrinkled her nose. "I'm not there with you, Claud."

"Oh, for God's sake," she huffed and pulled up a series of photographs. "Here is the 'rocket' carving that you pointed out on the small rock. Here are the two carvings from the first which I initially thought to be footprints owing to their proximity to what I thought were paw prints."

"Okay."

"But see how shape is actually quite similar to the rocket ship? Like if you jump from the paw print to the rocket ship to the footprint?" Claudia pressed a button and the three photographs flashed across the screen in sequence.

"Oh, shit."

"Have you ever watched a space shuttle launch? I don't mean up close, I mean from a great distance?"

"I see where you're going now," she took a last drag off her cigarette and threw it into the fire. "You think these might be representations of a comet?"

"Yes. And comets were a great portent in the past. And the paw prints, going from six dots to five?"

"What, you think whoever made this thought one of the stars fell out of the sky?"

"Well, I don't know, it could just be a coincidence but…"

"Or maybe they thought one could fall out of the sky?" Maya pulled on her pendant and stared at the screen. "Maybe this isn't a trail but a prophecy. This guy, the teapot guy, is like the chief. This under his arm is his ceremonial headdress, and in his other hand his staff. The dandelion clock thing by his leg is the Pleiades with five, six points if you include the, er, stalk, then the rocket/comet, and the next time you see it it only has four points."

"And two severed heads in between."

"What?"

"Well look at them," Claudia motioned at the screen as she reached into her bag for some food. "This one couldn't look more surprised that he's been beheaded and the one above still has the garotte floating under him."

"Jesus, Claudia…"

"I know, I'm sorry," she said around a mouthful of bread. "This is what learning about Tudor history from primary school age will do to a person."

"No, I mean I think you're right," Maya flicked through the photos again. "What if these are severed heads? What if it's not a trail, or a prophecy, but a story? What if it's showing that the falling of a star started this terrible chain of events that lead to the deaths of these people?"

"Okay. So who were these people?"

"Well, they'd have to be pretty important people to have their story commemorated like this. They have snakes woven in as well, and they wouldn't do that for just anyone. And then if you see it in conjunction with the larger rock, and our friend stick man on the ground with his...staff between his legs, it kind of looks like the fall of an emperor to me."

"Emperor?" Claudia sat up a little straighter. "Like the Incan emperor?"

"Could be Mayan, they worshipped the same deities. Could be wholly unrelated. Although Atahualpa was garotted."

"So how can we tell?"

"We can't. Not with any certainty." Maya poked at the fire and played with her necklace.

"Great, so we're back to square one." Claudia threw up her hands and reached for the bottle. "What do we do now?"

"Now we go to the lake."

"The lake? Why?"

"Cause you see this guy on the boat?" she pulled up the picture and showed it to her friend. "I don't think that's a boat. I think that's the tide going out."

"What? But Elaine said that…"

"I know what Elaine said, but just hear me out, okay? When I was a kid there was this place we used to go in the cove near our village. There was a cave formation that you got into high up in the bluff, and we used to dare each other to go as deep into it as we could. There was this one particular cave that was so far down that at high tide it was inaccessible, and when the waters rolled out of it it looked...well, it looked just like that."

"It seems a bit of a stretch, Maya…"

"I know, but look at this, right above stickman's head. Doesn't that look like an inlet to you?"

"Well, I guess it could be but…"

"And this, on the smaller rock," she flicked quickly onto a new screen. "Don't you think that looks like a cave opening?"

"Um, not really. It kind of looks like a man holding something above his head." Claudia shrugged a little, then squinted. "Or maybe a vagina?"

Maya tutted and shoved the laptop back at her.

"I'm sorry, Maya, but I think maybe you're just seeing things that you want to see?"

"Why would I want to see a goddamn cave?"

"Because it would mean we found something?" Claudia suggested tentatively. "That we had somewhere to go, that we didn't have to stay here?"

"God, whatever, Claudia, I just thought it was worth a shot," she took another drink from the bottle and passed it back to her friend. "Look, it's been a long day, my head hurts and I can't think about this shit any more. I'm going to bed."

"Yes, that's probably wise. I'm sure it will all seem clearer with fresh eyes."

"Yeah. Sure." Maya headed over to her tent and pulled the zip open before sitting in the opening and pulling off her boots.

"Maya?" Claudia called as she was closing the tent back up again. "We'll find it. We always do."

"Yeah. Night Claud," she smiled tiredly as she pulled the zip closed and rolled her sleeping bag out as she sighed. "We better."

Maya woke suddenly in the night, her heart pounding in her chest and her hand reaching blindly out in front of her. She sat up and rubbed her face, inhaling sharply as she waited for her heart rate to return to normal. What had she been dreaming about? She let her breath out slowly and looked around her tent.

"Great, now I need to pee," she muttered, reaching for her clothes and shoes.

As soon as she was dressed she unzipped the tent and climbed out, stretching in the cool night air and looking around for a suitably secluded spot. The fire had been covered over with sand but there were still a few embers glowing around the edges so she stepped forward and stamped them out before heading into the woods, the full moon offering her a guiding light.

"Well it's a marvellous night for a moondance," she sang softly as she made her way deeper amongst the trees. "With the stars up a…la la la lah…"

Giving up on the song she yawned widely and pulled her jacket a little tighter around her, eyes searching about for somewhere to relieve herself. She didn't know why she was bothering, it felt like she was the only person around for miles, but knowing her luck she would be discovered mid urination by a group of small children or something and, honestly, the ensuing lecture from Claudia would just not be worth it. Finally spotting some suitable foliage she squatted down behind it, her mind going over everything they had seen today.

As usual Claudia had been right, she was reaching, but it was just so frustrating. The images were telling them a story, she was sure of that now, and in her head that story ended at or near the lake. The problem was that she didn't know why, or where, or how to convince Claudia that they needed to trust her instincts. It was true what her friend had said, she did seem to have a habit of plucking answers from thin air, but it wasn't as simple as that. What looked to everyone else like her 'sleeping off her latest hangover' was actually her absorbing all the information and letting it swirl around in the crazy making place that was her mind before it came spewing out of her mouth like some sarcastic spit bubble of knowledge.

Maya sighed as she stood up and did up her pants. She knew what she looked like to all of them, all the preppy British kids she'd studied with, all the stuck up professors who'd treated her like shit til she turned in her first essay, then with suspicion til she sat her first exam. It had been the same way as she tried to find her first backer, rooms full of pervy old men referring to her as 'darling' and 'sweetheart' and looking at her like they were picturing her in her underwear. Thank God Elaine had come along when she did or she would most likely be in prison right now, whiling away her sentence reliving the moment where she kicked one of their fat asses through their expensive glass windows. Looking the way she did had its advantages, she wasn't so arrogant as to deny that, but in the world of academia she had stuck out like a sore hispanic thumb.

"Coño!" she swore as the branch she had just pushed past swung back and hit her in the face.

She leaned against the rock face and pressed her hand to her eye as she waited for it to stop watering. Eventually it did and she moved more cautiously along the rock, sliding her hand down it until she realised the indentations she could feel were carvings. She turned to kneel in front of it and swept the debris away, a smile splitting her face when she saw the image placed there.

"I fucking knew it."

By the time Claudia finally crawled out of her tent Maya was all packed up and ready to go, pacing about angrily as she smoked her fifth cigarette of the day, knowing full well that her lungs would chastise her for each and every one of them on the hike to their next destination.

"Okay, I'm up," Claudia said blearily, rubbing her hand over her face as she took in the unexpected sight. "What's going on?"

"I found it, Claud," Maya called, grabbing the kettle off the stove and pouring some coffee for her friend. "I found the fucking marker."

"What fucking marker?"

"The fucking marker that shows us where we need to go next!"

"Oh, right," she answered sleepily, blowing on her coffee before taking a cautious sip. "Let me guess, it takes us to the lake?"

"Well, yes, actually."

"Right." Claudia said again as she set her cup down. "Give me two minutes."

Fifteen minutes later they arrived at the spot Maya had found the night before and she pulled back the branches, pointing out the images on the rockface excitedly.

"See? The same guy in the boat/wave thingy, only this time he's on the water and there's a mountain behind him and this trail leading off of it."

Claudia yawned and raised her cup to her mouth as she studied the picture before her. "It could be anywhere, Maya. It could be the port. And how is he on the water without a boat?"

"The port? Come on, Claudia, there's all this...like foliage shit around it, where's that at the port?"

"Well maybe not the port but definitely along the coast," she shrugged and drained the cup.

"What?" Maya let the branches drop and stared at her friend in irritation. "Claudia, it's obviously the lake. It's round! Why are you acting like it's not obvious?"

"Why are you acting like it is?" Claudia replied angrily. "Maya, you are so determined to believe that the answers are at the damn lake that you are blocking out every other possible explanation! Now I'm not saying that you are wrong, I'm just saying if you make this great leap, even if it does turn out to be right, think of all the important information you could be missing and what that could mean for us later?"

Maya glared at her friend for a few moments as she let the words sink in then gave a defeated sigh and walked back out to the path.

"Alright. So, back to the rock?"

"We have all we need from the rock," Claudia dropped her bag on the ground and pulled the camera out. "Just make me some more coffee while I see what I can get from this one. What time is it?"

"I don't know. Ten?"

"Christ, Maya!" she yelled as she turned on the camera and saw the actual time. "It's five thirty! No wonder I'm so bloody tired."

Claudia wandered into the bush and started pulling the branches back, fixing them to the main body of it so she could get a clear shot. "You seriously need to get a watch. What time have you been up since?"

"I'm not sure," Maya answered as she set up the stove. "I woke up in the night and needed to pee. That's how I found it."

Claudia stopped abruptly and turned her upper body towards her. "Please tell me I'm not walking about in your piss."

"Of course not!" Maya answered quickly as she filled the kettle. "Just maybe don't go any further to your right."

"God, I hate you," she muttered as she retraced her steps out of the bush. "Hurry up with that coffee."

"Jeez, Claud, it's not like I can make the water boil quicker, it's a tiny stove."

"Maybe if I set you on fire we would have a more effective heat source?"

"Woah, easy with the hate!" Maya turned to her, affronted. "I thought you were meant to be a morning person?"

"That's because you never get up before noon!" Claudia snapped back. "Now be quiet, I'm trying to concentrate."

"I'm up now…" she muttered.

"Maya…

"Alright, I'm sorry."

"No, come and look at this." Claudia knelt on the ground and brushed the dirt with her hand. "There's another one down here but it's fairly covered and...promise me this is not where you urinated?"

"God," Maya muttered as she moved her out of the way. "Here, I'll do it. What is that? A turtle?"

"A turtle with arms? Maybe symbolic. You know like the Mayans depicted their deity Quetzalcoatl as a feathered serpent? Several ancient cultures revered turtles, although I don't recall any in South America," she said, snapping a picture of it. "And the boat/wave thing again. No man this time."

"And the cave again. But...three of them."

"Caves. Vaginas."

"Jeez, Claud, anyone would think you were the lesbian."

"I highly doubt that," Claudia checked her camera as she walked away. "Besides I'm too lazy to be a lesbian. It seems like far too much work."

"What?"

"Okay, so what do we think about this Great and Powerful Oz thing here?"

"Uh, what?"

"This weird, floaty head thing to the left of the caves?" Claudia pointed at the symbol as she retrieved the boiling kettle from the stove.

"I don't know, it's kind of…" Maya cleared some more of the dirt off it and sat back. "It's like the wave symbol next to it but inside something."

"Like the mountain."

"Yeah, maybe, or…" Maya stared down at it and tried to come up with an alternative.

"It's a mountain, Maya." Claudia sighed as she handed her a coffee. "It's a mountain, they are caves, it's not a boat, it's water. The indigenous people didn't have boats like that. It looks like…like a viking longship, or a galleon."

"So…"

"So I'm saying you are right. But you knew that. Now we just have to figure out where on the lake these caves are. Any ideas?"

"Um, I guess we go down to the shore and try to identify any landmarks from the glyphs." Maya tried to hide the smile on her face as she sat down next to her.

"Okay. But you're carrying the heavy stuff today," Claudia yawned. "I'm bloody knackered."

Chapter 7

By the time they reached the shore the sun was at its most powerful, beating down on them like they were ants under a magnifying glass. There had been a change in the air as well, rather than just being hot it was now stifling and muggy. Maya had made them stop several times during the trip because although Claudia had made no complaint she knew that her friend must be suffering. They had been walking for around six hours and covered close to twelve miles of difficult terrain.

She laid down her backpack under a large tree and started pulling out what she needed to make them some food as she waited for the redhead to catch up, fighting the urge to start looking for the caves immediately. She could feel the usual nervous excitement stirring in her chest at the prospect of really being on to something but she knew that they were both too tired and too hot to start out straight away. Better to get some food and rest and wait for the sun to abate a bit even though the anticipation was killing her.

This was the part of her job that she loved - connecting dots that no one ever had before, finding meaning where none had previously been known. She thought back to the first time it had happened. She and Claud had found fish bones where they had no right to be and used them as a starting point to prove that humans had settled there thousands of years before anyone had thought it possible. That had been their first dig together and they had never willingly worked apart since, their friendship growing stronger over all the highs and lows they had shared.

On paper she and Claudia should not be friends, she supposed. Claudia was from a solid middle class British background, her father was an engineer at a firm that built racing cars just outside Oxford and her mother was a charge nurse at the John Radcliffe hospital. Claudia attended local schools, worked hard and earned herself a place at Oxford University, to the delight of her parents. Being what the rich, privileged students referred to as a 'Townie' she wasn't included in many of their events, not that she would have attended if she had been. She preferred the company of her old school friends when they were in town, or travelling up to London to see the ones who had gone to university there, and had decided to stay living with her parents to avoid the extortionate student accommodation rents less than two miles down the road. This earned her a reputation for being a bookish, boring, homely type which only served to further alienate her from even the regular students, although had any cared to investigate they would have found that nothing could be further from the truth. Still, she kept her head down, worked hard and emerged with a first.

Maya, on the other hand, was from a poor family in Puerto Rico where she lived until she was nine, at which point her father got a lucky break with his job and moved them to Tucson, Arizona. There Maya was bullied for her thick accent and strikingly different appearance so built up her walls and avoided attending whenever possible, until the sixth grade when her father was killed in an accident at the plant where he worked. With the payout her mother received they packed up and moved to New York to live with Maya's aunt, a terrifying woman with a heart of gold who made damn sure that Maya studied hard and made something of her life. With the remainder of her father's life insurance the women shipped her off to England after she won her place at Oxford and left themselves short so that they could support her whilst she studied. It wasn't enough but she couldn't tell them that, so she worked at various bars and clubs around the city to pay her rent and studied on her breaks. When she wasn't working or studying, she let loose and gained herself a reputation as a party girl, so when she turned up to lectures looking wrecked from working til 5am people assumed she was hungover. She didn't bother to correct them, she had grown used to people making assumptions about her and what difference would it make anyway? She was already the hispanic chick with no money who probably got in on a technicality, so what did she care if they thought she always drunk and coasting through classes too? After a few close calls during finals week where she woke up ten minutes before she was due to sit her exam, she too emerged with a first.

During their first two years at Oxford their paths only crossed a handful of times. The first time was at the library where they both made a grab for the last copy of a textbook they needed for their course (Claudia gave up and let Maya have it after an impassioned plea, a burst of angry sounding Spanish and some thinly veiled threats). The second was one night that Claudia's friends were in town and they ended up in a bar where Maya was working (Maya remembered the book incident and kept slipping them free shots. She was fired the next day, not that she ever told Claudia). The third, a particularly rowdy party where they had both somehow ended up even though they didn't know anyone, didn't like anyone and they had spent most of the night drinking a bottle of tequila in the corner, cackling over how they would dispose of the body of a particularly odious boy who had taken a fancy to Claudia (they called him Eton Mess as his former school was all he seemed capable of talking about and, well, he was not a pretty man). From then on they would sit together in lectures and share cheap lunches at various places around town; Claudia invited Maya to spend Christmas with her family and persuaded her to sign up for a dig over the summer, even though neither of them could particularly afford it. Maya had been forced to live off beans on toast, that staple of British student life, for two months when she got back so she could afford her rent. She could barely stand to look at them now.

Still, that had been the dig where they had started to make a name for themselves and, more importantly, not killed each other despite the close quarters they had shared for the two weeks they had been away. Throughout Maya's endless complaints about the cold weather and Claudia's insistence on eating Pot Noodles at strange hours of the day they had forged a partnership that would serve them well in the years that followed.

Claudia dropped down heavily next to Maya and nodded her head in thanks as she grabbed the bottle of water the other woman held out to her.

"Well, that was...fun," she muttered after downing half the bottle.

Maya smiled and handed her a cigarette. "You mean this wasn't your favourite day ever?"

The redhead shot her a look as she searched for her lighter. "Do you remember that time we accidentally walked through that bog in Killashee and I lost one of my favourite shoes?"

"Oh, yeah, I remember," she chuckled as she stirred the pot. "I had to carry you four miles back to town."

"Not all the way!" Claudia protested as she exhaled sharply. "Only the last two after I sliced my foot open on that pottery shard. It wasn't even old enough for us to catalogue. Anyway, I still preferred that day."

"Well I can pitch the tents if you like? Get some food and then you can sleep while I check for landmarks?"

Claudia studied her face thoughtfully for a moment as she smoked her cigarette. "Alright, I give up. Who are you and what did you do with Maya?"

"Come on," she tutted and kicked her gently. "I just, you know, feel…bad about waking you up." Maya finished quickly, all her concentration on the stove.

"I'm sorry, what was that?"

"Come on, Claud…"

"No, it's just that that sounded an awful lot like an apology…"

"Alright, well you don't need to be a bitch about it."

"Alright, I'm sorry," she chuckled. "Thank you, Maya, that sounds lovely. And apology accepted."

"Dick," she muttered, smiling slightly as she kicked her again.

After they had eaten and set up camp Maya settled by the shore to check the pictures on the laptop as Claudia slept. The lake was enormous and surrounded by picturesque mountain ranges and forests, although it emitted a smell that was making her feel slightly unwell. The fact that there were mountain ranges on either side of the lake was also giving her some concern but she figured that the petroglyphs were most likely to be drawn closer to the area they referred to, or at least she hoped. Either way they were here now so may as well start with these ones and move onto the others if they didn't find anything.

She pulled up the image of the rock she had found last night and studied it for anything she could use as a landmark. The detail was pretty basic; a generic mountainous shape with a trail leading up from the water, trees to the left and right of it. There was a tiny glyph just above the waterline, two snakes with a blob in the middle, and when she zoomed in closer the blob took on a little more form. Extending out of the top of it were five circular objects, giving the image the appearance of a child's drawing of a hand. Underneath the image, below the waterline, was another drawing of the triangular shape with the line through it which Maya had taken to be the cave and Claudia had...had other ideas for.

But where was it? Maya studied the cliff face a few hundred feet in front of her and tried to find any similarities between it and the drawings. Nothing. Great. She flicked through the other pictures for a few minutes in the hope of finding something useful before snapping the laptop shut and throwing it unceremoniously onto the ground. Fuck the research, that was more Claudia's thing anyway. She had always been more of a 'kick it and see what falls out' kind of girl. She stood up and walked out from under the trees, shielding her eyes from the sun as she stared up at the mountains in front of her.

"So let's go kick it."

As she walked around the shore in front of the slope she pulled off her hat and waved it in front of her face to clear the bugs that were swarming around her. She looked up at the mountain rising above her and tried again to spot any identifying marks but, as expected, she saw none so she continued on her path around the corner and sighed in annoyance as the it dropped away where the rock face jutted sharply out into the lake.

"Well great." Maya huffed, putting a foot on the rock and climbing up to see if she could make it across. Slowly she tested her footing and started trying to work her way around, poking her head around the sheer face to see if it was possible to continue. Nothing. Just water lapping up against the cliff and a similar cut on the other side. She sighed and was starting to retrace her steps when the water dropped slightly and she saw a shape carved in the rock. She moved back into position quickly, too quickly, and slipped as a small wave washed over her foot.

"Coño!" she yelled as she fell into the water. As she broke back through the surface she spat out the fetid water she had inhaled and kicked her feet to keep her head above. "And I thought it smelled bad on the outside," she muttered as she grabbed her hat from the water and steadied herself on the rock. Well, now that she was already wet she might as well check out the thing that had caused her to fall in in the first place. She spat again to try and clear some of the foul taste from her mouth and kicked out towards the far cliff face. As she reached it she ran her hand down it and felt the rise and fall of a pattern beneath her fingers, but the algae filled water was covering it so she couldn't see what it was. Resigning herself she took a deep breath and ducked below the surface and as she peered through the murky water she could just about make out a blob and two wiggly lines before she had to close her eyes and kick for the surface again.

Buoyed with excitement she wiped at her eyes and blinked rapidly to try and clear the sting. This had to be it. Surely these were the same markings she had seen on the rock at the campsite? She turned to head back to shore and tell Claudia. They would have to find some way to get down deep enough to find the entrance to the caves but…

Claudia.

Maya stopped where she was and slowly swam back to face the cliff. She could hear the conversation in her head now.

"Are you sure, Maya? It seems awfully convenient that you just happened to fall into the water at the exact spot where blah blah diddy blah I'm always right blahdi blah."

She sighed and swam back to the cliff face, treading water as she took a few breaths to prepare herself and her eyeballs for the task ahead. Taking a deep breath she forced her head beneath the water and swam down as far as she could, her hand tracing the line of the rock. About fifteen metres down she felt the wall begin to slope away and she opened her eyes to look at what she was sure would be an opening. Instead she saw the cliff face disappearing into the silt that sloped back away from the stone and formed the bottom of the lake. Her lungs began to burn from lack of oxygen, too many cigarettes and sudden disappointment, so she kicked her feet and slid herself up the rock face, her eyes desperately trying to close as she searched again for the markings. She felt above her as she went and recoiled in disgust when her left hand touched something slimy, one eye closing against her will as she floated towards the surface. Her heart sank as she saw what it was that she had touched - a strand of seaweed suspended on a smooth, circular piece of coral protruding from the cliff face. She yanked it off as she swam past. So much for her snakes and hand print.

She took a gulp of air as she broke the surface and immediately started to choke on the skanky water. With one arm keeping her level and the other trying to clear her eyes she headed back the way she had come, disappointment weighing down her limbs. Goddamn Claudia. Why did she always have to be right?

Despondently she clambered up the rocks and out of the water, her white tank top smothered with green algae and her shorts plastered with God knows what. She slapped her sodden hat onto her head and trudged back towards the camp. She could see that Claudia was up and had the stove on but all she wanted now was what was stored in the left pocket of her bag.

"Ah, you're back!" Claudia greeted her cheerfully. "I've been doing some research and… God, you smell like a sewer. You haven't been in the lake, have you?"

"No, Claudia, of course not," she muttered, grabbing the bottle of bourbon out of her bag and wrenching the top off. "I decided to run back to the apartment and take a shower."

"Maya, that lake is completely disgusting. It is full of untreated waste, you could have caught anything!"

"It was an accident, okay?" Maya cried, flinging her ruined hat to the ground and tipping the bottle back to swallow far more than necessary. When she came up for air a stray droplet hit the back of her throat and she started to cough uncontrollably, beating her chest roughly in an attempt to regain control. As the coughing subsided she raised her eyes to the sky and then let her head drop down to her chest, feeling more pitiful than she remembered ever having felt in her life.

"Everything alright?" Claudia asked after a few moments.

"Yes," she replied sullenly, raising the bottle again but changing her mind before it reached her lips. "No! Everything is shit, Claudia! I mean, doesn't it just feel like everything we do on this one is just so...so..."

"Haphazard?"

"Yeah, like we're stumbling around blindly searching for… I don't know, like…"

"Anything that might even remotely fit?"

"Yeah, like we only have half the question and we're supposed to just…"

"Fill in the blanks?"

"Yeah," Maya sighed and took another drink. "You know?"

"Yes," she answered quietly, reaching for the bottle. "I know."

Maya pulled off her tank top and twisted it in her hands, watching the filthy water run out onto the grass. She stared out over the lake and into the forest on the other side, willing it to speak to her, offer up its secrets. Instead she heard distant bird calls and the flaring of the stove.

"It's just, I don't know, Claud," she sighed after a moment. "I just feel like we're missing something."

"That's because we are."

"What do you mean?"

"Come on, Maya, you said it yourself," Claudia said as she pulled her cigarettes out of her pocket and handed one over. "Elaine has given us some pretty slim leads before but we've always known what those leads were, um, leading to. This is nothing! 'Go to Fortín Solano, get Zuazola's journals, they may have something to do with the Inca.' I mean, really? That's it? Why go to all that trouble with no clear goal? She could have sent anyone to do that. Christ, she could have bought the journals for that matter, and made sure she got all of them and everything else pertaining to him. Why send us?"

Maya smoked her cigarette and looked at her friend. "Are you suggesting that Elaine is lying to us?"

"Yes."

"Why?"

"Why am I suggesting it or why is she?"

"I don't know. Both?"

"Well, I don't know why, exactly, and I'm not sure that 'lying to us' is the right term," Claudia shrugged and picked up the bottle. "But I can't shake the feeling that she knows more than she is letting on and she has sent us out here because she thinks that we are more likely to pick up the trail than anyone else."

"Trail?" Maya asked, reaching out her hand.

"Let me ask you something," she said as she passed the bourbon over. "What did she say when you told her Rebecca Bronstein was here?"

Maya took a drink and studied the redhead before she answered. "She said 'interesting'."

"That's it?"

"No," she admitted as she passed the bottle back. "She said something about Rebecca possibly having information that could be useful to us."

"And that didn't strike you as odd?"

"Well...not really. I mean, she was in the middle of telling me that I needed to keep it professional and, ah, well I thought…"

"You thought she was telling you not to shag her and ditch her because she might be useful later?"

"Hey!" Maya frowned at her before muttering. "You make me sound like some kind of rampant lothario."

"Sorry, I was just thinking back to..."

"Whatever, look, regardless of all that, why wouldn't Elaine just tell us if she wanted us to get information from Rebecca?"

"Because maybe she doesn't want us to work with her?" she shrugged. "Or maybe she just didn't expect her to be here?"

"Jesus, Claud, I'm too tired for this shit," Maya stubbed her cigarette out and rubbed at her sore eyes. "My brain hurts and I'm lost again. What are you saying?"

"I don't know," she sighed, opening her laptop and pulling up the pictures she had been working on. "I'm just as frustrated by this shit as you, Maya, I just didn't go for a swim in it."

"Okay. Just for that…" Maya glared at her and stood up, peeling her shorts off with a dramatic flourish.

"Of course," Claudia rolled her eyes and tapped at the keyboard. "Frustration aside I think I may have found something."

"What?" Maya paused mid way through wringing out her shorts and stared at her. "And you just thought to mention this now?"

"Well I was going to tell you when you got back but you seemed to be having some sort of breakdown and then we got slightly sidetracked with…"

"By all means, Claud, let's talk some more before you tell me what you found."

"Oh, I'm sorry. Am I boring you?"

"Right now?" Maya took a step forward and put her hands on her hips. "No, but I do want to smack you a little bit."

"Oh really?"

"Yes, really."

"Good to know." Claudia smiled tightly and shut her laptop, standing up quickly and striding towards her tent.

"What are you doing?"

"I'm going to my tent to wait for you to get over yourself," she shouted as she climbed in. "I may be some time."

"Claudia!" Maya called as her friend zipped up the tent. "Claudia, come on!"

"Get some sleep, Maya," came the angry reply. "I'll talk to you later."

"Come on!" she tried again. "Claud?"

She was met with nothing but a stony silence. She had seen this mood before, only a handful of times but she knew better than to push it. Claudia was patient, one of the most patient people she had ever met in fact, it was probably the main reason they were still friends, but when she lost that patience...well, the devil himself would think twice before engaging.

Maya sighed and threw her shorts on the ground. She turned and stared out over the lake again. If Claudia had information that needed to be acted on immediately she would tell her, she had no doubt about it. She trusted her friend implicitly and, much as it annoyed her, she would just have to wait. Also, as usual, Claudia was right; she was exhausted and could do with some sleep. Wearily she turned around and headed to her tent.

Maya woke suddenly, her heart pounding in her chest and her hand reaching blindly out in front of her. She sat up and rubbed her face, inhaling sharply as she waited for her heart rate to return to normal. She rubbed her face and reached for the zip on her tent. Shaking her head and forcing her eyes wide a couple of times she crawled out like a newborn foal, limbs flailing awkwardly in the darkness. Jolted awake by the sudden cold she reached back into the tent for her bag and grabbed some pants and a top, pulling them on quickly in an attempt to stop herself shivering.

"Look who's awake." Claudia said over her shoulder.

"What time is it?" she asked, staring up into the night sky.

"About half eleven."

Maya pushed the hair up the back of her head as she yawned and stretched her way over to where Claudia was standing by the edge of the lake. "What are we looking at?"

"The Pleiades. Do you see?"

"No," she yawned after a moment, rubbing her eyes as she did. "I see the moon. It's big."

"That's because it's full and we are close to the equator." Claudia said with a roll of her eyes. "Do you know your mental aptitude when you wake up is very similar to when you are drunk?"

"Whatever, I'm rapidly losing interest in this conversation," she muttered as she pulled her jacket on and forced herself to concentrate. "What are you doing?"

"Looking at the Pleiades," Claudia enunciated, taking hold of Maya's head and turning it in the direction she needed to be looking. "See?"

"Yes, grabby, I see. Why?"

"Did you know that the ancient Greeks had several myths relating to the 'disappearance' of the seventh star? One of them states that Elektra, devastated by the destruction of her beloved Troy, transformed herself into a comet and abandoned her 'sisters'. Ever since then the comet has been a symbol of doom."

"Fascinating."

"There are legends and tales about them all throughout history. They have different names in different places. The Aztecs called them 'Tianquiztli' which means the marketplace. The Inca called them the seed scatterer. Their appearance marked the start of the farming season."

"Since when do you know so much about this?"

"Since I did some research whilst you were off swimming."

"You know that's not what happened, right?"

"Hmm," Claudia murmured noncommittally as she returned to the fire. "So I also looked at the picture of the rock you found last night and tried to work out where this cave is. Of course, there is nothing in the picture to suggest that it is the mountain in the picture, it could be those on the other side of the lake, it could be the Andes for all we know."

"Not exactly making me feel better."

"I wasn't trying to," she shrugged, tapping at the keyboard. "I also researched the lake. Since 1970 the water level has risen by about ten metres. Before that the last serious change was in the mid 1700s when it also rose. By about fifteen metres."

Maya walked slowly towards the fire. "What are you saying, Claud?"

"I'm saying that since the petroglyphs were carved the water level in this lake has risen by at least twenty five metres. I'm saying that if there was a cave that was affected by the relatively small tidal fluctuations in this lake the opening would have had to be on the shore line, and the shore line that existed at that time would have been substantially lower than the one we are standing on now."

"So…"

"So if it's down there we will need proper diving equipment and either an exact location or a couple of months to search," she sighed, pulling two cigarettes out of the pack and passing one to Maya before lighting her own. "I'm sorry, Maya, but the only way we're going to find it otherwise is blind luck, and I'm assuming you've already tried that."

"Good guess," she smiled sadly, eyes locked on her cigarette. This was number seven. Not a good day for her lungs. "Why didn't you just tell me this earlier?"

"You were knackered, Maya. You're not the most rational of people at the best of times but with barely any sleep, smelling like raw sewage and looking like someone had stolen your puppy, I thought it best to try and buy myself some time before I told you we were basically fucked." Claudia sighed and pulled the bourbon out of her bag. "Plus, I was hoping I would be able to find something useful while you were asleep."

"I take it you didn't?" Maya asked as she opened the bottle.

"Knowing your tendency to lash out at the closest available person when you get upset don't you think I would have opened with the good news if there was any?"

"Hmm. I guess so."

"So what do we do now?"

"Now," Maya took a swig from the bottle and passed it to her friend. "We get drunk."

Chapter 8

Maya groaned and rolled out of her tent, blinking her eyes in the bright sun as her stomach gurgled unpleasantly. She opened her mouth and an unplanned sound of distress emitted from it, almost as if her body was trying to convey its displeasure with her at the amount of alcohol she had forced it to consume the night before. With that memory came the crushing realisation of why she had got so drunk. She had failed.

Letting the disappointment have its way with her she lay where she had landed, facedown half in half out of the tent, and breathed in the dewy scent of the grass until the stench of the nearby lake became overpowering. She honestly felt like this could be the moment for her annual cry, but she pushed the feeling away and struggled to her feet instead, forcing down the bile making its way up her throat as she walked unsteadily to the shore and stared out over the lake.

"Mierda," she muttered softly.

After a while she heard movement from Claudia's tent and turned back to the camp to try and find the stove. The place looked like some kind of cataclysmic event had occurred there; the stove and kettle were on their sides a few feet apart, Maya's bag was empty, its contents strewn around the area in which she had been sitting and there were two empty bottles lying end to end, as if pointing the way back to the tent. The fire, at least, had been taken care of properly, its perimeter intact and an excessive amount of sand covering it. It looked like someone had been trying to build a sandcastle out of it. Maya shrugged and leaned down to collect the fallen stove.

"Fucking hell, why do my hands hurt?" Claudia cried pitifully from inside her tent. "I can barely pull the zip. Urgh. I think I may actually die."

Maya chuckled a little before lapsing into a coughing fit. She dropped to her knees and waited for it to pass, then grabbed a bottle of water from the wreckage formerly known as her luggage. Sighing, she filled the kettle and lit the flame with shaky hands.

"Ow. Ow. Bloody hell!" Claudia finally crawled out of her tent on her hands and elbows, her hands held aloft in front of her. "What the fuck did I do last night? Look at my hands! They're all burnt! I...oh, for goodness sake, Maya…"

Maya turned to look at her in confusion and was greeted with the comical sight of her best friend with her face pressed into the ground, ass in the air and painfully red hands held in front of her as if in supplication.

"You okay, Claud?"

"Just dandy, thank you, Maya," she muttered into the grass. "However, my situation would be markedly improved if my head wasn't banging, my hands didn't feel like they had lost a fight with a blowtorch, and you weren't standing outside my tent stark bollock naked."

As her brain caught up with her friend's rant Maya looked down at herself to see that, yes, in fact, she was completely naked. With a tired sigh she sifted through her collection of clothes decorating the ground and pulled on the first things she could find. She picked up the first aid kit and walked over to her prone friend, taking her left hand gently and pouring some water into her palm, pulling a bandage out of their supplies and soaking it in water before wrapping it around Claudia's injured hand. She repeated the process with the other hand, then returned to the wreckage to find cups and the coffee.

She heard movement behind her again and after a few seconds she felt arms being wrapped around her shoulders as Claudia pulled her into a gentle hug. "Thank you. I'm sorry."

"I've got some cream somewhere," Maya said, patting her forearm. "I'll dig it out for you in a minute."

"'Dig' being the operative word. What happened to your bag?"

"I don't really remember," she admitted as she surveyed the mess. "I guess I was looking for something?"

"Are you sure it was you?" Claudia asked as she sat down next to her and gratefully took her coffee with her fingertips.

"Yeah, I have a vague memory of pulling things out of it." Maya scrunched up her face as she struggled to think back to the night before. "Was I screaming something about trying to find the point?"

"Oh, yes," the redhead giggled, before quickly wincing in pain and pressing her fingertips to her forehead. "Yes, that was about midway through the bottle of tequila as I recall."

The two of them sat in silence and nursed their coffees for a while. The sun was climbing steadily and Maya knew that they should start packing up and moving on, but part of her was still clinging to the hope that one of them would have a flash of inspiration and they would find the entrance to the caves. Plus, hangover. She sighed again and ran her hand over her face before grabbing her pendant. She couldn't shake the feeling that they were missing something obvious.

Her gaze was drawn to movement on her right and gradually her bleary eyes made out a man walking along the shore with what seemed to be fishing equipment on his back. Her stomach rolled at the prospect of eating anything that had previously lived in this lake and she found herself desperately hoping he had been trying to catch fish elsewhere.

"Hola," he greeted as he passed, tipping his hat at them before pointing at the sky to the east. "Miren. Viene la tormenta."

"Gracias, señor," she answered, studying the skyline but not really seeing his concern. "Tendremos cuidado."

"What did he just say?" Claudia asked as the old man disappeared up the hill.

"He said there's a storm coming in."

Maya sighed and put her hand on Claudia's backpack, essentially propelling the other woman up the hill. Every muscle in her body was screaming at her and the sweat was streaming down her face but she didn't want to stop yet. She knew now that the old man had been right, she could smell it in the air, and she didn't want to be halfway up this mountain when the storm hit. It was June, right in the rainy season in Venezuela and Maya knew what that meant. It wasn't a light English drizzle. No, this was the type of rain that when it hit you, you were wet, and you definitely didn't want it catching you halfway up a dirt track.

"Oh, thank God," Claudia exclaimed, breathing heavily. "I can see the top. Half a mile I reckon."

"Good," she answered, slowing slightly to wipe the sweat from her face and rearrange her hat. "Hopefully we will have enough time to find somewhere sheltered and set up the tents."

"Okay. Are you sure we shouldn't just head back to town?"

"No, if we are still out when the storm hits it could be bad. This area is notorious for mudslides and I don't want to risk it. We should just hole up somewhere and wait for it to pass."

"Surely it would have to rain for an extremely long time for there to be a mudslide?" Claudia paused to drink some water and gave her a sceptical look.

"Well, I'm not suggesting that we are going to get caught up in another Vargas, Claud, I'm just saying that I don't particularly want to be walking down a mountain when a thousand gallons of water comes rushing down the track towards us. Do you?"

"Not especially, no."

"Okay. Can we keep moving then?"

"Of course. After you." Claudia bowed her head and extended her bandaged hand up the path.

Maya scowled at her and stomped off, one hand dragging against the rock face that bordered the right of the path, her eyes scanning the sky above them for signs of the storm.

"If there is a storm coming how is it still so bloody hot?" Claudia muttered behind her. "It actually feels hotter than yesterday."

"Not for long," she answered. "You'll know when it's coming. The temperature will drop, the wind will kick in and just as suddenly vanish, then you'll be wet. Very wet."

"Good. I could do with a shower. So could you, in fact. You still stink from that lake."

"Ssh," Maya waved her hand behind her to silence her friend as she rounded the corner and saw tents in the distance.

"What is it?"

"Someone has set up camp here," she said, counting at least four tents slightly up the hill, around two hundred metres ahead of them on the left. She looked around to see what would have drawn them to this place and found nothing. To her right the line of the mountain dropped back down slightly, dense forest springing up in its wake and only disappearing again as the peak of the mountain rose up in the distance. The trail they were on opened up in front of them, a sea of grass with trees to the left and right of it until it met up with the rock face again fifty feet or so ahead.

Maya pulled her water bottle out of her bag, her dehydrated brain desperately trying to tell her something, seemingly prepared to kill her in the process if that was what it took.

"What?" Claudia asked.

"What?"

"You have that look."

"What look?"

"That 'I am about to have an epiphany' look."

"I have a look that says 'I am about to have an epiphany'?" Maya turned to her with a look of irritation.

"Well, yes but that's not it. That's your 'I'm about to say something quite startlingly hurtful' look."

"What is my 'maybe you should just shut up and let me figure it out' look?"

"That would be the same look."

Maya rolled her eyes and stared back at the clearing. After a few moments she huffed and started walking again. "Whatever it was it's gone now and we're wasting time. Come on."

"Wait, shouldn't we warn these people?"

"What? Why?"

"Well, aren't they a little exposed if the storm comes in?" Claudia gestured to the clearing they were bordering on. "Although they do have a lovely view."

Maya stopped in the middle of the clearing and looked up towards the tents on the left, then to the right where the rocks dropped away, much more sharply than she had first thought, and the forest took over. Over the treetops you could see the far side of the lake and the mountains on the other side. Despite the ominous black clouds looming over them it truly was a beautiful sight.

"Alright, but hurry," she gestured to the clouds. "The rain is already falling on the other side of the lake, it'll be here before you know it."

They covered the ground quickly and Claudia called out as they got within hearing distance. As they were about ten feet away a blonde head popped out from within the circle of tents and Maya's stomach dropped as she recognised one of the guys from Rebecca's table at the bar.

"Fuck," she swore as she pulled her hat down lower and turned back towards the path.

"Hi," Claudia greeted him, cheerfully oblivious. "We just wanted to make sure that you knew there was a storm coming in," she turned to wave towards the clouds, frowning slightly in confusion as she noticed Maya's retreat. "It might be safer if you head for higher ground."

"Aw, thanks, that's real nice of you," he called back, grinning so wide it nearly split his face. "We're okay though. We got our stuff rigged up real good back here. It'd have to be one hell of a storm to cause us any issues and it doesn't look so bad on the radar."

"You have a radar?" Claudia smiled incredulously.

"Yes ma'am," he smiled again. "All mod cons. Listen, if you guys wanna wait here til it passes you're more'n welcome?"

"No, we're good thanks," Maya called, forcing a smile into her voice. "Come on, Claud, let's go."

"Oh. Okay then," Claudia turned to wave at the blonde haired man and headed back towards the path. "Lovely meeting you!"

"You too," he waved back. "Y'all take care now."

Maya walked quickly up the hill, tossing a careless wave behind her as she tried to put some distance between herself and their camp. She scanned up ahead for any signs of Rebecca. Of course they would bump into her again now, the stench of failure and skanky lake water clinging to her, hungover as hell and all sweaty and gross from marching up a hill.

"Do you think they'll be okay?" Claudia asked as she caught up with her. "He was gorgeous and he called me 'ma'am'."

"He's with Rebecca."

"Really?" she asked, disappointed.

"Jesus, Claud, not *with* Rebecca, with Rebecca. Just you know, with her."

"Oh. Okay then," she smiled. "But I suppose that's still…you know, bad. Although technically…"

"Technically my ass," Maya stopped and looked back at the clearing. "They're looking for something here and I think I just figured out what it is."

"And? Care to share with the class?"

"Yes," Maya smiled at her and started back off up the trail. "But let's get to the top of this goddamn hill first."

Almost as soon as they had finished setting up their tents the heavens opened and transformed their idyllic hilltop camp into a soggy battle station. They huddled together in Claudia's slightly larger tent and Maya pulled up the pictures on the laptop.

"See when we looked at this before we saw the lake here, with the guy, then the trees on either side and the trail going up the side of the mountain, yes?" Maya said, pointing out each area as she spoke.

"Yes."

"Okay, but what if this," she circled the 'lake' with her finger. "Is not the lake? What if it is that clearing we just walked through?"

"I suppose it could be. But it could be anything, like I said before. That's the problem, right?" Claudia scratched her head and studied the picture. "And why is he on a boat if he's on grass?"

"Well we never established whether or not he is on a boat. In this picture there is no boat, right? Only in the first one."

"Right," she said, taking the laptop back and flicking through the pictures. "But really, Maya, there's nothing here to suggest that this is a clearing on a plateau halfway up a hill. Tell me honestly, aside from the fact that Rebecca and her team are there would you really have considered it an option?"

"Yes."

"Yes?"

"Yes!" Maya huffed in frustration. "Look, when we walked around that corner and saw that clearing it jarred something in my head. You said yourself I had an 'epiphany' look, right?"

Claudia shrugged and nodded slightly as she continued studying the photographs.

"So that is what was trying to come through! The 'sea' of grass, the trees on either side, the peak of the mountain up ahead, the trail going off to the side…"

"Okay, but did you see any caves?"

"Well, no, but…"

"So we are in exactly the same position we were in at the lake." Claudia sighed and started to pull the makeshift bandage off her hand. "Pass me the cream, would you? I'm not saying you're wrong, Maya, and we should certainly check it out, I just would like to have more to go on than your desire to beat Rebecca Bronstein and a hunch."

"Come on, that's not what this is about."

"Are you sure?"

"Positive. I'm just...I'm really not ready to give up yet."

"Me neither," Claudia squeezed some of the cream into her palm and winced as she tried to rub it in. "Help me sort out my hands and then we'll go back through what we've got, see if we can spot something we missed."

For the next couple of hours they sat in relative silence in the tent, listening to the rain bouncing off the canvas and the trees as they looked for answers. Maya reread Zuazola's journal and tried to find any indication that he had found the cave but, aside from the references to 'boca', came up with nothing useful. Claudia tried searching for information on cave systems in the area but the storm was interfering with their booster and she couldn't get the internet to connect for more than a few seconds at a time. Instead she went back to studying the petroglyphs in the hopes of finding some kind of marker that would tell them where to look.

"Maldita sea la madre que te parió." Maya huffed as she slammed the book down. "There's nothing here, Claud, just a bunch of whiny bullshit about nothing."

"I'm afraid I'm not doing much better," she sighed as she set down the laptop and removed her glasses. She rubbed her eyes, wincing as she put pressure on her palms.

"It feels like the answer is right here but I just can't see it. If this fucking rain would just stop we could at least go and look at the clearing. And I really need to pee."

"Hmm. Well maybe if you go and pee you'll find something else useful."

"Or maybe I would just drown or get swept away."

"It's an acceptable risk." Claudia yawned and lay down. "I promise I'll look for you when it stops."

"Yeah, right. Or maybe you'd just seek solace in the arms of your blonde texan."

"Ooh, maybe I would," she smiled. "He did have particularly good arms…"

"Oh, great," Maya swatted her leg. "Left to die because of good arms!"

"'Particularly' good arms, Maya. And I would think of you often, I'm sure."

"Often? I'm honoured."

"Yes. Quite often, I would imagine. Every time someone was overly sarcastic or inappropriately naked."

"Well, it's nice to know I will be remembered for such lofty achievements." Maya drawled as she sat up and grabbed her boots.

"What are you doing? You're not really going out in this are you?"

"It's either that or pee in your tent and I think that would lead to a discussion."

"Yes, that would definitely lead to a discussion."

"Alright then," she sighed as she pulled on her boots and unzipped the tent. "If I'm not back in an hour...well, I guess it's been kind of okay knowing you."

"Piss off, you know I would come after you really." Claudia scoffed, throwing her hat at her. "I love you even though you drive me insane and sometimes I imagine strangling you in your sleep."

"Aw, that might be the nicest thing you've ever said to me." Maya smiled as she put on her hat and dove out into the rain.

They had set up the tents under an outcrop near the forest, but before she had walked the three metres separating them she was soaked to the skin, the brim of her hat wilting under the weight and her tank top and shorts looked painted on. Deciding to go with it she stopped just shy of the treeline and let the rain wash over her, lifting her face to the sky and having her own private Shawshank moment. For a second she seriously considered going back for her soap, that way she could really get rid of the lake skank, but then the cold began to take over and her urge to pee came back with a vengeance.

She moved quickly into the forest and wondered if she would make it far enough away that Claudia would deem it an acceptable distance before she had no choice in the matter, but just as she was reaching breaking point she came to a small clearing full of tall grass with a rock in the centre.

"Won't you lay me down in the tall grass and let me do my stuff," she sang softly to herself as she wandered into a section of it still relatively protected by the trees. She made a quick scan of the area for snakes and bitey things and went about her business, keeping her eyes open for any other signs of life. She wasn't as weird about these things as Claudia but she certainly wasn't keen to be caught with her pants down.

Her eyes settled on the rock in the centre of the clearing and a strange feeling settled over her, not a feeling like she expected someone to jump out from behind it or anything, more like…

Suddenly there was a break in the clouds and sunlight poured in through the opening. As the rays landed on the rock it started to steam slightly as the warmth caused the water to evaporate. It gave the rock a sort of otherwordly look, almost like the pods in Alien, although less green, and Maya wandered over to have a look at it. As she rounded it she noticed that the front of it was shining in the light and as she got closer she saw that the rock was split open at the top with a jagged lump of quartz sticking out. The sunlight shone through it and cast a rainbow filter onto the bushes and trees in front of the cliff face opposite. She smiled at the sight and stood entranced by it for a few moments until the clouds covered over again and the rain renewed its intensity.

Holding her hat in place she ran back through the forest and jumped into the tent with a shiver, ignoring the squeals of protest from Claudia but accepting the towel she threw at her gratefully, rubbing vigorously at her arms and legs in an attempt to get herself dry.

"Whilst I am glad that you didn't die you are getting everything I own soaking wet!" Claudia complained, grabbing her bag out of Maya's way and pulling some dry clothes from it. "Loathe as I am to say it, take off your clothes."

"Over your texan already?" Maya chuckled. "I'm sorry, Claud, but I value our friendship too highly to…"

"Don't be absurd, Maya," she sighed, rolling her eyes in irritation. "Just put these on and get those soaking wet things out of my tent."

"Yes ma'am," she winked, pulling off her top quickly. "When it stops raining I have to show you what I found. There's this rock out there and it's all broken up on one side with these quartz crystals sticking out. It's beautiful when the sunlight hits it, it throws all these rainbows out against the trees and the cliff. It's like…I don't know, like being inside a crystal ball or something."

"How awfully poetic of you. Although I'm surprised there was any sunlight to cast…wait a minute. Rainbows?"

"Well, yeah. Quartz, you know?" Maya finished pulling on the trousers her friend had given her and looked over quizzically as she began tapping frantically at the keyboard. "What?"

"I'm not sure, it's just…" Claudia carried on tapping, her brow furrowed in concentration. "There, look! This glyph on the rock, and here again, on the second one!"

"The comet?"

"No, that one is the comet," she huffed, sliding next to her and pointing at the image to the right of the 'paw print'. "This one. See? It's a rainbow?"

"Is it?"

"Yes! When I was researching petroglyphs back in Puerto Cabello I came across some information about what we believe some of them meant, and this one is a rainbow. And here, see? It's repeated on the smaller rock, right above the cave."

"Well holy shit…"

"Of course, it doesn't necessarily mean…"

"Claudia!" Maya held her hand up for silence. "Let's just have this for now, shall we? We can get all disappointed again when the rain stops and there's nothing there."

"Well that's awfully bleak."

"Yeah, well, it's been that sort of trip."

Chapter 9

Just as Maya's patience was reaching the point where she would rather risk pneumonia and search blindly around for the caves the rain stopped as suddenly as it had started. The two of them grabbed their supplies and headed back into the forest where, after a brief moment of panic where Maya felt sure she wouldn't have made it so far without wetting herself, they reached the clearing and saw the rock in full sunlight for the first time.

"Oh my God," Claudia breathed. "It's so beautiful. The way the canopy holds the light inside and the refracted beams hit the rock face, it's almost ethereal."

"Yeah, that's what I thought," Maya smiled. "Although, with more aliens and crystal balls."

"Of course," Claudia shot her a look and walked across the clearing to get a better look at the rock. "This is just incredible. If I had discovered this place I would certainly have carved it into a rock. If I had any artistic skill at all, that is."

Maya murmured in agreement, distracted by the patterns being thrown on the foliage at the mountainside. She moved towards it and ran her hand through the beams, watching the way the movement almost seemed to cast a shadow the missing light was so brilliant. As she got to about five feet away she noticed the leaves in the centre moving slightly, like they were shifting in a hidden breeze, and as she continued on she could feel it on her skin.

"Claud, get over here," she said quietly, excitement building in her stomach. She pushed through the branches and strained her ears as she heard the distinctive sound of running water close by.

"Did you find it?" Claudia whispered behind her.

"I don't know, it sounds like…" she was cut off by Claudia letting out a blood curdling scream and grabbing hold of her. "What the fuck?"

"Get it off me! Get it off me!"

Maya span around to take hold of her friend's arms as she tried to calm her down and work out what was going on, not being helped in any way, shape or form by Claudia performing some sort of insane tap dance with her face screwed up in fear. Suddenly the dance seemed to reach its crescendo and she went into some sort of whole body spasm as she wheeled around, revealing the cause of her terror: a small snake on her backpack was slithering down her arm.

"Jesus, Claudia, you scared the shit out of me!" Maya said, reaching out to grab it and let it loose in the bush.

"I scared you?" Claudia answered, her voice taking on a hysterical pitch. "I scared you?!"

"It's just a snake, Claud, calm down," she tutted, turning back to her search.

"It could have killed me!"

"No it couldn't!"

"You don't know that!"

"'Red touches black, you're okay Jack'," Maya singsonged as she went deeper into the trees.

"What?"

"The rhyme about snakes. 'Red touches black, you're okay jack. Yellow touches red, you're dead'."

"Well, forgive me, terrifying Dora the Explorer." Claudia huffed as she shivered and ran a hand through her hair. "Just don't expect any sympathy next time you freak out because a wasp is within twenty feet of you."

"Hey," Maya span back around and pointed her finger at her friend. "That's different. Those things are a menace."

"Oh please, a bit of savlon and you'd be fine. Snakes, on the other hand…"

"Claudia, it was a milk snake. They're harmless. Besides," she turned back and pushed the branches aside, revealing the entrance to a cave and losing her train of thought. "Oh my God…"

"Maya…we found it. Have we found it?"

"I think we have."

Maya pulled her flashlight out of her bag as she rounded a corner. She had been walking for about twenty minutes and the light from outside had now reached the point where it was officially useless. She settled her hat more firmly on her head and tugged a little on the pendant around her neck as she pointed the beam down the sharply descending tunnel.

"Maya," Claudia's voice crackled over the radio on her hip. "Everything okay?"

"Pretty much the same since you checked in five minutes ago," she muttered, rolling her eyes as she pulled the thing from her belt. She took a calming breath before pressing the button and replying. "Yeah, all good. Still in a dark tunnel."

"I can tell when you roll your eyes at me you know," the crackly reply came back. "I just wanted to let you know that the rain is starting up again. It's not too bad but I'm going to head back to the tent and try to get a report on if it's likely to worsen. I'll keep you informed."

"Okay, thanks Claud."

She clipped the radio back on her belt and moved forward through the darkness. If the storm was closing in she needed to work quickly. The ground underfoot was wet from the previous downpour and in the steeper sections there were actually rivers of water running along either side. She definitely did not want to get stuck down here if it started again in earnest.

Maya scanned the walls as she went, hoping for some kind of sign that she would find anything other than hell at the end of this tunnel, and dropped further and further down through the rock. After about fifteen minutes she heard a noise and stopped dead in her tracks. She tilted her head to the side and listened intently for a few moments before realising, with absolute certainty, that she looked like a deranged cocker spaniel trapped in a coal pit. Tutting at herself she shook her head and started to move forward again.

"Shit!" she heard faintly from further down the tunnel. Quickly she clicked off the light and pressed herself up against the wall. Who the fuck would be down here? She rolled her eyes at the obvious answer to her own question and sighed as she pondered what to do.

As more noises echoed up the tunnel she started to slowly edge her way down the wall, deciding to leave the light off until she established that it actually was Bronstein and, as long as the woman wasn't in any danger, hopefully dodge past without her noticing. As she rounded the corner, however, she realised that that was not going to be an option.

Rebecca was wandering around a small chamber, her phone raised above her head as the beam of her flashlight roamed around the walls. Maya leaned against the opening and watched her for a little while, taking in her predictably stereotypical choice of clothing; a black tank top and the tightest, shortest black shorts she had ever seen on a person since Angelina Jolie made the outfit famous in the Tomb Raider films. She would have laughed had Rebecca not made it look so damn hot. Finally the beam flashed in her direction.

"Jesus!" Rebecca yelled, actually jumping on the spot as she clasped her phone to her chest. "What the fuck are you doing? You scared the shit out of me! Fuck!"

"Woah, easy!" Maya held her hands up, stifling the nervous laugh that was bubbling up her chest as she blinked in the harsh light. "I'm sorry, I thought I was the only one here too."

"Then why the fuck were you just standing there?" she shot back, fanning herself with her hand and walking away. "You could have said something, for God's sake, made a fucking noise! Have you not seen The Descent? Jesus Christ, I thought I was going to have a fucking heart attack!"

"I have, actually, and if you ever compare me to one of those butt ugly, snot covered, inbred monsters again I will drop your ass down the nearest hole I can find and leave you there."

Rebecca stopped her angry pacing abruptly and turned to face her slowly. Maya took a small step back at the look of anger on the shorter woman's face then sighed in relief when it dissolved into laughter.

"You're kind of scary, you know that?" Rebecca said.

"Me? I don't think I ever heard so many curse words come out of a person's mouth in such a short space of time before."

"Well I was scared, okay?" she smiled, sitting down on a boulder and letting out a sigh. "And I can't get a signal on my goddamn phone."

"That's because there's a huge storm outside and you're buried under about half a mile of rock." Maya smirked, pulling some chalk out of her pocket and drawing a cross on the entrance to the passage before fully entering the chamber and walking towards the other woman.

"Well I know that, I'm not an idiot," she scowled at her. "But it should work, it's a satellite phone."

"Of course it is. All mod cons, right?"

"What?"

"Never mind. Anyway, even satellite phones wouldn't work this far underground, especially with that storm interfering."

"They told me it would."

"Well 'they' probably saw you and your bank account coming from a mile away."

Rebecca stopped fiddling with the phone and looked up at her coldly. "You know, you really should try to get to know a person rather than let some half baked, preconceived notion dictate how you interact with them."

"Is that right?" Maya raised an eyebrow and folded her arms.

"Yes," she replied, standing slowly and moving to within half a foot of her. "It is."

They stood like that with their eyes locked, the only sounds their breathing and the steadily increasing flow of water cascading down the tunnel, neither of them wanting to be the first to back down. Maya's mind was racing from the different emotions that were flaring up in her; indignation at the statement when Rebecca was clearly working off some pretty big 'preconceived notions' of her own, irritation that she had the means to purchase all this fancy equipment but no clue about which pieces of kit would keep her safe, concern and anger that the woman was down here alone, separated from her team and obviously out of her depth, and a strange flutter in the pit of her stomach that she hadn't felt since…

The uncomfortable silence and gamut of emotions Maya was experiencing were interrupted suddenly by the crackle of her radio and

Claudia's voice blaring into the silence, causing the pair of them to start in fear.

"Maya, are you there?"

"Jesus!" Maya turned away to hide her embarrassment and pulled the radio from her belt. "Yeah, Claud, I'm here. What's up?"

"I managed to get online for about five minutes before the connection went down. The storm is coming in again and it looks like it will be worse than before. I'd say you have about an hour and a half before it kicks in properly. Did you find anything?"

"Er, kind of," she looked at Rebecca over her shoulder. "I'm about half a mile down, in a smallish chamber with four other tunnels leading off it."

"Okay, well keep in touch and don't do anything stupid. I'll let you know if the situation changes but if not I'll see you back here in ninety minutes, okay?"

"You know me, Claud."

"Yes, and that's what I'm afraid of. Ninety minutes, Maya."

Maya chuckled and clipped the radio back onto her belt. She turned back to see that Rebecca had wandered over to a tunnel two to the left of the one Maya had entered through.

"You have walkie talkies," Rebecca laughed softly. "Of course."

"It's not a walkie talkie, it's a cave radio," she muttered in response, walking around the chamber to work out which route to take, obstinately leaving the one Rebecca was at as the last option.

"What's the difference?"

"It's something to do with...the, er, frequency? Airwaves? I don't know, I didn't invent the fucking thing. Ask Claudia, she's the tech geek."

"Yeah, I'm getting that," Rebecca laughed, her face settling into that irritating yet maddeningly attractive smirk. "Maybe I will next time I see her. You didn't seem too keen on her knowing we were together."

"We're not together," she responded through gritted teeth. "I'm trying to find the next tunnel and you are...also here."

"It's this one."

"Why are you here?" Maya turned to face her again, ignoring her comment. "And why are you alone?"

"Why are you here alone?"

"Because I know what I'm doing."

"And I don't?"

"Not from what I can see, no," she huffed and went back to checking the tunnels.

"'Cause you've seen so much? I already told you, it's this one."

"I think I've seen enough."

"No, Maya, you saw what you wanted to see," Rebecca spat. "Some stupid little rich girl wandering about in the dark wondering why her cell phone didn't work, helpless for all her money and fancy gadgets."

"Don't forget the snazzy Lara Croft outfit," Maya scoffed, waving her hand disparagingly at Rebecca's clothes.

"Yeah, right, because yours is so much better," she smirked, folding her arms across her stomach. "Nice fedora, by the way."

Maya opened her mouth to reply but then glanced down at herself and saw what she must look like to Rebecca. She was still wearing the clothes that Claudia had thrown at her after she got soaked earlier; Khaki pants with a brown belt and a loose fitting shirt over a white tank top, plus the aforementioned fedora. All she was missing was a whip and a pair of testicles. The ludicrousness of the thought and the entire situation caught up with her and she burst out laughing, the pitch and intensity of it rising until she clutched her stomach and doubled over.

She dropped into a crouch and wiped the tears from her eyes, looking up at Rebecca to see her eyes dancing in amusement as she leant against the wall, waiting for her to recover.

"Feel better?" she asked as Maya pulled off her hat and ran her hand through her hair.

"Just peachy, thanks."

"Good. Then can we go? We don't have much time."

"What makes you so sure it's that way?" Maya asked as she stood up, curiosity getting the better of her.

"Because I have a map, Maya," she replied, pulling her phone back out of her pocket and holding the screen up for her to see.

"You have a map?"

"Yes. As soon as we saw the cave detail in the petroglyphs we looked up local systems and downloaded the schematics for this one. They were not particularly easy to find and I wasn't entirely certain we were in the right place until you showed up."

"If you have a map how are you lost?"

"I'm not lost."

"Then why were you trying to get a signal?"

"Because I wanted to check on the storm situation before I went any further," she shrugged. "Thanks to Claudia's walkie...sorry, 'cave radio' update, I know now that we have ninety minutes, so let's get on with it, shall we?"

With that she pushed off the wall and headed into the tunnel, leaving Maya to stare open mouthed at her retreating figure.

They progressed quickly through the tunnels, heading deeper and deeper into the mountain towards a chamber that Rebecca had marked as the most likely place to find answers. When Maya had questioned why she had picked that one Rebecca had launched into a complicated and overly verbose justification involving GPR and other technical jargon that Maya wasn't really interested in. Upon seeing the bored and unconvinced expression she wore Rebecca had stopped, shrugged and said simply "It's the furthest away and most difficult to get to."

Maya nodded at the admission. This was logic she could get onboard with. If she was going to hide the answer to some mystery she would make damn sure it was not somewhere that was likely to be stumbled across. That was, of course, if there were any answers to be had down here. They still didn't know what they were looking for, after all, and though she and Rebecca had reached a sort of understanding she still didn't feel particularly comfortable discussing the situation with her.

"So, Maya," Rebecca said suddenly. They had been walking for about ten minutes in near silence and Maya felt her heart sink at the tone of her statement. "You're Puerto Rican?"

"Yes," she answered simply, picking up the pace as much as she could without actually running away.

"And you went to Oxford?"

"Yes."

"How'd that happen?"

"I applied. I got in."

"Okay," Rebecca said slowly. "But how? I mean, I know you lived in New York by then, but it's not like…"

"Like what?" Maya said darkly, stopping abruptly and turning to shine her light directly into her face.

"Well, I just meant, er, well…" she stammered, raising her hand up to shield her eyes.

"You meant how did a low rent Spic like me end up at a fancy ass school like Oxford?" she said, her accent thick for effect.

"Hey, come on! No, of course I…"

"You seem to know so damn much about me, you figure it out," Maya spat and carried on down the tunnel.

"Maya!" Rebecca called after her, hurrying to catch up. "I'm sorry, I didn't mean to insult you."

"Yeah, well you did. I don't like other people all up in my business so back the fuck off."

"Okay. I'm sorry."

They carried on in silence for the next twenty minutes or so, Maya still stewing on the conversation and wondering how or why this woman knew so much about her. She hated people prying into her life. It wasn't that she was ashamed of where she came from, far from it. Her family had worked hard and sacrificed everything they could to get her where she was today, and she would never have anything but the utmost respect for them. She was just so used to other people looking down on them and thinking they knew so much about her because of the colour of her skin and her last name. And, yes, maybe she did refer to Rebecca as the jewish princess in her head, and that was not okay either, but it's not like she brought it up in casual conversation.

She slowed slightly as she heard the sound of rushing water up ahead and shone the beam of the flashlight around the tunnel in front of them.

"What do you think it is?" Rebecca asked quietly.

"I'm not sure. Underground stream, maybe?"

"Only one way to find out," she said, striding off down the tunnel.

Maya followed closely behind her directing the beam across the floor of the passage for any sign of danger. As they rounded the corner the sound got louder and soon they stepped out into a large cavern with something more like a small river running through it.

"God, it's beautiful." Rebecca whispered, her own flashlight illuminating the stalactites hanging from the ceiling.

"Yeah," Maya said. "But how do we get through it?"

"We swim," she shrugged, undoing her belt and dropping it to the ground before taking off her backpack and opening it up.

"Swim? Where?"

"The cave we want is through the passage to the left. From the map I thought it was just another tunnel but apparently not." Rebecca poked her tongue out in concentration as she dug around in her bag and gave a small sound of satisfaction when she pulled out a camera.

"Alright…" she said slowly, turning around to take off her shirt, radio and hat and setting them on the driest piece of ground she could find before tucking her flashlight into her bra strap. After weighing it up for a few moments in her head she undid her belt and took off her pants too. It wasn't like she was wearing particularly revealing underwear or anything, and she didn't feel like enduring the chafing that trekking back through the tunnels in wet pants would cause.

"Smile!"

"Jesus!" Maya swore as she turned around, bringing her hand up to her eyes as she was blinded by the flash. "What the fuck?"

"Sorry, couldn't resist," Rebecca chuckled. "Hot," she smirked, turning away as she looked at the screen on her camera.

"Goddamit," she swore under her breath, rubbing at her eyes to try and clear the spots that were swimming in front of them. She heard a splash and, when she could finally see again, looked up to see Rebecca in the water, shivering and splashing around to get warm, her camera around her neck. "Much as I would love it to break and destroy what is most likely an awful picture of me, should your camera be in the water?"

"Don't worry, it's waterproof to thirty metres. The picture is safe," she laughed, wiping the water out of her eyes.

"Great," Maya drawled. She took a breath and jumped in, clenching her fists as her mouth opened in shock at how cold it was. She kicked for the surface and spat out the water she had almost choked on. "Holy shit that's cold! Fuck!"

"What, you never did a polar swim?" Rebecca trilled, splashing her with water.

"No. I am a sane person and prefer to be warm."

"Come on, let's get moving, you'll soon get used to it."

"Hey, hold on a second," she held a hand up to stop her. She had been avoiding this conversation since they had bumped into Rebecca at the rock but they had now reached the point where she couldn't any longer. "Look, I, er, shit, I just need to know what it is that you expect to find in there."

Rebecca swam back over to her, stopping so that their hands and legs were almost brushing together as they trod water. "What are you asking Maya? If I'm expecting to find my parents bodies in there?"

"I, er...that's not…" she wracked her brain desperately to find the words as the heat of her awkwardness made her forget how cold the water was.

"No. I'm not."

"Oh. Okay."

"But thank you for asking," she said softly. "In your own weird way. Now come on before we freeze to death."

She turned and swam away, kicking cold water behind her in an act that Maya felt sure was deliberate. She followed as closely as she could, grateful for the brevity of the conversation and curious as to why Rebecca had seemed so certain. They swam to the edge of the cavern and into the tunnel, the roof of it only a foot or so above their heads. As they were going with the current their progress was fairly rapid and Maya couldn't help but look behind her and feel uneasy about what that would mean for their return journey, but her fears subsided as they emerged into a small chamber a minute later.

Rebecca swam over to the right bank and pulled herself out easily, sitting on the side before turning back and extending her hand to help Maya out. Resisting the urge to slap it away, Maya grabbed hold and pulled herself up, taking a moment to wring some of the water out of her hair and look around the cave. She pulled out her flashlight and stood up to swing the beam around the walls. Directly behind them was a small opening, small enough that they would have to crouch down to get through it, but it was the only other exit from the chamber so she made herself as small as possible and began moving through it.

The progress was slow because the passage was so low she would have been better off on her hands and knees, and had she not left her damn pants in the other cavern she would have been. As it was she moved as fast as she could in the cumbersome position she found herself in, and with the knowledge that Rebecca was following not far behind with a clear view of her not very covered backside. Thankfully Rebecca did not seem to have brought her flashlight with her so Maya's was the only light illuminating their way and was definitely held out as far in front of her as possible. However it did mean that when she was forced to make a sudden stop when the passage ended sharply, Rebecca did not notice right away and there was some not entirely appropriate touching.

"Shit! Sorry," Rebecca mumbled from behind her, with perhaps a hint of amusement in her voice. "What do you see?"

"A big drop."

"What?" she ducked her head under Maya's arm to see out, pressing their bodies uncomfortably close together in the process. "But the cave is supposed to be on the right! Shine the light down here."

Maya huffed a little and attempted to bend her arm around Rebecca's shoulders in an effort to direct the beam, meaning that effectively now they were not only pressed together but almost embracing. And soaking wet. Not good. Not good at all.

"There's a ledge here. It's narrow but I think it will work."

"And if it doesn't?" Maya asked, her legs already starting to shake a little as her not so small fear of heights kicked in.

Rebecca turned towards her, so close she could feel her breath on her face as she let out a soft laugh. "Then we plummet to our untimely deaths."

"Then let's hope it works."

Rebecca smiled and squeezed past her, stepping out onto the ledge carefully and pressing her back up against the wall as she stood upright.

Maya shone the beam on the ledge to guide her as she began to carefully move along it, then began to follow at a safe distance but close enough to grab her if the ground gave way. She gritted her teeth and tried to ignore the huge drop in front of her, and after a couple of minutes the ledge widened slightly and they were able to walk forwards. She kept one hand on the wall to navigate and with the other held her flashlight out to illuminate Rebecca's path, becoming slightly uneasy as the other woman surged ahead.

"Hey, slow down a bit," she said.

"It's okay, we're almost there." Rebecca turned to call back. As she did so the part of the ledge she had stepped on to crumbled away and she started to fall with it.

Maya's heart was in her mouth as she leapt forward, just managing to grab hold of Rebecca's right hand as the ledge gave way completely and she slid down with a cry. The sudden pull on her arm knocked Maya off balance and she fell forward, her right leg shooting forward to brace her on the other side of the gap and praying that the ground there would hold true. Thankfully it did and she was able to pull Rebecca back up, but just as they reached safety their feet tangled together and they fell to the ground.

Maya fought to get her breath and her heart under control, barely registering the cuts and scrapes all over her knees and arms in her relief, or the fact that she had landed directly on top of Rebecca with her cheek resting on her chest.

"Maya," she said, shaking her slightly. "Maya, we're okay, you can get off me now."

As the words startled her back to reality she pushed herself up and jumped to her feet in embarrassment. "Easy, princess, don't get excited."

"Maya," Rebecca smirked as she leaned on her elbow and draped her other arm over her hip. "Being held by you isn't quite enough to get me excited."

Standing up to dust herself off Maya begrudgingly nodded in appreciation that the woman had not only got her quote but reciprocated, and held out a hand to help her up.

"You okay?"

"A few scrapes but I'll live," she shrugged. "Thank you."

Maya shrugged and retrieved the fallen flashlight. She waved it along the wall until she found the next passage and then headed towards it. As soon as she stepped into it, though, she lowered the beam as she could see light coming from the other end. She moved quickly but cautiously along and when she emerged at the other end she saw a sight that took her breath away.

Chapter 10

The small chamber that lay before her shone with a golden light. There were no other openings save the one they had entered through but the wall above them glowed with thousands of phosphorescent fungi sprouting from every square inch of space. The surface in front of them was covered with a giant painting of an ornate temple-like building, its roof sloping upwards into a point. Sweeping up alongside it, its mouth open above the building as if was about to devour it, was an enormous green snake, a pattern around its eye and down its length painted with gold, as was the detail on the building, and down to the left of them was a life size figure wearing the ceremonial headdress and robes of the Sapa Inca, his staff and clothing also decorated with gold.

Maya stood and gaped at it in awe. The detail was absolutely astounding and it was huge, she had no idea how it had come to be created or how long it had taken but the result was enthralling and she could not look away.

"Oh my God," she heard Rebecca whisper beside her. "Have you ever seen anything like this before?"

She shook her head mutely and took a step towards it. Close up the detail was even more ornate, there were lines of colour weaving through the Inca's robes, his mascapaicha intricately rendered and the disc in the middle showing the double snake and rainbow of the Inca. The large snake's eye had a ruby in the centre, about the size of a toddler's fist, and the flash from Rebecca's camera caused it to flare like the intrusion had angered it. Maya followed the sweeping pattern running down the serpent's body and her eyes widened in astonishment as she noticed the marks surrounding it.

"Come and look at this," she said, waving Rebecca over. "Look at this detail running along the snake."

"Jesus!" she gasped as she took her place next to Maya. "It's unbelievable! What do you think it means?"

"I'm not sure yet," Maya murmured as she got as close to the images as she could without touching them.

The tip of the snake's tail was so close to the figure's outstretched hand it was almost connected and the pattern started here with a burst of gold before it thinned out into a meandering golden line. On either side were spread small but intricately drawn trees, each with a bare trunk that split off into varying numbers of offshoots and fanned into a canopy made up of fingerlike leaves. About a quarter of the way up there was a range of hills with a rectangular object on top highlighted in gold, tiny lines extending out of it like it was shining in the sun, and above it the trees started to appear closer and closer together until they formed into clusters, the makeup of the trees themselves changing until one was indistinguishable from the next. Above this the trail developed a shadow, a blue line that came out of the trees and fell against the gold line, getting thicker and thicker until it suddenly disappeared under it, about three quarters of the way up, and moved across the body of the snake as if it was wrapping itself around it. At the same point as this abrupt separation, in amongst the dense forest, there was a stylised drawing of a head, its eyes and mouth wide as if in astonishment, with two dolphins either side, their skin rendered in a light pink, their noses meeting above to form an arch. From there the golden trail crept on through the trees until it formed a chakana around the ruby of the snake's eye.

"There's more detail in the trees at the top but I can't make it out," Maya said, taking a step back and squinting up at it. "Can you zoom in on it?"

"I could but it would be a better resolution if I could get in closer."

"Well obviously, but you can't so we will have to make the best of your fancy equipment."

"Or I could get on your shoulders?" Rebecca pointed out.

"Get on my…?" Maya stared at her in disbelief. "Why do you get to go on my shoulders? Why don't I get on your shoulders?"

"Because you are taller than me and I have the camera."

Maya sighed and rolled her eyes before dropping begrudgingly down onto one knee.

Rebecca opened her mouth in preparation to make a comment about her position but appeared to think better of it and simply smirked as she climbed onto Maya's shoulders.

"Jesus," she huffed as she pushed up off the floor. "You're heavier than you look."

"Well, you know what they say," Rebecca laughed as she lined up the shot. "The camera adds ten pounds."

"Very funny."

"I thought so. Maya, if you could try and hold still that would really help, in case you hadn't noticed the light in here is quite low and the flash just makes everything flare."

"Well maybe you should stop wriggling, then!" Maya snapped.

"Oh, I'm sorry, am I making you uncomfortable?"

"Just get on with it," she huffed. Of course she was uncomfortable, she thought as she planted her feet wider to steady herself. She was hungover and exhausted. She had walked sixty miles in the last three days, broken into a museum archive, escaped through an ancient sewer system, been attacked by a hill, fallen into a festering lake and now she had a hot, half naked and soaking wet woman sitting with her legs wrapped around her neck.

"Okay, I think I have what we need," Rebecca said, patting her on the head. "Let me down."

She dropped back down to the ground and tilted her head forward to expedite the process. As Rebecca dismounted Maya stood up quickly, rubbing her neck as she turned back to study the painting once more.

"Ah, poor baby," Rebecca pouted as she ran her hand over Maya's shoulder blade. "Want me to rub it better?"

"Get off me," she huffed, shrugging her hand away. "Show me the pictures."

"Hey, come on, I'm only playing."

"Yeah, well stop it. We don't have much time."

"Alright," Rebecca said simply, sending her a sideways glance as she stood next to her and brought up the pictures.

She scrolled through them and Maya's brow wrinkled in frustration as she tried to make sense of the images on either side of the golden path. Rebecca had taken eight shots in total, the first of the whole scene, two closer shots showing the bottom half of the snake, one of its head and the top of the temple, and four focusing on the main areas of detail in the final third of its body. Maya stared at them and tried to work out what they meant; a circle of stones, a waterfall dropping into a lake, a series of steep steps… It definitely seemed like a map, but where was the starting point?

She sighed and clicked back through the pictures, stopping at the one of the snake's head that had caused the ruby to flash. Long fangs extended from its upper jaw, almost piercing the roof of the temple as its mouth opened around it.

"Boca," she whispered, looking back up at the painting. Her gaze dropped to the stylised picture of the head, it's mouth comically wide. "¿Dondé está la boca?"

"What are you saying?"

"Hmm?" Maya glanced back as Rebecca's question dragged her out of her head. "Oh, I, er, we found a journal. It's kind of why we're here. He kept saying...random stuff."

"Yeah," she laughed. "I've read some of those. All riddles, no answers."

"Answers…" Maya looked back at the painting, the other woman's words jogging a memory. "'La muerte llega con la marea alta, las respuestas llegan con la baja.'"

"Well that's...depressing."

"Yeah, I know," she muttered, an uneasy feeling spreading through her. "He was a depressing guy."

"Who was he?"

"Ah, a Spanish captain. Zuazola." Maya tore her eyes away from the painting, not sure why she had suddenly decided to share all this with Rebecca and regretting it already. "We should get back up to camp, we can study the pictures properly there."

"Sure," Rebecca smiled. "Your place or mine?"

"What?"

"Well, it's not like we came here together, so…"

"Whatever, I'll tell Claud to meet us at yours and we'll make copies." Maya said as she walked back to the entrance.

"And what if I don't want to give you copies?"

Maya turned back sharply and glared at her. "I really hope you're joking."

"Come on, Maya, I just don't see why we can't work on this together!" Rebecca threw her hands up.

"Look," she said, placing her hands on her hips and blowing a stream of air through her teeth. "I am sure that you are a wonderful person and great to work with but, as we have already discussed, I don't work with other people."

"But you're already working with me!"

"Only because it was either that or knock you unconscious!"

"Oh, come on! You have to admit we make a pretty good team?"

"No I don't and we're not on any team! I've known you for three days and have been actively avoiding you for ninety five percent of that time. The only reason we are here is because we got stuck in a cave together."

"And found something amazing," Rebecca pointed out, waving her hand behind her.

"Which I would have found by myself had you not been here."

"Yeah, but not as quickly, and if you had been down here by yourself it would have been you that fell when that ledge gave way and who would have been there to catch you?"

"It wouldn't have given way because I would not have been rushing across it like you were."

"But if it had…"

"Ay, Dios mío," Maya muttered, rubbing her hand over her face and shaking her head. "Look, we don't have time for this. Let's just go."

"Fine." Rebecca said after a pause, putting the strap of the camera roughly over her head and ducking quickly through the gap in the wall.

Maya sighed heavily and took a last lingering look at the images on the wall before following her through. As she came to the other end of the short passage she clicked on her flashlight and pointed it at the ledge to assess the damage where the rock had fallen into the abyss. There was a gap but it was only about a foot and a half wide and there was a handy rock sticking out of the wall about shoulder height that they could hang on to. She gave it a few quick pulls just to make sure it wouldn't come loose and then leaned over the gap to test the ledge on the other side. Once she was sure it was firm she jumped over and turned back to hold her hand out for Rebecca.

"I'll be fine, thank you, just move up and shine the light down."

Maya shrugged and did as she was asked. If Rebecca wanted to be pissy with her that was okay, just as long as she stopped with the teamwork bullshit. She waited til the other woman was safely across then continued on, flattening herself against the wall as the ledge narrowed and ducking into the tunnel as they reached it. As they got about halfway down the low passage she started to feel uneasy again but couldn't work out why, just that all her senses seemed heightened somehow, straining to work out what was different.

"Do you hear that?" Rebecca said uneasily from behind her, and as she did so Maya realised what was wrong.

"Shit!" She hissed. "How long have we been down here? I mean, since we last talked to Claudia?"

"I don't know. About an hour I think? Why?"

"Because that is the sound of water lapping into this passage which means that the water level has risen dramatically since we got in here."

"Are you sure? She said we had ninety minutes!"

"She said we had ninety minutes to get back to the surface and wherever that water is coming from, it's not the surface."

Sure enough when they reached the end of the tunnel they saw that the small chamber was now smaller still, the rock shelf that they had pulled themselves up onto was now under about ten centimetres of water and the passage they had swum through was completely submerged.

"Please tell me you're a good underwater swimmer?" Maya said, looking at their exit route.

"Uh, define 'good'?" she replied, looking slightly paler than before.

"Can you hold your breath for a long time?"

"I think so, but I've never really tried it under duress before."

"It'll be fine, you remember how far it is, right? Piece of cake," she smiled and shoved her in the shoulder playfully. "And just keep thinking about how pissed I'm going to be if I have to come back and save your skinny ass from drowning."

"Well that would almost make it worth it," Rebecca smirked, only her eyes betraying her.

"Yeah, well maybe you give me the camera now so I can just leave you to drown."

"Never going to happen, Maya," she smiled, jumping into the water. "You'll just have to try and keep up."

With that she ducked under the water and kicked off towards the now underwater passage leaving Maya to shake her head and jump in after her. She swam towards the opening and took as deep a breath as possible before ducking under and kicking out with all her might. It was pitch black ahead of her and she tried to angle the light as best she could without interrupting her stroke. Rebecca was about ten feet ahead and thankfully going strong despite the fact that she wouldn't have been able to see for the first few strokes, but the current was coming at them with some force and she knew it wouldn't be long before they began to tire. Sure enough, after about thirty seconds she noticed that she was gaining on Rebecca, even though she herself was beginning to lose her rhythm. She strained to see the other end of the tunnel, hoping against hope that it was shorter than she remembered and they would be out in the open in the next few seconds, but she saw nothing except for Rebecca's increasingly erratic movement.

Another fifteen seconds passed and her lungs were burning in her chest, her arms and legs growing heavy with the exertion and lack of oxygen. She was now level with Rebecca and she glanced over to see how the other woman was doing, pleased to see the look of absolute determination on her face. The sight gave her an extra burst of adrenalin and she pushed forward, shining the light blindly into the dark water ahead with a new certainty that they would be okay. But as they pressed on the water stayed black and there was no sign of it ending, the walls seemed to be closing in and she could sense Rebecca starting to panic slightly in the water behind her. She tried to push to the side and give her more room, to try and make sure her turbulent water didn't impede Rebecca's progress. Surely they had been going for at least sixty seconds? The current pushing against them couldn't have slowed them that much, could it? She felt the panic starting to bubble up in her own chest now, maybe they had somehow taken a wrong turn and were swimming down the wrong channel? In her efforts to get out of Rebecca's way she had drifted to the edge of the tunnel and as she struck out with her next stroke she punched the wall with the hand carrying the flashlight and it fell from her grasp as she grabbed her arm in pain and fought to keep her mouth shut. As quickly as she could she forced herself to start swimming again, kicking through the black water, her injured hand screaming pain through her body with every stroke, panic wrapping around her burning lungs.

Without the torch to light her way she had nothing to focus on except the murky water around her, and now she couldn't even see Rebecca. She swam diagonally to the right to try and find her but there was nothing and after a few moments she smacked into the other wall as well, not as hard but still enough to send her further down the panic spiral and her legs started to flail uselessly in the water. Her body was crying out for oxygen and her brain was fighting a losing war with itself, one half desperately struggling to keep moving forward, the other just wanting to open her mouth and scream, regardless of the consequences, like a child. Suddenly she heard her mother's soft but stern voice in her head telling her to pull herself together, and saw her tía flash in front of her, arms folded, head shaking.

"You got yourself into this situation, Maya, you better damn well get yourself out of it."

She closed her eyes and kicked, voices flying in the darkness around her, interspersed with the blood rushing in her ears, and when she opened them again she saw a dim light ten feet ahead and her heart leapt in her chest, desperately hoping it was real. As she swam out through the opening and kicked for the surface she heard noises from the chamber above and imagined it was her mother and aunt scolding her. She broke the surface and immediately gulped great mouthfuls of air, choking on stray droplets of water and thrashing about to keep her head above the water.

"Maya!" Rebecca cried as she grabbed hold of her, wrapping her arms around her and hugging her tightly as she held her above the water. "Jesus Christ, I was so worried! What happened?"

"Nothing, I'm fine," she coughed, grateful for the support but desperately needing air. She started to push for the wall and Rebecca got the hint, keeping one arm around her as they moved towards the side.

"But you just disappeared! The light went off and you were gone."

"I just swam into the wall and got a bit turned around. My own fault, sorry," she said, breathing deeply as she rested her arm on the wall and tried to calm herself down.

"Don't be sorry, I'm just glad you're okay." Rebecca replied, treading water in front of her as she reached out to gently push the wet hair out of Maya's face and tuck it behind her ear.

Maya's heart started racing again, but from a different kind of fear this time. Her eyes locked with Rebecca's, their faces so close, too close, and she felt her stomach clench uncomfortably. The chamber was deathly silent, despite the fast flowing river they were in, and her ragged breathing seemed embarrassingly loud in the space, like someone whispering in church. Rebecca's hand was still against her cheek, no longer clearing her bedraggled hair but softly stroking her face. She swallowed thickly, the wall behind her giving her no room to retreat as her eyes dropped against her will to Rebecca's lips.

"Maya!" Claudia's panicked voice blared across the silent chamber, startling them both and forcing them apart. "Maya, please answer me! If you have turned this damn thing off so help me I will… Maya, just answer me?"

Quickly she pulled herself out of the water, wincing as her battered hands reminded her of their injuries, and sprinted over to the radio.

"Claudia? Are you okay?"

"Am I okay? AM I OKAY? Christ, Maya, where the fuck have you been? I've been going out of my fucking mind up here!"

"I'm sorry, I left the radio with my clothes so it wouldn't get damaged!"

"With your…? Never mind, I don't even want to know. Where are you? All hell has broken loose up here."

"I'm still in the caves, about an hour out."

"An hour? I told you the storm was coming in and to get back here!"

"I know but I ran into a little... hitch." Maya said, glancing over at Rebecca, who gave her a filthy look in return.

"Yes, well, you're not the only one. The Americans are here and they are freaking out. Their camp got destroyed and…"

"Their camp got destroyed? How?"

"How do you think, Maya? It's like the bloody Wizard of Oz up here. I keep expecting to see Elaine fly by on a broomstick," Claudia huffed and continued. "Anyway, they're freaking out. Their camp is gone, their stuff is ruined and they can't get hold of Rebecca. They say she found a different entrance to the caves and they haven't heard from her in almost two hours."

"Well tell them she's okay. She's with me."

"She's with you?" Claudia asked after a pause.

"Yeah. We, ah, kind of ran into each other."

"I see. So you kind of ran into Rebecca, have been out of contact for at least an hour, and aren't wearing any clothes."

"Jesus, Claud!" Maya hissed, shooting an embarrassed look Rebecca's way before turning her back on her and snatching up her shirt. "We had to swim through a tunnel."

"Is that some kind of euphemism or…?"

"Shut up. Just tell them she's okay and we'll be back up as soon as we can. Secure the camp and let me know if anything else goes wrong, okay?"

"Why, certainly, m'lady. Anything else I can do for you?"

"No, that will be all, thank you. I'll see you in a bit," she huffed and put the radio on the floor as she pulled on her pants and shirt.

"So, your place then?"

She looked up to see Rebecca leaning against the wall next to the entrance, the smirk back in full force.

"Looks that way," she muttered, pulling on her hat and clipping the radio onto her belt. "Sorry about your stuff."

"It's just stuff," Rebecca shrugged. "All the information was backed up and the most important bit is what we got down here."

"I guess. Come on, let's get out of here."

"After you," she smiled as she pointed the beam of the flashlight up the tunnel.

Chapter 11

When they arrived back at camp the storm had died down slightly, the rain still fairly heavy but the wind no longer causing any issues. They were immediately confronted by an outraged Claudia marching towards them, spitting out insults and reprimands at Maya before grabbing her and pulling her into a fierce hug.

"Don't you ever do that to me again, do you understand?" she whispered into her ear mid crush. "I thought you were dead, you bastard."

"I'm sorry, Claud," she whispered back, patting her on the back in the hopes of release and wincing as she jarred her battered hand. "It won't happen again, I promise."

"It better bloody not," Claudia squeezed her once more and let go. "Rebecca. Tea? Coffee? Tequila?"

"Um, sure," Rebecca answered, looking at her with a combination of fear, amusement and confusion. "Coffee, please."

"Right. Your friends have gone back down to the camp to see if they could salvage anything. They should be back soon."

"Your friend is kind of scary," she whispered to Maya as soon as Claudia turned back to camp.

"She also has the hearing of a bat so be careful what you say." Maya whispered back with a wink.

They followed Claudia into the clearing and crawled under the tarpaulin she had put up between the two tents. She handed them both their coffee and let out a deep sigh.

"So, what happened? Please tell me you at least found something?"

"Oh my God, Claud, you should have seen it. It was incredible!" Maya held her hand out to Rebecca for the camera.

"Bloody hell, Maya, what happened to your hand? You're bleeding!" Claudia reached behind her for her bag and grabbed the first aid kit out of it.

"It's fine, I'll take care of it," she muttered, handing over the camera as wipes and bandages were forced into her hand. "Just look at the pictures. They don't do it justice of course, but it's the most amazing thing."

Claudia's face curled up in disapproval as she turned on the camera. "Well since what I am looking at appears to be a picture of your arse, I have to say…"

"Jesus!" Maya lunged forward and grabbed the camera out of her hand, skipping ahead to the next shot and moving to sit next to her friend as Rebecca stifled a laugh on the other side of the circle. "It's amazing. Look at the detail. Have you ever seen anything like it?"

"No, definitely not," she murmured quietly, lost in what she was seeing. "This is unbelievable. Well, I guess this rules out any doubts we had that it's something to do with the Inca."

"Yeah, but it's so weird. Why here?"

"Well, I actually had a thought about that," Rebecca said, reminding the two of them of her presence. "At the time when the Spanish invaded the Inca were fighting amongst themselves, right? I mean Huayna Capac had just died and his two sons were fighting for control. Huáscar was in Cusco and Atahualpa was in the north commanding the armies that had been expanding the Empire for his father."

"Right," Maya said slowly. "He was based in Quito."

"So almost at the northernmost tip of Inca territory, and only about 1800 miles from here," she continued, warming to her theme. "That's less than a third of the distance from one end of the empire to the other, less even than the distance to Cusco."

"Yeah, but Atahualpa marched south to fight his brother."

"He did, with his three generals. But the generals weren't with him when he was captured and killed by the Spanish, and one of them, Rumiñawi, came back to Quito and led the resistance against them from there."

"Okay," Maya admitted. "But he was killed, right?"

"Yes, but not before he had arranged for the removal of the Treasure of Llanganatis, ordered the people to flee and had the city burned. The Spanish captured him when they defeated his forces at Mount Chimborazo, tortured him for the location of the treasure and had him killed when he wouldn't give it up."

"You seem to know an awful lot about this," Claudia said, finally raising her eyes from the camera.

"I've always been interested in the Inca," she shrugged. "Obviously with what's happened recently I have stepped up my research."

"Recently?" Claudia asked, shooting a look at Maya. "You mean, with your parents?"

"Claudia…" Maya warned.

"Yes, with my parents."

"So you knew they were looking for something Incan?"

"Claudia, this is not our business."

"It's alright, I don't mind," Rebecca smiled at her before continuing. "At first, no. I tend not to get involved with what my parents do. I have my own life and they have theirs. But they would check in once a week, more so if they were off on an expedition, so when they didn't get in contact this time I knew something was wrong and I went to their office to see what I could find."

"And?" Claudia asked, leaning forward in rapt attention, oblivious to Maya tutting next to her.

"And...it had been ransacked."

"No!"

Maya gave a hefty eyeroll at her friend's dramatic reaction and reached in her bag for her cigarettes, changing her mind as she remembered her burning lungs in the cave. "How come this hasn't been all over the news?"

"Because I didn't report it," she shrugged. "Contrary to common belief I don't live my entire life on camera, and I prefer things to be kept private if at all possible. Granted, my parent's lifestyle doesn't really lend itself to discretion but I have grown up with that and have learned my way around the system."

"Meaning?"

"Meaning I hired people to look into it for me and keep it quiet."

"Right." Maya drawled.

"So what happened?" Claudia asked, leaning forward to offer a refill.

"I don't know yet. I have some information but nothing concrete," she looked down at the flowing coffee as if it held the answers. "The investigation is still ongoing, of course, and I have some ideas, but really I'm just trying to retrace their footsteps."

"So they were here?"

"Yes. San Esteban was the last place they contacted me from."

"And they told you about Piedro del...thingy?"

"No, they never discussed their work over the phone."

"Okay, I'm confused." Claudia pinched a cigarette out of Maya's pack and lit it.

"After I discovered the break in at their office I went to their house and they had left me instructions."

"Okay, hold up," Maya waved her bandaged hand and leaned forward. "So you're saying that their office was ransacked so you went to the house and it was all spelled out for you? What if the house had been gone through as well?"

"It was."

"What?" Claudia was literally on the edge of her seat now.

"So how come whoever broke in didn't find the instructions?"

"I'm sure they did. But unless you understand my parents the way I do you wouldn't know what you were looking at."

"So what were you looking at?" Claudia asked excitedly.

"They had pinned some things to my notice board and left one of my toys on my bed."

"What kind of toy?"

"Maya!" Claudia hissed, digging her in the ribs.

"Ow! For God's sake, Claudia," Maya snapped, rubbing her side. "I meant what kind of toy would point her to here?"

"Oh. Sorry."

"It was a toy llama they bought for me when we went to Peru," Rebecca replied, laughing at their exchange and Maya's obvious embarrassment. "And they had pinned some photographs of us on my board, from when we visited Fortín Solano, and..."

They were interrupted by voices approaching the camp and Maya jumped up to see who was coming, amazed to realise that the rain had stopped and none of them had noticed. Up the path walked the four Americans from Rebecca's group carrying an assortment of bags and equipment.

"Oh, hey, you're back!" the blonde texan greeted her cheerfully. "You bring our boss with you or dump her down a crevice?"

"Aw, Tom, your concern warms my heart." Rebecca smiled as she appeared beside her. "I see you looked after our stuff just like I asked?"

He smiled at her and laid his bag down on the ground. "Good to have you back, boss."

"God, Rebecca, we were so worried," the Reese Witherspoon type from the bar said earnestly as she pushed her way past him and flung her arms around Rebecca's neck. "What happened?"

"Well, Candace, let's just say that we will not be returning to Owens and Lloyd's for any of our future expedition kit," she sighed, disentangling herself and pushing the hair out of her face. "The information they gave me was not accurate."

"Aw, but they were such nice guys!" the blonde banshee cried as she pulled Rebecca into a one armed hug before wandering into the camp and peering into the tents, earning a glare from Maya.

"Nice guys who could have got me killed."

"Well I'm glad they didn't," the other guy said as he approached and kissed her on the cheek. "Good to have you back, Bec. Show us what you got."

"Thanks, Phil, you're gonna love it." Rebecca beamed at him and linked her arm through his, leading him over to where Tom was setting up the tarpaulin.

A few hours later they were all sitting round the campfire sharing a meal that Candace had prepared, something with quinoa and salad, entirely too healthy for Maya's liking. She glared around the circle and pulled out her bottle of tequila. This was definitely not on her list of things to do and she planned on making her escape first thing in the morning. For now, though, she figured her best plan was to keep her mouth shut, get drunk and pass out. Claudia, on the other hand, seemed happy as a pig in shit. She was sitting next to Tom, obviously, laughing uproariously at almost everything he said and taking every opportunity to touch him. Maya's eyes hurt from rolling them at her so often, not that Claudia had noticed.

"So," Rebecca said from her seat beside Maya. "What do we think we've found?"

"Well it's obviously a map," Phil offered. "But from where to where?"

"I thought the Inca didn't use maps though, right Maya?" Claudia asked, drawing the group's unwanted attention to her just as she was taking a hefty swig from the tequila bottle.

"Well," she coughed, trying to stop herself choking with as much dignity as possible. "Not usually, no, but then they weren't supposed to be in Venezuela either, so all bets are off."

"But we know now that they were, or at least that the people who made this painting were referring to them, so what do we think it's directing us to?"

"Well it has to be something big, right Bec?" Phil leaned behind him and pulled a bottle from his own bag. "I mean, someone did a number on your folk's place. That has to indicate they were onto something pretty big."

"I have to say I agree with you," she sighed, grabbing the tequila from Maya's hand without asking. "I just don't know what. My initial thought was maybe Rumiñawi's hidden treasure but...I don't know, it doesn't quite fit."

"Why not?"

"Just, well, I guess because the figure in the painting is clearly the Sapa Inca, which Rumiñawi was not, the snake is wrapped around some sort of temple, and if he had hidden the treasure in a temple it would have been found."

The group fell silent at this, each seemingly lost in their own thoughts. Maya glanced around them thoughtfully. She didn't know how much to say. She could join in the discussion, but she wasn't good with sharing. There were three people in the world she trusted; her mother, her aunt and Claudia. After that, well, she had lived with her abuela until she was six and her abuela's favourite saying was 'Del dicho al hecho hay un gran trecho', roughly translated as there's a long way between what people say and what is. Still, Rebecca was searching for her parents, she didn't have to tell them everything she had worked out, right? And maybe by giving them something she could work out what they were hiding. She took a breath and went for it.

"Did you ever hear of Paititi?"

"The lost city?" Phil asked.

"Are you serious?" Tom asked, his oversized mouth twisting up into a disbelieving grin.

"Well, yeah." Maya shrugged.

"I mean really serious? You really think we're searching for El Dorado? It's a myth; everybody knows that!"

"Well, actually El Dorado is a tale rooted in fact," she shrugged again as she toyed with a piece of grass. "It's just not about what most people think. 'El Dorado' literally translates as 'the golden', and while somewhere along the line people began to believe it referred to a city of gold, it actually relates to the tribal chief of the Muisca. He would cover himself in gold dust and dive into Lake Guatavita as part of a ritual."

"So what, we're hunting for some ancient C3P0?" he laughed holding his hand up in a high five which Phil shook his head to.

"No, pendejo, I'm just trying to explain how the stories got twisted. When the Spanish attacked the Incan Empire in the 1500s the Inca were forced to retreat because of superior weaponry and tactics, a vicious civil war and the outbreak of Smallpox. One by one their leaders were captured and executed, the last being Túpac Amaru in 1572, but somehow they managed to lose the Spanish and take what remained of their wealth deep into the jungle with the help of a tribe called the Antisuyu. Whether this was because the Spanish underestimated them and let them go, or couldn't navigate the land as well, or some other reason, the remaining Inca disappeared. Somewhere around 1600 a missionary called Andres Lopez sent reports back to the Vatican of local tales of a large city rich in silver, gold and jewels called Paititi, but there was some confusion over whereabouts these tales referred to. Obviously people have been looking for it ever since." Maya stared down at the flames and took a breath to prepare herself. "Over the last fifteen years there have been various expeditions into Peru and Bolivia, mainly focussing on the areas around the Madre de Dios and Beni rivers and recently, due to large areas of deforestation in Brazil, there has been a lot of interest in a few sites uncovered which seem to show large settlements in the Boca do Acre region."

"But the Inca were never in Brazil?" Candace said skeptically.

"That we know of, but they were never meant to be here either. They were retreating, driven out of their territory by the conquistadors, remember?"

"And you think they went to Brazil?" Rebecca asked, looking at her thoughtfully. "The last battles between the Inca and the Spanish were fought in the Vilcabamba Valley. If they headed towards Urubamba and up through the mountains that would take them towards Madre de Dios. It's plausible."

"But Boca do Acre? It's got to be...I don't know, 700 miles from Vilcabamba to there?" Tom pointed out.

"Well, sure but they had to know they were free, right?" Maya replied, nodding at him. "I mean, it's not like they would run round the corner, think 'Phew, we lost them!' and start building their last refuge. They tried that with Vilcabamba. They had to be sure. We're not talking about some little village here, Tex, we're talking about a fortified city where they could be safe."

"Alright. But what if the natives tales were exaggerated? What if there was no gold and all they had was their fortified city? What if it's already been discovered? Manco Pata, for instance?" Phil asked.

"Manco Pata is just a bunch of sandstone." Maya waved her hand dismissively. "It has absolutely no structure."

"Well, maybe they were in a hurry…" Tom shrugged.

"Look, the Incan Empire was incredibly advanced for the time and the resources available to them, and their architecture is breathtaking. They didn't just throw up walls to hide behind, everything was carefully designed for maximum effect and stability." Maya tugged on her pendant and stared down at the flames. "But my biggest reason for believing they haven't found it is this: the Inca worshipped three animals - the condor, the jaguar and the snake. Cusco, their capital, is built in the shape of a jaguar. Machu Picchu is like a condor. So where's the snake?"

The group fell silent again, the only sound the crackle of burning wood on the campfire. Maya felt something knock against her hand so looked down and saw Rebecca pressing the bottle of tequila against it. She glanced up as she took it and saw the other woman nodding, an impressed smile on her lips. Maya gave a quick smile back and raised the bottle to her mouth as she turned her attention to the rest of the group.

Claudia was looking at her with an odd expression on her face, like she couldn't quite believe her friend had been so open with this bunch of strangers and wasn't sure if she was okay with it, but her attention was quickly reclaimed by Tom as he passed her the bottle of whatever it was Phil had pulled out of his bag. Tom himself, Maya had decided, was not worth the effort. He clearly had some knowledge, particularly regarding geography, but the fact that he had not accompanied Rebecca down into the caves led her to believe that he was more the theoretical type than the practical, much as his ridiculously toned physique might suggest otherwise. Phil, on the other hand, was someone who Maya had several concerns about; he and Rebecca were obviously very close and he seemingly knew a lot about the Inca, and about the tech Rebecca's group were using. Outside of Rebecca herself he seemed to be the brains of the operation, but there was something about him that Maya didn't like, although it could just be the nagging suspicion that he didn't like her. Still, he had been the one to show the most cards during the conversation, but then again that could just be because the rest of them weren't holding any.

The two other women, for example, seemed at this point in time to be just filler. Candace and the banshee, or Vanessa, as Maya should probably get used to calling her, just seemed to swan about the camp and act as the Supremes to Rebecca's Diana Ross. Although, to be fair, Candace had cooked, albeit some hipster meal that Maya had not enjoyed at all. Vanessa had pretty much done nothing but sunbathe since the rain stopped, which was at least preferable to her singing. As she turned her gaze to that side of the circle the banshee reached into her bag, pulled out a tin, popped it open and started rolling a joint. So maybe she was the entertainment officer of this little tour group?

From that point on the conversation veered away from the task at hand and onto a wildly varied range of topics. Maya stayed mostly quiet until Claudia seemed on the point of telling the Cabo story, at which point she burst into a volley of rapid fire Spanish which successfully conveyed the point to her friend that no, she was not okay with the incident being shared. After that the group drifted off into mini discussions and it wasn't long before she felt Rebecca's gaze on her.

"So, you want to talk about earlier?"

"I thought we already did," she yawned, leaning back on her elbows. "Fire away, although I'm not sure I can come up with anything useful in my current state."

"No, not the painting," Rebecca said as she lay down next to her on her side, way too close. "The, ah, other interesting thing that happened in the cave."

Maya's stomach twisted and her head started to swim so she sat up quickly and reached into her bag for her cigarettes, huffing in frustration when she couldn't find them.

"There's nothing to talk about," she said quietly. "Stuff like that happens when you feel like you just nearly died."

"Oh really?"

"Yeah," she huffed again, rifling through her pockets desperately.

"Here," Rebecca slapped the pack against her bicep and sat up. "I never nearly died before, Maya, but I'm pretty sure that's not all there was to it."

She grabbed the pack and lit one, swearing under her breath as she dropped the lighter in the attempt. "Well, you're just going to have to trust me," she said as she blew out a stream of smoke. "That's all it was."

She looked around the group again, mainly because she could feel Rebecca's eyes burning a hole in the side of her head. Candace and Phil were both saying their goodnights which was something Maya was surprised about, they didn't seem like the likeliest couple. Vanessa was rolling another joint and Claudia and Tom were still deep in conversation.

"You know I don't get you, Maya," Rebecca murmured as she moved closer to the fire, closer to her.

"Don't worry," she snorted. "You're not the first."

"Can't you just…"

"Look, Rebecca," she snapped slightly louder than intended, drawing the interest of Tom and Claudia. She forced herself to take a deep breath and lower her voice before continuing. "Just forget it, okay? It was nothing. You don't get me because you don't know me. We're not friends, we're not anything, so just stop trying to work me out."

She flicked her cigarette angrily into the fire and linked her hands loosely around her spread knees. She knew she was being a bitch but she didn't care, she just wanted out of this situation and away from Rebecca, away from the confusion she kept stirring up in her. Again she could feel the woman's stare on her but she just kept looking into the fire, silently willing her to get up and leave, and finally she did.

"Alright, guys," Rebecca announced, stretching as she stood up. "I'm going to turn in. I'll see you all in the morning. Goodnight, Maya."

"Night."

As Rebecca walked off in the direction of her salvaged tent Maya let out a deep sigh, half relief, half frustration and flopped down onto the grass, her arm over her eyes. After a few moments someone sat down beside her and she waited in silence for Claudia's inevitable 'words of wisdom'. When none came she peered out from under the crook of her elbow and discovered that it was Vanessa who had come to join her, not Claudia, and that she was just staring up at the sky and smoking the joint peacefully.

"Could I have a drag off that?" Maya asked after a few minutes.

"Sure, mamacita!" Vanessa trilled after getting over her apparent surprise that Maya was there. "Knock yourself out! Although, you know. Not really."

"Thanks," she replied drolly, taking the proffered joint and inhaling deeply, savouring the bitter taste as it swirled around her mouth and reactivated her buzz.

"So what's your deal, Maya?" she asked, pronouncing her name like it was some exotic word she'd never used before.

"God, who knows at this point?" Maya answered, tipping her head back and staring up at the sky as she exhaled. "What's anybody's deal?"

"A very interesting question. One I think we are not in an adequate state of mind to address. Or possibly," she leaned over and poked her in the arm for effect. "The best state of mind to address. Did you know that John Wayne's real name was Marion?"

"Really?" Maya creased her brows quizzically and handed the joint back.

"Oh yeah. Marion Mitchell Morrison," she pronounced each word dramatically before taking another drag. "Makes you think, doesn't it? Growing up with a name like that and then turning into the archetypal male film star."

"Kind of like 'A Boy Named Sue'."

"Huh?"

"You know. The Johnny Cash song."

"Oh yeah."

They sat in silence for a while and passed the joint back and forth, watching as the stars stared down at them from the sky.

"It makes you realise how insignificant we all are, doesn't it?" Vanessa said quietly. "How we're all down here stressing the small stuff, looking up at the same stars that people thousands of years ago did, worrying about exactly the same shit."

"Maybe. But we're out here now looking for some of that shit, right? That has to mean something."

"Yeah, I guess. But then these people probably weren't writing instructions for people thousands of years later to find. They were most likely leaving directions for their friends to follow, like Bec's parents did for her. What if they were waiting to be rescued and nobody ever came?"

"Jesus," Maya muttered as she sat up. "That's fucking depressing."

"Yeah, sorry. Sometimes I go dark when I'm stoned," she smiled widely as she passed the joint back. "You're hot. Like super hot. I'm not into girls but I would totally make out with you."

"Yeah, I don't see that happening. But thanks."

"Whatever. You and Claudia ever do it?"

"What?" Maya choked out, looking quickly to see if Claudia had heard. Thankfully, and a little worryingly, Claudia and Tom had disappeared. "Jesus, no, she's like my sister."

"Hmm, I didn't think so but I thought I'd ask."

"Why?"

"You're not very good at gossip, are you?"

"No. I just don't get why people are so interested in other people's lives. I don't get why they're so interested in my life. I have absolutely no interest in theirs." Maya said as she flicked the ash into the fire.

"Well, maybe you should pay more attention." Vanessa smiled at her strangely. "You know, I'm getting a lot of tension from you and Becca."

"Well what can I say," she smiled and handed her the joint. "Some people just rub each other up the wrong way, you know?"

"Yeah, I don't mean that kind of tension. I mean the hot, sticky, panting kind," she took a drag and looked up at the stars as Maya stared at her in shock. "You guys look hot together too."

"Ah, Vanessa…"

"Plus you could totally knock her bitch of an ex on her ass if it came to it, which I would love to see," she yawned and stretched as she stood up. "Night, mamacita. See you in the morning."

"Not if I see you first," she muttered as Vanessa wandered off.

Chapter 12

Maya awoke in a panic as something vibrated against her arm. She jerked into an upright position in her sleeping bag and peered through the thin light to see what it was, desperately hoping it wasn't some kind of bug, especially not the winged kind. She sighed in relief when she saw her phone screen lit up and remembered that she had set her alarm for stupid o'clock so that she and Claudia could pack up and sneak off before the others woke up.

She rubbed her eyes, briefly startled by the rough sensation until she remembered her hand was bandaged, the jolt of pain reinforcing the point, and crawled out of her cocoon, stuffing it into its bag as best she could before pulling on her shorts. Carefully she unzipped the opening and crawled out, inching towards Claudia's tent and wishing bad things on her friend if she wasn't alone. She pulled the zip and peered inside, giving a quick sigh of relief when she saw only Claudia. She shook her gently and pressed a finger to her lips as her friend opened her eyes blearily, her brow furrowing in concern as she realised Maya was there.

"We have to go," Maya whispered. "Quietly and now."

Claudia nodded quickly and crawled out of her sleeping bag.

Twenty minutes later they were hurrying away from the makeshift camp, successfully having packed up their gear and got out without anyone waking up, still Maya couldn't help but keep glancing over her shoulder to make sure no one was following.

"Please tell me you didn't sleep with the banshee?"

"What?" Maya snapped her eyes up to Claudia's. "Of course not. Why would I do that?"

"Oh, I don't know. Maybe because you clearly fancy Rebecca but are desperately trying not to and sleeping with one of her friends would be a sure fire way to make sure nothing happens?" Claudia said, finishing with a yawn and stretching her arms up. "Just a thought, but I haven't had any coffee yet."

"Well you're way off."

"Right," she smiled. "So why are we sneaking off at the arse crack of dawn?"

"Because, I…" Maya glanced back again with a sigh and tried to think of how to phrase it. "She wants us to work with them and I…well, I don't think Elaine would be particularly happy about it."

"But you haven't spoken to Elaine in days, and the last conversation we had about it I remember having some doubts about her intentions, don't you?"

"I remember you having doubts about her."

"Of course you do," she scoffed. "Honestly, Maya, that woman could ask you to literally walk into hell and I'm sure you would do it. I can't understand the hold she has over you."

"Claudia," Maya stopped and turned to her friend, raising her hand between them as she tried to control her anger. "It's six o'clock in the morning, we've got ten miles to walk before we can eat or have any caffeine. Can we please not fight right now?"

Claudia made a face like she was biting her tongue before shrugging, adjusting the generator pack on her front and walking on through the forest. Maya sighed and followed her, exhausted and mentally drained. All she wanted to do was get back to the apartment and sleep for a week but she knew that once they got there the first thing she would have to do would be to ring Elaine and explain what they had found and, perhaps more importantly, who they had found it with. She honestly had no idea what the woman's reaction would be and at this point she was too tired to care.

Suddenly the trees cleared and they found themselves looking out over the park and down towards Puerto Cabello, the sea twinkling in the new light like it was laughing at a secret they weren't in on. Claudia had stopped to stare down at it so Maya walked up behind her and rested her arm on her shoulder, realising that this was the first time they had properly stopped to appreciate the beauty of the place since they had arrived.

"It's been an intense couple of days, huh?" Maya said softly.

"It certainly has been that," she replied with a sigh.

"I'm, uh, I'm really glad you're here with me, Claud. You know that, right?"

"I know. And I wouldn't miss it." Claudia smirked at her awkwardness and grabbed her bandaged hand with her own. "This trip really has it in for our hands, eh?"

"Kind of seems that way," she laughed, throwing her arm around her friend's shoulder. "Come on, I need coffee."

The two of them started down the hill in the breaking light; the lake, the cave and Rebecca behind them, the unknown ahead.

Four and a half hours and several cups of coffee later, Maya sat at the table in the apartment and stared out the window in preparation for the phone call she had to make. Claudia was in the shower scrubbing away the dirt of the last three days. She had offered for Maya to go first but Maya had a sneaking suspicion that she would need it more to relax after she had spoken to Elaine. She shifted her gaze to the counter and briefly contemplating drinking some tequila to calm her nerves but it wasn't even eleven a.m. yet and she knew once she started she wouldn't stop so she snatched up her phone and dialled the number.

"Maya," Elaine answered brusquely after one ring. "So good of you to call. I was starting to wonder if perhaps you had died."

"Yeah, I get that a lot recently."

"Well since you evidently haven't would you care to tell me what you have been doing with your time?"

Rolling her eyes Maya quickly filled her in on the events of the last few days; the petroglyphs, the cave, Rebecca's involvement, and her theory of what it all meant. Elaine listened in silence to her narration and when she was finished there was such a long pause that Maya pulled her ear away from the phone to check they were still connected.

"Paititi, eh?" she said eventually. "Interesting."

"That's it?" Maya said incredulously. "'Interesting'?"

"Oh, I'm sorry, maybe you would rather something like 'Ooh, Maya, how exciting! You truly are an exceptional person to have found all of that! Bravo! Bravo!'" Elaine said in her best patronising voice, which was really saying something. "Sorry to disappoint you, Maya, but I'm your employer, not your mother or one of your fangirls."

"I know that," she muttered, her skin prickling with embarrassment. "I just thought the fact we may be on the verge of the greatest Inca discovery since Bingham might warrant a little more than 'interesting'."

"Well forgive me but 'maybes' and obscure paintings are not enough for me to get over excited. I'm afraid I don't share your Latin temperament." Elaine said, sounds drifting through the line of a door opening and muffled voices. "Hold on."

Maya sat stewing in her rage and shame as Elaine conducted whatever business had suddenly cropped up miles away. Not for the first time she wondered to herself why on earth she continued to work for this woman who seemed to view her as some irascible child, driven by fits of pique and hormones. Eventually Elaine came back on the line and continued as if nothing was amiss.

"So what is your next move?"

"Well, I'm not really sure. I guess we go to Vilcabamba or Cusco, but I have a hunch that we could be looking at somewhere further east." Maya took a breath and hoped for the best. "Boca do Acre in Brazil. There has been speculation about it before and I think a lot of the information fits. What do you think?"

"I think that thinking is what I pay you for," Elaine snapped. "Although I would like to see the photographs you and the Bronstein girl took. Have Claudia send them over would you?"

"Of course. What do you want me to do about her?"

"Claudia?"

"No, Rebecca," she said, taking a breath as she waited for the answer.

"She's an interesting one, isn't she?" Elaine said, more to herself than to Maya. "I can't quite work out what she hopes to achieve in all this. Her parents are seasoned explorers, if they have dropped out of contact it's for good reason and it's highly unlikely that she will find them unless they wish to be found. Unless, of course…"

Maya sat and waited for her to continue, slightly surprised that she spoke of Rebecca's parents like she knew them. Although Elaine, whilst remaining a mystery herself, seemed to know everyone so really she should have expected it. Just as the silence was reaching the point that she felt the need to check the connection again she heard a rustle from the other end of the line.

"Well, it seems you have lost her for now, maybe that will be enough for her to give up. If not then just play along, see what happens. If you end up working with her then so be it, but it is entirely up to you."

"Fine."

"But Maya? Be very careful with this one. It seems very much to me like she is trying to play you. I have known many women like her before and they will do and say almost anything to get what they want."

"I'm not an idiot, Elaine," she muttered. "I know when I'm being played."

"That's what we all say until it happens. I just don't want to see you get hurt." Elaine said in an unexpectedly soft tone. Quickly she cleared her throat and continued. "Or distracted. Now send me those photographs and plan your next move. Call me when you arrive and give me your itinerary."

"Okay," Maya said to the dial tone. She put the phone down on the table and looked at it in confusion, no closer to knowing what to do than she had been before. Not that she had expected Elaine to have all the answers, the woman made the Sphynx look straightforward.

Sighing she got up and walked into the bedroom, flopping down on the bed to wait for Claudia to be done in the shower.

When she woke up she had no idea where she was and for a brief moment she thought she was back in her childhood home. Sighing deeply when she realised she was not she pushed herself up off the bed with her good hand and padded out into the kitchen where Claudia was sitting at the table in front of her laptop.

"Good evening," she greeted her cheerfully. "Feeling any better?"

"Mmph," Maya grunted, rubbing her eyes and wandering over to the kettle.

"I'll take that as a no then," she murmured as she pulled off her glasses. "I'm almost afraid to ask how it went with Elaine."

"Just peachy," Maya laughed. "She's delighted with our performance and wishes us all the luck in the world as we move forward."

"Really?"

"No, Claud, not really. She was ambivalent at best."

"Hmm. Well, I suppose we expected that. We could find the Holy Grail and she would ask us what took so long." Claudia looked over at her and clapped her hands together, the bandages producing a soft thud. "So, now that we're home and rested and the talk with Elaine is out of the way, would you mind telling me exactly when you figured out that the 'Boca' in Zuazola's journal was Boca do Acre and why you decided to go completely against character and share it with Rebecca's whole team before sharing it with me?"

"Oh…"

"Yes," she snapped, crossing her arms roughly. "Oh."

"It wasn't really like that, Claud, I swear." Maya stood opposite her and pleaded with her eyes. "In all honesty it just kind of happened very quickly. I saw the mouth on the drawing and it linked up with the 'boca', and the river on the snake made me think it could be, but I really don't know for sure. I do think that we are looking for Paititi and I wanted to get a feel for what they knew so I thought I'd throw them a bone."

"Pretty big bone to throw them. Especially since you're right."

"How can you possibly know that?"

Claudia turned the laptop round so it was facing Maya. On the screen was a photograph of a sign reading 'vuelva siempre' being held aloft between the noses of two dolphins. It stood on the banks of a large river with a dense forest behind it.

"Where is that?" Maya asked quietly.

"Boca do Acre, Maya," she smiled. "Just like you said."

"Jesus Christ."

"So, my extremely irritating and potentially savant friend," Claudia stretched and got up. "What are we eating?"

"I'll cook," she said distractedly, flicking between the photograph and the painting of the two dolphins on the snake.

"Oh, God, that weird tequila thing again?"

"Chicken a la Maya? You loved it!"

"I was drunk! More so after I finished it."

"Whatever," Maya stared at the picture the laptop, barely able to believe what Claudia had found. "We don't have anything in and I still need to shower so.."

"I'll go," Claudia sighed, grabbing her purse and heading for the door. "Do you want anything else?"

"No, I'm good, thanks."

"Okay, I won't be long."

Maya waved distractedly and smiled at the screen. Finally they had something, something big, and all thanks to a tourist's photo on a travel site. Of course, it could all just be a huge coincidence and there would be nothing there at all, but then the same had been true of everything else they had found, and this felt right.

She shook her head slightly, closed the laptop with a laugh and headed for the shower.

Twenty minutes later she wandered back into the bedroom in her towel, her excitement slightly dampened, no pun intended. They were on the verge of discovering something amazing, something people had been talking about for almost five hundred years, yet somehow she felt tired, confused, and kind of like something bad was about to happen.

She blew out a stream of air and shook her arms to try and snap herself out of it as she crossed over to her bag and grabbed a black bra. She just needed to get her head in the game, that was all. There was absolutely no point in worrying about anything else now, she would just deal with it as and when it happened. That was her forte, after all.

There was a knock at the front door and she sighed in irritation as she reached into her bag for the first pair of underwear she could find, pulling them on as she hurried to answer it. The knock came again as she was halfway there.

"I swear to God, Claud, if you forget your keys I cannot be held responsible for answering the door half..." she pulled it open to find Rebecca standing there. "Naked."

"Oh, I'm sorry, am I interrupting something?" Rebecca asked, her eyes darting towards the bedroom.

"No, I just got out of the shower."

"Right, yeah, obviously, because you're wet," she dropped her eyes as a slight blush rose to her cheeks and took in the outfit. "Nice colour."

Maya looked down at herself as Rebecca pushed past her into the apartment. In her haste to answer the door she had inadvertently put on a lilac thong, not her most discreet piece of clothing. She sighed and closed the door.

"Is there something I can help you with?"

Rebecca chuckled as she wandered into the kitchen and looked about the place. "I'll just stick with yes for now," she smirked as she sat down. "Do you want to put some clothes on?"

"Not really." Maya snapped as she followed her into the kitchen and leaned against the counter. "Do you want me to put some clothes on?"

"Not really." Rebecca smiled at her and crossed her legs, resting her hands on her knees. "So, you're probably wondering why I'm here."

"Actually I'm wondering how you're here as I don't remember telling you where we were staying."

"I have my ways."

"Right. Cos that's not creepy at all."

"Well you did kind of ditch me in the middle of the woods, Maya."

"And to you the reasonable response to that is to stalk me?"

"I'd hardly call it stalking." Rebecca huffed, her pout annoyingly making Maya soften a bit.

"What is it that you want, Rebecca?"

"I want to know why you won't work with me."

"Really?"

"Yes," Rebecca stood up and moved in front of her. "I've got the money and the resources. I've got a team in place that can help Claudia, and we already know that you and I make a good team, so why won't you just come with me?"

"Because I don't trust you." Maya said, the simple words causing the air to thicken around them.

"You don't trust me?" Rebecca took a slow step towards her and trailed a finger down Maya's bicep. "Or you don't trust yourself when you're around me?"

Maya's eyes dropped to Rebecca's hand and then slowly travelled back up to meet her gaze. The air between them was crackling and she swallowed thickly before answering.

"I don't trust you," she whispered as the door opened and Claudia burst in carrying several bags.

"Would you believe me if I said they were all out of tequila and we had to eat normal people food for a... Oh, hi Rebecca," she shot a quick look at Maya, clearly taking in her choice of outfit and proximity to the other woman. "Will you be joining us for dinner?"

"No," Maya said quickly, pushing away from the counter and heading towards the bedroom as casually as she could. "Rebecca was just leaving. I'll finish getting dressed and be out to start dinner in a minute."

She closed the bedroom door behind her, leaning against it and fighting to get herself under control. Her hands were shaking, for God's sake, how did this woman keep doing this to her? She needed to find a way to get over this and fast. From the kitchen she could hear the awkward murmurings of Claudia seeing Rebecca out and she breathed a sigh of relief as she heard the front door close. Quickly she pulled on some jeans and a top and headed back out to the kitchen, plastering a smile on her face as she went.

"So, what 'normal people' food did you get?"

"What the hell was that?" Claudia asked, hands resting on her hips, eyes bright.

"What was what?" Maya replied weakly, looking through the bags in an effort to hide from Claudia's rage.

"Don't play stupid with me, Maya. I come back to find you half naked and pressed up against the counter with her looking like she wants to eat you, then you kick her out and practically run into your room. What the fuck is going on?"

"Jesus, Claud, first you say I'm always half naked, then you act surprised when I am," she said wearily, putting away the groceries with her back to her friend.

"That is really not the point here, Maya. Talk to me. Tell me what's going on?"

"There is nothing going on!" Maya yelled, slamming the bag down as she wheeled around. "For fuck's sake, would everyone just stop treating me like a horny teenage boy who can't keep my dick in my pants?"

"That's not what I was…"

"Well that's what it fucking feels like, okay? And I'm sick of it," she snatched her cigarettes and lighter off the table and stomped towards the front door.

"Maya, please just calm…"

"Don't!" Maya snapped as she spun back around and pointed at her. Taking a deep breath she closed her hand into a fist and dropped it to her side. "Don't tell me to calm down, Claudia."

"Alright, I'm sorry." Claudia held her hands up and moved slowly towards her. "I'm just concerned about you. Please just talk to me?"

"There's nothing to talk about," she muttered as she wrapped her arms around herself, her bruised knuckles complaining as they knocked against her arm.

"Well clearly there is," Claudia said quietly. "You've not been yourself since we got here. You're drinking more, you're smoking almost as much as me, you're not as focussed, you seem two seconds from giving up every time we hit a dead end. Honestly I've not seen you like this since…"

"Jesus, not this again." Maya turned and pulled the front door open.

"Where are you going?"

"Out."

She slammed the door behind her and started walking down the hill into town, pulling out a cigarette and lighting it angrily. Claudia was right, of course, she hadn't been herself since they had got here and, thanks to her earlier confrontation with Rebecca, she finally knew why. Now all she had to do was sort it out.

Chapter 13

Maya took a deep breath and knocked on the door, steeling herself for whatever was waiting for her on the other side. The last thing she expected, though, was for Rebecca to open the door looking so visibly upset.

"Maya," she said, tightening her robe and fixing a smile on her face as she stood back to let her enter the room. "How did you find me?"

"It wasn't that hard," Maya shrugged as she walked into the large room and took in the tasteful decor. "This is the fanciest place in town. The front desk isn't very discreet, though. I just told them you were expecting me and they sent me right up."

"I'll be sure to mention that in my feedback," she muttered, moving over to the bar in the corner of the room. "Can I get you a drink?"

"No thanks, I'm not staying."

"I see. Well, what can I do for you then?"

"What is it that you want from me, Rebecca?"

"Excuse me?"

"Why do you keep showing up all the time?" she threw her hands up in exasperation. "It's like everytime I turn around there you are, smirking at me, making some innuendo, just generally throwing me off my game. So please, just be straight with me. What is it that you want?"

"I already told you what I want!"

"Yeah, you want me to work with you. But I already told you I don't want to so why do you keep pushing?"

"Because I need you, Maya!" Rebecca cried, breaking her cool exterior for once and surprising them both. "I need your help to find my parents. I've pieced together what I could and it's got me this far but I can't help feeling that they're running out of time and I..."

"Cut the crap, Rebecca, there are no cameras here for you to play to," she sighed wearily and shook her head. "There are hundreds of people you could have got to help you. You could have gone to the press and had half the world looking for them."

"Yeah, and once they found out what they were searching for when they disappeared what do you think all those people would be more interested in then? My parents would be at best an afterthought, at worst an obstacle."

"And what makes you think I would be any different?"

"Because of the way people talk about you."

"What, that I'm a bitch?" Maya snorted and folded her arms defensively.

"No! Well, yes, but they also say that you do things differently, make connections that no one else does, and that you care about the things that you find for the right reasons, not for how much they're worth."

"Yeah, right. Like who says that?"

"My parents," she sat down heavily on the bed and stared out through the open balcony doors to the waves crashing on the shore in the moonlight. "They have so much respect for you, Maya. That's why I came looking for you."

Maya stood in the centre of the room and watched her as she weighed her options up in her mind. Rebecca looked crushed, and although she was short in stature she had never seemed so small before. As she sat on the bed discussing her parents she looked for all the world like a lost little girl.

"So why didn't you just tell me that?"

"I don't know," she played with her hands in her lap as she spoke. "I guess I thought it would make me look desperate. I can't bear looking weak."

"Your parents are missing, Rebecca," Maya said softly. "You're allowed to be desperate."

"I know," she laughed drily. "And I'm reaching the point where I really am. It's a stupid pride thing I guess."

She stood in the middle of the room and stared out to sea as the thoughts ran riot in her head. Rebecca had all but admitted that their constant encounters were not a coincidence, she had told her that her parents admired her and that she had come looking for her. Presumably when they disappeared she had done her research, as seemed to be her way, and that was how she knew so much about her, but did that make it any better? How much could a person find out about her when they set their mind to it? That was a scary thought. Rebecca knew where she was from, where she grew up, most likely about her father and, from the way she was trying to get her to help her, about her sexuality.

Maya hated liars. She hated any kind of deception, regardless of the motivation. Tell a white lie, spare their feelings...no. People needed to hear the truth, that was what she believed, and putting on a pretence to get people on your side was just bullshit. If people didn't like you, they didn't like you, their problem not yours, cut your losses and move on. But desperation...that was something she could understand would force a person's hand. Desperation to save the people you love. Maybe that was something she could forgive. Forgive, maybe. But not forget.

"Alright," Maya said after a moment. "I'll help you."

"Oh, God, really?"

"Yes. But I have some conditions."

"Name them," she smiled, getting up and walking towards her. "I'll pay you anything you want."

"It's not about money." Maya spat, wrinkling her nose in disgust. "It's about what happens in Brazil."

"Okay…"

"I want you to stay away from me."

"But…"

"No buts," she held her hands up and backed away. "It's me and Claudia, that's the way it's always been, that's the way it will stay. We will report back to you with anything we find but that's it. Okay?"

"No."

"What?"

"I said no," Rebecca said, walking towards her and raising her chin. "They're my parents. I can't just sit in a hotel while the two of you traipse around the jungle looking for them. What if something happens to you?"

"Nothing will happen to us."

"Oh really?" she smirked. "Have you ever heard of Percy Fawcett, Maya?"

"No."

"He was an English explorer who lead several expeditions into the Amazon looking for a mysterious lost city called 'Z'. He was said to be invincible. It turns out he wasn't, as on his last attempt he and his two companions, his son and his son's best friend, disappeared. Do you know how many people, how many experts, went in trying to find them?"

"No."

"Over a hundred. And guess how many came back?"

"Alright," Maya sighed. "I get your point but what makes you think we have a better chance with five newbies tagging along?"

"Because these 'newbies' will bring with them any and all equipment you think we would need, a wealth of theoretical knowledge and, most importantly, will do whatever you say whenever you say it."

Maya tapped her fingers on her arm and thought it over. She hated the idea of dragging a bunch of randoms along with her anywhere, let alone deep into the rainforest, but she supposed there were certain advantages. If anything happened to her, for instance, at least Claudia wouldn't be left on her own.

"Alright," she said after a while.

"Great," Rebecca smiled, letting out a sigh of relief as she did. "So, why are you so sure that this Boca do Acre is where we need to be?"

"There are some details on the painting we found that tie up with some of our earlier research." Maya scratched her ear uncomfortably, not used to having these conversations with anyone except Claudia and Elaine. "I can, er, show you. I mean, if you want."

"That would be great. What was the second thing?"

"The second thing?"

"Yeah, you said conditions. As in more than one?"

"Oh, right," she took a deep breath. "If this is going to work I need to be able to trust you. I don't trust people easily and the way we've started off has not exactly helped your cause so from now on if you want something, just be straight with me. I'm not going to do something for you just because you make out like you want to sleep with me, okay?"

"Maya…"

"Just don't alright?" Maya turned to leave, heat rising to her face. "I'll see you tomorrow, Claudia and I are leaving at midday."

"Maya," she said gently, putting one hand on her shoulder and the other on the door. "Please believe me when I say that I never pretended that I wanted to sleep with you."

"I'm not an idiot, Rebecca. I know when I'm being played."

"Well obviously not because I have never once pretended to feel anything for you other than what I actually do."

"Oh come on," she turned to face her. "The bar? The cave? My goddamn kitchen?"

"Were all because I am insanely attracted to you and have been since the moment I met you." Rebecca said, blushing slightly and dropping her gaze. "And it's got nothing to do with me trying to get you to help me, quite the opposite in fact. If we'd met under normal circumstances I would just have asked you out, but we didn't so I've been trying not to act on it."

"You expect me to believe that?" Maya asked, a shadow of doubt creeping into her conviction.

"Why would I lie?" Rebecca shrugged as she leaned against the door and tucked her hair behind her ears. "You already agreed to help me and, if me embarrassing myself by spelling it out to you will help you to trust me then so be it. Like I said, I was trying to keep it professional."

"Well you're not doing a very good job," she couldn't help but laugh. "You were going to kiss me in that cave."

"You almost died!" Rebecca smiled, pushing her gently. "And you were totally going to kiss me back."

"And tonight? Claudia said you looked like you wanted to eat me. Which, now that I think about it, I will have to mock her for her choice of words later."

"Oh, God," Rebecca covered her face with her hands in embarrassment. "Claudia saw that? Shit."

Maya leaned against the door and smiled, allowing herself to believe for a moment that she had been wrong. There was no falseness in Rebecca's words, no hint of artifice, it was almost like some invisible curtain had dropped between the two of them. "Like I said, not doing a very good job."

"Well in my defence you were in your underwear and, my God," she uncovered her face and gestured at her. "Have you seen you? I really give myself credit for making it past the front door."

Maya chuckled and dropped her head, starting to believe Rebecca, but the realisation that the situation was now kind of awkward not far behind. After all, the attraction was obviously mutual but Elaine had warned her to keep it professional and she knew that was the right thing to do, especially now they were going to be stuck in the jungle together for who knew how long, but God help her did she want to kiss her right now.

"So, what happens next?" Rebecca said quietly as she moved a little closer and looked at her cautiously. "I mean, I tried not to do anything about this because I wanted us to work together, and now we are going to be working together, but I guess the cat's kind of out of the bag now."

"Yeah," Maya murmured as she turned her head. Rebecca's eyes, normally a chocolate brown colour, were now almost black, her lids heavy. She felt a quickening in her gut at the sight and clenched her hand into a fist to keep it at her side. "People keep telling me to be professional so…"

"Yeah, okay," she said, her voice thick with disappointment. She licked her lips and let out a shaky breath as she pushed away from the door.

Her heart was pounding and almost unconsciously Maya put her hand on Rebecca's wrist to stop her. She swallowed thickly and raised her eyes to the brunette's flushed face. "So I guess that means I'm not very professional."

Rebecca's eyes flicked back to hers, searching them as if to see if she understood.

"So…"

"So shut up and kiss me."

Maya propped herself up her elbow and ran her fingers languidly across Rebecca's stomach as she waited for her to recover.

"Well. That was…" she managed after a few minutes, letting out a shaky laugh as she pushed a hand into her hair.

"Yeah," Maya smiled.

"Something you picked up at Oxford?"

"No, that is definitely extracurricular," she laughed. "What kind of classes did they teach at Yale?"

"Please," Rebecca snorted. "I went to an all girl's boarding school. Anything I learned on this subject came long before Yale."

"You went to boarding school?"

"Well, yeah. You know what my parents do. What did you think, they would take the rugrat with them on their quests for fortune and glory?"

"Shit, I had no idea," Maya said softly. "I'm sorry."

"It wasn't all bad," she shrugged, interlocking their hands and massaging Maya's fingers with her own. "They tried to be home for holidays and birthdays and stuff, and when we went on vacation they always tried to make it about me, never about the work. At least I still had them both. Not like you."

Maya's hand tensed slightly and Rebecca immediately stilled her movements, her eyes snapping up to hers and full of regret.

"Shit, Maya, I'm sorry, I…"

"No, it's okay," she smiled tightly. "I just never really talk about it I guess. It's hard, you know?" She lay back down on the bed and stared up at the ceiling.

"How old were you?" Rebecca asked quietly after a while.

"Twelve," she sighed and ran a hand over her eyes. "I remember it so clearly, you know? It was a Tuesday. I was in class, which was rare, but it was History class. I never missed that class."

"You already knew you wanted to do this?"

"Nah, the teacher was hot." Maya smirked and raised her arm in defence as Rebecca swatted her playfully before grabbing her hand and pulling her arm around herself as she snuggled into Maya's side. "Anyway, they came and got me out of class and told me. I just couldn't get my head around it, it just didn't seem like it could be real. I went home and mami was just…broken. She just sat on the sofa and cried all night and I didn't know what to do so I just sat next to her and held her hand. The next day my tía arrived and bossed us both around til we got through the funeral, then took us with her to New York. I don't think either of us really registered what was happening until it was done."

"You miss him?"

"Every day," she said softly, her fingers going automatically to her necklace. "He was a good man, a great father. He was smart, strong, and so warm, you know? I used to get into a lot of scrapes as a kid, fighting with the boys, climbing trees, falling down stuff, and he would always tell me 'never let them see you cry, mona, don't let them know they got to you', and then he would pull me up and kiss my bumped head or scraped knee, wipe away my tears and stop mami from chasing me round the kitchen when she saw I'd ruined my clothes again."

"This was a gift from him, yes? " Rebecca guessed, her fingers reaching out to touch the silver monkey. "Mona like Monkey?"

"Mona Maya," she smiled. "He used to chase me round the house, his knuckles dragging on the floor as he made monkey sounds. When he caught me he would tickle me and pretend to pick fleas out of my hair."

"It sounds like you were a daddy's girl?" Rebecca chuckled.

"Oh yeah, totally! Mami used to get so mad at us. 'Ay bendito, you two will be the death of me!'" she laughed, mimicking her mother's thick accent and gesturing dramatically. "Then she'd roll her eyes, throw her hands up in the air and storm off to the kitchen til papi went to apologise."

Maya laughed softly at the memory, as conflicted as she always was when she thought about him. It had been almost sixteen years, longer than she'd had him for, but the wound had not healed and she didn't think it ever would. She felt Rebecca's hand stroking her cheek and was surprised to discover that she was wiping away tears that were suddenly there.

"Shit, sorry," she muttered, wiping at her face and attempting to get up.

"Hey, it's okay," Rebecca whispered, pushing her back down and kissing her gently. "Please stay."

She kissed her again, more firmly this time, cupping her face gently and tracing her cheekbone with her thumb. Maya gave into it and kissed her back, pushing her hands into her hair as their kisses became hungrier and the rest of the world dropped away.

She climbed out of the bed as gently as possible and walked out onto the balcony, leaning on the rail and watching the sun rise over the ocean. Rebecca had fallen asleep about half an hour ago but there was too much going on in Maya's head to join her. She sighed as she stared out to sea, the surf crashing onto the beach closely mirroring the waves of panic that were starting to wash over her. She squeezed her eyes shut and pounded her fist on the ledge as she tried to fight it off, wincing as her bruised knuckles reminded her of their presence. What was she doing? As usual she had proved everyone right and showed a complete lack of self control, worse than that she had opened up to Rebecca in a way that she hadn't done to anyone in years, and promised herself never to do again.

She hit the ledge once more, relishing the pain it caused, and softly cursed herself as she turned around to look at the woman still sleeping soundly in the position she had left her. This was crazy. She shouldn't be here. All she had done was start down a path that would end in nothing but pain and she had to shut it down now before it got any worse, for either of them, but how the hell was she supposed to do that when they were heading off into the Amazon together? She leaned back on the balcony and wrapped her arms around herself, shivering against a cold that had nothing to do the breeze sweeping in off the ocean. She would give anything to get back in that bed, wrap herself up in Rebecca and just go with it but that wasn't her and it never would be. She'd been there before and she couldn't let herself go back.

Her mind made up she crossed to the other side of the bed, gathering up her discarded clothes and putting them back on as quickly and quietly as she could. She paused at the exit, her damaged hand on the handle, her heart hammering in her chest, and rested her forehead on the door. It was for the best. What did she think was going to happen, they'd skip off through the rainforest, holding hands and gazing lovingly into each other's eyes? They'd find Rebecca's parents and the lost city then return home triumphantly to live happily ever after? Get over yourself, Maya, this isn't some goddamn Disney movie and you are definitely no princess.

She pulled the door open softly and crept out into the corridor without looking back.

Claudia was sitting at the kitchen table as Maya came out of the shower. She gave her a quick smile as she crossed the room to her bedroom and shut the door quickly behind her.

"I was just about to make breakfast, do you want some?"

"Ah, yeah. Sure." Maya called back. Her stomach was in knots and she wasn't at all hungry but they had a long day of travelling ahead of them and she knew she should at least try. She rubbed her face and sighed in irritation. She had been in the shower for half an hour and she swore she could still smell Rebecca whenever she moved. She was exhausted and felt like shit but she knew she had no one to blame but herself and she couldn't take it out on Claudia. She got dressed, finished packing up her stuff and then headed back out to the kitchen where her friend handed her a cup of coffee.

"How are you feeling?" Claudia asked carefully.

"Fine," she lied, avoiding her eyes and sipping at her drink. "How about you? All set?"

"Just about. A few more things to throw in the bag, tidy up around here and we're good to go."

"Excellent."

"I'm sorry about last night, Maya."

"It's not your fault," she shrugged, flashing her a quick smile before starting on her food. "The conversation with Elaine just got me all worked up. I shouldn't have snapped at you."

They ate in silence for a few minutes and Maya could feel Claudia studying her. Eventually she cleared her throat and tapped her fingers nervously on the table.

"I, er, I didn't hear you come in last night."

"Yeah, I was really late," Maya said quickly. "You know me, just lost track of time."

"Yes, that certainly sounds like you," Claudia smiled. "Did you go back to that bar?"

"No, I went to talk things out with Rebecca," she admitted, pushing her plate away with a sigh.

"Oh? How did that go?" the redhead asked delicately.

"Fine. I agreed we would help her find her parents if they do exactly what we say and don't get in the way. Are you done with your eggs?"

"What? Oh, yes. Thanks," she watched as Maya gathered up the plates and crossed her arms on the table. "Are you sure you're okay with that?"

"It's fine, Claud."

"You keep saying that."

"What?"

"That you're fine."

"Well maybe that's because it's true," she sighed as she washed their plates.

"Did something happen?"

"Claudia, please can we just drop it?" Maya dropped the dishes in the rack and leaned heavily against the sink, suddenly terrified that she was going to cry. She was exhausted and barely keeping it together. The last thing she needed was her best friend's judgement or worse, her pity.

"Okay," Claudia said after a pause, getting up from the table with a scrape of the chair. "I'm going to go and finish packing."

Maya let out a shaky breath as she listened to the footsteps receding across the room and squeezed her hands open and closed as she tried to get herself under control. She desperately wanted a drink and turned to eye up the tequila bottle on the counter.

"Maya," Claudia said quietly from her doorway. "Just...I'm always here. You know, if you want to talk about it."

She bit down on her lip painfully and raised her eyes to the ceiling, fighting desperately to keep her tears at bay. "Thanks Claud," she said quickly, relief washing over her as she heard the door close.

Two hours later Maya pulled the rental van up outside the apartment and beeped the horn to let Claudia know she was there. She climbed out, stretching her arms above her head and yawning as she walked round the back and opened the doors.

"Hi Maya."

She froze in position and closed her eyes as Rebecca's voice took her back to the night before. She heard it laughing, whispering, saying her name over and over. She took a deep breath and willed herself to hold it together. Slowly she brought her hand up to her pendant and turned around, forcing a smile to her face, immensely grateful for her sunglasses.

"Hey."

"So I was kind of surprised you weren't there this morning," Rebecca said, fiddling with the strap on her bag. "But I guess you had to pack."

"Yeah."

"Okay." Rebecca smiled nervously and took a step forward. "Did you get any sleep? I guess I got a couple more hours than you at least."

"I figure I'll let Claudia take the first shift, I'll get some sleep in the van."

"You're driving? I thought you would fly?"

"Well the quickest flight is fourteen hours to Cusco then an eighteen hour drive to Boca do Acre," she said, fiddling with the lock on the door as if it held the secrets of the universe. "We figured what with driving to and from various airports and check in times it would be the same just to drive. Plus I don't really like to fly, so…"

"Right." Rebecca nodded.

An awkward silence fell over them. Maya cast her eyes up to the apartment, desperately hoping that Claudia would appear and rescue her from this situation.

"So, are you going to fly or…?"

"What's going on, Maya?" Rebecca interrupted her.

"What do you mean?" she asked, her hands clenching at her sides.

"I just," she sighed and put her hand on her hips, eyes downcast. "Last night was...well, I just thought…well, I thought that we got through all this and, you know. Connected."

Maya took a breath and stared down at her feet. Her heart beating to a drunken disco track in her chest, her mind off on an unreachable retreat somewhere. Her hands were trembling even in their clenched position and she felt sick. She cleared her throat and looked out over the sea, readying herself for what she had to do.

"Last night was great but it doesn't mean anything, okay? It doesn't change the fact that I work alone and you and your team are there to back me and Claudia up."

"Are you joking?" Rebecca asked after a pause.

"No," she said, planting a hand on her hip to keep it steady and raising her shaded eyes to Rebecca's. "I need you to stick to our agreement. You said your team would do what we said."

"Yeah, of course," Rebecca said, shaking her head and grabbing both her backpack straps, her eyes searching Maya's face. "That's not in question. My team will do exactly what you say. But...last night didn't mean anything?" Her face twisted uncomfortably. "You can't seriously expect me to believe that last night meant nothing to you?"

"Look, Rebecca..."

"I know we got off to a bad start but..."

"Rebecca, please just stop." Maya held her hands up, desperate to end this before she couldn't take any more. "Last night was great, but it was just that. Think of it as my way of sealing the deal. I'm sorry, I thought you understood that it was just sex. If I've made things uncomfortable for you by all means find someone else to help you. But I have an obligation to fulfill and I'm going to do that, regardless of your involvement."

Rebecca took a step back as if she had been slapped, her hands gripping tighter to her straps. She bit down on her lower lip and dropped her gaze to the ground for moment before snapping back up angrily.

"You are unbelievable, you know that?"

"Look, I'm sorry if..."

"No, Maya, just forget it, alright?" she said angrily, her hands held up as she backed away. "I'm the one that should be sorry for not believing everyone who said you were a heartless bitch. Let's just keep it professional, okay? I'll have my people draw up the papers. You find my parents and we'll call it a day. I'll see you in Brazil."

With that she turned and walked off up the hill leaving Maya to stare after her, her insides feeling crushed into a little ball, like someone trying to protect themselves from a beating. A litany of curses poured through her mind and her heart started racing like it was trying to run after Rebecca, but her body couldn't move. It didn't matter now anyway. What was done was done and there was nothing she could do about it, except of course go after her like a normal, well adjusted person would.

"Jesus, you wouldn't believe what happened to me just now," Claudia muttered as she appeared with several of the bags. "That weirdo from downstairs just jumped out in front of me and started yelling about a party or something else equally unintelligible."

"Puedo ayudarte?" Maya sighed as she turned to help her with the bags.

"Fuck," she breathed, her face falling. "That means something nice, doesn't it?"

"It means 'can I help you?'" she muttered, throwing the bags into the back of the van.

"Bollocks." Claudia sighed, her shoulders dropping. "I was so rude to him as well. I really hope he doesn't speak English."

"Yeah," Maya said, looking up the hill as she headed towards the apartment. "Me too."

Chapter 14

The van bounced along the red clay road, kicking dust up behind it like a storm cloud, the jungle thinning out on either side as they approached the town. Maya looked up at the sign arching above the road welcoming them and sighed wearily as she nudged Claudia's sleeping form in the seat next to her.

"Hey, wake up. We're here."

"Really?" Claudia straightened up in her seat and rubbed at her eyes. "Are you sure because it seems like we have been driving for forty seven years."

"I'm sure," she smiled. "Welcome to Boca do Acre, Claud."

"Hmm, it looks lovely," Claudia commented as she gazed sleepily out of the window at the pretty wooden houses on stilts.

Maya shot her an amused look, unsure if she was kidding or not, and returned her attention to the town slipping by them. The houses were in a variety of shapes, sizes and colours, some of them little more than shacks, others almost palatial by comparison, and they gathered closer and closer together until they gave way to rows of shops, restaurants and hotels.

Maya pulled the van into the parking lot of their hotel and switched off the engine, jumping out and stretching like she hadn't been upright in a hundred years. Claudia walked around the back of the van and joined her in looking at the building in front of them, yawning and shielding her eyes from the midday sun.

"Our home for the next few days," she said unenthusiastically. "It's very, um, pink."

"I don't care," Maya laughed. "It was cheap and it has a bed. A real, goddamn bed, Claud, and a shower."

"Oh, God, I could kill for a shower."

"Well relax, you can have one without such drastic measures," she smiled. "Let's go check in, we can grab the stuff later."

They went inside and paid for their rooms, hurrying up the stairs and quickly agreeing to meet for dinner once they had freshened up. Maya pushed the door of her room open and threw the key on the table, flopping down on the bed with a sigh. She felt the tiredness of her limbs soaking into it and pulling her towards sleep so she forced herself to get up and turn on the shower, one hand stifling a yawn as the other checked the temperature. Once she was happy with it she peeled off her clothes and got under the spray, the sensation ripping a sigh of contentment from her body.

As she leaned against the wall and let the water wash over her, her mind drifted back before their long road trip to the last shower she had had, and the night preceding it, a wave of emotion washing over her at the memory. Her stomach tightened at the thought of Rebecca, warmth spreading through her to be just as quickly replaced by a sickening regret as she thought about the next day and the things she had said. She banged her forehead gently on the tile and cursed herself for being such a coward, allowing herself to wallow in remorse for a moment before she pushed it out of her head to focus on the task at hand.

Suddenly the spray went freezing cold so she quickly turned the water off with a yelp, stepping out of the shower and grabbing a towel from the rail. Maya sighed as she stared at her reflection in the mirror. She looked haggard. She didn't know where Rebecca would be staying in town, when she would be arriving or even if the deal was still in place, but for now she had an expedition into the rainforest to plan for and she couldn't just sit around waiting for her to show up. She wandered into the room and looked around for her bag, smacking herself on the forehead when she realised it was still in the van and she would have to put her old clothes back on again to get it.

She pulled on her shorts and tank top, grabbed her key off the table and dashed out the door. She ran a hand through her wet hair in an attempt to tame it as she descended the stairs, failing miserably and way too distracted by her efforts to notice Rebecca getting out of a shiny black jeep parked next to their beat up van.

"Maya," she greeted her coldly as she got about three feet away, scaring the crap out of her in the process.

"Jesus!" Maya swore, clapping her hand over her heart to control it. "Rebecca, hi. I, er, shit, I wasn't expecting to see you here."

"Yeah, I guessed that," she said, eyeing up the hotel distastefully.

"Did you have a good trip?"

"Yes, it was fine thank you," she smiled tightly as she flicked her hair over her shoulder, finally looking at Maya for the first time. "So I set up a meeting with a potential guide tomorrow morning. I figured that you and Claudia would probably arrive today but that you'd appreciate the time to recover before we start planning."

"Yeah, thanks for that." Maya looked down at her bare feet, shifting them uncomfortably on the hot asphalt, and when she looked back up she saw Rebecca's eyes raking over her body, a pained expression on her face. A lump formed in her throat and she fiddled with the keys to the van nervously. "Rebecca, I…"

"Here are the details for where we're meeting him, and the contract my people drew up for you and Claudia," Rebecca interrupted, clearing her throat as she stepped forward and handed Maya a file. "I'll see you both tomorrow at eleven."

She kept her eyes averted as she climbed back in the Jeep and started the engine, forcing Maya to move quickly out of the way as she reversed out of the spot with a squeal of tyres. She pressed herself up against the van, pulling away again quickly as the sun baked metal burned her skin, and watched as she disappeared up the road. She swallowed thickly and looked at the paper clipped to the front of the file, noting the address of a hotel and the name of the man they were meeting before folding it up and slipping it into her back pocket.

Maya unlocked the van and grabbed her and Claudia's bags out of it, slamming and locking the door before heading back to the hotel, her eyes drifting back to the road Rebecca had taken. A blast of a car horn brought her attention back and she waved in apology at the driver of the car she had just walked in front of, shaking her head as she jumped up onto the pavement and pushed through the front door of the hotel.

She knocked on Claudia's door and leaned against the frame, massaging the back of her neck while she waited. After a few moments Claudia pulled the door open wearing a towel.

"You, Maya Rodriguez, are now officially my hero," she smiled at her as Maya held her bag out. "I almost cried when I realised I'd have to put those sweaty, slept in clothes back on."

"Tell me about it," Maya smiled back as she handed over the file with the contract. "Rebecca just came by."

"Oh?" Claudia frowned as she opened it and scanned briefly through it. "How did she know we were here?"

"Ah, you know. She has her ways."

"Right. Cos that's not creepy at all."

Maya smiled sadly and pulled the paper out of her pocket. "She wants us to meet her there tomorrow at eleven. Are you alright to go get some food without me? I'm not really hungry any more and I'm kind of beat."

"Yeah, okay," she nodded, her eyes full of concern. "Do you want me to bring you something back?"

"Yeah, maybe. Thanks Claud, I'll see you later." Maya raised a hand in a brief wave as she turned and headed back to her room, feeling her friend's eyes on her the whole way. She unlocked her door and went inside with a quick smile in Claudia's direction, leaning heavily against it as it shut.

The next morning Maya pulled the van up in the parking lot of the hotel Rebecca had set the meeting up at, not at all surprised that it was the fanciest place they had seen since they got there. They were a little early so Maya decided to stay outside and have a cigarette to calm her nerves whilst Claudia went ahead and got them some coffee, which Maya was pleased about. Her friend had been sneaking concerned looks at her all morning and she was reaching the point where she really wanted to smack her.

She took a drag on her cigarette and looked up at the hotel, chuckling slightly as she marked the difference between it and the place they were staying. It was like an eagle standing next to a pigeon. Her gaze dropped to the foyer and the smile melted off her face as she saw Rebecca and Candace talking just outside the restaurant. Rebecca looked tired, her brow was wrinkled with a frown and she shook her head quickly in response to whatever it was Candace had just said to her. She held her phone in one hand and she kept glancing down at it. After a few minutes she held her hand up to silence Candace and pressed the phone to her ear. She talked animatedly to the person on the other end as she paced the lobby and Maya was just thinking she should stop staring at her like a creep when Rebecca suddenly glanced up and locked eyes with her.

Maya choked slightly on her cigarette, feeling as embarrassed as if she had been caught with her hand down her pants, and span away quickly, beating her chest to control her coughing fit. She stubbed her cigarette out on the bin and checked her reflection quickly in the black glass before taking a deep breath and heading into the lobby.

Thankfully Rebecca and Candace were nowhere to be seen and she quickly made her way into the restaurant to find Claudia seated at a table in the middle.

"Jesus, what happened to you?" Claudia asked as Maya sat down opposite her. "You look like shit."

"Gee, thanks Claudia," she spat, throwing a hand up in exasperation. "As if I wasn't dreading this enough already."

"Dreading it?"

Maya froze as she realised her slip. "Uh, just, you know…"

"Claudia, Maya, good to see you," Rebecca said as she appeared at their table. Maya heaved a sigh of relief and stood up to greet her, shaking the hand of the man hoping to be their guide as he was introduced to her, barely registering his name and forgetting it instantly.

Rebecca sat next to Claudia with the guide in between her and Maya, Candace taking the seat opposite. She told the man what they were hoping for, skilfully avoiding any mention of missing parents and lost cities whilst asking leading questions about his knowledge of the area and experience as a guide. Maya sat back and stayed silent, quite happy for Rebecca to take the lead and quietly impressed by the questions she was asking, things that she would almost certainly have forgotten about.

Claudia asked something about indigenous tribes in the area and Maya watched him as he explained that it would take up to a week to sort out the necessary introductions. She snapped her eyes to Rebecca at this piece of information as a week would surely be too long in her mind but the words caught in her throat as she saw that the brunette had clearly been staring at her. Rebecca quickly dropped her gaze and tucked her hair behind her ears, her face flushing with embarrassment.

Maya looked back to the guide and cleared her throat, addressing him instead to keep the focus off Rebecca. "A week? Is there anything we could maybe do to speed that up?"

"Please understand," he smiled. "It is a delicate process and would be unwise to rush."

"I do understand that and I wouldn't want to upset anyone but we do have a few...time sensitive issues," she glanced up at Rebecca again, pleased to see her back in control and her face its usual colour. "If we were to start off without introduction and hope they agreed before we got there..."

"It would be unwise," he smiled again. "Also I would need your route before I can begin to make the introductions as I need to know whose territory we will be passing through. Some of the tribes are more welcoming to outsiders than others. Of course they are selective about who they allow into their lands, dependent on what your motives are for requesting access."

"Of course, that's completely understandable," Rebecca said, shooting Maya a quick look. "We will have our route for you as soon as we make our decision."

After a further ten minutes or so they finished up the conversation and told the man they would be in touch as soon as possible. Candace showed him out as Rebecca turned quickly to Maya and Claudia.

"So, where are we on working out our route?"

"Uh, well..." Claudia looked at Maya with an eyebrow raised.

"Nowhere," she said simply. "We're nowhere with it."

"Great." Rebecca said with a sarcastic smile.

"But we will be. We know where to start and then we just have assume..."

"Excuse me, exactly how do we know where to start?"

"Well, we have the, ah, dolphins, you know?"

"No, I don't know, Maya, because you were supposed to show me your research and then," Rebecca pressed her tongue up against the back of her teeth as the colour rose slightly in her cheeks again. "Well, you didn't."

"Yeah, right," she realised, clearing her throat and glancing up at her friend who was leaning back in her chair and watching this exchange will a look of consternation on her face. "Um, Claud, could you show Rebecca the photographs, please."

"Sure," she said after a moment. She moved round so that she and Rebecca could both see the screen and pulled up the image of the snake. "Okay, so here is the painting the two of you discovered. We assume that this first section is the path through Vilcabamba valley; you have the huilco trees here, and we assume that this rectangle rendered in gold is Mandango, the sleeping Inca."

"That would make sense," Rebecca nodded as she looked at it. "People still believe he protects the valley, it would have been only natural that the Inca would have had some sort of lore about it as well."

"Right," Claudia clicked onto the next shot which focussed on the head and the dolphins. "So the trees get thicker, which we assume to be the start of the rainforest, and then this. The mouth. Or...well, I'll let Maya do the Spanish bits."

"Jeez, Claud, it's one word," she muttered as she rolled her eyes. "Alright, so remember I told you in the caves about the journal we found? That had the warning about the tide?"

"Yes, Maya, I remember. It was only four days ago."

"Ah, yeah. So also in this journal were a lot of references to 'boca', like he says '¿dondé está la boca?', and initially we thought it was referring to the caves, but then we saw the painting of the mouth and it's next to the river, and I remembered reading the deforestation article so…"

"That seems like a pretty big leap to make," Rebecca crossed her arms and gazed at her coolly. "'Boca' is not exactly an uncommon word."

"No, I know that Rebecca," she shot back, matching her gaze with a fiery one of her own. "I'm quite good at Spanish, being Puerto Rican and all. You want to let me finish, maybe?"

"So these dolphins are new," Claudia threw in after a short but painful pause. She cleared her throat and drew Rebecca's attention back to the screen. "They were more difficult to pin down as Amazonian river dolphins are present right the way along, and also in Venezuela and Bolivia, but when Maya mentioned Boca do Acre I started doing some research and found this photograph."

"Vuelva siempre," she read. "Always return?"

"Ah, apparently," Claudia held a hand out to Maya as Rebecca studied the photograph of the dolphin sign. "So we figured it could just be a coincidence but after a little more digging we found that the junction of the two rivers makes it a perfect place for the dolphins to live, so they are quite prevalent around here. Of course, it's not conclusive, but it's as good a lead as we're likely to get."

"And where is this sign?"

"It's in the courtyard of a food place on the edge of town, right by the junction."

"And you want to start there?"

"Well, we kind of wanted to go there first and check it out," Maya said. "But I think it's looking like a strong contender."

"Fine. Shall we say an hour?"

"You're, ah, you're coming with us?"

"Of course," she said, leaning back and folding her arms. "I think I was quite clear on that point. I'm not here to sit about in my hotel whilst you two go off searching for my parents."

"But it's such a lovely hotel," Maya muttered with a smirk, earning her a withering look from Rebecca.

"Ah, on that note, did you hear anything? About the break in?" Claudia asked gently.

"Yes, actually. We have a possible lead but I'm not sure anything will come of it," she sighed as she brushed her hair off her face, and Maya noticed again how tired she looked. "I've been asking around town, too, see if maybe anyone remembers them being here, trying to hire a guide or anything."

"And?"

"No," she shook her head. "It's possible, of course. There are a lot of guides around here but no one recognised their faces. They all seemed much more interested in the group that disappeared."

"A group disappeared?" Claudia asked, her voice going a little shrill as she shot a worried glance at Maya.

"Yes, apparently. Six of them, about a month ago." Rebecca seemed to notice Claudia's alarm and waved her hand dismissively. "Oh, don't worry, everyone has been quick to point out that their guide was young and inexperienced, a bit of a sketchy character by all accounts. But Felipe comes very highly recommended."

"Oh, okay." Claudia sat back in her chair, not looking particularly comforted.

"This group," Maya asked carefully. "You don't think maybe…"

"What?" Rebecca asked, her eyes fixing on her with a hard stare.

"Well, you don't think maybe your parents could have been part of it?"

"My parents would know better than to hire someone who didn't know what they were doing, Maya. They're very cautious."

"Well, yeah, but what if they weren't, you know," she paused, hoping that Rebecca would get what she was saying. Either she didn't or she was deliberately making her spell it out so she sighed and gave voice to what she was sure they were all thinking. "What if they weren't the ones in charge?"

The air stilled around the table as Rebecca's glare became icy. Maya felt rather than saw Claudia shift uncomfortably in her seat and she held her breath as she waited for Rebecca's response.

"If they weren't in charge," she said, her jaw clenching tightly as she got up from the table. "Then we are already too late."

She turned to walk away and Maya jumped up to follow her, grabbing her wrist as she caught up.

"Rebecca…"

"Don't," she spat as she turned round and pulled her arm away, taking a breath to calm herself down. "Don't touch me."

"Rebecca, I'm sorry," Maya said softly. "I didn't mean to…"

"Yes, I know," she smiled bitterly. "You never mean anything, do you?"

Maya took a step back, the brunette's words winding her like a punch to the gut, her usually soft brown eyes blazing with a hurt that she hated herself for causing. After a few seconds the fire died down and she smoothed her shirt with shaky hands, clearing her throat softly before she looked back up.

"I'll see you both back here in an hour?" she asked, like nothing had happened, then waved quickly to Claudia and turned to walk out.

Maya stared after her as she left the room. She felt hot and tingly, like she had just been slapped, and she really didn't want to deal with Claudia's reaction. She took a deep breath and went back to her seat, playing with her empty coffee cup to avoid Claudia's gaze, and the conversation that was about to happen.

"I think I saw a bar across the street."

Maya looked up in confusion to see her friend zipping the laptop into its bag and getting out of her seat. She walked to Maya's side of the table and waited there expectantly.

"Well?" Claudia asked when she didn't move. "Are you coming?"

She settled in her seat outside the bar and took a grateful sip of her ice cold beer, gazing out across the river as she waited for the onslaught. Claudia sat next to her and lit a cigarette, inhaling deeply and settling back in her chair as if they were just two friends sharing a relaxing drink on holiday. Maya would give anything to be those people. She had really messed up this time, and she didn't know how she was going to explain it to her.

"Well," Claudia said eventually. "That was awkward."

"You think?" Maya smiled sadly and took another drink.

"Are you ready to talk about it yet?"

"Not really," she sighed and pinched the bridge of her nose lightly. "I really fucked up, Claud, I'm sorry."

"Don't be sorry," Claudia said gently. "Just fix it."

"I don't know how to!" Maya groaned, leaning forward and putting her head in her hands. "I really hurt her, Claudia. And now we're all stuck in the fucking jungle together, looking for her parents who could well be dead…"

"Yes, well on that subject, it's probably best if you don't put it quite so bluntly next time."

"Oh, come on, we were all thinking it."

"That doesn't mean that it doesn't hurt to hear it, Maya."

Maya sat back in her chair and folded her arms, thinking back on the conversation, then all the other conversations where she had just blurted out the obvious fact that everyone else was skirting around.

"Jesus. I really am a bitch, aren't I?"

"You're not a bitch," Claudia said. "Maybe just a little...tactless."

"God, Claud. I just left." Maya said after a moment. "I just...freaked out and left her there. Then acted like it was nothing. Like I…"

She drifted off and stared out over the water. Claudia stayed silent next to her, waiting for her to continue. When she didn't the redhead leaned over and handed her a cigarette, lighting it for her as she studied her face.

"She'll get over it, Maya. She'll be furious and hurt for a while but it was only one night, after all," she leaned back in her chair and folded her arms. "The real question is, will you?"

"What?" Maya scoffed. "You make it sound like I'm in love with her, for God's sake."

"I'm not talking about Rebecca." Claudia said quietly.

Maya stiffened in her chair and flicked at the end of her cigarette with her thumb, biting down on her lip and willing her not to continue.

"It's been five years, Maya…"

"Don't, Claudia…"

"But you need to talk about it."

"I don't need to talk about it and I don't want to talk about it so just drop it, okay?" Maya stubbed out the barely smoked cigarette and snatched up her glass, slopping beer down the side as her hand shook angrily.

"I know you don't want to but you're clearly not over it so…"

"Of course I'm over it!" she barked. "Like you said, it's been five years, I'd be a fucking idiot not to be over her by now."

"I said it, not her. Meaning what she did to you. You're not an idiot, Maya, she really hurt you and I…"

"God, Claudia, will you please shut the fuck up?" Maya slammed the glass back down on the table, drawing stares from the rest of the people outside the bar. She pressed her palms to the hot metal to calm herself before she continued. "What happened between me and her has absolutely nothing to do with what's going on now."

"It has everything to do with it!"

"No it doesn't!" Maya clenched her hands into fists and turned to her friend, eyes shining. "Please, Claudia, I'm having a hard enough time here as it is, I really don't need you bringing up all this shit and making it worse. Please just drop it?"

Claudia looked at her with a worried expression for a few seconds and then held up her hands in submission. Maya nodded at her and huffed out a breath before picking up her beer once more and taking a gulp.

Chapter 15

The drive out to their agreed starting point was mercifully short, given that Maya and Claudia had barely spoken since Maya's outburst. They had headed back to the hotel and waited in the lobby for Rebecca to return which she did, with her whole team, thankfully on time. Maya and Claudia led the way in their van whilst Rebecca and the others followed in the jeep. The reacquaintance between the two groups had been fairly tense and Maya found herself both grateful that she only had to share the journey with one person she had upset, and apprehensive that there were now apparently five more in the vehicle behind.

She stared out the window as Claudia drove in silence, trying to summon up the words to apologise to her friend but failing miserably. She knew Claudia had just been trying to help, but she just couldn't talk about that part of her life, not with Claudia, not with anyone. The pain of the betrayal had been so bad that she had refused to deal with it, forcing it away from her with a sea of alcohol, drugs and sex until she could barely remember her own name, let alone the name of the woman who had broken her. By this process she managed to make it through the first couple of months, then pulled herself together enough to throw herself into work and denial instead, distracting herself with whatever random lead she could find until the untreated wound became an infected scar, a gangrenous line on her heart that only hurt when she knocked it.

Claudia pulled the van over to the side of the road and jumped out, heading over to the terraced area on the edge of the river. Slowly Maya followed her, watching as Tom practically ran over to greet the redhead, his enormous smile almost splitting his face. Maya walked past them towards the sign that had brought them here. Two pink dolphins, about six feet tall, climbed either side of a set of steps leading from the terrace to the river, a sign between their noses bearing the legend 'Vuelva siempre', literally meaning 'always return'. Above it was the original Portuguese sentiment 'Volte sempre', meaning come back often, so Maya could only assume the Spanish below was the result of an incorrect translation. Also, why it was in the middle of town at the edge of the river and not on the road out was a different question. It was tacky, pink, touristy, and she couldn't help but be grateful for it, whilst also hopeful that it had been inspired by something else, something long since forgotten.

She wandered underneath it and down the steps to the river, waving to a man offering boat hire and arranging to take one of the wooden paddle boats for the next couple of hours, all the while keeping an eye on the group on the terrace, talking and laughing together like old friends. She felt a pang of hurt as she took in the scene, but quickly brushed it off as she continued her discussion with the man. Why shouldn't Claudia get on with Rebecca's group? She wasn't the one who fucked everything up. Just because they had greeted Maya with all the warmth of a bucket of liquid nitrogen didn't mean they should be the same way with her friend.

She smiled at the man as she handed the money over and headed slowly back up the stairs, reluctant to break up the party. She cleared her throat hesitantly and gestured towards the boat.

"I got us a boat for the next couple of hours," she said, folding her arms uncomfortably. "I thought maybe we should cross the river and check out the forest directly opposite here?"

"Yes," Claudia jumped in, leaving her place at Tom's side and moving to stand with Maya as she addressed the group. "I don't know how much Rebecca has explained to you but we believe that the trail depicted on the last third of the snake begins here, with the dolphins, the point on the painting where the river moves away to the east and the golden trail crosses it and heads north."

"Cool, let's get on it then, shall we?" Tom said cheerfully as he started down the steps.

As the rest of the group followed him Maya turned to her friend and smiled gratefully. "Thank you," she said as she squeezed her arm gently.

"For what?" Claudia asked in confusion. "Maya, you might have pissed me off but it's only because I love you and I'm worried that you won't talk to me."

"Yeah, I know, I just thought…" she fumbled for the words and stared down at her feet in embarrassment. "I just felt...uh, kind of…"

"You know I think it's possible," Claudia laughed as she threw her arm around her friend's shoulder and led her down the stairs. "That you are the biggest dork I have ever met."

"Great," Maya said with a wry smile. "Thanks, Claud."

Maya peered off into the forest as Tom and Claudia secured the wooden boat to a post on the north bank of the river. She stood still and soaked up the atmosphere of the place, trying to let the jungle guide her to its secrets. It felt like she was standing on a precipice, like she just needed to take that final step and she would be rushing towards her goal. Unfortunately she also knew that if she took the wrong step she would be hurtling blindly towards something else entirely.

Her concentration was broken by someone approaching and softly clearing their throat. She turned around to see Rebecca and gave her an awkward smile in greeting.

"So," Rebecca asked. "What are we hoping to find here?"

"I'm not really sure," she admitted with a shrug. "Something that tells us we're in the right place I guess. Don't get me wrong, I'm fairly certain that we are, it would just make me feel better to know for sure."

"Alright," Rebecca walked past her and stared off into the jungle, just as Maya had been doing moments earlier. "And what makes you so certain this is the place? Tacky pink dolphins aside."

"I don't know, Rebecca," she sighed, expecting a snide response to her methods. "It just feels right. I can't explain it."

Rebecca turned her head and looked back at her, an expression on her face that Maya couldn't read. She returned her gaze to the trees for a second before turning fully and nodding at Maya.

"So where do we start?"

Maya looked up at her, taken off guard by the easy acquiescence, and tried to come up with a plan.

"I guess we just look around for anything unusual."

Rebecca raised an eyebrow. "Define unusual?"

"Er…"

"Well, she usually stumbles across it when she needs to pee but until then mainly something anachronistic, or similar to anything we saw in Venezuela." Claudia interrupted.

"Thanks Claud," she muttered, rolling her eyes at the unnecessary overshare and walking into the jungle, avoiding Rebecca's slightly confused look.

Maya pushed the branches out of the way as she made her way through the trees, her eyes scanning the ground as she went. She tried to recall her earlier composure but found that she couldn't. Usually she would wander about, soak up the atmosphere, allow her brain the time to sort out what was important and what wasn't, filter out the background noise in effect. Today, though, she couldn't do that. She felt a pressure she had never felt before and it was making her itchy.

She sighed and stared at the ground in front of her, willing the place to talk to her. She could hear the river behind her, the sounds of the others talking and laughing as they searched in the distance, the birds chattering in the trees above, but nothing of what she needed to hear. She pushed further through the trees, desperate to get away from the rest of the group and find some silence to think. After a few minutes she came across a fallen tree and sat down on it heavily, closing her eyes as she took off her hat and tilted her face up to soak in the sunlight filtering through the canopy.

Once again she wondered what she was doing and, unusually, if she was going to be able to do it. When she was out with Claudia the only pressure she felt was from herself, and she knew how to deal with that. Claudia was used to her methods and happy to concentrate on research and planning whilst Maya went off and did her thing, occasionally stepping in to tell her she was being ridiculous and talk through her ideas. Now, though, there were five other people counting on her to come up with something and the weight of that responsibility was interfering with her process.

"Everything okay?" Rebecca's voice broke her out of her reverie.

"Fine," she sighed, leaning forward and rubbing her face. "I'm just trying to concentrate. I'm not used to having so many people around."

"Well if you could be a little bit more specific we might be able to help you."

"It doesn't work like that, Rebecca."

"Really?" she snapped, folding her arms and staring down at her. "Would you like to tell me how it does work, then?"

"I'm not trying to be a bitch here," Maya said wearily as she stood up. "I just meant that if we were out here looking for something specific then sure, I could tell you and we'd all fan out, one of us would find it and we'd go off and celebrate. But that's not what we're doing and I just need some space to think."

"Yeah," she scoffed. "I bet."

"And what does that mean?"

"Nothing," she said curtly, turning to walk away. "It meant absolutely nothing."

"Alright, just stop," Maya snapped, squaring her shoulders and steeling herself for the conversation. "I know what I did to you was really shitty and I'm sorry, but we're in a situation now where we have to put all that aside or we might as well go home. So if you want to yell at me, slap me, tell me what you think of me, then you better do it now so we can get on with what we came here to do."

Rebecca stood with her back to her, her shoulders tense and her fists clenched at her sides. She took a deep breath and turned around. "You're right, I'm sorry, that was childish," she sighed. "Let's just try and be...professional. What do you need me to do?"

"I just need you to keep your eyes open, get your team to do the same, and give me some space to do my thing."

"Fine. Is there anywhere in particular you would like us to be? You know, so we don't get in your way?"

"Not really," she sighed, staring off into the forest. "I mean honestly, I don't have a clue what I'm looking for or where to start."

"And is that usual?" Rebecca asked, her voice even.

"It's not unusual," she replied, walking off to the left and scuffing the ground with her foot. "It just doesn't normally bother me so much."

"But this time?"

"This time...I don't know. It feels like I'm missing something."

"Well I hope you find it." Rebecca said softly, dropping her head as she turned to go. "I'll leave you to it."

Maya watched her leave, her stomach twisting at the words, a strong feeling washing over her that she had just had a very different conversation to the one she thought she was having. She sighed and turned away, pushing deeper into the jungle with a heavy heart.

An hour later she stumbled across a stream, like literally stumbled across it, the water filling her boots before she even noticed what was happening. She swore to herself and sat down on a rock, pulling her boots off and pouring the water out of them as she looked about. How had she not noticed the stream? Sure the jungle was much denser here than it had been up to this point, less light getting in through the canopy, but it wasn't that dark and…

That was when she noticed what she had been missing. The sound. Even sitting on a rock next to the stream she couldn't hear the faintest trickle of water, or any other sounds from the surrounding jungle for that matter. The place she now found herself in was eerily quiet and she felt the hairs on the back of her neck stand up as she looked around.

Where the fuck was she? She reached to her pocket for her phone, a lump forming in her throat as she realised that she had left it in the van, and whipped her head around quickly as she heard a cracking noise from behind her. She scanned the trees as she stood up slowly, seeing nothing but some kind of decaying hut about thirty metres away and hoping that the sound had been some rocks falling somewhere in the distance, not some kind of jungle cat stepping on a branch as it stalked her. Maya pulled her boots back on and jumped over the stream, concern flooding through her as she realised she had wandered here on automatic pilot and had no idea how to get back. How could she have been so stupid? Claudia was going to kill her.

She looked up at the canopy, hoping for some kind of indication as to which direction she should be heading, but it was too thick for any useful navigational purposes. She pushed back through the trees, keeping an eye out for any damaged foliage that would help her retrace her steps, and listening intently for any signs of life, an unprecedented feeling of unease settling over her. She had to get out of this place. Fast.

After about ten minutes she reached a pile of rocks, partially reclaimed by the jungle, vines and moss twisting around it as if trying to pull it down into the ground. A young sapling grew out of it at an odd angle, reaching up to the stray beam of sunlight breaking through the trees like an arm reaching out for help. Maya looked at it in despair. She had no memory of this place, and no idea at all where she was.

She took a deep breath to calm herself down and focus her mind. She had an amazing sense of direction and knew how to use her environment to navigate, but she had never been lost in the rainforest before and any clues it might be able to offer were completely alien to her. She stood where she was and looked around, the trees seeming to close in on her as she did. This was ridiculous. She was Maya Rodriguez, for God's sake, she didn't get lost, she explored. Except for this time, it would seem.

"Maldita sea," she muttered to herself as she moved on.

She scanned the ground, the trees, the canopy, pushing down the rising panic as best she could, and marched on slowly, desperately hoping that her internal compass would lead the way.

Suddenly she tripped over and landed with a crash in amongst the mulch of the forest floor, scrambling backwards in alarm as a snake reared up with a hiss.

"Coño!" Maya jumped up and backed away quickly, keeping her eyes trained on it in case it decided to strike, and then cursed again as she tripped over a hidden root and fell down a hill. She landed in a heap, the breath knocked out of her, and stared up at the sky in a daze. Slowly the shock wore off and was replaced by pain; her knees hurt from when she had fallen the first time, adding to the injuries she had sustained at the fort and the cave, she had also knocked her damaged hand again, and now her back hurt where she had landed with a thump at the bottom of this hill. She stared up through the trees, seriously contemplating just giving up and lying there forever when the realisation of it hit her. She could see the sky.

She sat up as quickly as her injuries would allow and looked around her for a twig, grabbing the first one she could and jamming it into a clear patch of ground. She marked the end of the shadow it cast with a cross in the dirt and sat waiting, counting away the minutes as best she could with no watch and her usual impatience dialled up to eleven.

After what seemed like an eternity, but was probably only about half the amount of time she should have waited, she marked the new position of the shadow and used it to work out which way was south, heading off that way feeling much calmer. She made sure to keep her eyes open for any other obstacles or potential hazards as she pushed through the trees, conscious of the fact that she had no idea what time it was or how far off track she'd gone, and that she hadn't found anything of use.

She walked on for about twenty minutes, humming various different songs to keep her mind away from panic. She was hungry, she had been bitten more times than she could count and she needed to pee. She chuckled to herself and was on the verge of just going for it and hoping for a repeat of her luck in Venezuela when she heard a sound from up ahead. She stopped and strained her ears to listen, almost at the point of believing she had imagined it when she heard it again.

"Claudia?" she yelled back, picking up her pace as she pushed through the trees.

"Maya?"

"Oh, thank God," she muttered, her heart lifting at the sound of her friend's voice. "Over here!"

She pushed on, Claudia's voice guiding her and a few minutes later came across the woman herself, her face contorted with rage and fear.

"Where the fuck have you been?" she yelled, throwing her arms around her.

"I'm sorry, I was just looking for…"

"You promised me, Maya! Four days ago, you promised me you wouldn't do this again!"

"I know, Claud, I'm sorry."

"I swear to God I'm going to get you chipped." Claudia huffed, releasing her from the bear hug and walking away.

"I'm not your dog, Claudia."

"No, my dog would have more sense than to wander off by herself in the bloody Amazon. Did you find anything?"

"No, I didn't."

"Well I'm so pleased you put me out of my mind with worry then," Claudia laughed bitterly. "Thankfully we did."

"What?" Maya grabbed her arm to make her stop. "You found something?"

"Yes. Well, Vanessa did."

"Vanessa did? Vanessa had difficulty finding her own tent! How did she find anything?"

"She says she was tired and bored so she sat down on a rock for a rest," she sighed, pushing her hair out of her eyes. "When Rebecca came to ask if she'd seen you they noticed the rock she was sitting on had carvings on it. She said she thought it was uncomfortable. She now has a perfect imprint of a snake on the back of her thigh."

"A snake?"

"Yup. Two snakes, facing each other, a rainbow linking their mouths."

"Jesus," Maya breathed, a smile breaking out across her face. "We were right."

"Yes we were. But we still have a route to plan before tomorrow and I'm starving so could we go back now, please?"

Maya nodded and followed Claudia back through the forest, excitement buzzing through her at the discovery the group had made. The symbol of the Inca, here, in Brazil, could be no coincidence. It meant that all the clues they had found and put together were real, that they were in fact following the trail of the last Inca who had fled their broken empire. Petroglyphs had been found in the Amazon before, she knew that. Pusharo, for example, discovered early in the twentieth century at the foot of the Pantiacolla hills and thought by some to possibly have been carved by the Inca as they retreated from the advancing Spanish, but nothing this far east and so obviously Incan in origin. She wanted to see it with her own eyes but she trusted Claudia and if she believed it was real then…

"I'm serious, Rebecca, we should just go by ourselves."

"We've already had this discussion, Phil. I won't have it again."

Maya and Claudia stopped and glanced at each other before creeping forward slowly, getting as close as they could whilst remaining hidden.

"I know we have but that was before this happened!" Phil said angrily. "I never understood why you were so adamant that she was the one we needed and she's already ditched us once. After her little disappearing act today I wouldn't be surprised if she's done it again. Who needs her anyway? She didn't even know what she was looking for and we found it without her."

"Phil…"

"And I'm sorry but I can't be the only one that's noticed the atmosphere between you two since we got here. What happened? Did she try something with you?"

"That's enough, Phil!" Rebecca said firmly, the silence that followed deafening. "If it hadn't been for her and Claudia we wouldn't even have known where to start. Whilst I appreciate you are an expert in your field the most exploration you have done before this week is into the nightlife of Princeton and the surrounding area. Trust me when I say that we need her."

"That didn't answer my question," he said after a few moments, causing Rebecca to sigh heavily.

"That is because your question was incredibly offensive, both to her and to me. Maya is not some predator, Phil, and I'm not some innocent little girl here to be corrupted. If something had happened it would have been because we both wanted it to."

"Is that a yes?"

"No it's not," Rebecca said angrily. "It's a that is none of your business."

"It used to be."

"For God's sake, that was six years ago. Don't be such a child."

"Jesus, Rebecca, I'm not talking about that, we were together less than a month. I'm talking about being your friend. You keep pushing me away recently and I'm worried about you. I just don't want to see you get hurt."

"Yes, well thank you but I'm a big girl and I don't need you to protect me," she said gently. "I make my own decisions and I live with the consequences, same as you do."

"Yeah, but you've got enough on your plate at the minute. I'm just looking out for you, Bec."

"And I appreciate it, but my decision stays the same. We need her and, even though she has her...issues, she's the best at this, and she's a good person. So if you could just not treat her with contempt for the remainder of this trip, that would be great."

Maya felt a wave of shame and guilt wash over her as she eavesdropped on this very private conversation, and she could feel Claudia trying not to look at her. She would give anything to be able to go back and fix this but she knew that she couldn't, that all she could do was try her best not to hurt Rebecca any more than she had already. She grabbed Claudia's arm and pulled her back into the forest, moving quietly along the tree line so that they could get back to the river at a different point and pretend they hadn't just overheard everything.

"Are you okay?" Claudia asked gently after a few moments.

"Just peachy," she muttered back. "Aside from the fact that I just got lost, had everyone looking for me, got outsmarted by a stoner who sings like a bag of cats being dragged behind a car and overheard a conversation that makes me feel like the biggest bitch in the world."

"Yeah, that's what I thought."

Maya huffed out a laugh and pushed through the trees leading out onto the riverbank.

"Hey, there you are," Vanessa smiled up at her cheerfully as she lay on the ground in a bikini. "People were seriously worried about you, mamacita."

"Yeah, well I'm back now. Where's this rock you discovered?"

"Ah, it's over there somewhere," she said, waving her hand vaguely upriver and yawning. "I forget."

"Seriously?"

"Come on," Claudia smirked, heading off in the opposite direction to the one Vanessa had gestured. "I'll show you."

"She's going to die on this trip." Maya muttered, glaring back at her.

"Well don't make it sound like a threat, Maya."

Claudia grabbed her hand and pulled her into the forest. After about five minutes they came to the rock and saw that Tom and Candace were already there doing some sort of test on it.

"Hey, you're back," he smiled up at her. "We were starting to get worried."

"Yeah, thanks," she muttered, kneeling down to get a closer look at the rock. It was just as Claudia had said, two snakes, facing each other, a rainbow between them. It was real. She sighed in relief and stood back up, making her way out of the forest to stand on the bank and gaze out across the river. She allowed herself a smile. They had found their starting point.

Chapter 16

The following morning found Maya and Claudia back at Rebecca's hotel, drinking coffee in the restaurant and waiting for Rebecca to arrive and go over the route they had planned out. She was already ten minutes late which seemed unusual, but then Maya supposed she didn't really know her all that well. She just wished she would hurry up because the news wasn't good and she wanted to get it over and done with.

She and Claudia had gone back to her room after they had found the rock to study the pictures from the cave and try to find some kind of context for them in the environment they now found themselves in. Not being able to assign a scale or any direction to the layout of the markers they had searched the internet for any mention of standing stones, waterfalls or steep stone steps in the rainforests of the surrounding area. Finding nothing they had started to painstakingly search through images from Google Earth, looking out for anything which might even remotely resemble the places they were looking for, and again coming up empty handed.

Despite her earlier feeling that she just needed to find her starting point Maya was apprehensive. Practically anywhere else in the world she would just head off and let herself be guided by instinct but here, in this place, she knew she couldn't do that. She had not gone much further than a couple of miles into the interior of the rainforest yesterday and been completely lost, and there was no way she would take an inexperienced team into that with her. They needed a guide and without a proper route that would be difficult to arrange, hence her concern over the conversation she was about to have with Rebecca. She sipped her coffee and glanced up at the door anxiously, her leg bouncing up and down under the table.

"Stop it," Claudia said tersely.

"What?"

"The leg. You know how much it irritates me."

"It's not like I'm doing it on purpose, Claudia," Maya muttered, leaning back in her chair. "I don't even know I'm doing it half the time."

"And I don't point it out half the time but you still do it and it's still irritating."

"Alright, I get it. God, what crawled up your butt this morning?"

"Well that's hardly appropriate humour, Maya. We are about to trek into the Amazon after all."

Maya pulled a disgusted face and put her coffee cup back on the table. She looked over at the door again and saw a harassed looking Rebecca making her way to the table.

"I'm sorry I'm late," she muttered as she sat down and gestured at the waiter. "I, er, overslept."

The waiter appeared and she ordered a drink in rapid Portuguese, causing Maya to raise her eyebrow slightly in surprise.

"Felipe will be here in about thirty minutes so shall we go through your plans?"

"Ah, yeah. Sure." Maya nodded and cleared her throat, leaning forward in her chair and spreading the paperwork out in front of her. "So, we put our starting point at the dolphins, then we should head north west as that is the direction the trail splits away from the river on the drawing. Obviously we don't have any kind of scale for it, or any kind of landmarks to pinpoint on the actual maps of the area, so we're kind of walking blind until we find the first marker."

The waiter reappeared with Rebecca's coffee and set it down in front of her with a flourish.

"Obrigada," she smiled at him, picking up the milk and tipping some into her cup. She looked up at Maya expectantly. "And?"

"And nothing," Maya shrugged. "You've seen the painting same as me. There's nothing in it that will give us a route unless we find those markers."

"So, we are going to tell Felipe that we want to go wandering about in the rainforest looking for a bunch of standing stones?"

"Well, yeah. Kind of."

"Okay," she smiled. "In that case I have a question. Are you joking?"

"Ah, no."

"Maya, do you have any idea what will happen if we tell the man we are paying to guide us through the rainforest that we just want to kind of wander about?"

"I'm not suggesting..."

"He is a very polite man so I don't think he would actually laugh in our faces but I am fairly confident that the conversation would be brief."

"Unless we told him what we were looking for."

"You want to tell him what we're looking for."

"No, I don't mean Paititi, or your parents, or any of that," Maya said quickly, glancing around to make sure they were not overheard. "I mean we tell him we want to go to the standing stones due northwest of here and let him do the rest."

"Are you…?" Rebecca stared at her and then turned to Claudia. "Is she serious?"

"Yup." Claudia said simply, picking up her coffee and smiling.

Rebecca turned back to Maya, shaking her head. "If we ask him that and he realises we don't know what we're doing he'll say no and word will travel to all the other reputable guides around here, none of them will take us. We can't afford to let that happen, Maya."

"We won't."

"You can't know that."

"No, but I'd be willing to stake a lot on it."

"Including my parent's lives?" Rebecca asked. "Because that's what you're asking me to do."

"Rebecca," she said gently, leaning forward and placing her hands on the table. "I realise that is seems like a huge risk, but it's the only play we have. Claudia and I were up all night researching this place, looking at anything and everything we could think of that has to do with stones, waterfalls, steps, scrolling through Google Earth in minute detail trying to see anything in that rainforest that isn't a tree, and there's nothing. The canopy is so dense that the stones could be anywhere. The only hope of finding them with the information we have access to is to be on the ground looking for them and trust me when I say that's not a great place to be if you don't know where you're going. Now if we say we want to head northwest to the standing stones maybe he knows what we are talking about and takes us there."

"And if he doesn't?"

"If he doesn't, maybe we ask him about the tribes that live in the area, maybe they know what we're talking about."

"This isn't the 1900's, Maya, you can't just go wandering into the rainforest talking to local tribes and winging it. We need a route."

"I know that! What I'm telling you is we don't have one and we need someone who knows the area to help us come up with it. If you have a better idea I'm all ears."

"Oh my God," Rebecca shook her head and leaned back in her chair. "Okay, I can call him and tell him we need more time. How long will it take you to find us a route do you think?"

"Rebecca, that won't help."

"Of course it will, just tell me what you need."

"Six months."

"Excuse me?"

"It would take about six months to plan an expedition like this properly," Maya continued, knowing full well that this was far too long for Rebecca's purposes. "We would need to apply for and be granted access to the records held by the RGS, the NGS or one of their equivalents, plan our route from some proper documentation, then apply to the Brazilian government for a licence to launch an expedition into the rainforest, explaining exactly what we were looking for and what we intended to do when we found it. If that was granted then we would have to find a guide, and then arrange contact with the various tribes whose territory we would pass through, again explaining exactly what we were hoping to achieve."

Rebecca sighed and picked up her coffee, staring over the rim of the cup, her eyes full of despair. Maya wished that she could give her what she wanted, that she could magically come up with the coordinates for the lost city and find her parents for her but she couldn't, although God knows she had tried.

"Alright," Rebecca agreed after a lengthy pause. "But just let me do the talking, you're a terrible liar."

"What?" Maya asked.

"She's right, Maya," Claudia piped up, of course choosing this moment to join the conversation. "You are really bad. Awful, in fact."

Maya looked between the two of them angrily, thoroughly put out by this recent disclosure, before giving up and picking up her coffee for something else to do.

"Whatever," she muttered, taking a swig of it and trying not to gag as she realised it was cold.

"How's your coffee?" Rebecca asked casually, gazing across the restaurant.

"It's fine," she lied, causing her 'friend' at the other end of the table to cackle like she was the world's greatest comedian. "Fuck you, Claudia. Excuse me, Rebecca, I'm going for a cigarette."

"I'll get you another coffee." Rebecca called as she walked away, Claudia's hysterical laughter following her to the door.

Felipe arrived shortly after Maya returned to the table, greeting them with his wide, open smile and shaking their hands warmly. Rebecca had phoned him the evening before and told him that they would like to work with him, so here he sat, all smiles and eager to know where he would be taking them. Maya sipped at her new coffee nervously and bounced her leg under the table.

"Ow!" she yelled, choking on her coffee as Claudia grabbed her knee and slammed her foot down into the floor. She glared at her before noticing Felipe and Rebecca staring at them from the opposite side of the table, Felipe in confused amusement and Rebecca with a look of supreme irritation. "Sorry," she muttered.

"Right," Rebecca said in a clipped tone. "Anyway, Felipe, thank you for coming. We just wanted to give you a little more information about our group before we set off. There will be five of us, Claudia, Maya and myself plus two more…"

"Five of us?" Maya questioned, earning a hard look from Rebecca.

"My associates Phil and Tom who you haven't met yet."

"And what exactly are you hoping to achieve on this expedition?"

"We're hoping to uncover evidence of human influence in the area dating back to pre-Columbian times," she replied smoothly. "Terra preta, artefacts, evidence of settlements, that sort of thing."

"I see," he smiled and leaned back, raising his cup to his lips. "You wish to emulate Heckenberger."

"Oh no," Rebecca smiled at him. "Our ambitions are nowhere near as lofty. Maybe in the future, once we've built up more of a complete picture. For now, though, we would be happy to just get a feel for the place, gather evidence of the scale of human activity in this region, what they were capable of."

Maya looked at Felipe with interest. Rebecca seemed to be trying to lead him but so far, at least, he wasn't giving anything away.

"So, you would like to show me your route?" he asked after a moment.

"Of course," Rebecca looked over at her. "Maya? Could you hand over the map?"

"Ah, sure," she replied nervously. The map was nothing. It was literally just a relief map of about a hundred square miles of the rainforest with a line drawn across it in a vague northwesterly direction, sticking largely to the lowlands and anywhere that she and Claudia had pegged as likely locations for the standing stones to be. She slid it across the table towards Rebecca and the guide.

"Thank you," she smiled at her as she took it. "So, as you can see, it's fairly rough at the moment as we were hoping to rely slightly on your expertise and knowledge of the area to get the best out of our time here. I'm assuming that is alright with you?"

"Of course," he studied the map with a slight frown on his face and circled a section in the middle with his finger. "This area may be problematic, the tribe here does not welcome outsiders. But I might suggest that you head further to the east anyway."

"Oh?"

"Yes, I believe there may be a site that will be of particular interest to you," he smiled up at them and pulled a pen out of his pocket, drawing a new route onto the map which came off their original route about thirty miles in and started north.

"And what might that be?" Maya asked, desperately hoping that it would just be that easy.

"There is a tribe near here," he said, drawing a star about twenty miles up the new route. "They are more welcoming than others and I have visited them many times. They have spoken of an area near them in a way that I believe points to a far earlier settlement."

"What do they say about it?"

"It is difficult to translate but their name for it roughly means 'dedos do diabo' in Portuguese. They have a legend that a battle was fought there between a great warrior and...well, what we would refer to as the devil. After many days and nights the warrior defeated the devil and sent him back to hell, but the devil grabbed hold of him in the final moments and tried to drag him down through the earth with him. The devil did not know that the warrior was anointed by the sun god and could not be taken underground so they were caught, the devil under the ground, the warrior on top, locked in the devil's grip. Eventually the warrior fought his way free but the hand which held him remained trapped, the devil's fingers still sticking out of the ground."

Maya's heart skipped a beat. She looked up at Rebecca and when their gazes locked she saw the same spark of hope in her eyes. The corner of her lips pulled up into a smile and she had an almost overwhelming urge to leap out of her chair and dance her around the room in celebration. Rebecca bit her bottom lip and smiled back, dropping her gaze to her hands quickly before turning back to Felipe.

"Well it sounds great, we would love to see it if possible. Thank you." Rebecca smiled at him, schooling her face into the calm, polite mask she had held in place for the entire conversation.

"How long do you expect this expedition to take?" Felipe asked as he sipped his coffee.

"We were thinking two weeks should be enough, with the possibility to extend to three if we came across anything that warranted further investigation."

Felipe looked back down at the map and studied it for a moment before nodding. "I believe that that would be enough time. Assuming you are all familiar with this kind of terrain?"

"Of course." Maya lied, causing everyone at the table to look at her suspiciously.

"We have varying degrees of experience," Rebecca covered smoothly, shooting Maya a silencing glare. "But we all know what to expect and are prepared for the challenges we will face."

"Very good," he smiled at her. "Okay, well if you are happy with this route I will file it with the authorities and begin reaching out to the tribe. I will be in touch with you as soon as I hear anything."

"That is excellent news, Felipe, thank you so much," Rebecca stood with him and shook his hand warmly. "I'll show you out."

Maya watched them walk out of the room and gave a yelp of pain as Claudia kicked her in the leg.

"Ow! What was that for?"

"Nice one, Pinocchio, you nearly blew the whole thing!" Claudia muttered, folding her arms and shaking her head. "And what was with the secret look between you and Rebecca at the devil story?"

"That really hurt," she pouted, rubbing her shin vigorously. "'Dedos do diabo'. It means devil's fingers. You know, kind of like how a superstitious tribe would view a bunch of rocks standing in formation in the middle of the rainforest?"

"Yes, thank you, Columbo, I got that part. It just seemed a bit odd that the two of you would be sharing a moment when we're supposed to be playing it cool and you're supposed to hate each other."

"We don't hate each other."

"Evidently not," Claudia smirked. "I thought you going to climb over the table and jump on her."

"For Christ's sake, Claud, I just looked at her."

"Yeah, and the temperature in the room went up by about fifty degrees."

"Alright, just drop it, okay?" Maya leaned back in the chair and rubbed her temples. "You're making a huge deal out of nothing."

"Fine. Can we go, then? I really need to sleep."

"Sure, we'll just wait for Rebecca to come back so we can say goodbye and then we can go."

"Do you want me to wait outside or…?"

"Oh my God, stop it!" Maya wheeled round in her chair. "You act like such a child when you're tired, I swear I…"

"Everything okay?" Rebecca asked as she returned.

"Yes, sorry," Claudia yawned as she stood up. "Maya and I just have sleepy sibling syndrome."

"You have what?"

"Nothing," Maya muttered. "It's just something she made up to explain why she's being a bitch."

"Yeah, that's probably it." Claudia smirked again, patting Rebecca's shoulder as she walked past. "Good to see you Rebecca. Maya, I'll be at the van."

"Me tienes harta!" Maya called after her, following her around the table and throwing her hand up for emphasis. God, she hated when Claudia got like this. She was glad the redhead had left when she did or she would probably have slapped her. Her attention was brought back to the moment by a gentle cough from behind her. She took a breath to clear her head. "So, that went well?"

"Yes, I think so."

They stood in the foyer facing each other, the distance between them slightly awkward, like neither of them knew how to position themselves around the other anymore. Maya looked at her feet, then up at Rebecca's face, finally fixing on the clock above the reception desk whilst Rebecca picked a spot somewhere across the street. She cleared her throat awkwardly, her hand flexing and tapping against her leg as she tried to think of something to say.

"So, I should probably get back upstairs," Rebecca said after about forty years. "Tell the guys the good news, you know?"

"Yeah, sure. Vanessa and Candace are staying behind?"

"Are you serious?" she furrowed her brow as she smiled at her. "You really think I would take Vanessa with me into the rainforest? She would get herself killed in about thirty minutes! Actually, she could probably do that anywhere if left unattended, which is why I've asked Candace to stay with her."

"Then why bring her at all?"

"Because she's a genius. And hilarious."

"Right," Maya nodded dubiously. "Well, I've yet to see either of those things so I'll just have to take your word for it."

"Yes, you will," she smiled, dropping her eyes to her hand and holding out a folded piece of paper. "Here. I thought you should have that. It's stupid that you don't have it already."

Maya unfolded the paper and saw a phone number written on it. She nodded and put it in her pocket.

"If you could, ah, text me yours. Or Claudia's, whatever," she said as she backed away.

"Sure." Maya called after her.

"I'll see you soon," she smirked over her shoulder as she disappeared around the corner.

Maya waved as she watched her leave. Thank God that smirk was back. She had missed it, she was surprised to discover, and it was a welcome change to the angry sneer that Rebecca had been directing at her since they had arrived in Brazil. She turned and walked out to the van, her mind drifting back to the last night in Venezuela, her body reacting before she realised what she was thinking about, and she could feel the flush rising from her chest to her throat. She shook her head to clear the flashback from her mind and climbed into the van.

"So, how did that go?" Claudia asked, the grin evident in her voice though her face was turned away.

"Shut up, Claudia."

Claudia chuckled as she started the van and drove off.

Chapter 17

Maya knocked on Claudia's door in the early evening and waited impatiently as music continued to play on inside the room but her friend did not appear. She was hungry now that she had woken up and wanted to go and get some food. After a few moments she banged on the door again, cursing Claudia's name as her stomach rumbled in protest. The music clicked off and she heard movement from the room.

"Oh, hey," Claudia smiled as she finally pulled the door open. She was dressed in her bathrobe with a towel round her head and a half made up face. "What's up?"

"I'm starving," Maya growled. "Are you going to be long?"

"What do you mean?" she asked with a confused frown.

"What do you mean what do I mean? Are you going to be long doing…" she gestured at her friend's attire. "Whatever this is. I'm so hungry I would eat a week old plate of half cooked roadkill if you happened to have one in your room."

"Did you not get my message?"

"Message?"

"Yes, my text message."

"Oh, I don't know, I didn't look," she shrugged. "Why?"

"Christ, Maya, I don't know why you even bother having a phone."

"How else am I gonna know what time it is?"

"You could buy a watch like a normal person," Claudia sighed and leaned against the door frame. "I sent you a message earlier to tell you that I am going out tonight, so you'll have to get dinner by yourself."

"You're going out? With who?"

"Well with Tom, obviously. Who else would I go out with?"

"Uh-uh. No way." Maya folded her arms and shook her head.

"Excuse me?"

"You're not going out with Tom."

"Er, yes I am."

"You can't, Claudia, that's not okay!"

Claudia took a deep breath and a step back into the room, one hand on the door and the other on the frame. "Maya, I am still quite tired and very hungry. I am not having this conversation with you because I fear I am about to say something I will regret. I will see you tomorrow."

"Claudia, don't be an idiot," she pushed against the closing door and found herself staring into Claudia's furious eyes. "You can't go on a date with a guy you're about to trek through the Amazon with."

"I can and I am, Maya, now get out of my doorway so I can finish getting dressed."

"Don't you see how awkward this is going to make everything?" Maya asked, leaning full against the door to keep it open and falling forwards into the room as Claudia suddenly stepped back and let go of it.

"I'm making things awkward? Me?"

"Ow!" she exclaimed from her crumpled position on the floor, grabbing her already injured hand to her chest. "That really fucking hurt."

"You think that the thing that will make this trip awkward is if I go out for dinner with Tom?" Claudia asked again, glowering down at her.

"Yes! It's obvious you guys like each other, I don't see why you can't just wait til after."

"Well it's not like I'm going to fuck him on the first date, Maya!"

"Oh, right, cos only a slut would do that?"

"That's not what I said, and you didn't even have a date."

Maya stared up at her, anger burning up from the pit of her stomach. "Fuck you, Claudia," she muttered, pushing herself up and out of the room as quickly as she could, her whole body shaking with rage.

"Oh, Maya, come on, I didn't mean...for God's sake, this is why I didn't want to talk about this now," Claudia called down the corridor. "Maya! Come back."

She ignored her and stormed down the corridor throwing herself through the door to the stairs and taking them two at a time until she reached the street. She marched off down the road without a clue where she was going or what she was doing, her only thought being that she needed lots of alcohol and she needed it now.

Three hours later Maya stumbled back up the stairs to her room, a bottle of bourbon in her hand and a half smoked cigarette dangling from her mouth. She sighed heavily as she clung to the handrail, bemoaning the fact that she had been given a room on the second floor. She pulled the cigarette from her mouth and cursed as half of the skin off her lip came with it, and quickly jammed her hand against her mouth, screwing her face up petulantly.

After a few moments of cursing her life, the world and everyone who lived in it, she continued her weary climb and leaned heavily against her door as she searched through her pockets for her room key. Once she had been through each of them four times and found nothing but some coins and a screwed up piece of paper she discovered that she was actually holding her key in the same hand that held the bottle and went about trying to open her door, sliding through it with a thump as it eventually gave way.

She wandered over to the bed and flopped down onto it, landing with a grunt as it ended up being further away than she had anticipated. She lay for a few moments breathing heavily to recover from her mountainous climb, then flipped herself over so she could have a drink, almost falling off the bed in the process and only just managing to brace herself with an unsteady leg. She pulled the lid off the bottle and gulped some of the liquid down, savouring the burn as it ran down her throat.

She felt like shit. This was not what she had planned when she had agreed to this job. She had assumed it would be the usual kind of thing, Claudia and her would go to Venezuela, find the book Elaine had instructed them to and then use it to track down whatever it said they were looking for. Sure, she expected a few complications along the way, references to places long since torn down, a few dots to connect, maybe the odd leap in logic to find what no one else had been able to, but not this, not myths and legends, a merry go round of coincidence and riddles. And she certainly hadn't expected Rebecca fucking Bronstein and her team to come along, throwing her completely off her game and causing issues between Claudia and her.

Maya sighed and took another drink. If she was honest with herself Rebecca and Tom had nothing to do with the situation between her and Claud, that was completely down to her and her jealousy of Claudia being able to act like a normal, rational person around people she was attracted to. She, on the other hand, had been totally blindsided by her feelings towards Rebecca, feelings that right from the off she knew were about more than just the fact that she was gorgeous. Something in this woman spoke to her and she couldn't deal with it, so she had convinced herself that she was being taken for a ride and kept herself at a distance. When that stopped working she had just given into it and then freaked out at how easy it had been to open herself up to this woman and bolted, totally fucking up everything in the process. She hated herself for it and she was taking it out on Claudia. So now she was drunk and alone, feeling like crap and sinking fast. There was only one thing she could think of to sort this out.

She picked up her phone before she could change her mind and dialled the number, flopping back on the bed as she listened to the dial tone.

"Hola, mamá," she smiled as the woman picked up. "Qué tal?"

"Maya! I didn't expect you to call while you were working," her mother said, the rattle of pots accompanying her words. "Did you make it to Brazil? How is it going? How's Claudia?"

"She's fine. It's fine."

"Are you okay, mija? You sound sad."

"I'm fine," she lied. "Just tired I guess."

"You're a terrible liar, Maya," her mother said softly. "You always were."

"So people keep telling me."

"People?"

"Never mind, ma," she sighed, getting up and walking over to the window. "What are you making?"

"Pastelón. You know it is your tía's favourite."

"I do," she smiled, picturing her in the tiny kitchen of the apartment she shared with her aunt. Her stomach rumbled as she thought of her mother's cooking, reminding her that she had not actually eaten anything.

"Are you sure you're alright, mija? You don't sound yourself. Is the trip not going well?"

"It's fine. If we find what we're looking for it'll all be worth it."

"So what is it then? Is it about a girl?"

"No, ma, Jesus!"

"Maya," her mother admonished. "Must you always use blasphemy?"

"Alright, I know, I'm sorry," she help her hand up in a vague attempt to placate the woman thousands of miles away.

"If your abuela heard you it would be the hot pepper for you."

"Mamá, I'm almost thirty…"

"Do you think she would care?" Her mother chuckled. "'You are never too old for eternal damnation, Maya, you should remember that.' That is what she would say to you."

"How could I forget?" Maya chuckled at her mother's impression.

"'Well it seems you have, what with those awful tattoos all over your body,'" she laughed, hamming up her accent as she played her part.

"I have two tattoos, abuelita!"

"'And don't think I have forgotten the time you came home blind drunk with that boy whose mother was a hairdresser…'"

"Oh, come on," Maya scoffed. "Even she wouldn't bring that up. I was sixteen!"

"And of course that was the last time it happened," she chuckled. "You sound a little drunk now."

"I'm fine."

"Maya…"

"Ma, please," Maya sighed, sitting up and rubbing her eyes. "It's been a really long day, week, whatever, and I'm tired. Please just let it go right now, okay? I just wanted to hear your voice."

"Alright, mija, I just worry about you," she said sadly. "You are always so busy and so far away."

"I was home last week."

"Yes and spent the whole time you were here with your head stuck in a book. You ate hardly any of your mofongo."

"I had two portions."

"You need to eat, Maya, you are too skinny."

"Mamá," she sighed again.

"I know, I know. Ay bendito, what will I do with you?"

"Enough about me. How are you?"

"I'm fine," she said quickly, pots clattering again in the background. "Your tía is out again this evening. If you ask me she has some fancy man on the go."

"Well good for her." Maya chuckled.

"Hmm, not if he is anything like the last one."

"And what about you? No fancy men for you?"

"Please," she scoffed. "Where would I find the time? Speaking of which, I must go, mija, I have to get this finished before I go to work, and this must be expensive, calling me all the way from Brazil. Honestly, Maya, what a life you lead."

"Yeah, I know," Maya sighed and plucked at the edge of the table with her nails.

"And whatever it is that has you so sad, you'll figure it out. You always do. You are strong that way. I'm so proud of you, mija," she said tenderly. "I know your father would be too."

Maya jammed her knuckle against her mouth and swallowed down the lump in her throat, taking a moment to collect herself before answering. "Te quiero, mamá. I'll talk to you soon, okay?"

She disconnected the call and grabbed the bottle off the bedside table, ripping the top off and taking a gulp from it in an effort to force down the emotions bubbling up inside her. Drunk Maya was not a good place for emotions to be, unusual and regrettable things tended to happen. She threw the phone down on the bed and pulled open the sliding doors, squeezing out onto the plank of wood that they were trying to pass off as a balcony and lighting a cigarette.

God, she needed to pull herself together. Here she was, on the verge of one of the greatest discoveries in a hundred years, and she was balancing on a plank of wood two storeys up, protected by a guard rail that looked like it was made out of balsa wood, drunk out of her mind and wanting nothing more than to crawl up on the sofa next to her mami and cry like a little girl. It was pathetic, really.

And Claudia. God, she had been such a bitch to Claudia. She took another gulp from the bottle and stared out over the construction site behind the hotel. At least she thought it was a construction site. There didn't seem to be any actual construction going on. Why had she done that to Claudia? Why could she not just let her friend go out and have a good night? Because she couldn't? She sighed and took a drag from her cigarette, cursing herself again for fucking things up so spectacularly.

Why had she slept with Rebecca? For God's sake, she knew it was a bad idea. Not the act itself, that had been amazing, but she was not the kind of person that slept with people she would have to see again, at least not these days, so why had she done it? And why could she not stop thinking about her? This was not what she did. She didn't fawn over people like some lovesick teenager, she didn't get close to them and she absolutely did not go back for more. So why was that all she could think about?

She threw the end of the cigarette over the balcony and negotiated her way back into the room, hurling herself back down on the bed with a groan. She was going to have to do it, like actually do it. She was going to have to apologise to Claudia. She sighed again and picked up the phone, squeezing one eye shut so she could focus on the letters.

I'm a fuxking idiot. I'm sorry. Have a good night.

The effort of her grand statement complete she rolled over on the bed and shoved her hand in her pocket, staring at the yellowing ceiling and letting the bourbon spread its numbing magic through her body. She hoped Claudia was having a good time, though she couldn't really imagine how she would be. Tom seemed to her to be about as interesting as a bucketful of beige paint, but then maybe Claudia was more interested in the bucket than its contents. She still didn't get why she couldn't just admire the bucket where it was, she didn't have to take the damn thing out to dinner. Maya herself had admired plenty of buckets without dragging them into some fancy restaurant, sometimes maybe to a club or back to the bucket's house, not that a bucket would have a house. Whatever, stupid metaphor anyway. Was it a metaphor? Whatever.

She pulled her hand out of her pocket to stifle a yawn and looked down in consternation as something tickled her stomach. She plucked the offending bit of paper from where it had landed and held it up to her face, squinting to make out the writing and then blinking to make sure she had understood. Rebecca's number. Rebecca had given her her number and asked her to text. Well, if the king of bad ideas and the queen of drunken logic got together and had a child, this would be it. She absolutely should not text her now.

Hi. It's Maya.

A violent buzzing pulled her out of her dream and she sat bolt upright, the action causing her head to pound like someone was using her brain as a speedball. She looked around in alarm for the source of the noise and grabbed hold of the offending phone, bashing wildly at the screen to make it stop.

"Hello?" Claudia's voice blared out of the speaker.

"Oh, God…" she groaned, flopping back down on the bed.

"Er, Maya…please tell me you're alone?"

"What?" she asked breathlessly, not understanding the question.

"Maya!" Claudia said loudly. "You have me on speaker! I can hear…whatever it is that you're doing!"

"Jesus, Claudia, stop yelling! I know you can hear me."

"Oh. Well okay then. It just sounded like…never mind," she muttered.

"What?"

"Nothing. So, as I am assuming you are quite hungover this morning I thought maybe we should go and find some greasy food to make you feel better before we go shopping."

"What?" Maya rubbed her face and tried to make sense of her friend's words. So many words…

"Right. So I see this morning is not ideal for normal methods of communication therefore I will try a different tack," Claudia sighed. "Maya, get out of bed and get in the shower. I will be at your door in fifteen minutes and I expect you to be washed, fully clothed and ready to go. Understood?"

"Uh, yeah," she yawned, sort of understanding but not really in any state to argue.

"Good. I'll see you shortly."

The call disconnected with a beep and Maya lay still for a moment enjoying the blissful silence, only for a moment though as loud music blasted through the wall, a not so gentle reminder from Claudia next door that she was not to go back to sleep. Sighing heavily she pulled the covers off and got out of bed, padding over to the tiny bathroom in a daze, bouncing off the door frame as she misjudged its width.

She stood under the spray and let the hot water work its magic on her, then yelled in shock as it suddenly turned ice cold.

"Me cago en tu madre!" she barked at the shower as she jumped out of the spray, almost slipping in the process, and hastily turned the thing off.

Standing in the centre of the tiny room, and breathing as heavily as if she had escaped death, she turned to look at herself in the mirror and pulled a disgusted face at what she saw. Her eyes were bloodshot, the bags under them big enough to carry a week's worth of supplies, her olive skin was so pale she looked jaundiced and her tongue looked like she had been eating chalk.

She huffed at her reflection in irritation and pulled out her toothbrush, almost making herself gag with her vigorous efforts to make her mouth presentable again. Next she grabbed a towel and wandered back into the room, drying herself off as she hunted for a suitable outfit to wear. They were going shopping, Claudia had said. She didn't remember agreeing to this plan. She hated shopping, it was like her idea of a nightmare. There were almost always other people there and they kept walking around and getting in her way, or worse, speaking to her. Or even worse, touching her. She shivered at the thought and pulled on her top, running her hands through her hair to try and create some semblance of order before sitting heavily on the bed, tiredness washing over her.

As she sat and waited for Claudia, her eyes closed and her posture stiff, trying desperately to will her hangover away, something started nagging at her brain. She opened one eye cautiously, as if the action could either call the memory forward or banish it forever. Slowly she glanced around the room trying to pinpoint the source of her discomfort, and eventually her eye landed on her phone. She reached out a hand fearfully, hovering above it like she was afraid it would attack, before picking it up gingerly and unlocking the screen.

Rebecca (8)

"Shit," she whispered, dropping the phone onto the bed and closing her eyes. What the fuck had she said? She rubbed her face with her hands and let the pain of her hangover wash over her.

"Fuck it," she sighed, picking the thing up again and unlocking it quickly.

Hi. It's Maya.
8.34

Hi. Thanks for giving me your number. I'll let you know when Felipe gets back to me.
9.46

Okay. What are you doing?
9.54

Not much. Just looking into a few things before bed.
9.55

Sounds like fun. Need an extra hand.
10.03

Maya, are you drunk?
10.10

No. Maybe. Why?
10.14

I'll talk to you tomorrow.
10.21

Maya stared down at the phone. Well, that wasn't too bad, she hadn't said anything incriminating, not really. Her ham fisted attempt at innuendo was a little embarrassing, sure, but it wasn't so obvious that it couldn't be denied if it came to it. All things considered it could have been a lot worse.

There was a loud knock at the door and she pushed herself off the bed, slipping the phone into her pocket as she went, her hangover guilt receding slightly as she opened the door to see Claudia's smiling face. At least she had fixed one situation last night, although now presumably she would have to hear the details. The thought made her stomach churn.

"I need coffee," she greeted her friend as she grabbed her key.

"Alright, drunkie," Claudia laughed. "Let's get you sorted."

"How did you know I was drunk?"

"You apologised."

Maya gave a resigned shrug of acknowledgement and closed the door behind her.

Chapter 18

Maya rested her head on her hands as she waited for Claudia to return with their coffee. She was starting to feel a little bit like she might actually die at any moment, and the thought was not entirely unwelcome. If was definitely preferable to having to deal with feeling this shitty for an undetermined period of time.

"Here," Claudia said, returning to the table and shoving a coffee at her. "Drink this, eat something, tell me what's going on."

"Oh God," she groaned as she tried to sit up. "Can't I just drink this and go back to bed?"

"No, Maya, you cannot. You've been wallowing in self pity for days now and I'm sick of it," Claudia leaned back in her chair with a sigh. "I realise that you don't want to talk about it, that you never want to talk about it, but there comes a point where you have to and I would say that time is upon us, wouldn't you?"

"No," she said sullenly, blowing on her coffee. "I'd say that that time is when I'm like eighty and on my death bed."

"Well I would say that if you think you're going to live til you are eighty with the way you're carrying on you are delusional."

"Come on, Claud, I'm not that bad."

"Oh really?" Claudia smiled and leaned forward, folding her arms on the table. "How much did you drink last night?"

"Look, last night was just a hiccup, alright?"

"Okay. What about the night before we found the cave? We drank a bottle of bourbon and a bottle of tequila between us and I'm fairly certain I was too pissed to speak, let alone carry on drinking after the first few shots of tequila."

"I don't really remember if…"

"And the night before we found the rock? You finished the bottle then as well."

"Yeah but it wasn't full."

"And the night of the campfire?"

"Come on Claudia, give me a break," she sighed and leaned back in her chair. "So I've been drinking a lot this week. What's the big deal?"

"Because the last time you were drinking this heavily I didn't think you were going to be able to stop and it scared the crap out of me," she answered quietly, studying her from the other side of the table. "I can't lose you, Maya. No one else can annoy me quite like you can."

Maya let out a dry chuckle and looked at her friend as she drank her coffee. She was right, of course, she was drinking more than usual, but she wasn't anywhere near as bad as she had been before. That had been an exceptional circumstance and one that she would never let herself get into again. She took a deep breath and removed her sunglasses, wincing a little at the brightness of the sun.

"I know you're worried and I know I've been out of control but trust me, it won't be like it was then. What led to that, what happened with Nina," she spat, shivering involuntarily as her ex girlfriend's name passed her lips for the first time in years. "I won't ever let anyone do that to me again. Ever."

She leaned back in her chair and put her glasses back on, not feeling great about the way Claudia was looking at her. She knew that look. It was a look that said she was about to come out with something that would smash through Maya's carefully constructed shield and force her to admit something to herself that she really didn't want to.

"At what cost, though? It seems to me you're doing far more damage to yourself trying to keep Rebecca at arms length than she could ever do if you let her in."

"Claudia," Maya sighed. "This thing with Rebecca and me is…I don't know what it is, but I do know that now is not the time or the place to be getting into anything. We're about to go trekking through the jungle together, that's not really a great place to start hooking up."

"Why, because you wouldn't be able to keep your hands off each other?"

"What? No, of course not."

"So, because you wouldn't be able to romance her? Take her out for fancy dinners?"

"Claudia…"

"No, wait, is it because the setting is so romantic you're worried you wouldn't be able to top it on your anniversaries?"

"Why are you being such a dick?" Maya said angrily, slamming down her coffee cup and glaring across the table at her.

"Because you are being ridiculous and you have this whole web of paper thin excuses built up in your head to stop you from being with this person who could actually make you happy and it's bullshit, Maya."

"They're not excuses, Claudia, they are valid reasons! In case you haven't noticed the rainforest is quite a dangerous place to be and it would do neither of us any good to go in there distracted."

"Oh, of course. Sorry. So it is that you wouldn't be able to keep your hands off each other."

"Claudia…"

"I expect you're worried about how the rest of us would cope as well, having such a hotbed of sexual energy in our expedition party."

"Alright, now you're just being a bitch," Maya muttered, throwing some money on the table as she got up to leave.

"Maybe I am but it's only so that you will see that no one is buying this, not me, not her, most likely not even you at this point."

"And what does that mean? Have you been talking to her?"

"No, of course not Maya," she sighed wearily. "Sit back down would you, you look like you're about to collapse."

"Then what do you mean she's not buying this?"

"Well it's fucking obvious that you regret what you did. You look kind of like a naughty puppy whenever she's around."

"What?" Maya asked in embarrassment, sitting down quickly as her legs began to wobble.

"Like half 'I'm sorry I peed in your shoe' and half 'but look at how cute I am. Love me! Love me!'. It's gross. Really."

"Honestly," she cleared her throat and steadied her hands on the table. "Did I do something to you that I'm not aware of? Cause you're really making me feel like shit here."

"I'm sorry, I don't mean to," Claudia tutted and reached forward to take one of her hands. "It's just that I'm tired of watching my best friend make herself deliberately miserable for no good reason and I don't know how else to get through to you."

"And telling me that I am behaving like a pathetic lovesick animal is really your best play?"

"I never said pathetic," she shrugged, leaning back again. "It would only be pathetic if it were one way, and it's definitely not."

"It's not?"

"Oh my God, woman, are you blind?" Claudia laughed. "She looks at you like she's composing sonnets to you in her head! Seriously the more time she spends around you the more that carefully constructed 'I'm ready for my close up' demeanour falls away and she visibly relaxes. It's weird. Like watching a time lapse video."

Maya let this thought float around her head for a minute, a small smile dancing on her lips. She didn't know why it pleased her so much, seeing as it didn't change anything, but it made her stomach tingle and she was content just to focus on that for a minute.

"Oh my God, you are bloody useless at times," Claudia muttered, standing up and waving her hand for Maya to follow. "Come on. We have to go and meet Tom and Candace."

"What? Why?"

"We're going shopping, remember? To get the kit sorted for the trip."

"Oh, God. Can't you just go? I feel like shit."

"Well you should have thought of that before you drank a whole bottle of bourbon alone in your room like some sad old lush."

Maya rested her head on the back of the seat and closed her eyes. They were parked outside Rebecca's hotel and Claudia had gone inside to find Tom and Candace, leaving Maya to 'get herself together', something neither of them were particularly confident would happen in the allotted timeframe. Still, she was grateful for the momentary silence, not even slightly appreciative of Claudia's new 'tough love' approach to her current downward spiral, and happy to let her mind wander.

She still had no idea why they were going along on this shopping trip. She understood that Rebecca's team needed to replace what had been damaged in the storm but their own stuff was fine. Sure, they needed a few practical things like mosquito nets, bits and pieces for the first aid kit, but nothing like the tech that they were being dragged along to look at. She sighed and stared out the window, ducking down in her seat awkwardly as she spotted Rebecca walking out the front door with a beautiful Brazilian woman. They stood talking just outside of the glass fronted lobby, the woman rubbing Rebecca's arm gently as she spoke to her, Rebecca nodding with a smile, her eyes tired. Quickly the woman pulled her into a tight hug, leaning back after a moment to kiss her on the cheek, lingering a little and resting her hands on her shoulders.

Maya's stomach churned uncomfortably, her hangover washing over her with renewed vengeance. Well, that would certainly explain why she looked so damn tired all the time. She looked away in irritation. What did she care? Rebecca could sleep with whoever she wanted to, it had nothing to do with her. Let her fuck half the girls in Brazil if she wanted, it was no skin off her nose. She rubbed her stomach and closed her eyes as she took a slow breath to try and stave off the wave of nausea creeping up her throat.

Suddenly the doors popped open and Claudia, Tom and Candace piled in, Rebecca loitering outside the van as they chatted amongst each other loudly.

"Just make sure that you don't go crazy, Tom," she said, leaning on Claudia's open window as she closed the door. "We have to carry all this stuff, remember? We need only the essentials, the more lightweight the better."

"Yeah, I know. It'll cost more though."

"That's alright, within reason. Candace, keep an eye on him." Rebecca cleared her throat and addressed Maya. "Good morning. How's the head?"

"Just peachy, thanks," she muttered, smiling thinly.

"Hmm, I can imagine. It certainly sounded like you were enjoying yourself."

Maya turned her head slowly to look at her. She had a strange look on her face and she couldn't tell whether it was amusement, anger or both. What did that mean? How was she getting that from one possibly inappropriate text? "Uh, yeah."

"Okay," Claudia interrupted quickly. "Let's get going then, shall we? Rebecca, see you later."

"Yeah, sure. Have fun guys," she clapped the side of the van and walked off leaving Maya to stare after her in confusion as Candace and Tom started up a discussion about what was essential and what was not.

"You talked to her last night?" Claudia asked quietly.

"No," she replied, a hollow feeling starting in the pit of her stomach.

"Are you sure?"

Maya stared out of the window and wracked her brain to remember before pulling out her phone with a dry mouth. She unlocked the screen and went to her call log.

Mamá. 19.43.

Rebecca. 23.12.

"Shit."

After they had dropped Tom and Candace back at the hotel with all the stuff Maya and Claudia returned to their own rooms to clean up and head back out to meet them all for dinner. Maya walked down the road half listening to Claudia's chit chat, a ball of nervous energy playing havoc with her stomach. What the fuck had she said during that phone call? She had been thinking about it all day and still couldn't remember a damn thing. Consequently she had no clue how she should act around Rebecca, if she could just get away with laughing it off or if she had said something completely inappropriate that she would have to try and apologise for.

They arrived at the restaurant to find the others already there, seated at a round table in the middle of the room. The lighting was low and there was soft music playing through the speakers, the atmosphere completely at odds with her inner turmoil. As they approached the table she assessed the seating arrangements, the round table leaving her little chance to avoid being in Rebecca's line of sight and Tom's position destroying it completely. As expected Claudia slid into the seat next to him leaving Maya in between her and Vanessa, directly opposite Rebecca.

"Hi," Claudia said as they sat down, smiling around the table warmly at their greetings before focusing her attention on Tom.

Maya looked around the table, trying to smile as best she could when she felt like she might vomit all over the place, feeling both relieved and panicked when Rebecca didn't meet her gaze. If the others noticed the awkwardness between the two of them they didn't acknowledge it and the conversation flowed freely as the wine and food arrived at the table, subjects ranging from news of back home, stories about Tom and Phil's time at Princeton, to the shopping trip they had been on this afternoon.

"Well I was actually surprised at how little you bought," Phil smiled. "Very restrained, Tom, bravo."

"Restrained?" Claudia choked on her wine. "I thought there must have been some sort of mistake when they rang the bill up. That's a year's rent to me."

"Well, I'm still bummed I didn't get that profiler," Tom sighed, shaking his head as he picked apart a piece of bread. "That shit was cool, guys. Like Alien cool."

"It would have been a lot less cool after you'd been carrying it for three days, Tom." Candace pointed out. "You got your GPR, I don't know why you needed the profiler too."

"Yeah, I know, but it was still cool," he said leaning forward and checking to see if they could be overheard. "And speaking of needs I still think y'all are wrong about the guns."

"What?" Maya piped up, slightly louder than anticipated and drawing stares from the other diners.

"We're not wrong, Tom," Rebecca hissed, glancing at Maya with her hand up placatingly. "And we are not having this conversation again."

"But we're going into the jungle, Rebecca, there will be things there that are trying to kill us!"

"Are you fucking serious?" Maya glared at him, Claudia shifting slightly in her seat in case she had to intervene. "What the fuck do you think is going to happen to us?"

"Well I don't know, we could be attacked by something, like a jaguar or an alligator or something."

"And you think shooting at it will help?"

"Guys," Phil said, eyes darting around at the other patrons. "Let's just drop it shall we?"

"Well it couldn't hurt."

"Oh, it could hurt," Maya laughed. "It could hurt a lot. When you missed and just succeeded in pissing it off more? That would hurt."

"Well then I just wouldn't miss," he shrugged, picking up his drink and smiling at her arrogantly.

"Right, of course not," she smiled dangerously. "You probably been shooting BB guns at bunny rabbits in tin can alley since you were knee high to a grasshopper, huh cowboy?"

"Maya…" Claudia said quietly, shifting closer to her.

"What? Are you even hearing this? Jesus, Claud, I can't believe you like this guy," she muttered, grabbing her drink and knocking it back.

"Yeah? Well at least I'm man enough to do something about it." Tom laughed, slurring a little as he slammed his glass back down on the table. "I'm not the one who…"

"That's enough, Tom," Rebecca said evenly, raising her hand to signal the waiter. "I think it's time we left."

"Yeah, I think you're right," Maya said through gritted teeth, dying a little inside as she glanced around the table. Tom's face was beet red, his eyes flashing with indignation, Phil and Candace were staring down into their laps, Phil's hand fiddling with the stem of his wine glass, and Vanessa was just gazing vacantly at the ceiling, almost as if she was not a part of their group. Did they all know? During the conversation she had heard at the river it didn't seem like Rebecca had told any of them but maybe that had changed. Maybe they had been there for the phone call.

Next to her Claudia was staring straight ahead, arms folded, fury coming off her in waves, although whether it was directed at her or Tom or both of them Maya couldn't tell. She reached into her pocket for some money and threw it on the table.

"I'm going for a cigarette," she said with as much dignity as she could muster. "Excuse me."

"What?" She heard him mutter as she walked away from the table. "She started it."

She shoved the door open and burst out into the street, shame and rage washing over her as she lit a cigarette with trembling hands. What the fuck was she doing here? Why had she ever thought that this was a good idea? The door opened behind her and Claudia appeared next to her.

"Can I have one of those?" she asked with a sigh.

Maya held the pack out and watched warily as her friend pulled out a cigarette and lit it, inhaling deeply before blowing out the smoke and leaning against the wall.

"Claud…"

"Just forget it, Maya, alright? I honestly don't know why I expected anything different."

"Hey, come on. I didn't mean to…"

"Embarrass us both in front of the people we have to spend the foreseeable future with? Well you did."

"Oh, cause he was so much better, right?"

"No, he was being an arse as well." Claudia shook her head and took another drag. "I just don't understand why you always have to make things difficult."

Maya smoked her cigarette in silence, stung by her friend's words. The guy was being a prick, her reaction was justified, right? What was she meant to do, just let him go wandering around the jungle with a loaded gun? Maybe shoot his own dick off in the process? And what kind of a friend would she be if she let the guy Claudia was crushing on do that before she had even had a chance to sleep with him. Or maybe she had. She cringed internally as she realised that she had been so wrapped up in her own bullshit that she hadn't even asked how Claudia's date had gone. Apparently that's what kind of friend she was. She sighed and ground the cigarette butt out with her heel, looking up as the door opened again and Rebecca walked out, Phil and Candace behind her with Vanessa and Tom bringing up the rear, the latter looking very much like a scolded child.

"Hey, Tex," she said, marching over to him. "You're an asshole. So am I. Buy you a drink?"

As the initial look of shock wore off his face split into a wide grin and he shoved his hands in his pockets, nodding his consent. "Sure. But only if you let me buy you one back."

"I'm not sure we could stand each other's company for that long but we'll see," she smirked at him. "Anyone else? First round's on me?"

"Can we go somewhere loud?" Vanessa asked, linking her arm through Maya's and apparently oblivious to look of disgust on her face. "I want to dance."

"Sounds like a plan," Claudia laughed, linking Maya's other arm and helping Vanessa drag her down the street. As they walked Claudia squeezed her arm gently and shot her a grateful look which almost made her discomfort worth it.

"Maybe somewhere with karaoke?" Vanessa mused.

"Oh, dear God," Maya muttered as she tried desperately to escape.

Two hours later she was leaning against the bar watching Claudia and Tom grind up against each other in what she felt confident was the worst club in the world. It honestly looked and felt as though they were in a small barn that someone had stuck a bar and a cd player into, thrown up some lights and got their drunk, tasteless friend to come round to play the most random, awful music they could find. The beer was warm, the shots were watered down, and the clientele she could only assume had got drunk somewhere else and stumbled in here on a dare.

Phil and Candace wandered over to join her, raising their glasses in greeting but not making any effort to speak over the din. She preferred it that way, she wasn't a fan of attempting small talk in clubs, especially with people who didn't particularly like her. Candace managed to convey that she was going to the toilet and wandered off across the dancefloor, passing Vanessa who was in the centre of the room, dancing up a storm to music clearly different from the latest horror blaring out of the tinny speakers. Rebecca had disappeared about an hour ago having not spoken to, or even made eye contact with Maya since they had arrived.

Suddenly one of Vanessa's chaotic dance moves went wildly out of control, sending her spinning into a table and knocking all five of the drinks over their owners. With a careless wave of her hand she went back about her business whilst the five people jumped up and yelled angrily after her.

"Oh, shit," Phil said, the look on his face conveying his words to Maya as the sound was lost amongst the racket. "Help me!"

"What? Why me?"

"Because we need to calm them down and I don't speak Spanish!" He yelled over the song.

"What makes you think they do? They're probably Brazilian."

"Well I don't speak Brazilian either."

"Oh my God, how drunk are you? I thought you were the smart one," she laughed. "They speak Portuguese here."

"Jesus, whatever, I obviously can't speak it," he shook his head and looked on in worry as the two men from the group started moving angrily towards Vanessa. "Shit, please just help me, okay?"

She sighed and followed him over to the two men, putting a hand gently on one of their arms as he yelled at an oblivious Vanessa.

"Tu ta me tirando?"

"Lo siento, señor," she shouted over the music, pulling his attention away from the twirling blonde and onto herself and Phil. "Mi amiga está muy borracha y es idiota."

The man looked down at her hand angrily and then up at her face as he understood what she was saying. His friend had stopped and came back to them, looking to see if there was a problem.

"Please," Phil held up his hands. "She didn't mean anything by it. Can we buy you all a fresh drink?"

"That would be great, thank you," a voice said from beside them. A woman from the table had come over and, after speaking to the two men in rapid Portuguese, took Maya's arm and guided her to the bar. Why did people keep grabbing her arm today? Was she giving off some sort of vibe?

The woman ordered their drinks and leaned against the bar, turning to look at Maya with a smile. She smiled back briefly, wondering where Phil had gone and spotting him over by the table, apparently attempting to clear up the spilled drinks with some napkins he had found God knows where.

"Hi. I'm Alexia."

"Maya."

"It's good to meet you, Maya," she smiled again, her eyes dancing in the low light. "What brings you to Boca do Acre?"

"Oh, you know."

"No, I do not or I wouldn't have asked," she laughed, reaching out to tap Maya's forearm gently. Maya glanced down to where the touch had landed, then back up at the woman's face. Was she flirting with her?

"It's kind of a long story."

"Well I'm not going anywhere," she smiled, her lips wrapping around her straw. "Are you?"

Okay. So this was definitely happening now. She looked at the woman more closely. She was pretty, deep brown eyes, even face, curly, shoulder length brown hair, caramel skin, toned arms...on paper all good but Maya felt nothing. She smiled at her and looked away, her eyes immediately connecting with Rebecca's across the room. Of course. She hadn't seen her all night and now there she was, tucked in a booth with the chick from the hotel.

"What about you?" she asked as she flicked her gaze back to Alexia and tried to look interested. "What are you doing here?"

"Working."

"Oh yeah? What do you work as?"

"I am a travel writer. It takes me all over but I am based in São Paulo. Where are you based?"

"New York."

"I love New York!" Alexia cried, running her hand up Maya's side and and leaning in close. "The city that never sleeps. My kind of town," she winked.

Maya forced herself to smile and reached for her drink uncomfortably. "Yeah, so we should probably get these drinks over to your friends before they think we forgot them."

"I had forgotten them," she shrugged. "But you are right, we should take them over. Then maybe you and I could go somewhere a little quieter?"

Maya's gaze drifted back over to Rebecca's booth. The two women were now locked in conversation, their faces close and the Brazilian rubbing up and down Rebecca's arm. "Yeah," she said, smiling as she returned her eyes to Alexia's. "Maybe."

Alexia smiled wickedly and grabbed hold of half the drinks, setting off to the table as Maya collected the rest and followed her. She set the drinks down and stiffened slightly as the woman rested her hand proprietarily on her lower back as she talked to her friends. She looked around uncomfortably and her heart sank slightly when she saw Rebecca's booth was now empty. She gave the place a quick scan, desperate to catch a glimpse of her and not sure why, eventually giving up the search as she realised she was being spoken to.

"Sorry, what?"

"I said," Alexia leaned up and whispered in her ear, her breath hot on her face. "Do you want to get out of here?"

She felt her hand drift down from her back to her ass and took a breath to control the wave of revulsion that spread through her. What was wrong with her? This woman was gorgeous, normally they'd be halfway back to hers by now.

"Ah, you know what? I'm not feeling too hot right now." *I'm sorry, what?*

"Are you sure? You look pretty hot from where I'm standing," she winked and moved in closer.

Yeah, no. "Yeah, I don't know what it is. Maybe something I ate?" *Lame, Maya. Really lame,*

"Oh," the woman dropped her hand and moved away slightly, disappointment evident on her face. "Okay."

"Sorry about that." *So, so sorry.* "I hope you have a good night. It was great to meet you. Really."

Maya smiled quickly and backed away, seeking out Claudia to tell her she was leaving and exiting the club like it was on fire.

Chapter 19

Maya woke up and reached out to stop her alarm. She picked it up and yawned, trying to focus her eyes on the message alert.

Rebecca - Felipe called. He has good news. Meet us here at 11.

She clicked out of the message and checked the clock. 9.30. Plenty of time. She quickly sent a message to Claudia and climbed out of bed, heading to the bathroom for her three minute shower. Afterwards she dried and dressed herself before checking the phone for a reply, her brow creasing in confusion when she saw there was none. She stared at the wall between her room and Claudia's as she noticed the lack of sound coming from there and hastily headed out to knock on her door.

Five minutes later she returned to her room and sat on her bed, staring at her phone, unsure what to do. Apparently Claudia was not in, which meant in all likelihood she had not been home. Should she call her? What if she was still...busy?

Maya stood up and grabbed her stuff off the table to head out to the van. If Claudia was not here she was most likely at Rebecca's hotel already so she could just meet her there. She fired off another text telling her exactly that and climbed behind the wheel, rolling down the window to let in some air and try to disperse the sweltering heat which had gathered inside.

So Felipe had good news. She guessed that meant they had got permission to go which was great, and sooner than expected. She had figured it would take at least four days. Maybe he knew someone? Anyway, they still had to wait for confirmation from the tribe they were meeting so it would still take a few more days. After the meeting with Felipe was over she figured it would probably be a good idea to head back into the Jungle, try and acclimatise herself a little more. The temperature here was not that much hotter than it had been in Puerto Cabello but it was muggier, like it had been there before the storm, and constant. The air was so thick she felt like she could almost chew on it.

She pulled into the car park of the hotel and climbed out, stretching as she looked up at the place, not for the first time envious of their air con and pool facilities. She could really use a good swim right now, burn off some of the frustration she had clogging up her system. Judging by the terse text she had received off Rebecca the drunk dial was still a thing, and she still had no idea what she had said. At this point she didn't really care anymore, Rebecca was fucking someone else so what did it matter? Sure, it was a little bit embarrassing, maybe a lot embarrassing depending on what she'd said, but Rebecca obviously didn't want to talk about it and neither did she, so the best play here was just to pretend it had never happened. That was something she excelled at.

She pulled out her phone and checked the time. 10.45, not too bad. Time to get a coffee and relax a bit before the others showed up. She strolled into the hotel restaurant and looked around for a table, her inner cool leaking out of her like a rusty bucket when she saw Rebecca sitting alone in the centre of the room reading the paper. She briefly thought about leaving, or sitting somewhere else like she hadn't seen her, then squared her shoulders and walked over.

"Hi," she said cheerfully, her knees practically knocking as she gripped the back of the chair for support. "Mind if I, er…"

"Please do," Rebecca replied too quickly, gesturing at the chair and returning to her paper, barely glancing in her direction.

"Thanks."

Maya sat and ordered her coffee from the apparently omnipresent waiter, then shifted uncomfortably and pulled out her phone, willing there to be a message from Claudia.

"Did you have fun last night?" Rebecca asked from behind her paper, a slight edge present in her voice.

"Er, yeah," she muttered, pulling on her pendant as she thought back on the night. "Not really my kind of place though. I decided to get an early night."

"Yeah," Rebecca laughed dryly, turning the page of her paper sharply. "I bet."

"Excuse me?"

The waiter reappeared with her coffee and took his time setting it down, running through food options as she tried to work out what Rebecca was being such an ass about. Most likely she was referring to her hangover and still pissed about the phone call. Maya smiled at the waiter and waved him off, letting the silence hang between them as she tried to work out what to say next.

"I, er, I thought about heading out this afternoon," she said after a moment. "You know, wander about a bit, try and get to grips with the local terrain."

"What, you didn't 'get to grips' with the local terrain enough last night?"

"What?"

"I can't this afternoon," Rebecca sighed, finally looking at her as she held her paper with one hand and lifted her coffee to her mouth with the other. "I'm meeting with someone."

"Right," Maya said, the image of the handsy Brazilian woman flashing across her mind like a hot knife.

"I'll ask Phil and Tom though. It would be good for them."

"Yeah, okay. Great."

Maya smiled quickly and picked up her coffee, rolling her eyes as Rebecca disappeared back behind her paper. She poked at her phone on the table, cursing Claudia and her lack of appearance.

"Where's Claudia?"

"I was just wondering that myself," Maya chuckled. "I haven't been able to get hold of her this morning."

"Oh? You haven't been home?"

"No, she…"

"Good morning ladies!" Felipe interrupted enthusiastically. "I am so glad to see you. I have excellent news."

Rebecca stood up and folded the paper quickly before shaking his hand with a warm smile. Maya followed suit and sat back down, shooting a glance at Rebecca as she did so. Something weird was going on, this was more than the phone call but she didn't know what. Was Rebecca upset about Tom and Claudia? No, that couldn't be it, only crazy people got upset about their friends hooking up. She turned her attention back to Felipe as he finished ordering his drink and beamed at them both.

"So, how do you feel about beginning our trip the day after tomorrow?"

"Really? That soon?" Maya smiled over at Rebecca who met her eyes for less than a second before turning back to their guide.

"That would be amazing, Felipe, thank you so much," she said excitedly. "This is much quicker than I had dared to hope for."

"Yes, we are very lucky," he nodded. "My contact from the tribe happened to be in town on the day we last met. I didn't want to tell you on at the time in case he would not agree, but I talked with him and he is more than happy to meet with you."

"That's fantastic, thank you."

"After that it was just a question of filing our route with the authorities and getting authorisation to continue. Thankfully I have a friend," he tapped his nose and laughed. "He pushed it through quickly."

"I'm so relieved," Rebecca sighed and leaned back in her chair.

"So, what happens now?" Maya asked as the waiter returned with Felipe's coffee.

"Now we go," he shrugged. "I will need tomorrow to prepare my things, check a few last minute details like conditions, etc, then I will meet you here on Friday morning, say ten? And we go to the starting point you indicated and begin. Does that sound good?"

"It sounds perfect," Rebecca smiled.

"I have the route that I filed with me," he said, reaching into his bag and pulling out a folder. "I will talk you through it then leave you with a copy so that you can discuss it with your team. We will be covering up to twenty five miles on some of the days, although I have started us off at only fifteen."

"That should be fine," Maya nodded.

"The terrain will be difficult for those not used to it and, although you have assured me that your team is prepared, I have taken the liberty of including exit strategies should it come to that."

"Thank you, Felipe, I appreciate that, although hopefully it will be unnecessary." Rebecca flicked through the folder, placing it down after a few seconds so that Maya could see but still firmly avoiding her gaze. Maya frowned slightly and leaned forward to get a better view.

"Is, ah, is everything okay?" Felipe asked Maya, a slight look of confusion on his face.

"Hmm? Yeah, sure, everything's fine," she lied, smiling her biggest smile. "So, day three seems to be mostly uphill. Do you think twenty miles is realistic?"

"I thought you may question it but the forest is not so dense here and day two will be the biggest test as our bodies adjust to the situation. I find that once we have broken through that barrier on day three we feel a new burst of energy," he smiled at them both as he turned to day four and began eagerly outlining the easy days and the stressful ones. Maya smiled back and concentrated on his explanations, trying to ignore Rebecca's frosty attitude and focus on the task at hand.

Maya pushed her room door open wearily and sat down on her bed, bending over with a groan to pull off her shoes, checking the time on her phone as she did so. It was almost ten and even though she was starving she didn't have anywhere near enough energy to go and find food. She threw the phone down and wandered over to the shower, deeply regretting checking into this hotel and willing to sell her soul for a bath.

After the awkward meeting with Felipe she had waited in the restaurant for Phil and Tom to appear, driving them and a flustered Claudia back to their hotel so Claud could change, before heading out to the dolphins to do some prep. To be fair to them they handled the seven hour trek well, particularly Tom and Claudia who didn't appear to have gotten much sleep the night before. There had been a slightly awkward moment where Phil had tried to engage her in a discussion about Rebecca, but he seemed to realise fairly quickly that she wasn't having any of it and moved onto safer topics, like what kind of animals would be trying to kill them.

She stood in the tiny cubicle and let the ineffectual spray tease the dirt and sweat off her skin, staying in as long as she could bear the cold, then wandered back into the bedroom, shivering in her thin towel. She sat down heavily on the bed and checked her phone again, secretly hoping for a message from Claudia saying that she was bringing her food but not particularly hopeful as she could hear soft music coming from the next room. She sighed and lay back on the bed, sending out all kinds of prayers that some way, somehow, Claudia would suddenly appear at her door with a pizza, her heart leaping in excitement as a knock suddenly came.

She wrapped her towel around her more securely as she practically skipped towards the door, an action which saved her from an embarrassing wardrobe malfunction as her hand dropped in surprise when she saw Rebecca on the other side of the door.

"Rebecca," she said, taking in the other woman's flushed appearance. "What are you doing here?"

"What the hell are you doing, Maya?"

"Getting dressed?"

"Don't play dumb with me," Rebecca spat, the scent of alcohol drifting off her as she pushed past her into the room. "What makes you think that you can behave like this?"

"Uh, Rebecca, I don't know what you're talking about," she muttered uncomfortably, closing the door and wrapping her arms around herself.

"You don't know what I'm talking about?"

"No."

"Did I do something to you?" Rebecca said angrily, her hands on her hips as she faced her. "Did I say something or act a certain way that made you want to hurt me?"

"I didn't mean to hurt you, Rebecca, honestly, I just…"

"Just what? Decided that leaving in the middle of the night and telling me it meant nothing wasn't enough, you had to hook up with some skank right in front me and fuck her two days before we head off into the jungle together?"

Maya shook her head in confusion before she realised what Rebecca had been thinking and embarrassment swept over her. "Oh, shit…"

"Oh, shit. Right." Rebecca turned to face her, her eyes flashing. "How dare you? How dare you do that to me?"

"Rebecca, I…"

"Don't you dare say you're sorry," she snapped, taking a step towards her. "Do you have any idea what I'm going through? What I'm dealing with at the moment?"

"I know, I didn't…"

"The way you treated me after we slept together really fucking hurt, Maya, and I am trying really hard not to let that get in the way of what we're doing here. There are much more important things at stake than my feelings."

"I'm sorry, I…"

"But I can't do this if you're going to keep batting me about like a cat with a mouse. I'm not your play thing, Maya, you can't just call me up when you're drunk and horny and expect me to come running then pick up someone else in front of me when I don't."

"Hey, that's not what happened." Maya held her hands up and took a step towards her. "That wasn't what I wanted."

"Oh really?" Rebecca folded her arms and moved closer, a dangerous smile on her face. "So what exactly were you referring to when you said 'I want to come over and keep you up all night'? An in depth discussion on the agricultural practices of the Inca? A particularly intense game of chess?"

Maya's mouth went dry and her heart was pounding, mortification flooding over her as she started to remember what she'd said. "No, I don't mean I didn't want to…I mean, I'm not saying…shit."

"Well what the hell are you saying?" Rebecca threw her hands up in exasperation. "First you tell me to leave you alone, then you sleep with me, then you tell me it was just sex and it meant nothing, then you call me up and tell me you can't stop thinking about me, then you fuck someone else and I can't take it Maya, I just can't."

"I'm so sorry," she said, shivering with embarrassment as she stood in her towel and hating herself for putting Rebecca through this, all because she was too much of a coward to deal with her feelings when she was sober.

"Well sorry isn't good enough!" Rebecca yelled, her hand balling into fists at her side as she moved closer, causing Maya to step back quickly and slam into the wall. "You just can't play with people's emotions Maya, don't you understand that?"

"Of course I do, I was just…"

"You were just drunk, yeah, I got that from the way you were slurring down the phone at me and talking about how good I sound when I…"

"Oh, God, please, I'm sorry," Maya hung her head and pressed her palm against her eye, dying a little as that part of the conversation came flooding back.

"Do you not think I've thought about it? Because believe me, I have, but I wasn't about to call you up in the middle of the night and start replaying it down the phone to you because you made it pretty clear that it was a one time thing and I respected your wishes, hard as that might have been."

"Rebecca, please…"

"And the one thing that made it easier to do that was allowing myself to believe that you didn't care, that you weren't lying when you said it meant nothing, because you know, Maya, sometimes when you look at me I feel like I can't breathe and I…" Rebecca stopped suddenly, her eyes going wide and the fire going out of them as she realised what she had said. She backed away quickly and headed for the door.

"Rebecca, wait…" Maya said, reaching out to catch her hand.

"Don't," she replied thickly, still facing the door.

Maya pulled gently on her arm, persisting when she held her position and eventually reaching out with her other hand to turn Rebecca around to face her. Her eyes stayed fixed on the floor and there were angry tears sliding down her cheeks. Maya brushed them away with her thumbs, her heart clenching in her chest, feeling terrible about herself and desperately wanting to fix the situation.

"I didn't sleep with her, Rebecca," she said gently. "I didn't even kiss her."

"Yeah, right," Rebecca sighed, swaying slightly as Maya's hands caressed her face.

"I swear to you I didn't. I thought about it. God, seeing you with that woman almost drove me crazy and I…"

"What woman?" Rebecca looked up at her, brow creased in confusion.

"That woman you're always with," she muttered. "The hot, handsy Brazilian with the gorgeous...eyes."

"Madalena?" she said. "You thought I was seeing Madalena? Jesus, Maya, she's my contact! She's been trying to find out about my parents."

"Oh."

"God, she's old enough to be my mother!" Rebecca laughed softly. "And she's straight. And married."

"Alright, I'm sorry," Maya smiled and raised a hand to her head in embarrassment.

"You're an idiot, you know that?"

"Yeah, I know that."

"You really didn't sleep with her?" she asked after a moment.

"Of course not."

"Why not?" Rebecca asked quietly, looking up at her through her eyelashes, colour rising to her cheeks.

Maya thought about what to say in reply. She could tell the truth, be honest for once, say that the thought of being with anyone else made her sick to her stomach, that all she had wanted to do since the moment she ran out of Rebecca's hotel room was go back and tell her she was sorry. But she couldn't do that. She couldn't just leave herself open like that. At least not with words. She leaned forward and gently pressed her lips to Rebecca's face, her stomach tightening as she heard the other woman's breath hitch. She reached out her hands and tilted her face up, moving her kisses down her cheek softly, Rebecca's eyes locking with her own as she kissed the corner of her mouth. She pulled back slightly, their faces inches apart, feeling Rebecca's rapid breaths on her mouth as she waited for her response.

Chapter 20

Maya woke with a start, sitting bolt upright with her heart hammering in her chest. After a few seconds she recognised the heat of the sun shining in through the open window and blinked wildly against it, wondering why she felt so naked and alone.

Rebecca.

She looked down at the bed beside her, knowing that it was empty before she did, but her heart fell anyway. She flopped back down and gazed out of the window. She deserved that, she supposed. She just didn't think that Rebecca would be that vindictive. She rolled onto her side with a heavy sigh, cursing herself for having been so stupid as to let the woman in again, her eyes flicking towards the bathroom in surprise as she heard the toilet flush and water flowing into the sink.

After a few seconds the door opened and Rebecca reappeared, pausing nervously as she saw that Maya was awake.

"Hey, good morning," she murmured, her arms moving in front of her like she didn't know whether to cover herself or not.

"Good morning," Maya smiled, unable to control her face as the relief washed over her.

"I, er," Rebecca hovered around the bathroom, her cheeks reddening with embarrassment. "Is this...I can go if you…"

"Rebecca," Maya said softly, sitting up and holding out her hand. "Come back to bed. Please."

Slowly Rebecca crossed the small room and sat on the bed, looking so unsure that Maya inwardly cursed herself again. She ran her hand gently over Rebecca's back, running her fingers lightly up her neck as she leaned forward and kissed her.

"I may be an idiot but I'm not stupid."

"You realise that makes no sense," Rebecca laughed softly as she ran her hand through Maya's hair.

"It makes perfect sense to me," she smiled back, holding up the covers and pulling the other woman under them. "And I have no intention of making the same mistake twice."

"So, what do you want to do now?"

"I can think of a few things," Maya smirked, running her hand over Rebecca's body.

"Yeah, me too," she murmured, her gaze dropping to Maya's lips as she licked her own, before she shook her head and stopped Maya's hand. "But I wasn't talking about that and we have things to sort out today. In case you've forgotten we're about to depart on a trek through the rainforest, we can't waste the whole day in bed."

"I wouldn't exactly call it a waste," she said softly, kissing along Rebecca's jawline and down her neck as she trailed her hand lightly across her stomach.

"Maya…" Rebecca pleaded, her breath catching. "You know what that does to me."

"I know," she smiled against her neck.

"So stop. We need to get up."

"In a minute."

Four hours later they sat in the restaurant at Rebecca's hotel with the rest of the group going over the route Felipe had marked out for them and highlighting the most likely points in the journey for communicating back to Candace and Vanessa. If their plotting was correct the longest period of time with no contact would be two days, days five and six. Felipe had warned them not to advertise that they had means to contact the town when they were with the tribe so that would rule out day three as well, unless they had a chance to stop somewhere during the day.

"It's unlikely, though," Maya said studying the route. "Day three is the longest day we will have done. Let's put it as a possible black spot."

"It should be fine, I don't see us having anything to report back by then anyway." Rebecca agreed from the other side of the table. "How did you guys feel about carrying the kit yesterday?"

"Yeah, it wasn't too bad," Phil said. "Shoulders are a bit sore today but a lot better than I expected. I hate to have to say it but Tom did a good job."

"What was that? Did you just compliment me on something?" Tom smirked. "It's alright, dude, you can say it. You're cute when you blush."

"I would like you all to bear witness to the reason I don't compliment him often." Phil gestured at the group, shaking his head wearily.

"Alright, if we can move on from the uncomfortable bromance and back to the task at hand," Maya said, smiling in spite of herself as she turned the page. "After we leave the tribe there is this area here where I guess the stones will be. You see the distance he has put in for us is much shorter than the day before, shorter even than day one, so I am assuming he's leaving us time to explore the area."

"But you don't think we'll be able to get a signal there?" Phil asked.

"If it's the right place I highly doubt it. Claudia and I scoured this area online and saw nothing so if it's there it's well enough hidden from view that it can't be picked up by satellite, which most likely means it's covered by a thick canopy."

"Right. But our camp for the night will allow us to send back what we find?"

"Yes, it's on higher ground. But, assuming we find anything, we may not camp there."

"Why not?" Tom asked with a frown.

"Because what we hope to find is a pointer to the next location," Rebecca explained. "And that location will probably not be along Felipe's route."

"Okay, so days five and six might not be black spots then? If we change route?"

"Maybe not but whichever direction we head after day four, unless it's back, will lead us into this valley, so I would say that we leave it as most likely no contact." Maya said, pointing out the area on the map.

"So basically what we're saying is that after day four all bets are off?" Phil asked. "The route we've filed will be totally irrelevant?"

"Pretty much, yeah."

"And this Felipe guy is alright with that?"

"Well, he doesn't exactly know about it."

"Right," he smiled and leaned back in his chair. "So what if he says no?"

"Then we're on our own."

"We're on our own?" Phil glanced at Rebecca then back to Maya, his voice slightly raised. "I thought the whole point of getting a guide was so that we wouldn't be on our own? Because we haven't got a fucking clue what we're up against out there?"

"Ah, what Maya is trying to say is that whilst we will do everything in our power to convince him," Claudia interrupted with a nervous glance around the half empty room. "If the worst comes to the worst we will continue on alone. We have already put in the groundwork for various different routes using the information we have, located several areas of high ground that should make for good communication and vantage points, and once we have the information from the first marker it will be much easier to plot a new route and convince the guide to follow it."

"And if he won't?"

"Then we communicate the new route to these guys and go on without him." Maya shrugged, gesturing at Vanessa and Candace.

"But, of course, we hope it won't come to that," Claudia said, shooting a meaningful look at her friend and rolling her eyes when she simply shrugged again.

"Candace, Vanessa, are you guys all set up here?" Rebecca asked.

"Yes, I think so," Candace replied, glancing at Vanessa who was, as usual, seemingly preoccupied with an entirely different set of events. "I've secured our contacts back home for if you find anything we can't handle here and I am due to meet Madelena on Sunday morning."

"Excellent. I will see her this afternoon and I think you should come with me, see where we are up to and what we think will happen next."

"Okay."

"So, Phil, Tom, if you could get the rest of the supplies while Candace and I meet with Madelena," Rebecca asked. "Then I guess just get some rest before tomorrow. Vanessa...Vanessa?"

"Hmm?"

"If you could just check through one last time and make sure you have all you need?"

"Aw, it's all good, Becca, don't you worry about me," she smiled broadly.

"Actually I'm more worried about us so please just check for me?" Rebecca asked with a tight smile.

"Sure thing, lady."

"Alright," she turned to Claudia, then to Maya, a slight blush creeping into her cheeks as she did. "So you two are going to work on alternate routes some more?"

"Yeah," Maya replied, the corner of her mouth twitching. "I thought maybe we could do it here. You know, with your fancy equipment?"

"Good idea," she nodded, pulling her eyes away quickly. "Tom, could you show them around please?"

"Sure," he drawled, smiling at Claudia.

"Um, maybe you guys should just check out of your hotel and stay here tonight?" Rebecca said, glancing at Maya before continuing quickly. "On me, of course. By which I mean I'll pay. For the room. Rooms. You know. Obviously."

"Yeah, sounds good," Maya cut in, trying desperately not to laugh at the hole Rebecca was talking herself into. "You alright with that, Claudia?"

"Definitely," Claudia said, looking pointedly at Maya. "The facilities at ours are awful and the walls are incredibly thin."

Maya's eyes shot up to meet her friend's, realisation washing over her as Claudia raised her eyebrow and turned to smile sweetly at Rebecca.

"Oh...okay then," Rebecca attempted to smile back, her face bright red as she turned to her bemused friends. "Shall we get on with it?"

They all stood up and gathered their various belongings before leaving the table, Vanessa wandering out towards the pool, Candace chatting to Phil as he shot Rebecca a suspicious look, Tom inviting Claudia to see the various pieces of equipment they had upstairs with a suggestive smirk. Rebecca watched them all leave and sat back down with a groan, covering her face with her hands.

"Smooth, Bronstein," Maya smirked down at her as she gathered her papers. "Very smooth."

"Oh, God, don't," she moaned. "That was so embarrassing. Do you think they realised?"

"If they didn't then I'm not sure how comfortable I feel going into the jungle with them," she laughed. "And you know you just kind of called me a whore?"

"Jesus, I'm pathetic!" Rebecca cried, throwing her hands up dramatically. "I bet even Vanessa noticed."

"Hey, don't beat yourself up," she chuckled, slipping into the next seat and rubbing Rebecca's back softly. "Vanessa is surprising perceptive about these things. She called me on it back in San Esteban."

"Really?"

"Yup," she shook her head as she thought back to the extremely awkward conversation, her hand drifting up to Rebecca's neck, fingers tracing patterns around her nape. "She probably didn't actually notice your little meltdown cos she assumed we've been doing it since then."

"Maya," Rebecca said shakily, her eyes looking slightly drunk. "You need to stop that or I'm going to embarrass myself even more."

"What?" Maya asked innocently, leaning closer and drawing the tip of her finger lightly across the back of her neck. "This?"

"Jesus," she whispered, her eyes falling closed, her breath shallow. Maya closed the gap between them and kissed her softly, smiling when Rebecca's eyes stuttered opened as she pulled away and held out her hand.

"Come on," Maya smiled as she stood up, pulling a shaky Rebecca with her. "Show me what you got."

"What?" Rebecca asked, coming out of her stupor slightly.

"Your equipment?"

"My what?"

"Your tech, Rebecca," Maya laughed at her wide eyed expression and put a hand on her back to guide her out of the room. "Honestly, such a filthy mind for such a proper young lady."

Maya grabbed a slice of pizza out of the box and moaned slightly as she shoved it into her mouth.

"God, this is so good. I'm starving."

"I bet," Claudia smirked at her as she jotted down some coordinates in her notebook. "Worked up quite an appetite, did we?"

"You're one to talk," she muttered, throwing her a filthy look. "At least I didn't miss an important meeting."

"No, just held it up for several hours," Claudia shot back. "And at least I didn't wake you up with my...shenanigans. Honestly, Maya, I thought you were being attacked! You're lucky I didn't break down the door."

"Alright, alright," she laughed, throwing a bit of pizza crust at her friend. "So what have we got?"

"Apart from sunburn from having to walk the streets since eight o'clock this morning?" Claudia smirked, sweeping the crumbs from herself and moving closer. "A few possible sites on this ridge here if we follow route A. Route B is a little trickier and we'll be lucky if we reach high ground by the end of day seven. I can't see any clearings along it either, unless we veer off to the south."

"How far south?"

"Ten miles?"

"No, it's too far," Maya shook her head and grabbed another slice. "If we do that we're almost doubling back on ourselves."

"Agreed," Claudia pulled the book back and made a note by the route. "So, route B leaves us dark for most likely three days."

"Not great but maybe we'll get lucky."

"I could make a comment," Claudia sucked in a deep breath and spread her arms. "Nope, I have chosen to rise above it."

"Very impressive, Claud, I'm proud of you," Maya muttered, clapping her hands sarcastically. "Route C?"

"I'm really hoping it's not route C."

"Why not?"

"Because route C splits off from route B at the end of day 5 and continues along the valley floor to the west," Claudia set the map on the floor between them and drew the line with her finger. "This is where our original route was meant to go and here is where Felipe said the, er, unfriendly tribe was."

"Hmm, pretty close."

"Yes, that's one way to put it. Another way would be to say that if we follow route C we would be setting up camp within five miles of a potentially hostile tribe on days six and seven, having been out of contact with the rest of the world for two days and unlikely to regain contact for at least one more."

"Why six and seven?" Maya frowned down at the map. "Surely we can go further than that on day six? How far is that?"

"It's ten miles but look at the gradient. And that is the best route I can find once we break off from B, it starts to get steeper again after this point."

"Alright, well let's hope it's not route C. Although…"

"What?" Claudia asked, eyeing her friend suspiciously as Maya pulled out the prints Rebecca had made of the pictures from the cave.

"I'm just thinking," Maya rifled through them until she found the one she was looking for, holding it up for her friend to see. "Where better to find steep stone steps?"

"Good point, dramatically made." Claudia shrugged and reached for the pizza. "I'd still rather avoid the people trying to kill us with poison darts."

"Nice stereotype, Claud. This isn't Apocalypto you know."

"Of course not," she scoffed. "Apocalypto was about the Mayans. We're way too far south."

"You're ridiculous." Maya laughed, flicking through the photos.

"And you are in an awfully good mood," Claudia smiled, nudging her with her foot. "I'm glad to see it."

"Shut up," she muttered with another laugh, kicking her gently in reply. "Come on, let's get on with this. I don't want to be stuck in here with you all night."

"Yes, I bet."

"As if there isn't somewhere you'd rather be as well?"

"That is very true," Claudia conceded, putting down her pizza and going back to the map. "Let's crack on."

Later on Maya decided to make use of the facilities as Tom had returned with all the supplies and she suddenly felt very much like the third wheel in the room. Rebecca was still out at her meeting and they had not yet sorted out the sleeping arrangements so she went for a swim whilst she waited, the conditions in the pool decidedly less stressful than the last time she had swum and her choice of outfit much more suitable for a public setting.

The water calmed her nerves as she completed length after length. She was dealing with the situation infinitely better than she had the last time she had slept with Rebecca but that didn't change the fact that she was unnerved by the turn of events. Last night, and this morning, had been amazing and honestly she was hoping that Rebecca's offer of getting her a room had been for show and that they would be spending tonight together, but that in itself was giving her pause. This was definitely not the kind of thing she did.

But then again, why not? It wasn't like anything had to be decided right now. This was a highly unusual situation and once it was over and done with she could deal with the ramifications in a more normal environment. She realised then that she was being extremely arrogant, maybe Rebecca wasn't looking for anything either, maybe this was all just stress relief to her, a bit of a distraction whilst she tried to solve her parent's disappearance. Either way, there was nothing she could do about it now, there was no way she could repeat her actions from last time and she realised that she didn't want to.

She stopped at the end of the pool, folding her arms on the edge and resting her chin on them, breathing hard in the warm night air. Tomorrow they would begin their journey, that was what she should be focussing on. If the routes she and Claudia had mapped out had shown them anything it was that they were most likely heading into the unknown with no way of contacting the outside world for far longer periods of time than they had initially thought.

"Hey," Rebecca smiled down at her as she walked over. "I wondered where you were. I tried calling you."

"I just got the urge to...well, swim. Obviously." Maya smiled back, pulling herself out of the pool and definitely not missing the way Rebecca's eyes travelled over her body appreciatively as she did so. "So, how was Madelena?"

"Not great. She thinks she might have found something but she wants to check it out properly before she tells me fully."

"Shit, really?" Maya frowned as she grabbed her towel off the chair and dried her hair. "She does realise we're leaving tomorrow?"

"Yes, but she says there's nothing to indicate that they're here, just that they might have been," she sighed and folded her arms. "She says we should go and she'll get the information together by the time we make our first contact. I guess it makes sense. I just wish I knew."

"I'm sorry, that sucks." Maya wrapped her towel around herself and pulled her into a hug, kissing the top of her head gently. "Do you need me to do anything?"

"This is good," Rebecca smiled. "Although you know how I feel about you in a towel."

"Hmm, I vaguely remember you having some thoughts on the subject last night."

"Vaguely? Maybe we should go upstairs so I can reiterate them."

"Well I would but I don't exactly have a room, so…"

"Oh, right," Rebecca pulled away, a small frown creasing her brow. "Sorry, I, er, I said I would get you guys some rooms sorted. Come on, I'll…"

"I think Claudia is okay, actually," Maya said quickly as Rebecca moved towards the hotel.

"Oh?"

"Yeah, I left her in Tom's room with our stuff and she looked pretty settled for the night."

"Right, so just you then."

"Unless…"

"Unless?" Rebecca asked hopefully, turning to look up at her.

"Well, you know I did let you crash in my room last night," she shrugged. "Maybe you could return the favour."

"I think I would be okay with that."

Chapter 21

Maya stood in front of the dolphin archway and contemplated the words there. 'Vuelva Siempre'. She sent up a silent prayer that they would, after all they were headed into a dangerous world, one that for all her assurances to Felipe none of them were adequately prepared for. She knew she was being reckless and she was okay with that, reckless was kind of how she operated, but the rest of her team...well, she had never been in this situation before and, given the option, she wouldn't be now had time not been so much of the essence.

She walked through the arch and down to the water's edge. She only wished they had time to prepare properly. She felt sure that the RGS would have information that would help them immensely but there was no time for that. As much as Rebecca was putting a brave face on things Maya knew that she was becoming increasingly concerned as time went on and that the news she had been receiving from her investigators, both back home and here in Brazil, was not doing anything to ease her worry.

At some point during the previous night Rebecca had shared with her some of the information she had been able to gather and it did not look good. Apparently they had found some evidence at her parent's office that suggested a link to Martin Amaric, a very unscrupulous character within their world who, despite never officially undertaking any kind of expedition, had managed to get his hands on several well known artefacts thought lost forever. Although numerous investigations had been centred on the man and his activities nothing had ever been proven and he continued on, several antique dealerships in his name providing a perfect cover, and no one willing to come forward to dispute any of his claims as to where he had acquired such rare objects.

Maya had emailed Elaine whilst Rebecca was in the shower and told her that there may be a connection, not wanting to divulge too much of what Rebecca had shared as it wasn't her business, but not wanting to disappear off into the unknown without informing her employer of the potential risk either. So here she was, standing literally on the edge of the most important and dangerous expedition of her life, without the faintest idea of how it would pan out. Would they find Rebecca's parents? The missing Inca city? Would they make it out?

"Hey," Rebecca said from behind her. "You okay?"

"Yeah," she sighed staring across the water into the forest on the other side. "Just, you know, getting in the zone."

"Oh, sorry, I'll just leave…"

"No," Maya interrupted, surprising them both. "Stay."

"Okay," she said softly after a few seconds, moving closer to her.

"How about you?" Maya asked, playing with a piece of grass as she glanced nervously at her. "You doing okay? Are you ready for this?"

Rebecca gave her a strange little half smile and ran a hand through her hair. "As much as I can be I guess. I mean, the timing is not great but sometimes you just have to go for it and hope for the best, right?"

"Ah, yeah," she answered, once again not entirely sure if they were talking about the same thing. "Well, Felipe seems to know what he's doing and this is the perfect time of year, climate wise, so at least we have that."

"Yes. And we have you and Claudia. I'd say we're looking pretty good given the speed with which we've been forced to throw this thing together."

"And what about them?" Maya asked, tipping her head in the direction of Rebecca's team. "Do you think they'll be okay?"

"I would say so," Rebecca nodded firmly as she watched Phil and Candace saying their goodbyes. "They're good guys, you know? Up for a challenge but not too impetuous."

"Alright."

"How did you and Claudia get on yesterday?" Rebecca asked as she took a step closer and flicked her hair over her shoulder with a wry smile. "I, er, didn't get a chance to ask you last night."

"Oh, you didn't get a chance?" Maya chuckled softly. "Really?"

"Well, I was a little distracted."

"Hmm, I can't say I blame you," she smirked. "There were more interesting things going on."

"That's one way to put it," she dropped her eyes as a faint blush rose in her cheeks and she moved closer again. "But now that I have regained my focus did you find anything?"

"We planned a few routes that could work for us but it's like before, we won't really know til we get out there," she shrugged and turned to look back across the river. "We, ah, did maybe find a likely area for the steps, but it's, ah…"

"What?"

"It just keeps us below the communication line for longer than we would like," she finished quickly. No point in bringing up their major concern until they had to. Rebecca gave her a strange look but nodded silently and folded her arms as she turned to follow Maya's gaze, now standing so close that she could feel the heat radiating from her body. They stood together by the water, looking out into the trees and silently thinking about what lay ahead. Maya closed her eyes and took a breath, holding it in as she let her mind clear itself and focus on the task at hand.

"Good morning, ladies," Felipe's voice broke through her reverie. "Are we ready to begin?"

"As we'll ever be," Maya replied, turning to face him with a smile as she practically leapt away from Rebecca. "How does it look?"

"Very good," he smiled back. "The weather pattern looks set to hold and there have been no concerning reports from the area over the last few weeks."

"Ah, concerning?" Phil asked cautiously as he joined the group.

"Animal attacks, hostile activity," Felipe shrugged and gazed up at the sky. "That kind of thing."

"Great," Phil smiled tightly, pulling at the straps on his back pack.

"Anyway," Rebecca said, way too brightly, as she rolled on the balls of her feet. "Shall we get going?"

"Absolutely," Felipe smiled and wandered off towards the boat.

"You okay, Phil?" Rebecca asked, stepping towards him and rubbing his arm.

"Just great," he grimaced. "What could possibly go wrong? There have been no 'concerning reports', our 'route' is logged and approved, and our guide seems as laid back and observant as Vanessa."

"Sounds good to me," Maya shrugged. "Let's get on with it."

"Lead the way," he sighed, extending his arm towards the boat.

They had been walking for four hours down a relatively clear and easy path. Felipe had explained that they were following the route the tribe used to get back and forth to the town and although Maya was pleased that the route for their first day was easy she couldn't help but wonder if they were missing anything. She supposed that if there was anything of interest in the area so close to the town it would have been spotted and documented by now though so she followed their guide in silence, eyes scanning the terrain for any signs that could be of use. The group was quiet, the silence broken periodically by a slap and a curse as the local bugs launched stealth attacks on exposed pieces of skin. Felipe led the way followed by Maya, Claudia and Tom, Rebecca and Phil bringing up the rear.

The temperature had been climbing steadily all day and the pressure under the canopy was intense, like walking through a steam room with a small child strapped to your back. The vines and foliage were low hanging and so thick the light was struggling to get through. There was a steamy vapour coming off the trees and ground and the unfamiliar calls of various animals made the whole journey feel like they had wandered into some kind of alien planet. Maya could only imagine what it would be like in the summer season.

"Shit," Tom swore softly as he slapped at his neck again. "I swear to God some sort of bug memo went out. They are definitely biting me more than the rest of you."

"Probably," Maya shrugged back at him. "Is your blood type O?"

"Yeah, why?"

"Mosquitos prefer it. They also prefer guys over girls. Except if they're pregnant which none of us are," she glanced at Claudia. "As far as we know."

"Okay, but why aren't they biting Phil?" Tom huffed, missing the sneer that Claudia shot at her friend.

"Type A, bro," he called cheerfully.

"Also, you're bigger than he is, so you're giving off more heat," Maya smirked as she ducked under a branch.

"Damn right I am."

"Just be thankful you didn't get drunk last night, they'd eat you alive," Rebecca pointed out.

Maya swung her bag off one shoulder and pulled a small bottle out of the side pocket, passing it back to Tom as she continued on. "Try this."

"Jesus," he said in surprise as he sprayed it on his arms and neck. "It smells like lemons."

"That's cos it's basically lemon juice," she laughed. "They don't like it. Your blood will have to be really good for them to fight through that."

"Cool, thanks."

"No problem, Tex."

They walked on in silence for a while, the heat of the day and effort of traversing the unfamiliar terrain dissuading them from idle chatter, which Maya appreciated greatly. She looked about her as she went, trying to tune into her surroundings, and watched Felipe closely to see if there were any navigation techniques she could pick up from him. For all Rebecca and Claudia's reassurances to the rest of the group she needed to be prepared in case when the time came to tell Felipe of their plans he would want no part of it and they were left on their own. If it came to that Maya wanted to be as prepared as she could with only four days to learn their environment.

So far, though, their guide just seemed to be wandering through the forest without a care in the world which led her to believe that this was a route he had taken many times and therefore had no need to check the area for directional markers. If that was the case from here to the tribe's village then she would have no option but to ask him to teach her how to read the landscape and that was not something she enjoyed doing. Still, this time it wasn't just her and Claudia muddling their way through, there would be three other people relying on her, so she would just have to suck it up.

"You okay?" Claudia asked as she fell into step beside her.

"Yeah, I'm good. Just thinking."

"I can tell, your frown is so deep I could park a bike between your eyebrows."

"Nice image, Claud," she chuckled. "Not at all psychotic."

"You know what I mean," Claudia laughed. "Your bitchy resting face is out in full force."

"Great."

"Anything I can help with?"

"Not really, just trying to get to grips with…well, this," she gestured around her with a sigh.

"You'll get it," Claudia said with a nod. "And, er, last night? Everything okay?"

"Yeah, really good," Maya grabbed the straps of her backpack, a smile tugging at her lips. "You?"

"Yes, good, thanks," she answered, a similar smile on her own face. "I'm not sure that Phil is overly thrilled to be suddenly trekking through the rainforest with two couples."

"Hey, woah, we're not a couple," Maya said quickly.

"Oh, calm down, Maya, I just meant with everyone having sex," she huffed. "But good to know you're still, well, you."

"Whatever," Maya rolled her eyes and tugged on her straps.

Claudia looked over her shoulder to check the distance before speaking quietly. "Did you tell her about route C?"

"No."

"Are you going to?"

"I will if it comes to it. No point in telling her beforehand, is there?"

"I suppose not, I just…" Claudia looked back again as she thought how to phrase her statement. "I just think the earlier she is aware of it, the more time she will have to make a balanced decision. Spring it on her once it's inevitable, the more likely she is to just jump in."

"Well if it's inevitable there's no choice to be made, Claud."

"Except on whether or not to turn back."

Maya's glanced up at her friend briefly before turning her attention back to the path ahead. She had only known Rebecca for a matter of weeks but she was fairly certain that there was nothing on earth that would ever cause her to make the decision to turn back.

At around 7.30 Felipe brought the group to a halt as they reached the area he had marked to set up camp. Once the tents were all up they gathered round the campfire and prepared their meal in relative silence, their bodies and minds tired from the day's walk. There was a brief animated moment when Tom pulled out a cast iron skillet to start cooking their meal on and Phil questioned why he had brought one of the heaviest pieces of cooking equipment known to man along on a trek through the rainforest. The discussion died down quick enough when Phil became too tired to continue his incredulity and Tom pointed out that he was the one carrying it and Phil should just get over it. As she grabbed her food Maya noticed Felipe gazing around the group thoughtfully. She took a seat next to him and looked at them all, trying to see what he was seeing. As she sat he turned and smiled at her, raising his cup as he did.

"Successful first day, no?"

"Well, we made it," she smiled back. "So I guess that's a win."

"You are right," he nodded. "That is all we hope for in this kind of endeavour. Everything else is a bonus."

"That's a little bleaker than I would have put it but, yeah," she laughed and tore a piece of bread, putting it in her mouth as she felt his eyes settle on her.

"You have never been to the rainforest before."

"What makes you say that?" Maya turned and met his gaze, trying to work out what was going through his mind.

"A feeling," he waved his hand and turned back to his food. "Through the meetings you let the others lead but the questions you asked suggested experience in exploration. Today you kept your eyes on me, and your approach changed as we walked, like you were trying to learn the landscape through me. It makes me wonder."

"It makes you wonder what?" Maya queried, her eyes narrowing.

"What it is that you hope to achieve out here," he answered, smiling enigmatically.

She looked around the group again and ate some of her food, her eyes drifting up to the forest as she contemplated his words. Apparently he was not as oblivious as Phil had thought, not that she had ever agreed with the man's assumption of him. She would never have entrusted her life to someone that she didn't credit with a certain amount of intelligence. But how to respond? Knowing someone suspected an ulterior motive was one thing, but confirming it was something else entirely. That required trust and trust had to be earned.

"You're right," she shrugged. "I've never been out here before. I like to discover new places and I like to know how to navigate them. You seem to know what you're doing, at least I hope so or what are we paying you for?"

"A good point," he laughed. He took a sip of his water as he looked at her. "But you didn't answer my question."

She fixed her gaze on him. "What was it you were hoping to achieve when you first came out here?"

Felipe smiled and set his cup on the floor. "A deeper understanding of where my people came from I suppose. An appreciation of the land and how it has shaped our history."

"And did you find it?"

"In part. But there is so much left to be uncovered. I am not sure we will ever fully understand."

"Agreed," she said with a rueful smile. "I don't think we're capable."

They ate in silence for a while, the unfamiliar sounds of the forest a strangely perfect soundtrack to the thoughts spinning through her head. As she looked up she met Rebecca's eyes, a tired smile on her face. She smiled back and raised her cup before taking a sip.

"Tomorrow will be harder I think," Felipe said as he set his plate on the ground. "The path will still be fairly clear as we are following a well travelled route but there may be some things I can show you if you like?"

"That would be great, Felipe, thank you," she smiled.

"And maybe then we can have a further discussion on your motivations."

She shot him a look from the corner of her eye as he stood up and wandered over to clear off his plate. After a few seconds Rebecca took his place, smiling over at him as he lit a cigarette.

"Everything alright?" she asked quietly.

"Yeah, fine," Maya smiled, finishing her water. "He just knows we're not being completely honest with him."

"Oh?" Rebecca scratched her jaw, glancing out into the forest in an apparent effort to look casual. "Do you think it will be a problem?"

"Not sure yet," she shrugged and mopped up the rest of her food with her bread. "Maybe, maybe not. Could actually work in our favour."

"How so?"

"Well, if he thinks we're lying and he still brought us out here then he is obviously more interested in the money and we can use that."

"I suppose you're right but it still makes me feel a little uneasy," Rebecca sighed. "Anyway, problems for another day."

"Yup."

"So we sorted out the sleeping arrangements," she said quickly, tossing her hair over her shoulder. "Tom and Claudia wanted to share…"

Maya scoffed. "You will note my complete lack of surprise."

"And, er, Phil has agreed to bunk in with Felipe so that leaves you with me, if that's okay with you?"

"I think I would be okay with that," she said, turning to face her with a smile. "I guess you're okay with my snoring at this point?"

"I can deal with it," Rebecca laughed softly. "Alright, well I'm going to wash up. I'll see you in there?"

"Great."

Rebecca stepped over the log they were sitting on, using Maya's shoulder as a support and giving it a squeeze as she went. Maya watched her leave and then shook her head, mentally chastising herself for behaving like a moony teenager, and reached into her bag for her notes. Her hand knocked against Zuazola's journal and she looked down at it with a frown, a strange feeling hitting her suddenly that she had missed something. She closed her fingers around it and went to pull it out but stopped halfway, an unexpected paranoia creeping into her. She turned her head and saw Felipe leaning against a tree smoking at the edge of the camp. He smiled broadly at her and waved so she pulled her hand from the bag and waved back, huffing out a laugh as she told herself she was being ridiculous. Still, she left the journal in the bag and pulled out her own notebook instead, reading back over everything they had gathered so far in the hopes that something useful would jump out at her.

Chapter 22

The next morning Maya woke up and rubbed her eyes as she peered around the tent. The door was open with the bug screen still in place and the sounds of the forest outside reminded her of where she was. She stretched as she sat up, noticing as she did so that she was alone in the tent, and pushed out of her sleeping bag as she crawled towards the door.

Phil, Rebecca and Claudia were seated around the fire eating breakfast and chatting quietly amongst themselves, the other two nowhere to be seen. She opened up the tent and climbed out into the clearing, stretching her hands above her head and cracking her neck.

"Good morning, starshine," Claudia greeted her with unnecessary cheerfulness. "Coffee?"

Maya grunted in response as she moved towards the group, rubbing her eyes as she accepted the offered cup gratefully and sat down next to Rebecca. The coffee was hot, strong and bitter and she let out a happy sigh as it worked its way through her system.

"Sleep well?"

"Yeah, I guess so," Maya yawned. "Don't remember waking up."

"You were late getting to bed last night," Rebecca said before blowing on her coffee. "Find anything interesting?"

"Bits and pieces," she shrugged, hunching over and digging her toes into the forest floor. "You were dead to the world."

"Well, I haven't been getting much sleep recently," Rebecca said quietly, trying to keep a straight face as Maya nearly choked on her coffee.

Maya coughed into her hand and nudged her playfully with her knee, trying to ignore Claudia's eyes flicking between the two of them whilst

Phil stared up into the canopy like it held the secrets of the universe. Thankfully at that moment Felipe wandered out of the brush and greeted them all warmly.

"We should probably leave within the next half hour," he said as he glanced at his watch.

"Of course," Rebecca stood up and threw the remnants of her coffee into the fire. "Claudia, can you wake Tom while we start striking camp? Maya, you should maybe get dressed?"

She looked down at herself in alarm and, after giving a small sigh of relief as she saw that she was suitably covered, she smiled up at Rebecca and nodded her head.

"Sure, give me five minutes and I'll pack up."

"Thanks," she smiled back and headed over with Phil to start gathering up their belongings.

They had been walking for six hours when Felipe called a halt for lunch, their progress much slower than the previous day as the terrain became more difficult and their limbs started to feel the effects of the unfamiliar strain. Maya could tell that Felipe was becoming concerned by their pace even though he said nothing.

"Everything alright?" she asked casually as she sat down next to Phil. He had been bringing up the rear all day and he looked exhausted.

"Fine. You?"

"Yeah, I'm good. Couldn't help but notice you're looking a bit tired, though."

"We all look tired, Maya," he said sullenly. "We're marching through the Amazon."

"Yeah, but, ah," she looked around the group as she weighed her next words carefully. "Some of us seem to be handling it better than others."

"Look, what do you want me to say?" Phil turned to face her, his eyes angry. "I'm doing my best and I will continue to push myself. I just need to adjust, alright?"

"Alright," she held her hand up in apology and turned her attention back to her food. "Just checking in."

"Yeah, well, go check in with someone else," he muttered, setting his plate down on the floor and pushing himself up. "I'm going for a piss."

Phil strode off into the trees, pushing branches angrily out of his way as he went, crashing through the undergrowth like an angry bear. Maya watched him leave and hoped idly that he didn't disturb anything as he went. She really didn't want to have to deal with the aftermath if he did.

"What was that about?" Rebecca asked as she sat down beside her.

"Nothing, just checking he was okay."

"Oh. That explains the storm off then."

"What do you mean?"

"He tends to get a little angry with himself when he's not doing as well as he thinks he should be," she explained as she ate. "You confirming that to him would have made it even worse."

"Well it's not like I said anything bad."

"Bad?" Rebecca cocked her head with a small smile. "Or bad for you?"

"What the fuck is that supposed to mean?"

"Oh, come on, Maya," she chuckled as she ran her hand up her leg. "You're not exactly the most tactful of people."

"Yeah? Well maybe sometimes…"

Maya's retort was cut short by a scream of pain from the jungle and she immediately flung down her plate, grabbing her machete from her pack as she ran in the direction Phil had gone.

"Phil!" she yelled, vaulting over a fallen tree trunk and hacking at vines blocking her path. "Where are you?"

"I'm over here," he called back, his voice shaky. "Fuck!"

She spotted him seconds later, hobbling towards her as he clutched his leg, blood rolling down his calf. Maya grabbed his other arm and pulled it around her shoulders, supporting his weight as they headed as quickly as possible out of the trees. Felipe and Rebecca were not far behind her and Felipe grabbed his other arm as Rebecca cleared their path.

"What the fuck happened?" Maya asked, her heart still racing.

"Fucking snake," he said weakly, fear and pain contorting his face. "I stood on it and it bit me. Fuck, I'm going to fucking die."

"Of course you're not going to die, don't be such a drama queen," she chuckled as they broke back out of the forest into the clearing and sat him down on a log.

"You don't know that!" Phil yelled. "I don't even know what kind of snake it was!"

"Whatever it was it wasn't venomous, so calm down," she said, inspecting the wound as Felipe rummaged in his bag for a first aid kit.

"Again, you can't possibly know that!"

"You're bleeding, Phil," she sighed as she began to clean out the wound. "If the bite was venomous there would be no blood, the area would already be numb and would be starting to turn blue, so calm down, have a drink and let us clean you up."

"She is right," Felipe said calmly as Claudia appeared with a small bottle of rum. "It will be painful, especially with all the walking, but you will be fine."

"Christ," Phil muttered after a big swig of alcohol. "As if I wasn't slow enough already."

"Well, look on the bright side," she smiled up at him as she wrapped the bandage around his leg. "At least now you have a legitimate reason for moving at a glacial pace."

"Fuck you, Maya," he chuckled. "And thank you. You know, for, ah, coming after me."

"Coming after you?" Maya stood up and wrinkled her nose. "I was just coming to tell you to stop being such a little bitch. I guess I'll have to wait now till you're feeling a little better or whatever."

"Great," he laughed. "Thanks for the heads up."

"No problem," she smiled and turned away. "Tex, get over here. We're going to have to divide up slowpoke's stuff now he's got himself bitten."

"Aw, man," Tom moaned as he grabbed hold of Phil's pack. "That means I'm gonna sweat more which means more mosquitoes, right?"

"The curse of your healthy manstink, my friend," Maya patted him on the shoulder with a sigh. "You're just going to have to suck it up."

Tom gave her a serious look and a grave nod of the head as he began removing the heavier articles from Phil's pack. She chuckled slightly and wandered back over to the trees to try and find a suitable stick for Phil to use as a crutch, glancing over her shoulder as she heard someone following.

"Can I help?" Rebecca asked.

"Ah, sure. We're looking for a sturdy stick about 5 foot, preferably with a fork at one end that he can lean on," she said with a cautious glance up. "Are you okay?"

"I was scared as hell when he started shouting," Rebecca said with a nervous laugh. "And of course I'm worried about him but not anywhere near as bad as I would have been if we'd been out here on our own. Thank you, you know, for helping him."

"No problem," she answered uncomfortably, redirecting her focus to the ground.

"And I'm sorry about what I said. It was unnecessary."

"You were probably right," she shrugged. "I'm not exactly the best when it comes to talking."

"You are when you want to be," Rebecca said quietly as she pulled a decent looking stick out of the brush. "And what you said to him back there was exactly what he needed to hear. I'm so grateful you agreed to come with us."

"Ah, yeah, sure," she muttered, inspecting the stick and deciding that it would do. She turned and headed back to the others.

"Um, are we okay?" Rebecca asked as she followed.

"Yeah, of course. Why wouldn't we be?"

"You just seem a little uncomfortable."

"I'm just not very good with gratitude." Maya said, focussing her attention on stripping the leaves from the stick.

"Yeah, I get that," she said quietly, putting a hand on her shoulder to stop her before they reached the others. "It's not too much, this…you know. You and me. Out here."

"No, it's fine."

"Oh, God," Rebecca sighed, turning away and running her hands through her hair. "Please don't say it's fine."

"What?" Maya frowned, thoroughly confused by what was happening. "Why not?"

"Because that's what you say when you're lying!" she said as she turned back and threw her hands up.

"Is it?"

"Yes! Every time!"

Maya stared at the stick as she considered the validity of this statement, then shrugged and approached the woman pacing nervously in front of her. "Maybe that is what I say when I'm lying, but not exclusively," she said as she threw the stick on the ground and put her arms around Rebecca's neck. "Honestly? I was a little worried about it before we started, but now that we're here it just feels… I don't know how else to say it other than fine, I'm sorry."

"It's okay," she smiled as she kissed her. "You said it fine."

"Does that mean you're lying?" Maya asked with a frown.

"No," Rebecca laughed as she bent down to retrieve the stick and pulled Maya back towards the others. "I don't have any tells."

"Good to know," she laughed as she wrapped her arms around Rebecca's waist and kissed her neck, an uneasy twinge in her gut at the words.

The rest of the day was slow going. Phil tried to keep his pace up but his leg was clearly bothering him and the rest of the group were feeling the effects of the previous day's exertions and the extra weight of Phil's divided baggage, minimal as it was between the five of them. Still, any additional stress was bound to cause issues and one of their party being bitten by a jungle predator, no matter that it was relatively harmless, had definitely taken its toll.

As the sun dropped beneath the horizon Felipe turned to Maya expectantly. She looked back at him with a shrug. The light was dim but they could still see for now. He pushed on, his pace slightly slower than before and his eyes shooting to the sky more often, his hand firmly on the handle of his machete like he was expecting to have to use it. Maya followed suit but keep her gaze at ground level, trusting their guide's judgement but wanting to cover all angles.

About thirty minutes after nightfall they came to a clearing and Felipe called a halt to their march. Quickly they set up camp and cooked their evening meal, everyone falling into their role with a weary precision. As they collected their food Felipe dropped into the seat next to Maya as he had the night before, his glances around the group more furtive this time.

"How bad is it?" Maya asked quietly.

"It depends on how tomorrow goes."

"Felipe," she murmured. "You don't know me so well but I'm pretty sure you've figured out I'm the practical one. How bad is it?"

"Tomorrow was planned as the toughest day," he sighed. "I was concerned about it as I was not sure of your group's capability. Based on your assurances I went with it."

"How short are we?"

"About two miles."

"So we planned to cover twenty miles tomorrow, today fifteen," Maya recalled as she stared down at her food. "Actually today we've covered thirteen…""

"More like twelve," he sighed.

"Which means we need to do twenty three tomorrow," she said, practically whispering as her gaze settled on Phil. "And one of us is injured."

"It is certainly not how I had hoped." Felipe shrugged.

"Is there somewhere we can camp before there?"

"There is," he nodded as he turned to look at her. "It is actually only about three hours walk from here. I had planned to camp there if today had gone better than expected, and where we could have stopped to check in on day three if not."

"I would like to think we can manage more than three hours, Felipe," she chuckled.

"I am sure that you can. I am not sure he can," he gestured at Phil. "As I said, it is a place where we can contact your friends and, more importantly, a place where we can call for him to be picked up."

Maya looked up at him, her mind whirling as she processed his words. "You think we should get him out?"

"This is not your world, Maya," Felipe shook his head with a smile. "In your world a scratch or a bite is treated and allowed to heal. In here even the smallest injury can summon death with alarming speed."

"Felipe…"

"I see your skill, Maya. Your knowledge, your aptitude, but even you do not know what it is that you face," he spooned the last of his food into his mouth and stared into the trees. "This is an unforgiving place and I would hate to be the cause of an unnecessary loss."

He stood up and wished her good night, heading over to wash up his bowl as the sounds of the rainforest replaced his quiet voice. Maya stared down at her own food, largely untouched, and thought it through. She saw the validity in his words but for the first time she didn't know what to do. If Claudia had been bitten she would have absolutely no qualms in dropping her off at the nearest safe haven and continuing on alone, no way would she put Claud at risk. But this wasn't her confidante, it was Rebecca's, and that meant it wasn't her decision. She glanced over at the brunette, sitting next to Phil and locked in deep conversation. She guessed that tonight would be the best time to discuss it, when they were alone in the tent, she just really didn't want to.

She shovelled a forkful of food into her mouth and looked up at the stars. The Pleiades, of course. She smiled as she tried to force some more food down, then stood up and wandered over to wash up her bowl and headed out into the forest to pee, taking care to sweep the area for local inhabitants before she did so.

Five minutes later she unzipped her tent and unrolled her sleeping bag, taking a moment to put Rebecca's in position before she undressed and crawled in. She lay there and listened to the sounds of the jungle, relishing the relative lack of bugs in the tent, and tried to work out how she would sell the idea of leaving Phil behind to Rebecca. Her thoughts were interrupted by the harsh sound of the zipper being pulled and Rebecca sliding through the gap with a sigh.

"Hey," she said tiredly as she pulled her tank top over her head.

"Hey. How's Phil?"

"He's okay," she sighed as she shimmied out of her shorts and into her sleeping bag. "A little sore, a little bummed out that he let everyone down."

"He hasn't let anyone down." Maya said slowly.

"He feels like he has," Rebecca zipped up her sleeping bag and turned to face her. "He's slowing us down. You know it, I know it, he certainly knows it."

"Yeah," she said quietly. "Felipe says there's a place about three hours out where we could get him picked up."

She felt Rebecca's eyes on her in the darkness and held her breath unconsciously as she awaited her response.

"Good," came the quiet answer. "It's safer that he gets out."

"Yeah, I agree," Maya sighed. "I'd hate for a simple bite to turn into something worse."

Rebecca made a small sound of agreement as she huddled up next to her and wrapped her arm around her waist. "I'll talk to him in the morning. Goodnight."

"Night," she said quickly, a little shocked at the lack of discussion. She wrapped her arm around Rebecca's shoulder and stared at the roof of the tent, her mind working through everything that had happened up until this point, and wondering why it felt like it was all about to change.

Chapter 23

The trip to the next camp ended up taking about five hours as Phil's leg was far worse than it had been the previous day, even with different members of the team helping him the sweat pouring off him from the exertion and excruciating pain left no one with any doubt that they were doing the right thing getting him out. They arrived at the place, a small farm, around midday and Phil was quickly escorted into a little hut where he was cleaned up, given painkillers and told in no uncertain terms to get some rest until help arrived.

Maya, Claudia and Tom set up their camp whilst Rebecca tried to contact Candace and Vanessa for an update and let them know about Phil and Felipe went to catch up with the farmer. When they were all done Tom and Claudia started to prepare lunch, laughing and shoving each other in an overly cute and loved up way that was, frankly, killing Maya's appetite to the point of nausea, so she headed off up the hill next to the camp in the hopes of stumbling across something interesting, or at least less sickening, and give them some privacy.

The climb quickly became fairly steep but she pushed on, her thighs burning slightly as she reached the top and was met with a breathtaking view of the valley below, the river shining from the bottom like a snake encrusted with diamonds. She stared down at it as she waited for her breathing to even out, a soft smile on her face as she realised how lucky she was to be seeing this. She turned her eyes to the right, taking in the winding path in the distance that Felipe had pointed out to her as they approached, the route they would take tomorrow as they got back on their way. He hadn't been joking when he said this would be the most challenging part.

Maya followed the path until it went out of sight, rising steadily for a few miles before levelling out and disappearing into the trees, and then she stared off into the distance as she wondered if they would really find their next marker out there. She had a strange feeling about it all, a sort of excited expectation tinged with a sense of foreboding that didn't sit well with her at all. She plucked some grass and rolled it between her fingers as she looked out at the alien landscape and tried to get herself in sync with it, breathing in its scents and sounds in the hopes of understanding it a little better.

As the sun reached it's highest point she turned with a sigh and headed back down the way she had come, her stomach growling as the smell of the food cooking drifted up from their camp as she approached.

"Just in time," Claudia greeted her. "See anything out there?"

"Not what we're looking for," she said quietly, smiling gratefully at Tom as he held a plate out to her. "Is Rebecca not back?"

"No, not yet."

Maya glanced off towards the farm and sat down to eat her food, frowning slightly as she wondered if it were a good thing or a bad thing that Rebecca had been talking to Candace and Vanessa for close to an hour. Maybe she had stopped in to see Phil on the way back? Claudia joined her and handed her some water.

"What are you thinking?"

"Nothing," she shrugged. "I guess Candace must have found something."

"Maybe," Claudia answered non-committally. "Maybe she's just not getting a connection."

"Yeah, maybe," she nodded, raising the cup and taking a swig. "How are you doing?"

"Better than I thought I would, actually," she laughed. "Yesterday was hard and I expected to be a bit sore today, but I seem to be okay."

"Tramp," Maya smirked, earning her a punch in the arm from her friend.

"You know that wasn't what I was talking about!"

"I'm not sure I do with how gross you two are acting," she laughed, nodding her head at Tom as he bent over the stove. "You're too cute, it makes me want to hurl."

"Oh, shut up," Claudia replied with a blush and a smile creeping onto her face. "Just because you and Rebecca have decided to be overly professional doesn't mean Tom and I can't have a bit of fun."

"Hey!" Maya said with a playful glare. "Just because we're not all over each other all the time doesn't mean we're not having any fun."

"Please," she scoffed. "If you two were having 'fun' none of us would get any sleep."

"Fuck off," she shot back with a tut. "We weren't that loud."

"Maya, I had to leave the hotel. And…"

"Hey," Rebecca said, appearing behind them suddenly. "Everything okay?"

"Fine," Maya answered at the same time as Claudia said "Nothing."

"Okay," Rebecca said slowly as she shifted her gaze between the two of them, a sceptical look on her face. "I'm going to grab some food."

Maya smiled at her as she walked off and then snapped her head round to her friend with a glare. "Look, I'm sorry we woke you up…"

"And kept me up, and caused me to have to leave," she whispered back.

"Whatever, I'm sorry I had loud sex in a hotel with paper thin walls, I was kind of in the moment, but will you please stop going on about it?"

"I've mentioned it twice, Maya."

"Three times, and that's at least two times too many if you ask me," she huffed.

"Fine," the redhead laughed as she cut up her food. "I won't mention it again."

"Thank you."

"Just remember canvas is even thinner."

Maya opened her mouth to fire off an angry retort but stopped herself as the other two made their way towards them, turning to Rebecca instead. "How'd it go?"

"Fine," she replied with a tight smile. "Candace is worried about Phil but relieved that he's coming back at least. They'll meet him at the hospital when he gets back."

"That's good."

"Yeah," Rebecca nodded, the fake smile still plastered on her face. "The equipment is all set up if you want to contact anyone?"

"Thanks," she smiled back, studying her face in an effort to work out what was wrong with her.

They ate in silence for a while and then discussed the plans for the next part of their journey. Felipe had suggested they stay where they were for the night as the plane couldn't get there until five and they wouldn't be able to make the next camp in that time. His only concern was that the weather was due to turn slightly worse tomorrow and he didn't know whether they would get caught up in it or if it would pass behind them. Still, none of them wanted to leave Phil behind until they knew he was safe so they had made the decision to wait.

"Have you seen Felipe?" Claudia asked Rebecca.

"No, not since he showed me where to set up," she answered with a shake of her head.

"Should we save him some food or do you think he'll eat with them?"

"I'm not sure," she said as she set her empty plate down and stood up. "I'm going to go and take some to Phil though, see if he's awake. Maybe save some for now and I'll see if I can find him."

"Okay," Claudia nodded gathering up their empty dishes and heading over to the makeshift cleaning area.

"Maya, want to come with me?"

"Sure," she answered, following Claudia over to clean up her plate as Rebecca got some food together for Phil.

When they were done she and Rebecca headed out of the camp. Maya glanced over her shoulder to make sure they were out of earshot of Tom and Claudia before she spoke again. "Are you okay?"

"Honestly? Not great," she said quietly. "I'm trying desperately to believe it's nothing to worry about, which is why I didn't want to mention it in front of the others, but Madalena didn't show up to her meeting with Candace and she hasn't answered her calls."

"Well that's not good," Maya answered with a frown. "Do you know where she lives?"

"No," Rebecca sighed. "Vanessa is trying to find out now. I'm hoping she is just following up a lead or something and hasn't been able to make contact. The meeting was only scheduled for this morning."

"Right, so no need to panic just yet."

"Exactly," she smiled, concern still clear in her eyes. "She's probably just in the thick of it and can't get away, right?"

"Yeah, I'm sure that's it." Maya smiled in a way that she hoped was reassuring, patting Rebecca's back for emphasis. "I'm sure she's fine."

"Maya," she laughed softly, turning to face her and putting her hand on her waist. "Has anyone ever told you that you are the worst liar ever?"

"Recently it seems to be all anyone has to say about me," she huffed, rolling her eyes and folding her arms across her stomach.

"Well, that's not true," Rebecca said softly, dropping her gaze and moving closer. "There are a few other things I've said about you recently as well."

"Yeah," Maya smirked. "I definitely preferred those."

"Oh yeah?"

"Yeah," she smiled as Rebecca looked up at her.

"Ladies," Felipe said as he appeared from nowhere. Rebecca took a step back and ran her hand through her hair nonchalantly. "I hope you have everything you need?"

"Ah, yeah, all set up," Maya said with a cough. "Thanks."

"Yes, thank you Felipe," Rebecca smiled. "We saved you some lunch if you haven't already eaten?"

"No, I have not," he smiled back. "Very much appreciated, thank you."

They stood there for a few moments, the three of them smiling at each other awkwardly before Rebecca took a step back and gestured between the plate in her hand and the small building behind her.

"I'm going to see if Phil is awake, bring him some food," she said. "See you guys back at camp?"

"Sure," Maya nodded. "See you in a bit."

Rebecca smiled and headed into the hut leaving Maya and Felipe to walk the short distance to the camp. As they were about halfway there Felipe stopped and turned to glance up to the path they would take the next day.

"I saw you took a walk earlier," he said. "Tell me your thoughts?"

"It looks steep," she shrugged. "I'm pretty sure we can handle it though, once we don't have an injured person to guide through it. Thank you for arranging to get him out, by the way."

"You are welcome," Felipe smiled. "Although it was largely selfish on my part. I do not wish to have any unnecessary complications on what should be a straightforward trek."

"Well, of course not," she said, following his gaze as he stared up into the hills. "Who would want that?"

He turned back to face her, a serious look settling on his face. "The night before last I asked you why you came out here was and you did not really answer me," he said, glancing over to where Tom and Claudia sat in the distance. "I understand that you did not wish to share your true reasons because you do not fully trust me, and I respect that. In fact I would do the same. But I need you to be honest with me on one point."

"And what is that?" Maya said cautiously as she folded her arms.

"Are you attempting to follow someone?" Felipe asked, his eyes locking with hers, his brows furrowed in concern.

"No," she answered, surprised. It was the truth, in a way. Sure, they were hoping to discover a path laid out centuries ago, but follow someone? "Why do you ask?"

Felipe studied her for a few seconds and then turned away with a nod. He stayed silent for a few moments, the look on his face indicating he was trying to decide what to say. "The man who owns this place shared some concerns with me about a group he spotted a week or so ago," he said eventually. "He did not interact with them but from what he tells me they did not seem like your usual hikers. And they were not local. In any case they were unusual enough for him to share his thoughts with me and he is not a man for, how do you say, idle gossip."

Maya nodded at the phrase. "Well, if he's concerned I suppose we should take that on board but I can assure you, Felipe, I don't know anything about it. All we are trying to do out here is dig up some history, and our reasons are purely academic."

"Academic," he turned back to her with a curt smile. "Yes, of course."

Felipe turned and headed over to the camp, leaving Maya to stare after him in confusion. With a shake of her head she turned to follow before remembering that she had to contact Elaine and bring her up to date. With a last look at him she turned around and headed for the farm, wondering what it was the farmer had seen that would concern him so much he would share it with Felipe.

Maya rubbed her eyes and took a deep breath as she stared at the screen. She had spent half an hour writing a message to Elaine in an effort to avoid actually having to speak to the woman. It had been a long couple of days and she really wasn't up for listening to her barbed comments and generally disdainful attitude. She was sure she couldn't possibly have read the message in the time that had elapsed since she had sent it, let alone digest everything that it contained, yet here was was the reply staring back at her and giving her a headache.

Call me.

How could two words fill her with such dread? She sighed and loaded up her Skype account, her hand hovering over the call button and pulling back in surprise as Elaine's picture flashed up with an incoming call. She rolled her eyes and clicked to answer.

"If it takes you that long to follow a simple instruction like 'call me' I'm not surprised you haven't found what we're looking for yet," Elaine snapped in greeting, her attention seemingly on whatever she had been doing before she made the call.

"Hello to you too," she muttered.

"Don't be petulant, Maya, I think we're both a little busy for pleasantries," the older woman said, finally looking into the camera and sitting back in her chair. "Now tell me properly, what did this man say?"

"Just what I told you in the email," Maya replied, rubbing her face tiredly. "He asked me if we were following someone and when I asked him why he would think that he told me the farmer had some concerns."

"And what were these concerns?"

"Like I said, nothing specific."

"Maya," she sighed. "The reason I asked you to call was because I was hoping the vague nature of your email was due to some long suspected but hitherto cleverly disguised semi illiteracy on your part and that speaking to you in person would allow you to make up for your woefully inadequate written account. So please, tell me again, exactly what did he say."

Maya bit down on her rage and took a moment to try and compose herself before she answered. "He said," she started through gritted teeth. "That the farmer had spotted a group about a week back that didn't seem like hikers, not local, and that he was concerned."

"And?"

"And he asked if we were following someone, if that was why we were out here."

"And?"

"And I said that we weren't," she said, irritably. "That our reasons were purely academic."

"And?"

"And what?" Maya asked, throwing up her hands, already completely over this conversation.

"And you didn't think to get more information from him?" Elaine snapped back, turning her attention back to the papers on the desk in front of her. "I mean, that is what I'm paying you for, isn't it? To find out information that will enable you to retrieve artefacts for me?"

"Yes," she admitted, closing her eyes to try and calm herself down. "But he doesn't trust me and it's not as easy as…"

"Well then make it that easy. You're paying him to guide you, tell him you need to know what's going on." the woman tutted. "Honestly, sometimes I wonder if my confidence in your abilities is misplaced."

"Technically I am not paying him anything," she pointed out, ignoring the backhanded compliment. "I will talk to him again later when he's had a chance to calm down."

"Maybe if you'd handled it better he wouldn't need to calm down," Elaine sighed, removing her glasses and rubbing at her eyes. "Speaking of the money, what does the little princess think about all this?"

"I haven't exactly had a chance to tell her yet," Maya said reluctantly. "She's sort of preoccupied."

"Preoccupied?" she laughed. "What could possibly be more important? And please don't tell me this is to do with you?"

"What? No, of course not," she huffed, folding her arms defensively. "Her best friend is injured and having to be airlifted to safety and her contact is missing."

"Missing?" Elaine sat forward and put her glasses on quickly. "Why didn't you tell me this?"

"Because," she answered with a shrug, shifting uncomfortably in her seat. "I, uh, didn't think it was that important."

"You didn't think it was that important," she answered with a tight smile before sighing and tapping something into the keyboard. "Of course you didn't."

"She's only been out of contact a couple of hours, Elaine, she could be doing anything."

"Not everyone has your capricious attitude, Maya," she said, looking at her over the top of her glasses. "Some people set a lot of store in keeping to their appointments."

"Hey, I keep my appointments," Maya shot back, leaning forward and jamming her knuckles into her knees. "And I'm not capricious."

"Really? What about…?"

"Cabo was a one off," she interjected, tired of that one incident being thrown in her face.

"Well," Elaine smiled, her lips pulling back and giving her the appearance of a wolf about to deal a fatal blow to its prey. "Since I was about to say Mytilene I'd say that was untrue, wouldn't you?"

"Whatever," she huffed, rolling her eyes and wondering once again how this woman made her feel and behave like a teenager.

"Do you at least remember her name?"

"Her name?" Maya felt the heat rise to her face as she thought back to Mytilene.

"The contact, Maya, not your sad little conquest."

"I know that," she said quickly. "I just...I only know her first name. Madalena."

"And is she local to Boca do Acre?"

"I, er, I don't know. She wasn't staying at the hotel."

"Oh, well then she must be," Elaine spat sarcastically. "Obviously we are getting nowhere here. I suggest you get yourself back out there and do some digging then come back to me with some proper information. Do you think that is within the realm of your capabilities?"

"Of course it is."

"After this conversation I am not so sure," she sighed, taking off her glasses again and leaning back. "But I suppose there is a reason I keep sending you out so I will try and give you the benefit of the doubt."

"Thanks, I'm honoured," she muttered.

"Oh, I'm sorry, have I offended you?" Elaine folded her arms and fixed her with an icy stare.

"No more than usual," she shrugged, willing herself not to shrink under the pressure.

"I don't have time to spare your feelings, Maya," the woman snapped. "In case you hadn't noticed you are wandering through the jungle in search of something you have only managed to glean the bare minimum of information about, being led by a man you don't know, who doesn't trust you, who now has reason to believe you are willfully leading him into a bad situation, something you have completely failed to nip in the bud, and suddenly your companion's contact has mysteriously disappeared. Your companion who, as you also seem to have forgotten, has missing parents who have somehow managed to get themselves mixed up with some very bad characters. It you had managed to provide me with any useful information at all I would have been able to do some digging and find out what it is that you are dealing with. I am trying to make sure you and your team are safe out there so forgive me if I don't have time to take your fragile ego into account. Now grow the hell up and go get me what I asked for."

Maya opened her mouth to reply just as Elaine disconnected the call so she sat there for a moment staring at the blank screen as her rage bubbled through her. "Fucking bitch," she muttered as she shut down the laptop and ran her hand through her hair. She took a deep breath and stood up, striding out of the room with a scowl on her face and heading back to the camp.

As she walked she thought back over the conversation, her rage slowly dying down and being replaced with something altogether more unsettling. Why was Elaine so concerned about some random farmer's vague rambling and a woman who had been out of contact for a couple of hours? What did she know that she wasn't letting on?

"Oh, shit," Claudia said quietly as she approached. "I take it you spoke to Elaine?"

"I wouldn't put it quite like that," she muttered as she sat down. "She spent ten minutes insulting me, then told me to grow up and ended the call."

"Nice," her friend chuckled. "Didn't she say anything constructive at all?"

"No," she sighed, rubbing at her face. "I could really do with a drink."

"That, at least, I can help with," Claudia smiled, reaching into her bag and pulling out a quart of tequila.

"Claudia, I kind of love you, you know?" Maya chuckled.

"I know," she winked as she offered her the bottle.

"You better hold onto it," she said with a shake of her head.

"Are you joking?" Claudia said with a frown. "Who are you and what have you done with Maya?"

"That's the only bottle we have and something tells me we might need it later," Maya sighed as she turned to stare out at the forest. "I've got a bad feeling about this."

Chapter 24

Maya watched the small plane approaching from the south, skirting over the trees and twitching its wings like a surfer dragging their hand through the water. It dropped down into the valley then rose up above her and circled in for landing, its engines sputtering as the pilot made his approach. She headed back down the hill towards the camp quickly, the conversation with Elaine still occupying her thoughts and giving her an unsettled feeling not even the tranquil view could shift.

As she walked through their camping area and on up to the farm Claudia fell into step beside her and they made their way to the hut where Phil had been resting in the makeshift bed. As they got closer they saw the pilot climbing out of the plane and starting towards them, his copilot opening the door at the rear of the plane and pulling out a stretcher before she followed him. She reached the entrance to the hut at the same time as Maya and Claudia and they all stopped outside a little awkwardly.

"After you," Maya said, gesturing with her hand.

"Thank you," she smiled back, her eyes lingering on her for a few seconds before she stepped through the door.

Claudia walked past her with an amused snort and a shake of her head, stepping into the already crowded room and leaving little room for Maya to follow so she leaned on the door jamb and folded her arms as she watched the scene. Rebecca was sitting on the edge of Phil's bed, his back pack in her hand, talking to her two friends quietly as the pilot chatted with Felipe.

"Alright," Felipe said a minute or so later. "Are you ready, Phil?"

"Yeah, I guess," he answered dejectedly before pointing at the stretcher. "I don't need that. I may not be able to keep up with you guys but I can still walk."

The copilot nodded and walked back out, placing her free hand on Maya's hip with a smile as she she squeezed through the doorway, causing her to hold her hands up and back out with an apologetic mutter and a bemused smirk. She watched the woman as she walked back towards the plane, taking in the exaggerated sway of her hips which she assumed was for her benefit and returning the smile she shot over her shoulder.

"Maya?"

She snapped her eyes back into the room and saw Phil hobbling over towards her, Rebecca standing behind him looking a little pissed off.

"Give me a hand?" Phil asked as he reached her, handing over his backpack and grabbing her shoulder for support.

"Ah, sure," she answered, her brow furrowing in confusion as she walked with him. "You okay?"

"Yeah, just feeling a bit stupid, you know?"

"Yeah, I know," she nodded, shooting him a smile. "Could be worse, though. You could have got yourself killed."

"True," he laughed. "Listen, I wanted to thank you. For coming after me, I mean."

"You already did."

"Yeah, but, ah, well, you know. I was kind of an ass to you and I never really…"

"Come on, man, don't do that," Maya sighed, stopping and turning to face him. "You didn't know me, you still don't. I know what it's like to be asked to put your faith in someone you don't have a read on yet. And I've been told I can be quite abrasive, so…"

"Yeah," he laughed loudly. "Well, you certainly can be that. But you're also the best person she could have picked. You know, for this."

"Ah, I don't know about that," she muttered, looking over to where Felipe and the pilot were talking animatedly.

"She does. And so do I," he smiled down at her sadly. "Just, er, look after her, alright? She's like my best friend and my kid sister all rolled into one, and I'd never forgive myself if anything happened to her."

"I'm not going to let anything happen to her," she replied, turning back to him with a nod. "If I did I'd have to put up with your guilty, vengeful ass on my case for the rest of my life, right?"

"Right," he chuckled before shooting a glance at his friends talking to Claudia back by the hut. "I know she seems tough, like she has it all together all of the time, but it's an act, you know? She may seem like she's handling it but she's not. She's just so used to keeping it together in public she can't let go."

"Phil," she sighed and put her hands on her shoulders. "You're worried about her, I get it. But this isn't some reality show, there are no cameras out here, and she isn't alone. Even if she isn't entirely comfortable around me and Claudia she has Tom here, and we're all looking out for her."

"Yeah, I think she probably feels more comfortable around you than Tom at this point," he said with a smirk. "So lay off the blatant eyefucking with the hot, blonde pilot, maybe. I don't think Becca was particularly thrilled with that."

"What?" Maya said indignantly, her pitch rising unconvincingly even as she rolled her eyes. "Come on, that's not…"

"Look, I don't know what's going on with you two, and it's none of my business," he chuckled. "The way you look you must get tons of people flirting with you. I'm just saying maybe tone it down a little, alright? Bec likes you. A lot. And it's been a long time."

"Phil," she said tightly, turning him and leading him towards the plane. "I really don't think she would appreciate you telling me all this. Just drop it, okay?"

"I guess you're right," he sighed. "I just...don't hurt her, alright?"

"Come on, don't be a dick," Maya muttered as they reached the plane. "I'll see you on the other side."

"You better," he replied as she helped him up onto the plane, the co pilot taking his other hand and pulling him up into his seat.

Maya waved and took a step back as Rebecca, Tom and Claudia walked up to say their goodbyes. Once he was all strapped in the blonde climbed out of the plane and opened the door to the cockpit, glancing back at Maya as she did so.

"You're not coming with us?"

"Ah, no," Maya answered with a smile, stepping closer to Rebecca and putting her arm loosely round her waist. "Got stuff to do out here."

The copilot shrugged and climbed up into cockpit, her eyes drifting back towards them as she fastened her harness. Maya looked over at Felipe and the pilot again, still locked in conversation, the pilot's arms folded and his hand on his mouth as he stared down at the floor, nodding occasionally at Felipe's words.

"What are you doing?" Rebecca asked quietly as she shuffled out of Maya's grasp and turned to face her.

"What? Nothing," she said quickly, snapping her eyes back and noticing the looks on the group's faces ranging from confusion to amusement and, in Rebecca's case, annoyance.

"Well in future I would prefer it if you would leave me out of your 'nothing'," she hissed, colour rising to her face. "I'm not your damn prop, Maya."

"Wh…?" Maya frowned after her as she climbed up into the plane to give Phil a hug, and turned to Claudia in confusion. "What did I do?"

"Well at least you didn't pee on her," the redhead whispered, amusement evident in her voice. "Although you might as well have."

"Shut up, Claudia," she snapped, walking over towards Felipe and the pilot with a scowl.

As she approached the two men were shaking hands and saying their goodbyes so she stopped and waited for Felipe to come over to her as the pilot climbed up into the plane and started the engine.

"Everything alright?"

"Fine," he smiled at her. "Just getting some information from back home."

"We've been gone less than three days, Felipe," she chuckled. "Not homesick already, are you?"

"You know it is not that, Maya," he replied, tilting his head towards her.

"Yeah, I know. Anything we should be worried about?"

Felipe stayed quiet as he watched the plane turn around and start taxying down the short, makeshift runway. Maya gave him time, watching the plane take off and disappear into the distance, waiting until he eventually spoke again.

"Shall we take a walk?"

"Sure," she shrugged. "Cos we never do that."

An hour later Maya walked back into camp with a frown on her face and headed straight over to her tent, ripping the screen open and rooting through her bag until she found her cigarettes. She held them in front of her and stared at them with a sigh, feeling the last of her resolve melting away as Felipe's words swarmed her brain.

"Fuck it," she muttered, sending up a silent prayer that there would be no more underwater swimming for her on this trip as she wanted nothing more than to sit and smoke the entire packet whilst drowning her discomfort in Claudia's tequila. She zipped the tent back up and walked up the hill to the spot she had found earlier.

Somewhere around her third cigarette she made the decision that she would have to tell Rebecca what she had learned, but how much to tell her? And really, what had she learned? That there were a bunch of guys walking round the jungle with rifles who appeared to have a man and woman with them that were possibly bound? What would that possibly achieve other than totally freaking Rebecca out for potentially no reason?

Maya ground the cigarette out and linked her arms loosely around her knees as she looked out at the sunset, letting the melting colours settle her mind. After a few minutes she heard a rustle in the grass behind her glanced down to her left, recognising Rebecca's boots as she came to a stop beside her.

"Beautiful," she commented as Maya looked up at her, her arms crossed as she stared out over the valley.

"Yeah," she agreed as she turned back.

The two of them held their positions in silence as the sun slowly dropped out of sight, Maya's mind searching for a way to begin the conversation she needed to have, how much she should say, and also wondering why Rebecca was here. Was she expecting an apology? She hoped not as she still wasn't entirely sure what she had done wrong and really she didn't have the time or energy for yet another discussion about feelings. She honestly didn't understand why this stuff had to be so difficult, or why it was that Rebecca seemed to be able to read her like an open book while she was pretty much clueless about what was going on in the other woman's head. It was one of the things that frustrated her the most about herself, that she could be so good at reading landscapes and so bad when it came to people.

"Are you okay?" Rebecca said eventually, taking her completely off guard as she knelt down in front of her in the fading light.

"I'm okay," she shrugged, dropping one of her knees down and resting her chin on the other. "Just thinking."

"It's so peaceful up here," she said softly, plucking a blade of grass and twisting it between her fingers. "Quiet."

"I like the quiet," Maya smiled as she watched her fingers work.

"We saved you some food."

"Thanks."

"I was a little worried when you didn't come back," Rebecca said, her eyes still on the grass. "I'm sorry I made you mad earlier."

"What?" Maya looked up at her in confusion. "You didn't make me mad."

"Oh, right. Sorry, I just thought…"

"You were the one that yelled at me, right?"

"Maya," Rebecca chuckled softly, finally looking up at her. "That's why I thought you were angry."

"Yeah, well, Claud said I might as well have peed on you so I figured I kind of…overstepped, or whatever," she shrugged.

Rebecca laughed and stroked Maya's leg as she tried to draw her gaze. "You didn't overstep, I just took your 'stuff to do' comment the wrong way. I'm sorry."

Maya looked up at her in confusion, casting her mind back in an effort to work out what she was talking about, her eyes going comically wide when she realised. "Oh, shit, you thought I meant that you were the stuff I had to do? Rebecca, I…"

"I know, don't worry," she said quickly as she moved closer. "I was just rattled cos that woman was so obviously after you and you obviously liked it, but then you put your arm around me and I… I just felt…I don't know."

"I'm sorry, I guess after what Phil said I thought it would make you feel better."

"No, it did, I just…wait, what?" Rebecca said, her hand stopping suddenly on her leg. "What Phil said?"

"Oh, shit…" she muttered, squeezing her eyes shut as she realised what she had said.

"What did he say?"

"Nothing, really. It doesn't matter."

"Maya," she said, her voice dangerously low. "What did he say?"

"I don't remember exactly," she sighed and leaned back on her hands. "Just that you didn't like the way I was acting with her and…well, that you like me and maybe it had been a while so I, er, well he kind of told me not to hurt you."

"That fucking asshole," Rebecca spat, her eyes narrowed as she looked up at the sky. "Now I wish I'd made him stay and walk a hundred miles on that fucking leg."

"Hey, come on," she said softly, leaning forward again to take her hand. "He was just looking out for you."

"How? By making me out to be some sort of fragile kid? By making you feel sorry for me?"

"I don't feel sorry for you," Maya said quickly.

"Right," she laughed humourlessly. "You just said you put your arm around me to make me feel better."

"Yeah, but not because I felt sorry for you!"

"Why else would you need to make me feel better, Maya?"

"Because," she said, sitting up and putting her hands on the other woman's shoulders, feeling her anger vibrating up her arms. "If she'd been flirting with you I would have been mad as hell and I wanted you to see that I didn't want her."

"Maya," Rebecca shook her head as she stared at the floor. "I don't need you to…"

"I'm not doing anything, Rebecca," she said softly, her hands shifting up to cup her face. "Look at me. I care about you and I don't want some blonde bitch making you feel like shit. And sure, I could have dealt with it better but I think we both know I'm not very good at that stuff."

"Stuff," she chuckled, running her thumb over Maya's hand on her cheek. "You're pretty good at some stuff."

"Well, yeah, but if I'd tried that to get her to back off I think some people might have got a bit uncomfortable, don't you?"

Rebecca laughed and leaned in to kiss her. "You're infuriating, you know that?"

"It's not the first time it's been said," she smiled, pulling her back in.

Rebecca's hands slid into her hair as the kiss deepened and Maya felt the stress of the last few days start to lift from her shoulders as she dropped her own hands from Rebecca's face to her hips, pulling their bodies together. Something in her mind wouldn't let her fully enjoy the moment, though, and after a few seconds she pulled away slightly, resting her forehead against the other woman's as she caught her breath.

"I have to tell you something," she said quietly, feeling Rebecca tense up immediately.

"What?"

Maya took a breath and leaned back, leaving her hands in place in the hopes that it would somehow make the conversation go better. "I don't know what it means and I don't know how important it is but I feel like you should know anyway."

"Know what?" Rebecca asked, pulling back a little further with a sceptical look on her face. "You're kind of freaking me out right now, Maya."

"I'm sorry, I just…I've been thinking about how to tell you, like, if at all and how much, you know?"

"No, I don't know, obviously," she said, throwing up her hands in frustration. "I don't have the first fucking clue what you're talking about! What is it? Are you married?"

"What?" Maya said, shaking her head in confusion. "No, of course not! Jesus…"

"Okay," she sat back on her heels looking slightly relieved. "So just tell me what it is before either of us make this anymore uncomfortable."

"Good idea," she breathed, running her hands through her hair as she steeled herself to begin. "The farmer told Felipe that he saw a group of people near here a while ago. He thought they seemed…well, Felipe said unusual, I'm taking that to mean sketchy, so he and his son kept an eye on them."

"Sketchy how?" Rebecca asked with a frown. She folded her arms across her chest tightly, her shoulders tensed, as if in preparation for what she was about to hear.

"Sketchy like they had rifles. They didn't get close enough to see exactly but from the sounds of it they were pretty heavy duty."

"Alright," she nodded. "And?"

"So apparently there were five of them, four with weapons, one most likely a guide, and they came through the valley about a month ago, then back the other way about four days later, then back again the following week, returning, again, about four days later," Maya clasped her hands in her lap and looked down at them as she prepared for the next part. "So by this point the 'guide' is looking a bit skittish…"

"I thought they didn't get close to them?"

"They didn't but they were watching them and the routes he was taking them seemed a little off," she explained with a shrug. "Either way, the farmer's son was concerned enough that he decided to track them, expecting them to be heading back towards town, which they did, but they stopped at a makeshift camp by a creek about three hours walk from the river."

"Okay," Rebecca said cautiously. "So, what? You think they'll come back? I don't really…"

"No, that's not…" Maya sighed and flexed her hands nervously. "There were more of them at the camp. At least four more guys with guns and two others. A man and a woman, by themselves, off to the side. He says they looked like they might be in some sort of restraints."

Rebecca sucked in a breath at this and hugged herself tighter, her face going pale in the dying light. "Go on," she said quietly.

"The son headed into town and got a group of his friends together…"

"His friends?" Rebecca spat angrily. "Why didn't he go to the police?"

"Because they don't trust the police, and they didn't know what they were dealing with," she answered quickly, desperately hoping that Rebecca wouldn't start freaking out. "In any case, when they got back to the camp they had cleared out. They tried to track them but they couldn't tell if they were following new tracks or the same ones as before, so when they got back here," she pointed down into the valley. "He came back up to let his father know what he'd found and he said they had passed through the day before with more people and he had already contacted the pilot. Apparently they've been doing sweeps along possible routes from here on in but haven't seen any trace of them."

"So what?" Rebecca shrugged. "That's it? They're just gone?"

"No, they're still looking. The son and his friends carried on but Felipe says there are certain areas they won't go to, so if the trail leads them there, then…"

"Then what? My parents are on their own?"

"Rebecca, we don't know that it is your parents, it could be anyone."

"But it could be! Fuck," she swore as she got to her feet and stared out over the valley. "How long have you known about this?"

"Felipe mentioned it to me at lunchtime…"

"You waited eight hours to tell me this?" Rebecca shouted as she spun round to face her.

"No! I, fuck, he asked me if we were following someone," she explained as she stood up and took a cautious step towards her. "I said no, that our reasons were purely academic and he got all closed off and walked away. After we loaded Phil up I asked him what was going on and he told me. Since then I've been up here trying to make sense of it all and working out what and how to tell you."

"You don't get to decide what to tell me, Maya," she said angrily. "You tell me everything, I thought we already went through this? I'm not some little kid you're here to protect. I asked for your help to find my parents. If you're keeping things from me that's obviously not going to work."

"I'm not keeping anything from you!" Maya shot back. "I just didn't want to worry you til I had all the information!"

"Worry me?" Rebecca laughed. "Don't you think I'm already worried? Don't you think I'll be even more worried now I know that you might not be telling me things in case my delicate sensibilities can't handle it?"

"Alright," she sighed and held her hands up as she backed away. "I've pissed you off, I get it. I should have told you sooner, I'm sorry I didn't. I think it's best if I just leave you alone for a bit to think it all through, so just come find me when you want to talk about it."

"Yeah, sure," she smiled, her eyes hard. "Great idea, Maya. I'll just see you later, once you've had a chance to report everything back to Elaine."

"Come on, Rebecca, I don't know what else…" Maya started with a sigh before her brain caught up. "What did you just say?"

"Oh, for God's sake," she huffed, rolling her eyes as she turned away.

"No, really," she said, her anger bubbling dangerously close to the surface. "I'm really going to need you to tell me how you know that name."

"Everybody knows that name, Maya, same as everyone knows yours," Rebecca shot back, still facing away from her. "Honestly, I don't how you can be so blind to the impact you have. Just because you don't play up to the press doesn't mean word doesn't get around."

"So let me get this straight," she said, her voice shaking with the effort of keeping her temper under control. "When you met me you knew exactly who I was, exactly who I worked for, and yet you thought that this would somehow go better if you pretended like you didn't?"

"Come on, we already talked about this," Rebecca sighed, turning around to face her. "I didn't tell you that I knew who you were because I didn't want to look desperate."

"Fuck that, Rebecca," she snapped, taking an angry step towards her with her fists clenched at her sides. "You didn't just know who I was, you knew everything about me. Everything. And you lied about it! And worse than that, you slept with me, a lot, and made me feel like shit for trusting my instincts. Do you have any idea how much of an idiot that makes me feel?"

"Not everything, just who you work for, and I didn't..."

"Yeah, and where I grew up, and where I went to school, and about my father," she reeled off, her whole body shaking now. "You probably know where I live, my local bar, my favourite band. I bet you had some creepy private investigator follow me round taking pictures of me too, huh?"

Rebecca opened her mouth then quickly closed it again, folding her arms defensively.

"Jesus fucking Christ," Maya swore, her lip curling as she shook her head. "Who the fuck are you?"

"Maya, I..."

"For all your snooping there is obviously one thing you didn't pick up on," she said through gritted teeth, her voice quiet and steely. "When people lie to me, they only do it once."

Maya felt a small ping of satisfaction at the fear on Rebecca's face and she turned quickly to head back down the hill towards camp. She didn't use her quiet voice very often but when she did whoever the unfortunate soul was on the receiving end, they knew they had crossed a line there was no coming back from.

Chapter 25

Maya stormed back into the camp, her rage pumping through her body like a molten stream of lava. Claudia was sitting on Tom's lap, giggling at some stupid joke he was telling as she played with the hair at the back of his neck, her laughter dying on her lips as she saw her friend's face.

"Maya, what…"

"Alcohol. Now."

"What happened?"

"Now, goddamit!" Maya yelled, coming to a halt in front of them and clenching her hands into fists as she tried to get herself under control.

"Okay," she said quickly, jumping up and taking hold of her arm to lead her towards the tent, having the good sense not to speak again until she had retrieved the bottle from her bag and handed it over.

Maya ripped the lid off and chugged a third of the bottle, wiping her mouth with the back of her hand as she came up for air.

"Maya," Claudia said gently, concern written all over her face. "Please, talk to me. What happened?"

"Pack your shit," she muttered back as she turned to leave. "We're out of here as soon as I talk to Elaine."

"What?"

"Pack your shit, Claud," she called over her shoulder. "And don't trust any of them."

She marched over to the hut, swigging on the bottle as she went in an effort to calm the storm in her chest. She knew she shouldn't have trusted her, why hadn't she just listened to herself? Now she was stuck in the middle of a fucking jungle, stumbling after a bunch of heavily armed psychopaths, and for what? A couple of good orgasms and a shot at finding a city that had been hidden for half a millenium? Well fuck that. She didn't need this shit. And what would happen if she did find it? The place would be trashed, turned into another tourist attraction to line the pockets of the rich and destroy the ecosystem of one of the last untouched places on earth.

Maya punched the door of the hut open and sat down heavily in the chair, finishing off the bottle as she waited for the laptop to load up. As soon as it was done she logged into Skype and called Elaine, grateful that the woman seemed to live next to her computer and answered on the second ring.

"Maya," she began with the fakest of smiles. "Always a pleasure. I take it you got what I asked for?"

"Oh yeah, I got what you asked for," Maya snapped. "And a lot more besides."

"Drunk being one of them?"

"I'm not drunk."

"Please," she said, pulling off her glasses and setting them on the desk. "I can smell the tequila from here. Alright, what have you found?"

"Where to start?" Maya laughed. "So there are at least 9 guys out here with guns, they have two, possibly three hostages with them, potentially including the Bronsteins, they're heading northwest along the valley floor and have the Hardy boys of the Amazon on their tail. Also, that fucking privileged, attention seeking, duplicitous bitch has been lying to me since the minute we met. She knows all about me, all about you, fuck, she probably already knew exactly who had her parents and exactly what she was leading us all into, so I'm done. Me and Claudia are heading out tonight and will be on the first flight we can get to New York. I'll bring you everything I have and we can start planning a proper expedition to find whatever may or may not be out here."

Maya sat back in her chair and rubbed at her face angrily, taking a moment to catch her breath after her rant and looking cautiously back at the screen when she realised she had received no response. Elaine was sitting calmly, her hands folded on the desk, her gaze cool.

"Are you finished?" the older woman asked after a moment.

"Yes," she answered uncertainly.

"Good. Then here's what I want you to do. Go back to camp, drink a lot of water, sleep it off, get up tomorrow and continue on to your next checkpoint."

"I just…"

"When you reach it contact me again and I will give you the information I have uncovered. I am still waiting on a few final details and you are currently in no state to…"

"Did you not hear what I just said?" Maya slammed her hands on the desk. "I'm done, Elaine. Done. Claud and I are coming home."

"Maya," she sighed. "I grow weary of having this conversation with you. You are fully aware of how little I enjoy repeating myself and we are rapidly approaching the point where I will stop and you will find yourself unemployed."

"You can't seriously expect…"

"What I expect," Elaine interrupted forcefully. "Is for you to do your goddamn job, Maya, and stop whining! Now I assume that you have, as usual, ignored my instructions and let yourself become personally involved with Rebecca Bronstein?"

"That's not…"

"And now you have found out that she has not been completely honest with you and had your delicate little heart crushed?"

"Fuck you, Elaine."

"That language is uncalled for, unprofessional and entirely unappreciated," she snapped, whipping her glasses back on and picking up a pile of papers. "Now…"

Suddenly there was a commotion outside the hut and Rebecca's raised voice rang through the door.

"Get your hands off me! Right now!"

"I will not!" Claudia's voice answered. "You are not going in there!"

There was a short series of muffled bangs and Maya whipped round in her chair just in time to see Claudia and Rebecca crash through the door and land on the floor in a tangled heap, grappling with each over in a way that Maya found absurd, infuriating, hilarious and weirdly a little hot all at the same time.

"What the fuck are you doing?" she yelled, jumping up to pull Rebecca off Claudia quickly.

"Your friend attacked me!" Rebecca spat.

"I didn't attack you!" Claudia shot back, jumping up off the floor with an angry glare. "I told you not to come in here, I asked you nicely but you didn't listen!"

"Because you wouldn't listen to me! I only wanted to talk to her!"

"Well she obviously doesn't want to talk to you! Whatever you said to her in your last conversation made her down half a bottle of tequila and tell me to pack up!"

"Hey, I am standing right here," Maya tried to interject.

"You don't know what you're talking about, Claudia, and it has absolutely nothing to do with you," Rebecca said, ignoring Maya completely as she smoothed down her top.

"Of course it does, she's my best friend and the last time I saw her this upset she…"

"Claudia!" Maya shouted, stepping in front of Rebecca and putting her hands on her friend's shoulders. "I appreciate what you're doing, I really do, but I think we all just need to calm down, alright?"

"My my," Elaine's voice chuckled out from the laptop. "Maya Rodriguez, the voice of reason. Time to buy that lottery ticket, I think. Hello, Claudia."

"Elaine," Claudia replied with as much dignity as she could muster with her hair in disarray and her shirt ripped. "Good to see you."

"I wish I could say the same," she replied with a smirk. "I see Maya's influence is rubbing off on you?"

Claudia held her tongue and turned away to straighten her clothes, rolling her eyes at Maya as she did so.

"Ah, good, more eye rolling," Elaine chuckled, turning her attention to Rebecca. "Ms Bronstein. You seem to be having an interesting night?"

"You could say that," she answered with a shrug. "Almost as much fun as last fourth of July."

"Ah, yes. Whatever happened to that young man?"

"He…"

"You've got to be kidding me," Maya said incredulously. "You two know each other?"

"Of course we do, Maya," Elaine sighed. "Our line of work makes for a very small world, everyone knows everyone in this business. Except for those who choose not to, like you, obviously."

"I don't fucking believe this," she whispered, backing up to the wall, the room suddenly feeling way too small and claustrophobic, nausea building up inside her at an alarming rate.

"Hey," Rebecca said gently, reaching out to her.

"Don't fucking touch me," she gritted out as she swatted her hand away.

Rebecca held her hands up and backed away as Maya pressed her palms against the wooden wall and bent over slightly, feeling dangerously unhinged and on the verge of throwing up. The smell of the room flooded her nostrils and made her stomach churn, earthy and damp, sap and fertilizer, the blood pounding in her ears as the shame of being so completely oblivious flooded her brain and made it spin with anger. She felt hot, angry tears fighting to reach the surface and forced them back down with everything she had. Damn tequila always made her want to cry, even when she wasn't in the middle of one of the biggest betrayals of her life. Why the fuck did she drink the stuff?

"Claudia, be a dear and help Maya to the seat before she keels over, would you?" Elaine's voice sounded from the distance. She stiffened slightly as she felt her friend's hand slide softly across her back, then started to slowly calm down as she rested it there and settled the other one on her arm.

"When we get out of here," Claudia whispered softly in her ear. "I'm going to shit in a box and post it to her house."

As the words registered in her brain the fog and nausea started to lift and she let out a shaky laugh, gripping onto Claudia's arm as she stood up and followed her lead to the chair, part of her wondering which 'her' her friend had been referring to and then realising she would be just as happy with either. She sat down heavily and took a breath to calm herself down before looking up at the screen.

"Thank you, Claudia," Elaine said as she leant on the desk. "I'm sure whatever you said was in no way inappropriate. Rebecca, I am afraid I am going to have to ask you to leave."

"What?" Rebecca exclaimed. "No way, I need…"

"I don't care what you need, Rebecca," she said, cutting her off calmly. "You will have your answers in due course. Now. Please."

Rebecca glared at the screen for a moment, colour rising to her face, before nodding tersely and walking out.

"Good," the older woman nodded, turning her attention back to the remaining pair with a smile. "Now Maya, I realise that you are not having the best night but I need you to listen to what I am about to say without being churlish, alright?"

"Sure," she answered, folding her arms with a shrug, not trusting herself to say more and immensely grateful for Claudia's calming hand on her shoulder.

"Thank you, I appreciate how difficult this must be for you given your trust issues and, although I already know you don't believe it, I am truly sorry for not informing you of the extent of my knowledge regarding Ms Bronstein and her current predicament," Elaine said in a strained voice, her eyes downcast for the moment. "When I sent you to retrieve Zuazola's journals I was aware that the Bronsteins had gone missing, obviously, and I also knew that they had been looking around that area in the hopes of finding information pertaining to the whereabouts of Paititi."

Maya and Claudia stared at the screen in silence as Elaine reached out of shot and retrieved a bottle of vodka, pouring a large measure of it into a glass with some ice and taking a healthy swig before continuing.

"I have known the Bronsteins for many years, they are good friends of mine, and I often discuss their expeditions with them. As such, I knew that they had access to information taken from Zuazola at the time of his incarceration, and that had led them to Piedra del Indio. I sent the two of you in to find out if the journal was still at the fort and bring it back here for safe keeping if it was."

"Why?" Maya asked.

"Because if there was more information in the journal than Zuazola's thief had realised, whoever took David and Daniella would need to go back to the source to find out what was missing. If I had that source they would need to go through me and I would have a shot at helping my friends."

"Or getting yourself killed."

"I am too high profile a target for them to kill, and far too devious," she said with a tired smile. "You two, on the other hand, are entirely disposable."

"Gee, thanks," Maya drawled.

"Which is why I didn't want to give you any information that would allow you to draw attention to yourselves, why my instructions were deliberately vague," Elaine took another drink and pointed at Maya. "Your mind works differently to anyone else I have ever known. I knew that you would find your way to what we were looking for via a completely different route, and I was right."

"You don't know that."

"Oh but I do," she chuckled. "You told me yourself that Rebecca and her team worked their way to the caves via maps and with specialised equipment, you and Claudia arrived at the same place, in less time, using scrawled gibberish in a centuries old notebook and a blacklight."

"And pee," Claudia muttered.

"Anyway, after you had found the caves I had intended to bring you home and pass the information on to people more equipped to deal with Martin Amaric's band of scum and villains, but then you told me that Rebecca had seen it and was trying to enlist your help, and I knew that she would end up going with or without you. I knew that without your help she would most likely end up getting herself killed and so I had no choice but to let you continue and hope that your skill at keeping yourself and Claudia alive and out of danger would also extend to Rebecca. Of course, I also had people watching over you."

"Oh, God," Maya said with a disbelieving shake of her head. "Please don't tell me Felipe is one of yours as well?"

"Of course not," she scoffed. "Don't you think if I had someone who knew the Amazon well enough to guide a group of untested fake students through it I wouldn't have sent them out looking for the Bronsteins instead of you?"

"At this point I honestly don't know," she sighed. "So that is what you want us to do, then? Track a bunch of armed lunatics through the rainforest?"

"Ah, excuse me?" Claudia said suddenly. "Armed lunatics?"

"For goodness sake, Maya," Elaine said. "You didn't tell her?"

"Tell me what?"

"Uh, I have been a little busy tonight, you know finding out everyone has been lying to me this whole time?" Maya said indignantly. "And anyway, I thought we were leaving so I wouldn't have to tell her."

"Tell me what?" the redhead repeated, her pitch rising slightly.

"Just, er, it's kind of involved. I'll tell you later."

"At any rate, no," Elaine said before finishing her drink, completely ignoring Claudia's protestations. "I want you to continue on the path you have planned out. Follow the markers, try and find your way to the city. Keep in contact with me as often as you can and give me your exact coordinates. Tell me where you are, where you are planning to go, and when you expect to reach the next point of contact. If you see them, or any sign that they might be near, you get out of sight, get to high ground and contact me, understood? I plan to have a team on the ground by this time tomorrow and they are heading to the last known position. These people are dangerous, ladies, and I don't want you anywhere near them. They have at least a week on you so hopefully your paths shouldn't cross before my team has had the chance to neutralise them."

"Great," Maya muttered.

"Remember your promise, Maya," Elaine tsked at her. "Now, unless you have any further queries I suggest you get to work on clearing that hangover."

"Just one," she said, shifting uncomfortably in her seat. "When I told you we were coming to Brazil and that Rebecca wanted our help you said you thought she was playing me. Did you know or did you just assume from observing her past behaviour?"

Elaine swirled the ice around her empty glass for a few seconds before looking up at Claudia. "Would you give us a moment please, Claudia?"

"Alright," she nodded, squeezing Maya's shoulder before turning to leave. "I'll be right outside, waiting to hear what fine mess you've gotten us into this time."

Maya shot her a tired smile and then turned her attention back to the screen where Elaine had removed her glasses and was pinching the bridge of her nose. She gave her a few moments, studied the dark wood panelling of her office to distract herself from the lead weight settling in her chest.

"I've known Rebecca since she was born," Elaine said, tiredness heavy in her voice. "She's a remarkable woman, strong, smart, resourceful, and she was always so kind and loving. Of course, she's not perfect. She can be stubborn and belligerent, just like you, when the mood takes her, and she was a wilful teenager. If you had asked me that question five years ago I would have said absolutely not, never in a million years. But she went through something a few years ago, and it changed her, made her harder, more guarded. And now this, with her parents...she is so close to them, Maya, she would do anything for them."

She sighed and picked up her glasses, putting them back on and picking up a stack of papers without looking back at her.

"I want so much to tell you that she's not," she said sadly. "But the truth is I honestly don't know."

Maya took a breath and rubbed absently at her eyelid as she let Elaine's words sink in. "Okay," she said after a moment. "Thank you. I'll talk to you tomorrow."

She disconnected the call and closed the laptop, resting her hands on top of it as she tried to gather her thoughts. Instead all she got was a faint ringing in her ears and a familiar empty feeling creeping through her chest. She sighed and stood up, slowly making her way out of the hut and over to where Claudia was sitting on the floor having a cigarette. She pulled out her own pack and lit up before lying on the ground next to her friend and staring up at the night sky.

"So, something about armed lunatics?" Claudia said after a while.

"Yeah, so it turns out there's a shady looking group of guys with guns and a couple of hostages who passed near here a couple of weeks ago," she answered, blowing out a plume of smoke. "So that pretty much sucks."

"Hmm," the redhead murmured thoughtfully as she took a drag. "Well, you seem awfully blase about it so I guess I'll just go with it and use you as a human shield in the event of an emergency scenario."

"Sounds like a solid plan, Claud."

"Did you bring any earplugs?"

"No," she answered, squinting up at her in confusion. "Why?"

"Cos you snore like a bastard when you're drunk and since I'm stuck sharing a tent with you again I was hoping to be able to protect myself a little."

Maya rubbed the bridge of her nose and silently cursed the tequila again as drunken tears of gratitude sprung to her eyes. She cleared her throat softly before she responded. "Are you sure Tom won't be a little upset about that?"

"If he is he can fuck off," she snorted and stood up, holding a hand out to help her up. "No way I'm letting you share a tent with that manipulative bitch."

Maya chuckled softly as she got to her feet, pulling her into a quick hug before draping her arm around her shoulder and walking back towards camp.

"Just to clarify," Maya said with a quick glance at her friend. "Tom won't be staying with us, right?"

Claudia shot her a wicked grin and took a last drag on her cigarette.

Chapter 26

The next morning Maya and Claudia got up early and went about their business as usual, performing their morning ablutions, preparing and eating their breakfast, washing up and packing away their plates, all the while talking quietly between themselves about anything that was unrelated to the events of the previous night. Rebecca emerged from her tent about half an hour after they got up and headed off into the forest, shortly followed by a sleepy looking Tom who, thankfully, got himself sorted out quickly and kept her talking as they ate before sending her off to pack up the tech stuff while he dealt with the tent. When Felipe wandered over twenty minutes later he took a seat next to Maya and went through the day's route whilst Claudia packed up their kit, and he seemed either oblivious to the tension in the group or was completely ignoring it.

Just after seven thirty they said their thanks and goodbyes to the farmer and headed off to start their trek, their pace high as they attempted to make up some lost ground. From the discussions she had had with Felipe during the planning stages and for the first couple of days she knew that today was going to be hard and she was grateful for it, covering the first five miles in a fog of seething anger, her slight hangover spurring her on like someone poking her with a sharp stick. As the morning wore on and the sweat cleared the alcohol out of her system she started to calm down a little and instead just felt incredibly stupid for being taken on such a ride.

"How are you feeling?" Claudia asked, dropping into step beside her as if on cue.

"I'm fine."

"That good, eh?"

Maya shot her a sarcastic smile and carried on in silence, grateful for her friend's presence and support but really not in the mood to talk. Thankfully Claudia seemed to realise this and walked next to her without further comment for the next few miles, the only sounds the noise of the jungle and the occasional slap and curse as someone, usually Tom, was bitten by a bug. Felipe was in his usual position at the head of the group, about fifteen feet ahead, and Maya watched him like a hawk the whole way, knowing that it was more important than ever to learn from him now. There was no way she would ask him to lead them on now. If they really were walking the same path as the people who held Rebecca's parents, that was absolutely not what he had signed on for.

They stopped for lunch in a clearing at around one o'clock, Felipe telling Maya that they had covered around ten miles, good news as they had got the hardest part out of the way fairly early on, and he seemed confident they would reach the village before nightfall. Maya tried to respond enthusiastically but the look on his face made it clear he knew something was wrong and, after they had got themselves settled, he took a seat by her.

"Is everything alright?"

"Fine," she smiled, turning her attention quickly to her food.

"You know, you are not a very good liar," he chuckled.

"So people keep telling me," Maya huffed, pushing her hair out of her face and staring out into the trees.

"You are fighting with your girlfriend?"

"She is not my girlfriend," she snapped.

"My apologies," he said quickly. "I just thought...it does not matter what I thought, I am sorry. It is none of my concern."

Maya sighed and set her plate down beside her, chewing on her lip to try and control her anger and figure out what to say. "She just...we made an agreement about this trip and she...there's just been a bit of a...discussion," she muttered. "Don't worry, it won't be a problem."

"You do not wish to turn back then?"

"No," she said quickly. "No, we keep going. It'll be…"

"Fine?" Felipe interrupted with a raised eyebrow.

"Yes, but really," Maya chuckled. "It will be totally fine."

Felipe nodded and concentrated on his food for a few moments. "You are not concerned about what I told you yesterday?"

"I'm concerned about it, yeah," she shrugged. "But it's a big place, you know? And they've got like, what, a week on us?"

"True," he said thoughtfully.

"Are you concerned?"

Felipe finished the last of his meal and looked out at the forest, clearly thinking the question over before he gave his answer. "Truthfully I am concerned. I still feel like you are not being completely honest with me, and that is not a good feeling."

"Felipe, I…"

"I do not believe you mean any harm," he cut her off, waving his hand for emphasis. "Or I would have stopped this expedition back at the farm, but I would like you to think very carefully about your next move before we reach the village. These people are good people, they will help you all they can, but if they suspect you are lying to them they will not take kindly to it."

"I promise you, Felipe, all I want at this point is to see the stones."

"And after that?"

Maya looked at him for a few seconds as she made her decision. "That depends on what they tell us."

"That is what I thought," he said with a nod. "This afternoon you should walk with me. I have some things to show you."

With that he stood up and went to clean off his plate, packing it away and walking over to the edge of the clearing to smoke. Maya picked up her discarded meal and tried to eat some more of it as she thought over their conversation. She was starting to trust the man more and more and would like to be able to tell him what they were doing, but the secret wasn't entirely hers to share and, after the events of yesterday, her faith in her own abilities to judge whether or not someone was trustworthy had definitely been called into question. As if to illustrate the point Rebecca suddenly appeared and sat down beside her.

"Look, I know you don't want to talk to me…"

"And yet, here you are," she sighed, giving up on her food completely and standing to leave.

"Maya, please," Rebecca said quietly, grabbing her hand as she stood up and flinching slightly as Maya ripped it out of her grasp and wheeled round to point her finger in her face.

"I swear to God, if you touch me one more time, I will leave you out here so fast your head will spin."

"Alright," she stammered, holding her hands up in submission. "You're right, I'm sorry. I've upset you and I…"

"Upset me?" Maya laughed harshly, her lip curling up into a sneer, her eyes flashing dangerously. "Oh no, Rebecca. You haven't 'upset' me. If anything you've made me feel just peachy."

"Maya…"

"See, I knew from the moment I met you that I shouldn't fucking trust you and once again my instincts have proved to be absolutely right. You can be damn sure I won't make the same mistake of not listening to myself again, not fucking ever."

"I didn't…"

"Don't even try it, Rebecca," she said, her voice shaking with anger. "I am still here for one reason and one reason only, because I owe Elaine everything I have. I will help you until we find what we are looking for, or she tells me I can leave, but until then you stay the hell away from me unless you have something to say that involves this expedition. Is that clear?"

Rebecca bit her lip, her chin trembling slightly, then sucked in a breath, squared her shoulders and nodded once before walking away. Maya stayed where she was, a shudder of anger and disgust rolling through her body, and exhaled a few shaky breaths to calm herself down.

"You know," Claudia said quietly as she got within earshot. "I bet it wouldn't be that hard to find another snake."

"You're petrified of snakes, Claud," she muttered.

"I know, but I reckon it would be worth it."

Maya huffed out a laugh and turned to collect her stuff. "Yeah, maybe it would."

The afternoon passed slowly, the heat oppressive and heavy like it was trying to mirror the atmosphere of the group. Maya walked with Felipe, listening closely to any advice he had to give, grateful for the distraction from the pathetic mess she allowed herself to become embroiled in. Again. Rebecca walked a few feet behind them with Claudia and Tom a little further back, sometimes laughing and joking with each other but for the most part as sombre as their friends. Only Felipe seemed unfazed by the heat and tension.

Finally, as night was falling, they reached the village and greeted their hosts tiredly, accepting the food and water they offered gratefully and sat down with them to eat as Felipe made the introductions and explained what they were hoping to see. As the night wore on they were shown where they could camp and the villagers said goodnight, leaving them to themselves for the rest of the evening which Maya was definitely happy about. She wanted nothing more than to slip away and get some sleep, the best way she could think of to avoid unwanted questions from the tribe and another possible encounter with Rebecca, however unlikely that seemed after that afternoon's conversation.

Just as she was getting herself settled Claudia appeared and crawled into the tent with her, fixing her with that look that meant they were going to have a talk. Maya's heart sank and she lay back, closing her eyes in the hopes that Claudia would take the hint.

"How are you doing?"

"I'm fine, Claud. I just want to get some sleep," she sighed.

"Yes, me too," Claudia replied, lying down next to her and propping herself up on her arm. "So, are you going to tell me what happened?"

"What happened when?" Maya huffed as she pulled her legs up. Apparently her friend was not going to take the hint.

"What happened in the last episode of Game of Thrones," she said with a roll of her eyes. "Come on, Maya, the sooner you tell me the sooner I will leave you alone. I don't see why we have to go through this rigmarole every time."

"Because you always try and get me to talk about it before I'm ready," Maya muttered, adjusting her pillow under her head, her eyes still closed.

"If I waited until you were ready I would have bigger problems to deal with, like the intense cold which had recently caused hell to freeze over."

"Then I suggest you start looking for a warmer coat now and leave me in peace."

"Maya…"

"Jesus Christ," she muttered, rolling onto her back and staring up at the canvas. "I told her about the people the farmer had seen, and that they had a male and female hostage and she started freaking out…"

"Understandably."

"Of course," she said with a wave of her hand. "Then she started accusing me of keeping things from her and getting really pissed off so I told her I was going to go and give her some time to calm down and she made some comment about me running off to talk to Elaine. I asked her how she knew about Elaine and she said that everyone knew that I worked for Elaine…"

"Which is kind of true." Claudia cut in.

"Do you want to hear this or not?" Maya said with an angry glare.

"I'm sorry. Please continue."

"So I asked her why she had made out like she didn't know anything about me and she just said that all she knew was who I was and who I worked for, so I reminded her that she also knew where I grew up, where I went to school, about my father…"

"She knows about your father?"

"Yeah, she knows everything, Claudia! Like seriously, everything," she said, sitting up and wrapping her arms around her legs. "And she just keeps on lying to me about it. Like every time I find out something that she knows about me it freaks me out but I've just kept on pushing it back because I like her, you know? But this time I couldn't and I made some joke about her having some creepy private detective follow me around and take pictures of me and she got this really guilty look on her face and I realised she had and that's when I saw the extent of it. These aren't things she's overheard or found out in casual conversation, she has paid someone to violate my privacy. You know how I feel about people lying to me, Claud. If she'd been honest about it from the start, it wouldn't be so bad, but how can I know that she didn't use what she knew to totally play me for an idiot? How can I possibly trust anything she says?"

Claudia sat quietly for a few moments, her fingers playing with the zip on her sleeping bag as she took in everything she had heard. Maya ran her hands through her hair and shook her head, a sadness like she hadn't felt in years washing over her and making her want to scream.

"So, you already knew that she hadn't been completely honest with you?" Claudia asked after a few minutes. "I mean, before last night? You already knew that she knew about your father?"

"Yes."

"When did you find out?"

"In Venezuela."

"In the caves?"

"Uh, no. After," she said, her mind drifting back to that night against her will.

"Oh, right." Claudia said with a slight nod. "And you didn't ask at the time how she knew so much about you?"

"Well, no. Not really."

"Not really?"

"No, Claud, it wasn't really...I mean, there was...we kind of had other stuff going on, you know?"

"But surely when she casually brings up the topic of your father you could stop what you were doing long enough to find out how she knew?"

"Jesus, it wasn't like that, okay?" she sighed, scratching absently at her eyebrow. "We were just talking about her parents and she said something about how she still had both of them growing up, and then she asked me about him and I...well, I guess I just kind of got lost talking about him and it didn't occur to me to ask and then, well, you know what happened next, and there wasn't really an opportunity."

"Until you slept with her again."

"Like I said before, there was kind of other stuff going on."

"Maya, you were in that room together for a good twelve hours!" Claudia chuckled. "You can't just have been fucking each other the whole time. Surely you talked at some point?"

"Uh...not really."

"Oh," she said, a slight frown on her face as she turned to look at her. "Really?"

"We slept for a couple of hours," she replied with a shrug.

"Oh." Claudia stared at the door for a few moments before shaking her head and turning back to her. "At any rate, you have known that she had this information for a week or so now, I'm not sure I fully understand why you got so angry that she knew about Elaine? I would have thought her knowing personal details would have bothered you more."

"It did. It does," she sighed as she lay down and dropped her head back onto the pillow. "It's just the sheer scale of the deception, you know? Like it just keeps coming, wave after wave of lies. And you're right, if we'd talked about it, if she'd just told me straight off, or even when we got to Brazil, then maybe I could have dealt with it. But the fact that she just kept lying and made me believe that there was something between us…"

"Well, I honestly don't think she's lying about that part. But you're right," Claudia added quickly. "How can you trust anything she says? She's fucked up massively with this and put us all in a bad situation. Which leads me to my next question; what happens tomorrow?"

"I guess we head out to the stones, see if they're what we're looking for and take it from there," she said with a sigh, relieved to be on to a different topic. "If they are the first marker there should be some sort of sign and we use the position of them to work out which direction we need to head in to find the waterfall."

"And what about Felipe?"

"I'm not sure yet," Maya admitted as she rubbed her eyes. "Despite my recently reinforced trust issues I feel like I want to tell him the truth and ask him to come with us, but it's not my decision and I'm really not sure he'd come in any case, seeing as we already know what's out there."

"So you need to talk to Rebecca first."

"Yeah," she sighed again. "And I really don't want to."

"Understandable," Claudia said as she patted her on the knee and stood up. "But I'm afraid you're just going to have to get over it. I'll be right there with you, ready to put her into a headlock if you give me the signal."

"Thanks, Claud," she said with a chuckle.

"I'm going to say goodnight to Tom. Sleep well."

"You too."

She turned over as her friend left the tent, resting her head on her hands and staring at nothing as she thought about what tomorrow would bring. If the stones truly were the first marker, and if they found proof that that was the case, would that proof come in the form of a key to show them how to get to the next one? More importantly, if they weren't the marker, or they couldn't find any information to confirm it, what then? Did they give up and go home? Elaine had people out searching for Rebecca's parents now, Maya didn't understand why she still wanted them to continue. Surely it would be better for them to go home and get this planned out properly?

She sighed and turned over heavily. It just didn't make sense. Nothing on this entire trip had made sense. And she had the feeling it was going to get a lot worse before it got better.

Chapter 27

The next morning Maya was the first one up, more an indication of how well she had slept than of her enthusiasm for the day. Her mood was one that should not be inflicted on those of a normal disposition and she recognised that, the only issue now was avoiding people until she had a handle on it. Quickly she gathered together the ingredients for coffee and breakfast and got everything going in the hopes that someone else would appear once the coffee was brewed and take over, leaving her to drink hers in peace on the hillside and ignore everyone for a while.

Unfortunately the next person to emerge from their tent was Rebecca. As the sound of the zipper broke through the silence Maya felt her whole body tense and fought to keep herself from turning to leave. After a moment Rebecca walked over to her and cleared her throat.

"Need some help?"

"You can take over here if you like," she said as she moved away from the stove, coffee cup in hand.

"Okay," Rebecca replied, moving into Maya's spot and taking over. "Are you staying? I wish you would, I know you don't want to talk but I…"

"Rebecca," she said quickly, holding her free hand up. "Just…no, okay?"

Maya had walked halfway to the hill before she realised she hadn't poured her coffee. She stopped with her back to the camp, her caffeine addiction and her desire to not deal with Rebecca waging a harsh war in her brain and keeping her rooted to the spot. After an embarrassingly long period of deliberation she turned slowly back to the camp, scowling when she saw the thinly veiled look of amusement on Rebecca's face. She stomped back over and poured her coffee without acknowledgement, turning to leave again just as Claudia climbed out into the clearing with a yawn.

"Ooh, coffee," she smiled as she rubbed her eyes and held her cup out. "Grab me one will you?"

Maya glared after her in annoyance as she wandered off, toothbrush in hand, then sighed as she turned back to where Rebecca was holding up the coffee pot. Slowly she made her way back over and held up Claudia's cup, willing herself not to throw the scalding hot liquid in the woman's face. Although that would wipe the smile off of it and put her on the first plane back to civilisation. Maya shook her head quickly, a little alarmed by the fact she was considering disfiguring someone just so she wouldn't have to look at them anymore. Not a good sign. She chanced a glance up at her and saw that her look of amusement had turned into a wary frown, something that definitely cheered her up a little bit.

"Thanks," she said with a clipped nod, turning to leave and almost walking straight into Felipe. "Shit, sorry!"

"No problem," he smiled down at her as he dodged out of the way. "Next time I will make more noise."

"Probably a good idea, I'm not really at my shiny best first thing in the morning," Maya muttered.

"I shall keep that in mind," he smiled again. "So we should be ready to leave within the hour. As I mentioned before, I wouldn't use your equipment within the village but there is an area near to where we are going that you could set up and our guide is my contact, so he will be fine."

"Should we bring all of our stuff?" Rebecca asked. "Will we be coming back here?"

"I suppose that depends," he answered with a cryptic look at Maya. "But our route takes us onwards so I would say that we take everything, and remember that we are a day behind. Once you have seen the stones we should discuss the remainder of the journey."

Maya nodded her agreement and took a sip of her coffee, holding out the other cup to Claudia as she reappeared, and then she headed over to their tent to start packing things up. She had just finishing rolling up the sleeping bags and was backing out of the door when she heard Claudia approaching so she shoved the bags out towards her friend, catching herself awkwardly in the chin with one of them which caused her to fall backwards and land with her hair in her face. She reached blindly to grab hold of an offered hand and pulled herself up as she swiped at her face to try and regain her vision, irritated to discover when she did so that it was Rebecca, not Claudia, who had come over.

"What did you say to him?" Rebecca whispered, standing way too close.

"What?" Maya hissed back, taking a step away as she tried to tame her hair, currently running as wild as her temper. "Nothing. He just knows we're not telling him everything."

"How?"

"I don't know, Rebecca, probably because he's not stupid?"

"Or maybe because he insists on talking to you and you are a terrible liar," she muttered with a roll of her eyes.

"Yeah," Maya shot back, her voice dangerously sweet. "Whereas if he'd been talking to you he would have happily walked into hell without the slightest inkling that anything was wrong."

"And just what is that supposed to mean?"

"That you lie better than you tell the truth," she smiled, walking away from her to pull the guide ropes up.

"I didn't lie to you, Maya," Rebecca snapped, quickly looking up to see if anyone had heard before lowering her voice and following her. "I just didn't tell you everything, there is a difference."

"Yeah, the difference between being a straight up liar and a manipulative cunt," she hissed, her face right in the other womans as her anger boiled over. "You have done nothing but play me since the minute you met me and there is nothing you can say or do to make me forget that, so why can't you just do the one thing I asked and back the fuck off?"

"That's not what happened, why can't you just let me explain? Maya, please, just listen to me for two minutes?"

"You had your chance to explain, back in Venezuela," she snapped, desperately trying to keep her voice down. "And again here, in your hotel. Instead you chose to fuck me. Figuratively and literally."

"Look," Rebecca sighed, holding her hands up and stepping back slightly. "I made a mistake. I should have been honest with you, I get it…"

"No, you don't, Rebecca," she spat, throwing a peg down at the floor. "You don't get it at all. You will never understand what you have done here, so just do like I asked and stop trying to talk to me about it, okay?"

With that Maya continued working her way around the tent, her hands shaking with anger and her brain streaming with curses in any and all available languages. As she reached the front again she was surprised and annoyed to find Rebecca still standing there, staring down at her hands as she played with her fingers. Maya stopped in front of her, hands on hips and a glare that could cut glass, until eventually Rebecca looked up, her sad eyes only making Maya want to slap her more.

"I fucked up. I should have told you. But you're not the only one who has been hurt, Maya, and with everything that's gone on over the last six months you are definitely not the only one with trust issues," she said quietly. "It was never my intention to 'play' you, and I don't care what else you think about me but I'm no one's whore. I would never sleep with anyone for any reason other than that I wanted them. I really like you and I'm sorry that I hurt you. I hope one day you can forgive me."

"Don't hold your fucking breath," Maya muttered, turning back around to gather up the pegs and stuff them in the bag. This entire conversation was making her head hurt and she just wanted it to stop. Eventually she heard movement behind her and after a moment she glanced over her shoulder to confirm that Rebecca had left. She dropped to sit on the ground with a heavy sigh and stared up into the trees as she tried to calm down. Why had she not just listened to her instincts? She knew this was a bad idea from the start.

"Are you okay?" Claudia asked quietly as she approached.

"Peachy, Claud," she chuckled drily as she stood up. "Just fucking peachy."

True to his word, within the hour Felipe led the group through the village as they all said their thanks and goodbyes to their hosts. The walk out to the stones was set to take about six hours and the path was not an easy one as not many people came out this way, Felipe explained, and they would spend a lot of time cutting their way through overgrown areas. Claudia walked by Maya's side and as the day progressed and their route took them downhill through thick jungle the two of them found themselves smiling, their thoughts clear to each other. This was definitely the kind of place they wouldn't have been able to see when they were conducting their search. It was extremely dark down here, no sunlight getting through the thick canopy at all, a perfect place to find something which had been lost for five hundred years.

They stopped for lunch beside a small stream in a slightly less gloomy area and Maya stared up through the trees to try and see the sky, her brain cycling through the lessons Felipe had been giving her about navigating through deep jungle. Claudia sat down next to her and also looked up, as if she was trying to see what she was looking at.

"It's looking pretty good, right?" the redhead murmured. "There could be anything down here. I feel like I'm in the Lost World or something."

"Well I could do without the sudden appearance of dinosaurs," she smiled as she looked at her friend. "But let's not get our hopes up too much. It's a big place and we're just kind of stumbling around here."

"Yeah, I know, but we could really do with a break right about now," Claudia shrugged as she took a bite of her lunch. "I don't think I'm exaggerating when I say that this whole thing has gone tits up."

"No," she chuckled. "I would agree with that assessment."

They sat for a few minutes in silence, the sounds of the bubbling stream and distant birdsong settling on Maya the kind of calm that she so badly needed right now. The rest of the group were scattered about the clearing, Felipe and his contact furthest away eating their food and chatting together amiably, Tom and Rebecca a little closer, their conversation seeming more downcast and sparse. Tom leaned in to say something, his hand on her back, pulling away and looking out into the forest when she shrugged and shook her head.

"I'm sorry, you know?" Claudia said quietly. "For pushing you. I honestly just thought you were being, well, you about the whole…"

"Claudia," she sighed. "It's not your fault. I didn't do anything I didn't want to do. Just shouldn't have done it. That's all."

"I know, I just…"

"Look, just forget about it. You thought she liked me. So did I. We were wrong. It happens," Maya set her plate down and rubbed at her face wearily. "Let's just do what we came here to do and get out."

"Of course," she said as she gave her a cautious look. "And I'm not apologising for saying she liked you, I know she did and still does, I'm…"

"Claudia," she said quietly. "Unless the next words out of your mouth are to do with completing this task and are in no way related to my situation with Rebecca fucking Bronstein I strongly suggest you stop talking."

"Alright," Claudia said, her voice way too cheerful. "Let's crack on then, shall we?"

"Good idea," she muttered as they stood up and went to get themselves ready, the others quickly following suit so that within a few minutes they were back on the road again.

They followed the line of the stream for a while as it wound its way down through the forest, the trees bending over the top of it protectively and meeting in the middle like a cloister. After a few miles their guide turned them abruptly to the right and they started to head slightly uphill, away from where the stream dropped down to the left. Maya worked up front alongside Felipe and the guide, hacking away at the branches and vines that blocked their path, the sweat pouring off her in the muggy heat. Claudia, Tom and Rebecca followed them up, carrying their packs and keeping an eye out for anything they might disturb on the way.

Eventually they broke through into a clearer section and Maya sighed in relief, spinning around quickly to grab a bottle of water and almost decapitating Rebecca with her raised machete in the process.

"Jesus Christ! What are you doing?" Maya yelled, her heart hammering in her chest as she shoved the offending item into her belt.

"Bringing you some water!" Rebecca snapped back, her eyes wide. "I didn't realise you were going to spin round with a raised weapon!"

"That is precisely what I've been doing for the last hour! Fuck me, I almost took your goddamn head off," she muttered, grabbing the water out of her hand and shaking her head.

"I'm surprised you didn't," Rebecca muttered back as she walked over to Felipe.

Maya glared after her as she walked off, drinking some of the water before taking her hat off and pouring a little of it over her head. Claudia held out a cloth for her to wipe herself down with, an amused expression on her face.

"Well, that could have been nasty," she muttered, barely suppressing a laugh.

"It's not funny, Claudia," Maya shot back as she wiped her face.

"Well, no, not really," she said with a slight cough. "I was just picturing you trying to explain it to Elaine."

Maya paused and dropped the cloth from her face. "You have real problems, do you know that?"

"Of course," Claudia smiled happily as she held out Maya's bag. "That's why we're such good friends."

Maya glared at her and threw her backpack on as she turned and followed the rest of the group, her heart rate finally coming back down to an acceptable level as she caught up and fell in line a few paces behind Rebecca and Tom. The area they were walking through now was unlike any they had experienced so far, the canopy above them was thick but there was very little growth on the ground except for lush green grass. She supposed it had to do with a nearby water source but they had left the stream a fair way back. A separate stream below ground maybe? Either way, it was much quieter here, almost peaceful though, not the oppressive silence of the place she had been lost in on that first day.

Maya's pace slowed as she thought back to it, the memory stirring something in her. That place had had seriously bad vibes, like something terrible had happened there, this place was totally the opposite. The silence brought a sense of reverence to the place, and it felt almost hopeful here in the middle of nowhere. The last place, though, so close to town, around two hours walk, and it had felt…

Like she was being watched. Her blood ran cold as she thought back to the moment, the feeling of unease almost bordering on panic as she had tried desperately to find her way back. What was it that had made her so nervous? The silence or the fact that she had felt eyes on her? She had to be making it up, right? Just her mind playing tricks on her? There was no way she had gotten herself lost within striking distance of where Rebecca's parents were potentially being held hostage, it was too big of a coincidence. Sure, she was about the same distance away from town, and the timeline maybe fit, but...no. No way. Maya shook her head sharply. There was no way that had happened. It was just a weird place, that's all. Just some dank little hole in the middle of nowhere with a weird vibe.

Still, if she had been there when they were maybe she could have found a way to stop all this. Or maybe she would have just gotten herself killed. She sighed and shook her head again. Why was she even thinking about this? There was nothing she could do about it now anyway, even if it had been real. And anyway...

She pulled up sharply and just managed to avoid walking smack into the back of Rebecca and Tom as they came to a sudden halt.

"What's happening? Why have we stopped?"

"Look," Rebecca whispered as she reached blindly for her hand and pulled her past Tom.

"Oh, my God..."

Chapter 28

The five rocks stuck out of the ground at irregular intervals, standing around eight feet tall with thick bases and tapering off to jagged points about a foot from the top. Four stood in a vague crescent shape, their tips jutting out at odd angles, the fifth standing alone a few metres in front and slightly larger than the rest but around a foot shorter. Maya could definitely see how the legends about them had got started, they did resemble a claw reaching out of the ground, and that coupled with the way the canopy diffused the light and the heat caused the whole area to steam slightly, the place had an almost mythical feel.

She pulled on her pendant and skimmed her fingers over the rocks as she walked between them and took in the scene. Where had they come from? She hadn't seen any large rock formations during their travels but that obviously didn't mean there weren't any in the surrounding area, it just made her question who had brought them here and why? She ran her hand up and touched the sharp edges. There were definitely tool marks here but they were too old and weathered to be able to judge what kind just from looking. The Inca had no metal tools, that was a large part of the reason they were beaten by the relatively small group of conquistadors, but they were obviously master stone masons. They could have created this place, but for what purpose?

Maya turned and looked behind her, watching as the group wandered around the site, only Felipe and his contact hanging back. She caught his eye and returned his smile with a nod before making her way over to where Claudia and Tom had set down their stuff outside the circle and were pulling various bits of kit out of the bags.

"What do you think?" Claudia asked as she approached.

"It's beautiful," Maya said as she took off her hat and pack, laying them down next to Claudia's. "It has a similar feel to the entrance of the caves in San Esteban, but that could just be the light. There's nothing yet to say they are...what we hope they are," she finished quietly, running her hand through her hair and glancing discreetly up at the two men off to the side.

Felipe had his hands in his pockets and his back to them, talking quietly with his friend who was leaning against a tree with a disinterested expression, his eyes staring out into the forest blankly. She turned her attention to the rest of her group just as Tom finished assembling whatever expensive toy he was working on and started wandering around the first stone, stopping every few seconds to take a reading and record it. Maya sat down tiredly and pulled out some water, watching him work without the faintest clue of what he was doing.

"So we're just sitting here?" Claudia asked as she dropped down beside her.

"For now."

"Until your spider sense starts to tingle?"

"Maybe," she smirked as she offered her friend the water. "Or maybe your Texan will find something and we can all go home."

"Surely if he found something that would send us home that would mean we lost," Claudia said with a frown. "Unless this place turned out to be...what we were looking for. And I have to say, beautiful as it is, that would be a bit of a let down."

"Yeah," she said, huffing out a laugh as she watched Rebecca and Tom discuss a particular marking. "Just a bit. Like being invited to Liberace's new digs and finding out he'd moved to a studio in Queens."

Claudia shot her a look. "That is by far the most bizarre analogy I have ever heard you make."

Maya chuckled and stood up, pulling her kit out of her bag and making her way over to the furthest rock, looking all around it for any kind of sign. Finding none she dropped to a squat and pulled her knife from her belt, marking an area into the earth where she would start to dig to try and establish how much it had risen since the stones were placed. She had been working for around twenty minutes when a shadow fell over her and blocked her light, causing her to look up in annoyance.

"Sorry," Rebecca said, dropping to her knees to get out of the way. "Any luck?"

"Not yet, but it will take time," she replied. "I don't want to damage anything."

"Okay. Can I do anything?"

"You can stay out of my light."

"Sorry," she muttered as she shuffled slightly further away.

"How's the cowboy doing?"

"Alright. He's still gathering samples though so it'll be a while."

"What is he doing anyway?" Maya asked, leaning back and looking over at him as she wiped the sweat from her brow.

"Taking readings from the rocks to gauge their age and establish where they came from," she answered as she followed Maya's gaze. "Of course, we would need a sample to match it to before we can confirm their origins but we should be able to pinpoint the general area based on mineral content and density."

"From out here?" Maya said incredulously, feeling a little old fashioned in her methods suddenly.

"Well, yeah," Rebecca answered, looking at her in confusion. "Like we did in San Esteban? Of course, we'll need somewhere to set up a connection before we can read the data he's collecting, and Phil is better at the analysis. Don't tell Tom I said that, though."

Maya shrugged and went back to her painstaking task of carving out a mini test pit in the ground in front of the rock. She had barely made a dent in it and knew it would be at least a couple of hours before she had anything of use, by which time Tom and Rebecca would likely have skipped off to higher ground to analyse their data, but maybe she would get lucky. Maybe she would get a few centimetres down and find Atahualpa's embalmed head staring back at her.

"What are you doing?" Rebecca asked after a few minutes. "Do you think they maybe put markings at the base of the rocks and they've grown over?"

"Well if they did we'd have to dig round them all and that would take weeks to do properly, so let's hope not," she chuckled drily.

"Oh," she said with a frown. "So what are you looking for?"

"I…" Maya stared intently at the floor as she scraped away the dirt, annoyed with herself for being embarrassed about her methods now she knew Tom had the means to do the same thing quicker. Still, maybe she would find something in the fill that would make it worth it. With a sigh she sat up and looked at the other woman in irritation. "I'm just trying to concentrate, Rebecca. Was there something you wanted?"

"I'm sorry, I didn't mean to disturb you," she said, her cheeks reddening slightly, though with annoyance or embarrassment Maya couldn't tell. "I just wanted to talk to you about what happens. You know, if we find something. But it's a little difficult to discuss anything with them here."

Maya glanced over at where Felipe was sitting, arms folded around his knees and watching them silently. His friend now appeared to be sleeping propped up against a tree, the site they were so interested in apparently old news to him. She frowned and returned to her task, as she thought over their options.

"Well, how about you ask him to show you to the camp? It didn't look that far on the map," she said after a moment. "They can take you and

Claudia there with the stuff, Tom and I can keep working, you guys set up and then make your way back here."

"Okay. What if they want to come back with us?"

"I'm sure you'll think of something, Rebecca," she scoffed as she focussed on her task. "You're pretty good at getting people to do what you want."

She saw Rebecca tense slightly out of the corner of her eye then, after several moments of frosty silence, she stood up and walked over to Claudia, exchanging a few words with her before heading over to Felipe with a smile. Maya watched discreetly as he jumped up to greet her, listening to her suggestion and nodding quickly. After a few minutes the four of them were off, leaving Maya and Tom alone in the clearing to continue their work.

Two hours later Maya sat up and cracked her back, rubbing at her neck to try and smooth out the kinks. She looked over to where Tom was now sitting on the ground doing something with his equipment as he drank some water, a look of deep concentration on his face. She stood up and walked towards him, stretching her arms above her head and shaking out her stiff legs as she went.

"Hey, Tex," she called out, apparently startling him with her approach. "Get what you needed?"

"Shit, I forgot you were here," he laughed as he looked up at her. "Never known anyone to be so quiet."

"Yeah, well, you know," she shrugged as she rummaged through her bag to find her book. "Concentrating."

"Sure."

"So, did you solve it?"

"I don't know," he answered, rubbing his head as he yawned and leaned back. "Maybe. Just need to get this stuff uploaded so we can see what's going on. How about you? Find anything useful in your...hole?"

"Trench," Maya muttered back, shooting him a glare. "And maybe."

"Okay," he laughed, lying down and draping his arm over his eyes. "Whatever, dude. Wake me up when the girls get back."

Maya rolled her eyes and walked back over to the rock, flicking through her book and pulling out the chart she needed as she reached the shallow trench and stepped into it. She held it up against the side wall as she dropped down, testing the colours to get a reading as best she could, although really she had no clue having never dug in this type of environment before. Two and a half hours of sifting through soil and she hadn't turned up anything but some scary looking bugs and a bunch of unreadable dirt.

"Hey," Claudia called from behind her.

"Fuck! Jesus, Claud, you scared the shit out of me," she breathed, her hand clapped over her heart. "Make some noise when you're sneaking up on me, would you?"

"That would kind of defeat the point, don't you think? Budge over," she smiled brightly as she dropped down next to her, almost stepping on her foot the trench was so small, and taking the chart out of her hand. "So, what does Munsell have to say?"

"Not much," Maya sighed, sitting on the edge in defeat and giving Claudia more space to work. "Plus the stratigraphy is so different to what I'm used to working with I'm not really sure what I'm seeing."

"Hmm, I suppose we should have expected that. I mean the deposition here would be vastly different from a populated area," she murmured as she crouched down and compared the layers to the chart. "Nothing useful in the fill?"

"No," she sighed, brushing stray bits of dirt from her bare legs and rubbing her hands on her already filthy shorts, idly wondering how many clean pairs she had with her.

"And in the trench itself?" Claudia asked, turning to look up at her. "Nothing inorganic?"

"Just nothing. No midden, no shards, no coins," she sighed. "Nothing to prove that anyone was here ever, other than the fucking rocks, and definitely nothing to say who they were or what they were doing. I don't know what this place was, Claud, but it certainly wasn't part of a settlement."

"Hmm," Claudia said again, sifting gently through the pile of back dirt Maya had created and looking around the area. "Or maybe we're just looking in the wrong place."

"Well maybe but I figured that if this was some sort of dwelling the most likely place to find evidence of that would be here in the middle," Maya gestured to where she had dug the trench. "Like if there was a covering at some stage that disintegrated it would have fallen in and been buried over time."

"True, but it would most likely have been plant based and therefore mixed in with all the other debris so you probably wouldn't be able to differentiate."

"Yeah, I guess."

"And if the site is Incan any dwelling they built would be far more complex."

"Yeah, but it's most likely not," Maya sighed, flopping back to lie on the ground, her legs still in the trench.

"I'm not so sure about that," Rebecca said, appearing over her suddenly and scaring the life out of her once more.

"Jesus!" Maya yelled, leaping back up and swinging her legs out of the hole. "Don't you guys realise we're in the middle of nowhere? What's with all the sneaking about?"

"I'm sorry," she said, attempting to keep the smirk off her face. "I thought you knew I was there. Impressive hole."

"Thanks," she muttered before walking back over to her stuff and grabbing some water.

"But you can't seriously tell me you don't think the Inca did this?" Rebecca asked as she followed her. "Look at the way the rocks are cut? They're almost identical to the death steps at Machu Picchu."

"Well they are hardly unique, Rebecca."

"Not now, but at the time they were."

"Their positioning, maybe."

"Well of course the positioning," she said in frustration, throwing her hands in the air. "But whilst we're on the subject of positioning, do you see any large deposits of rock nearby that these stones might have been brought from?"

"No, but that doesn't mean anything, we walked here from the south via one trail," Maya shot back with a hand on her hip. "We have no idea what is in any of the other directions."

"True, but from what we've seen on the whole trip so far it seems unlikely in this type of environment."

"You don't think there are any rocks in the Amazon?" Maya asked in amusement.

"Of course I don't think there aren't any…" she stopped short and took a breath. "Why are you being so difficult?"

"I'm not being difficult at all, Rebecca," Maya said as calmly as she could, thinking that given the circumstances she was being incredibly professional. "I just think you are reaching to make this fit because you want it to so desperately, and I know the feeling. So just take a step back and look at them."

Rebecca glared at her for a few moments and then turned to face the stones in front of them, throwing her hands up in a shrug before letting them fall with a clap onto her thighs.

"I mean really look at them," Maya sighed, stepping up behind her and taking hold of Rebecca's shoulders, forcing the shorter woman to focus on the area. "Look at them with an objective eye and tell me if you see anything in them, anything at all, other than the fact that you want them to be, that leads you to believe these stones were cut and placed by the Inca?"

They stood in silence for a few minutes as they looked at the scene, taking in the detail of each stone, and as the time ticked by Maya felt Rebecca's shoulders begin to drop in defeat. "No," she said quietly.

"Right. Then stop making assumptions and help us find something useful," Maya said as she let go of her shoulders and walked back over to Claudia. "Anything?"

"No," the redhead answered with a smirk. "But I did just realise that you do occasionally listen to me."

"What?"

"You sort of stole my speech there, Rodriguez," she chuckled. "Of course, I am the master of dealing with tunnel visioned women. You've given me years of practice."

"Shut up," Maya muttered, handing her the water with a small smile. "So what do you suggest, master?"

"I suggest we borrow Tom's GPR and do a sweep, see if there's anything buried around here."

"Seems unlikely."

"True, but we only have about two hours of light left and we have to start somewhere."

"Yeah, I guess," she sighed, turning to where Tom was sleeping on the ground. "Tex, wake up! We need your equipment."

"That's what all the ladies say," he muttered from under his arm.

"You wish, pendejo," she scoffed, giving his leg a less than gentle kick as she reached him. "Get up and show me how this thing works."

Maya sat down with a heavy sigh and stared at the middle stone, rising up out of the ground in the fading light like it was giving her the finger. Claudia, Rebecca and herself had taken turns over the last couple of hours to sweep the site, Tom having gone back up to the camp to start analysing the data he had gathered. In desperation she had taken to scanning the stones with her blacklight for the last half hour, hoping against hope that maybe they would flare up like the rock at Piedra del Indio but, as she expected, nothing.

"This is not looking good," Claudia murmured as she sat next to her, the two of them watching Rebecca work at the opposite edge of the circle.

"Tell me about it," Maya replied, pulling at her pendant in frustration. "I don't know what to do."

"Maybe you should pee?"

"You're not funny, Claudia," she huffed, her friend's words making her suddenly realise that she desperately needed to go.

"Of course I am, but I'm also serious," Claudia said. "We seem to be at that stage again where if we don't get a serious blast of Mayavision we're fucked."

"We're not fucked, we'll just, I don't know, sleep on it," she sighed. "But now you've made me have to pee so I'm gonna go up there."

"Okay," Claudia chuckled. "Good luck. Really."

Maya laughed as she walked away and up the hill towards the forest. Mayavision. She liked that. Maybe she should patent it? She pushed through the leaves and branches, all the while scanning the ground for anything dangerous or useful, until she found a good spot. Quickly going about her business she headed back through the trees towards the rocks, realising with a heavy heart that the light was much dimmer than it had been even a few minutes before and that they would have to start heading up to the camp if they wanted to make it before dark. She got to the top of the hill and looked down at her friends, her eyes going wide as she saw the stones from this angle.

"Claudia! Rebecca!" Maya called out, a smile breaking over her face. "Get up here now, bring the camera!"

Chapter 29

Claudia reached her first, camera in hand and a hopeful expression on her face. Maya pointed excitedly back down the hill, spinning her friend round so wildly she almost made her fall and laughing as Claudia gasped at the sight. Without saying a word she got the camera out and started taking photos, handing the bag to Maya so she could pull out the prints from San Esteban and compare the two.

"What is it?" Rebecca asked breathlessly as she reached them, her eyes going wide as she turned around and looked back down the hill. "Oh my God! It looks just like…"

"This?" Maya said, holding up the photograph of the petroglyph with the 'emperor' on it and pointing at the 'dandelion clock' at the top of the picture.

"Yes!" Rebecca said as she grabbed the picture from Maya's hand. "I knew it! I knew this was it!"

"Alright, but don't get excited," she said, standing up and looking back at the stones. "Sure, they look like the drawing on the rock…"

"Exactly like the drawing on the rock…"

"But it could just be a coincidence," she continued, ignoring the interruption and the derisive snort that followed. "And even if it isn't, we still don't know what it means."

"Well it obviously means something!" Rebecca said, her voice rising as her obvious frustration grew. "Come on, Maya, you can't seriously expect me to believe that you, of all people, can't see that this means something?"

"I didn't say…"

"I mean, come on, do you really hate me that much that you're going to dismiss this just so you don't have to agree with me?"

"Okay, you need to calm the fuck down right now," Maya hissed, her eyes narrowing as she pointed at the other woman. "Don't you ever accuse me of ignoring shit for such a pathetic reason, or any reason for that matter, and how the hell are you so arrogant that you think I care more about you than finding Paititi, huh? Jesus Christ, Rebecca, get over yourself."

Rebecca held her ground and glared at her, the atmosphere between them growing so heated and the silence so sharp that Claudia stopped taking pictures to turn round and see what was going on.

"Go fuck yourself, Maya," Rebecca hissed after a minute, her lip curling into a snarl. "I don't need to take this shit from you, and I'm definitely not the one that needs to get over herself."

With that she turned and walked off down the hill, stopping to pick the GPR up from where she had dropped it and stalking off in the direction of their camp. Maya watched her go, her hands clenched into fists at her sides, before turning away to let out a huff of frustration and kicking at the ground.

"We should go after her," Claudia said after a moment. "It's not safe, it's getting dark."

"I know," she muttered. "Just give me a second or the most danger she'll be in is from me."

"Okay, I'll get a few more shots. You go and pack up the kit so we can go as soon as your rage bubble bursts."

Maya grunted her agreement and stomped down the hill, furious with Rebecca for ruining this moment and furious with herself for letting her. She loved finding stuff, it was the main reason she did this job, and now instead of basking in the excitement of a new discovery she just wanted to kick and punch stuff till she wore herself out. How did this woman have the ability to rile her up so much? It was infuriating. She stuffed her kit back in her bag and looked down at the filled in trench with a frown. If only she had needed to pee as soon as they got here she wouldn't have needed to dig, and sure, she had worked as carefully as she could but the trench would definitely leave a scar.

"Ready?" Claudia asked as she joined her, squinting up into the fading light with a worried frown.

"Yeah," she sighed, taking a last look at the stones as they walked through them. "I hope you got what we needed."

"I'm pretty sure I did. I shot from as many angles as I could and I already took a ground plan earlier. If there's a pattern we'll find it."

"I hope so or this will have been for nothing."

"Come on, Maya, you don't really believe it's nothing," Claudia said softly. "It looks exactly like the drawing, she was right about that, and you saw it too or you wouldn't have called us up there."

"Of course I saw it," she snapped as they pushed through the jungle up the trail towards the camp. "And I'm not saying it means nothing, I'm just saying that without context we don't know what it means. Why am I the only one being objective here?"

"I don't know, why are you?"

"What?"

"Why are you so reluctant to believe we found it?" Claudia asked her with a questioning look. "Usually you are the first one to get all excited and I have to try and calm you down. Why are you suddenly so rational about it all? Pessimistic even?"

"I don't know, Claudia," she spat, pulling out her machete and hacking at a timid looking branch blocking their path. "Maybe it's because we are in the middle of the rainforest with no idea where we're going and in the vicinity of a bunch of armed maniacs whose potential hostages are most likely our benefactors parents?"

"Maybe," her friend shrugged. "Or maybe you just don't want to find it."

"What?" Maya stopped and looked at her angrily. "That's absurd. Why would I not want to find it?"

"Because you think she's freaking out and will put us all in danger."

"God, you're annoying," she sighed after a moment, turning to continue quickly up the path. It was much darker now and within ten minutes it would be night. "How is it you can always do that?"

"Years of practice," Claudia chuckled from behind her. "You are quite easy to read, you know, once you look past the bluster."

"I do not bluster."

"Yeah, okay," she laughed. "Just keep telling yourself that. You know you're going to have to talk to her, right?"

"Why me? Why can't you talk to her?" Maya asked indignantly.

"Because you slept with her and now she's going crazy so I'd say it's your fault."

"Well you were the one who wrestled her to the ground. She wasn't crazy till that happened. I blame you. You talk to her."

"Maya…"

"Alright," she sighed after a moment. "I'll talk to her."

They walked on in silence, picking up their pace as the evening grew darker and listening for any sign of Rebecca on the trail ahead. After almost ten minutes they caught sight of her about thirty feet on and called out but she didn't stop and a few moments later they lost sight of her again. They pushed on, catching a glimpse of her every few minutes and apparently gaining on her but she made no acknowledgement so they just followed in silence, letting her have her moment.

Fifteen minutes later night fell completely and Maya was relieved to see the glow of a fire in the near distance guiding them home, or what she assumed was home having never been there before. She realised then that she had been following Rebecca which was perhaps not the best idea given her apparent state of mind. She supposed Claudia would have said something had they been going the wrong way, but then Claud wasn't really renowned for her sense of direction so…

"Don't worry," her friend said, breathing heavily from the pace they had set. "It's our fire."

"I wasn't worried."

"Of course you were, ye of little faith."

Maya tutted but allowed herself a small smile as they stumbled out of the dark forest into the campsite, her mouth watering and stomach rumbling as she smelt the food cooking over the fire. She headed over to where Tom and Felipe were sitting and accepted a plate gratefully, taking a seat opposite Rebecca and glancing at her briefly as she ate her meal. She seemed to have calmed down a bit and now just looked sort of sad if anything. It made Maya feel bad and she frowned at the thought. Why should she feel bad? Rebecca was the one who told her to go fuck herself. She was the one who spied on her and lied to her. Okay, obviously she was also the one whose parents were missing, possibly being held hostage by madmen…

She sighed and drank some water. She would finish her meal, give her a little more time to calm down, then go and talk to her. This little meltdown she was having needed to end or they were all going to be in trouble, and if talking this shit out would help that then that's what she would have to do, like it or not. And she really did not. She looked around at the small group gathered around the fire and thought back to their makeshift camp in Venezuela. Everything had been so different then, even though she had felt uncomfortable and irritated she had been excited that she might be on the path to discovering Paititi and, much as she had tried to deny it, attracted to Rebecca in a way she had never thought she would feel again. Now, she wished that that part of her had actually been as dead as she had once believed, and the prospect of uncovering the lost city with someone like Rebecca filled her with dread. She knew that it was too big a discovery not to be of international interest but she had really hoped that somehow it could be done in a way that would have minimal impact of the city itself and the surrounding area. The involvement of the Bronsteins, and despite Rebecca's protestations Maya now truly believed she was exactly like her parents, pretty much guaranteed the discovery would be a media circus.

Every step she had taken to get here had pulled something from her, she felt it in her bones and the exhaustion that had settled on her in the last two days was unlike anything she had experienced before. The group that had shared that night in Venezuela was gone, two of them having stayed behind to relay information, one pulled out through injury, and one in such a state of meltdown that it would have been better if she'd gone with him. Maya saw that now, once again too late to do anything about it. She sighed and set her plate down, turning her attention to Tom to find out where the computer had been set up.

"I'll show you, it's a little temperamental," he said with a smile, standing up and jerking his head towards the furthest tent.

"You know, I'm pretty good with computers," she muttered as they made their way over.

"I know," he said quietly. "I just wanted to show you what I found. Claud told me what you guys saw and I just wanted to let you know Phil and Candace backed it up."

"Phil is with Candace and Vanessa?"

"Yeah, they gave him a shot and he was good to go," Tom smiled. "If you ask me he's just a lazy ass."

"No argument from me," she chuckled as she pushed into the tent, surprised by the relief she felt at hearing he was okay.

They huddled in front of the screen as he talked her through the technical jargon of how they had processed the samples he took and how they had matched the stones to the same period they were hoping for. Maya didn't quite get it, her geoarchaeology class had always been really early in the morning and she had usually been more focussed on her coffee, but Tom was very convincing and really she just wanted to get started on the photos and check in with Elaine. After about ten minutes Tom left and she was able to get on with making sense of the pictures. She plugged in the camera, uploaded the data and started scrolling through the images, cross referencing the shots Claudia had taken with the pictures from San Esteban and the caves in the hopes of making some kind of link.

After a while she heard someone enter the tent and looked over her shoulder to see Claudia opening the zipper and pushing her way in.

"Any luck?"

"No, not yet," she sighed as she moved aside and offered Claudia the laptop. "I mean, there are a few things that I think could give us an idea, but then I think I'm just reaching and then I think maybe I just think I'm reaching cos I don't really want to know, and then I want to punch myself, and you for suggesting it and then…"

"Okay, alright, how about if we just breathe a little," her friend said, holding out a placating hand. "Why don't you talk me through it?"

"Yeah, good idea," Maya rubbed at her eyes and clicked on the first picture. "So, the positioning of the rocks is almost identical to this one, here, that we found on the larger rock in Venezuela, the last…pawprint, comet, whatever in the sequence, right? The one with only five points. And then here, in the cave, we recognised straight away that we were looking for some sort of stones, but they never put in the pattern, like they draw them in profile."

"Right, but if they had put them like the, er, pawprint, I suppose we wouldn't have known what we were looking for."

"I guess," she said thoughtfully. "But they wouldn't care about that, right? I mean, if they wanted their friends to find them…"

"Their friends?" Claudia asked quizzically. "What makes you say that?"

"What?" Maya looked up in confusion. "Oh, nothing, just something Vanessa said. Anyway, the picture in the cave is clearly a map of sorts, so why draw the stones without any way of determining which way you go from there? I mean, I thought maybe there would be something at the site to show us but unless they drew it right at ground level, like Rebecca suggested, and it's grown over…I just don't get it."

"But maybe the layout is the the pointer?" Claudia said, flicking through the photos. "Maybe they left the painting but to be safe hid the key somewhere else. Like, they showed that the marker was a set of stones, but you couldn't tell which direction the stones were pointing you in until you had the key?"

She turned the laptop to Maya with a smile. On the screen were two photos side by side, one of the last pawprint on the rock at San Esteban and the other of the stone circle. Claudia had positioned the pictures so that the pawprint matched the direction of the stones, with the 'thumb' stone at the top right. There was a line running above the pattern on the rock and the angle of the stone circle photograph clearly showed the river in the valley below following the same trajectory.

"Jesus," Maya breathed. "Are you serious?"

"I think it's possible," she said with a small shrug. "The next marker is a waterfall. If it falls into a lake which feeds into this river then…well…"

"Claudia, you are my fucking hero," Maya beamed broadly, grabbing her face in her hands and kissing her forehead. "You just broke the motherfucking case."

"Alright, Serpico, calm down," she muttered, rubbing her forehead with her hand. "It's not definite yet, and..."

"No, but my spider sense is tingling," Maya chuckled, grabbing the laptop back and jabbing buttons to find her file. "We need to let Elaine know where we're headed next and.."

"Maya, stop," she said firmly. "Look at where we would be going."

"What? I am," she frowned. "Along the valley, find the waterfall."

"And what is along the valley?"

"The waterfall?"

"No, Maya," Claudia sighed. "I mean, maybe, but remember? Route C? Unfriendly tribe? Poisoned darts?"

"Oh. Yeah. That."

"Yeah," she huffed. "That. And you still need to talk to Rebecca."

"Oh, God," Maya groaned, running her hands through her hair. "Alright. But then you need to message Elaine and tell her what's going on. She said we had to get in touch asap, she's probably already calling for my blood."

"What? No way, I'm not doing that."

"Fine," she smiled with a shrug. "I'll call Elaine, you talk to Rebecca."

Claudia glared at her for a few seconds then opened up her email. "I'll let you know what Elaine says."

"Great. I'll be back soon," Maya muttered with a roll of her eyes. She stopped with her hand on the zipper as something caught her attention and turned back to her friend as she sniffed the air. "Can you smell burning?"

"What?" Claudia's eyes went wide with alarm as she checked over the equipment. "No. Really?"

"Maybe it's just you," she shrugged with a wink. "Smoking's bad for you, Claud. You should cut down."

"Yes, I'll do that," she huffed. "As soon as you stop drinking. Now piss off."

She chuckled as she opened up the tent and crawled out into the night. She looked around to see Felipe pacing over by the trees as he smoked a little way off and gave him a small wave as she headed back, hoping desperately that Rebecca would have gone to bed by now. She could see the fire was still lit though, meaning that someone was still up. God, she had never wanted to see that goofy cowboy so much in all the time she had known him. Sadly, although obviously for the best, as she drew closer she saw Rebecca sitting by the fire, Tom yawning by her side.

"Hey," she said awkwardly as she reached them. "Can I, er, can we go somewhere and talk for a minute?"

"I can go if you…" Tom stuttered.

"No, it's better if we…" Maya said, jerking her head towards Felipe before looking back to Rebecca. "That okay?"

"Sure," she answered stiffly, standing up and following her around the campfire and into the forest. "Are you sure it's safe out here at night?"

"Yeah, I noticed on the way up that it drops off towards the valley out here to the right," Maya nodded, folding her arms across her chest against the chill night air. Mostly. "It should be okay and the view will be awesome."

"Great."

They walked in silence for the next ten minutes or so, the full moon and increasingly sparse canopy making their way easier, the sounds of the jungle making the atmosphere uncertain and calming in equal measure. Finally they broke through the treeline and found themselves at the edge of a sharp drop, the view over the valley breathtaking.

"Wow," Rebecca breathed, stepping closer to the edge than Maya felt comfortable with.

"Yeah," she murmured, moving back slightly and sitting on a fallen tree in the hopes Rebecca would step away from the edge and join her. After a moment she cleared her throat to grab her attention. "So, we might have found something useful."

"Really? I thought it didn't mean anything," she called over her shoulder.

"Come on, Rebecca," she sighed. "I never said that."

"Uh, yes you did," Rebecca laughed bitterly.

"I said we didn't know what it meant."

"And obviously you were right."

"Well, yes, but I think we might have found something so…" Maya sighed. This conversation was wearily familiar. "Would you just come and sit down so I can talk to you?"

Rebecca shook her head softly before taking a deep breath, squaring her shoulders and turning around with a smile on her face. "Sure, Maya," she said breezily as she walked over and sat next to her. "What did you find?"

"Okay," she said uneasily. "So, we think that the picture in the cave was a map, but you need a key to unlock it. Like the map tells you that the stones are the second marker but it doesn't show you the configuration, or how to read it."

"Right. But the pictures on the glyph tell you how to read it."

"Yeah," she said with a frown. "That's what we think."

"Okay," Rebecca said with a nod, tucking her hair behind her ears. "So how? The solo stone is a pointer? "

"Uh, yeah," she said softly, scratching at her eyebrow as her frown deepened "It looks like we head down into the valley and follow the river till we get to the waterfall."

"And?"

"And?" Maya asked looking up in confusion.

"You have that look again," she said simply. "Like you have something you don't want me to know."

"It's just," Maya winced slightly and looked down at her hands, wondering why everybody could suddenly read her so easily. "Remember when we first showed Felipe the route and he said we should head north because there was a hostile tribe to the west?"

"Yes?"

"So that's where the valley takes us," she said. "Back at the hotel Claudia and I plotted various routes from here on out to try and see where the black spots where. This was the one we were really hoping wouldn't come up."

"Right," Rebecca nodded. "But you decided not to share that."

"Come on, Rebecca," she sighed, clasping her hands between her legs. "Don't start this again."

"Don't start what?" Rebecca said blithely. "Pointing out that you're a hypocrite?"

"What? How am I a hypocrite?"

"Because you have all this information that you don't share with me and that's okay, you're doing it to protect me. But when I don't tell you everything I'm a manipulative cunt?"

"Okay," she laughed harshly, shaking her head and gripping her knees, her anger beginning to bubble up again. "Please tell me you don't honestly think me not telling you about a possibly dangerous route that we might not even have to take when you are already incredibly stressed is in any way the same as you not telling me that you paid someone to stalk me?"

"I didn't pay someone to stalk you," Rebecca scoffed, folding her arms and staring out over the valley.

"Did you or did you not have someone follow me around?"

"That's not…"

"Rebecca!" Maya snapped, clapping her hands together before pressing a fist to her lips, taking a breath before allowing herself to speak. "Did you or did you not have someone follow me around? It's a simple question."

"Yes, but…"

"No buts," she smiled thinly. "That's it. End of. Now please can we get back to the task at hand?"

"Maya, please," Rebecca looked at her imploringly, reaching out to take her hand but stopping herself at the last minute. "I didn't know you then. I didn't trust anybody. I just needed to know you were the person my parents thought you were."

"Listen to me very carefully," she said softly. "I don't care. You broke my trust. We're done. Can we please just put this aside and get on with what we came here to do?"

Rebecca bit down on her lip and crossed her arms in front of herself, taking a few moments to collect herself before nodding quickly. "Fine. I want to go. Tonight."

"Tonight?" Maya asked with a frown. "What do you mean tonight?"

"I mean before dawn," she said with a nod. "I want to go back to the camp, sleep for a couple of hours, get up, pack up quietly and leave before Felipe and his friend wake up."

"Why?"

"I don't trust him."

"Felipe or the friend?"

"Either of them," she said with a shake of her head. "Ever since we got out here I've been more and more suspicious of Felipe and as soon as we got to the village I became sure."

"Why?"

"Nothing specific," she shrugged. "I'm just very good at reading people and I don't trust him."

"Seriously?" Maya laughed. "You expect me just to pack up and go wandering about without a guide because you," she pushed her tongue into her cheek and chuckled. "Don't trust him?"

"Honestly," she sighed and ran her hands over her thighs as she stared out into the night. "I don't care. I am leaving at 4am. If you want to come, come. If not Tom and I will go alone."

"Oh, so Tom is in on this as well?" Maya asked as the other woman stood up and walked back into the forest. "Rebecca?"

She huffed in frustration as she stared out over the valley, her mind reeling at this latest piece of information. Great. So Rebecca was leaving with or without her. Part of her just wanted to let her go, at least then she would be free of all this crap and could just go home. But the other part, the larger part if she was honest, knew that she couldn't just let her go out there alone. Obviously Elaine would kill her if she allowed that to happen, but there was also the fact that, if she was really, really honest about it, she didn't want her to get hurt.

Chapter 30

Maya rolled over in her sleeping bag and huffed in frustration. It was no good. She had been trying to sleep for hours and had failed. When she had got back to camp she had filled Claudia in on Rebecca's crazy plan and her friend had listened stoney faced before nodding her resigned consent. They both knew this was a terrible idea but what choice did they have? Tom wouldn't let Rebecca go alone and Rebecca knew that, and Maya knew that they couldn't just abandon him either.

Part of her just wanted to tell Felipe what they were planning and Rebecca would just have to live with it, but that would be an epic breach of the other womans trust and that wasn't Maya's style, despite everything that had happened and even if it did mean putting herself in a potentially perilous situation. Also she knew that if Rebecca didn't trust him she would take the earliest opportunity to leave him behind, and this time she wouldn't be asking Maya to join so that was the end of that. Her only consolation was that Claudia had spoken with Elaine and told her where they were and where they were planning to go, although obviously at that stage she had not been aware of the crazy pre dawn start.

Elaine had told Claudia that she had managed to get a team on the ground and that they were not far from them. So far her team had not sighted the other group but they had found evidence of where they had been, although strangely they had found nothing to suggest there was a third party following them. What that meant Maya wasn't sure exactly but she assumed that either the farmer's son and his friends were very careful or they had given up and gone home. Still, she felt a little better knowing that they weren't alone out here, even if they had no way of contacting Elaine's team, or even Elaine herself for the next couple of days as they would be travelling up the valley floor and therefore have no signal.

She sat up with a sigh as she heard movement from the next tent and checked the time on her phone. 3.55 a.m., right on schedule. She shook Claudia awake gently and packed up her sleeping bag as quickly and quietly as she could, opening up the tent a small way and sliding out into the chilly night air to come face to face with surprised but hopeful looking Rebecca.

"I don't suppose you changed your mind and just got up to pee?" Maya whispered in her ear. Rebecca pulled back slightly and shook her head softly. She sighed and nodded, moving away from the tent and looking back at it with a sinking heart. Tom had packed up all the computer equipment and the tent that housed it the night before so that they could leave the others standing as they made their escape. Of course, that meant the four of them would be sharing from here on in, not a prospect that filled her with joy. They moved swiftly out into the forest, only Maya sparing a backwards glance at Felipe's tent, half hoping that he would emerge and make them stop.

They walked the first thirty minutes in absolute silence, the atmosphere between them tense and heavy. Rebecca led the way, her stride purposeful, Tom following with Claudia close behind him and Maya bringing up the rear, keeping her eyes peeled for danger in the dim light. Rebecca had obviously done her research as a few moments later they broke through the treeline near the start of a steep track which seemed to wind its way down to the valley floor. She immediately started down it, dimly lit as it was by the light of the fading moon.

"Rebecca, wait," Maya called softly, moving passed Claudia and Tom to where the woman had stopped. "Are you absolutely certain you want to do this? It's not too late to turn back."

"I'm certain," she said with a determined nod. "I don't trust him, Maya. I don't know why but I'm sure I'm right. I'm sorry that you all think I'm putting you in danger but believe me when I say I think we would be in more trouble if we stayed with him."

"It's okay, Bec," Tom said as he stepped forward. "She's good at this, guys, when she gets a feeling about someone she's usually right so it's best to just go with it."

"Alright," Maya nodded. "Then let's go with it."

Rebecca nodded back and started off down the path again, Maya following her closely as the gradient got steadily steeper, the early morning dew making the task increasingly dangerous. About a third of the way down Rebecca's foot slipped out from under her and Maya grabbed hold of her pack just in time to stop her careering off down the hill. After that they took things a little steadier, each following close behind the other, their hand on the strap of the person in front in case of incident. In this way they made it to the valley floor safely and picked up the pace again, wanting to put as much distance between themselves and the camp as they could before the sun came up.

About an hour later, as the first rays of sunlight started creeping over the hill, Rebecca pulled them off the flat and into the treeline, wanting to keep them as much out of sight as they could be whilst still maintaining a decent pace. Maya had to agree with the logic, if they walked along the riverbank out in the open all it would take would be for Felipe to look out from the ridge and they would be found, if he even cared to look for them. He had had half his money up front and would the other half really be worth chasing after them for? He didn't really seem like the type, and she was sure Rebecca would honour the agreement once they got out of here. Assuming, of course, that they did get out of here.

They walked all day, the gradient steadily rising as the river to their left rushed past them. They ate their lunch as they walked so as not to lose any time, their mood uneasy except for Rebecca. She seemed happier than Maya had seen her since Phil had been bitten, at one point humming to herself as she walked and plucking leaves from the trees. Maya stayed a few feet behind her with a frown on her face as she puzzled over the woman's behaviour. Sure, they were one step closer to finding the city and, hopefully, Rebecca's parents, but that outcome was nowhere near guaranteed so Maya couldn't understand what in the hell she was suddenly so happy about.

Maya herself was not in the least happy. The whole situation was crazy and had her feeling totally off kilter and unable to concentrate. Lack of sleep was almost certainly not helping and throughout the day she had become increasingly uncomfortable and almost paranoid, and every ten minutes or so she found herself scanning the tree line on the opposite bank, a strong suspicion washing over her that they were being watched. After she had checked for about the fortieth time she shook her head and dismissed it as Rebecca's crazy rubbing off on her and ran her hand across the back of her neck in an effort to calm herself down.

Suddenly an unfamiliar sound broke through the noise of the jungle and the four of them stopped in their tracks, looking about in a panic. The noise started to build, a low rumble at first which turned into a steady drone and Maya's eyes went wide as she realised what it was. She turned to Rebecca and saw that she also understood by the way she was gesturing for them all to move further back into the forest.

By the time the small red plane passed overhead they were a good fifty metres off their original path, completely hidden under the dense canopy. Rebecca heaved a sigh of relief as the sound started to recede, but Maya couldn't help feeling torn. If the plane was flying along the river that surely suggested they were following the route the other group had taken and, given the fact that the group apparently kept doubling back on themselves, that would most likely not end well.

"At least we know they're still looking for them," Claudia said quietly. "We're not completely alone out here."

"Or maybe they're now looking for us." Rebecca answered tersely.

Maya gave her a look as the statement settled on the group. Could she be right? She supposed if Felipe had been able to summon the plane so quickly to get Phil out it was certainly possible, and he was responsible for their safety. She sighed and walked after Rebecca, her pace having picked up significantly with the appearance of the plane.

"How far do you think it is?" she asked over her shoulder.

"No idea," Maya shrugged, rolling her shoulders to shake the uneasy feeling. "Assuming it is in this valley fifty, sixty miles max."

"Fifty?"

"Or sixty," she shrugged again. "If it's even here."

"Oh, it's here," Rebecca smiled as she snapped another branch off. "I know it. We'll just need to walk quicker."

Maya shot a look over her shoulder at Claudia and accelerated to keep up with the woman on a mission, shaking her head softly as she wondered how long she would keep up this pace. As the light started to fade seven hours later she got her answer - indefinitely. This relentless march was unexpected and Maya had no idea what toll it would take on them all tomorrow or, indeed, if Rebecca even intended to stop for the night.

"Alright," she called out to her. "It's getting dark. We've been marching at mach maniac for the last eighteen hours and I'm starving. We need to find somewhere to camp."

"It's not that bad yet," Rebecca called back. "We'll stop when it gets worse."

"No, Rebecca," Maya said firmly, stopping dead in her tracks next to a suitably open area. "We stop now. There's a good spot right here."

"And there will be another one when we're ready to stop," she snapped, turning to face her and putting her hand on her hip. "We have to get as far as we can today to make sure he doesn't catch up with us."

"What makes you so sure he would even try?" Maya asked with a frustrated sigh. "For God's sake, you already gave him half the money and he has all your contact information. Why the fuck would he come looking for us?"

"I don't know, Maya," she said, her eyes hard. "But what if he does? What if he was in that plane?"

"What if he was, huh? If he comes after us then that has to mean something, right? Sure, he'll probably be pissed, I know I would be if I got ditched in the middle of the Amazon, but if he comes after us surely that means he's on board."

"Or it could mean something much worse."

"What are you talking about?" Maya scoffed.

"Just forget it, alright?" Rebecca said with a wave of her hand. "Let's just keep going."

"Uh, Bec?" Tom said, stepping forward quickly as she made to leave. "I'm sorry, but I think Maya's right. I'm kinda beat and I don't think he's going to come after us. The last thing we need is for one of us to get hurt cos we're roaming around in the dark."

Rebecca stared at him, a look of betrayal on her face that eventually gave way to a stony glare. "Fine," she said, pushing through the trees into the clearing and throwing her bag down on the ground.

Maya glanced over at the other two and raised her eyebrows. Tom shrugged in return and followed his friend through the trees, pulling the tent out and beginning to set it up with a worried look at Rebecca. Maya huffed in irritation and turned to Claudia.

"Come on, I'll help him get set up if you can make some food?"

"Sure," Claudia said with a nod. "You think she's okay?"

"No," she answered with a look over her shoulder. "I'd say she's about twenty four hours away from total meltdown."

"And that doesn't concern you?"

"Of course it concerns me, Claudia," she said as she grabbed the bag. "I just don't know what to do about it."

Maya pushed through the trees and walked over to help Tom, sending him a small smile of gratitude as he looked up. Although she assumed his intervention was mostly to do with tiredness on his part she appreciated it nonetheless, and more so the fact that he had pointed out the danger Rebecca's crazy mission was putting them all in. She sighed and started work on the pegs, her mind playing through all the ways letting Rebecca continue this downward spiral could end, none of them good. Well, maybe one, but that involved a boat and a bunch of Oompa Loompas so would most likely not happen. Once they had finished she sat down on the floor of the newly erected tent and stowed away their bags before looking over to where Rebecca was sitting, her arms wrapped around her legs as she stared into the flame of the camp stove, occasionally swigging out of a slim bottle.

Wait, what? Quickly she got up and crossed the clearing to where the other woman was working her way quietly through a quart of vodka.

"What are you doing?"

"Settling in for the night," she answered as she stared into the flame, slurring slightly already.

"Give me the bottle, Rebecca."

"No."

"Seriously?" Maya held her hand out and beckoned for it. "Come on, this isn't going to help if you want to do the same kind of distance tomorrow."

"Why do you care?" Rebecca huffed, pulling the bottle closer to herself. "It's not like we're being followed, right?"

Maya looked up at Claudia for a little help and rolled her eyes when she received a shrug in return. With a sigh she sat down next to Rebecca and mirrored her position. "Well, are you at least going to share?"

Rebecca turned to look at her suspiciously, apparently seriously considering it before handing the half empty bottle over.

"Thanks," Maya said, raising it to her lips before taking a large swig. "So, you want to tell me what's going on?"

"I would have thought it was obvious, Maya," she scoffed. "We know where the next marker is, at least roughly, and I want to get us to it as soon as possible so we can find the last one and hopefully my parents. Is that so hard to understand?"

"No," she said with a shrug. "It's just I'd like us to get there in one piece is all and, no offence, it's just you seem a little...unhinged right now."

"Thanks," Rebecca chuckled drily. "I'm surprised you noticed."

"Come on, Rebecca, don't do that."

"What?"

"The self pity thing," she muttered. "There's a time and place and the middle of the fucking rainforest is not it."

"Self pity?" Rebecca spat, turning to face her with fire in her eyes. "Really? You think that's what this is?"

"Well, kind of. Yeah."

"In case you hadn't noticed I am in the middle of an extremely stressful situation here, Maya," she spat as she grabbed the bottle. "You're pissed at me, I get it, but I don't think a little bit of compassion is too much to ask."

"Look, I know this is shitty for you but…"

"Shitty? That's what you're going with? Shitty?"

"Rebecca…"

"No, just forget it," Rebecca spat, jumping up and staggering slightly as she reached for her bag. "I'm really not in the mood for another one of your talks about what an asshole I am and how I just need to get over it and 'be professional'. I'm a person, Maya, not a fucking robot. I have feelings. Sometimes they get the better of me, sometimes I screw up. And you're no fucking saint yourself."

"What has that got to do with…?"

"Screw this," she muttered, shaking her head and heading for the tent. "I'm going to bed."

Maya watched her leave with a frown, an uncomfortable feeling settling over her that she had just made the situation a hundred times worse. But the what the hell could she do when Rebecca was being so unreasonable?

"Well, that went well," Claudia mumbled from behind the stove. "Maybe Tom should talk to her next time?"

"You think?" Maya answered with a glare.

"And she took the bottle."

"Yeah, well," she said, getting up to grab some food. "At least if she's drunk she won't try and ditch us in the middle of the night."

"Are you sure about that?" Claudia asked. "As I recall that's your favourite trick when we go out. You get wildly drunk, say you're going to the toilet and disappear off home."

"It may have escaped your attention, Claudia, but we are in the middle of the jungle, not some club in Soho."

"Same principle," she shrugged.

"Not even," Maya said, shaking her head vehemently. "When I do it it's because I realise I am about three and a half minutes from making a complete fool of myself and I need to be where others are not. She's just, I don't know, upset."

"And the understatement of the year award goes to…"

"Oh, shut up. You know what I mean."

"Yes, I do," Claudia said as she took a seat next to her and ate some of her food. "Because I know you very well and am not currently 'upset'. But she's right, Maya, you could try showing a little compassion. She is having a monumentally bad time at the moment, even if she did bring part of it on herself."

"Are you serious?"

"I'm not saying you should kiss and make up," Claudia said quickly. "What she did to you was not right and if her being all heartbroken was the only thing going on I'd be telling you to fuck her off, but it's not, and maybe you could just be a little more tactful. You know, less you about it all."

"Jesus, Claud, you make me sound like a sociopath," she muttered, ignoring her friend's shrug. "And she is not heartbroken, don't be so dramatic."

"Actually, she kind of is," Tom said as he sat down next to Claudia and kissed her cheek. "It's weird. You must be really…"

"Tom," Claudia cut in quickly, clapping a hand on his knee. "I think it's probably best that you don't finish that sentence."

"No," Maya said, her eyes narrowed. "I'm curious to know how it ends. Spit it out, cowboy."

"Ah," he looked between the two of them in confusion. "Just you must be really important to her. I haven't seen her this upset in a long time. Normally she's so together, you know?"

"Well, you know, her parents are missing, probably kidnapped, and she is stuck in the middle of the Amazon with you," she spat, rinsing off her plate and standing up with a sigh. "And me. Alright, I'll talk to her tomorrow. Try and show some, uh, empathy. Or whatever."

"That's the non-sociopathic spirit," Claudia beamed. "Bravo."

"Whatever," she sighed. "I'm exhausted. I'm going to wash up and try to pretend this sleeping arrangement is completely normal. I'll see you guys tomorrow. Tom, if she leaves in the night I'll hold you responsible so if you are a fan of all your appendages I suggest you don't let that happen, capiche?"

"Of course."

Maya nodded and headed over to the edge of the clearing, rubbing at her eyes and yawning as she went.

"Is that really what you were going to say?" Claudia whispered to Tom before she was quite out of earshot.

"Of course not," he whispered back. "But your friend is scary and I'm quite fond of my nuts."

Maya smiled to herself as she brushed her teeth. At least she would be able to sleep tonight safe in the knowledge that no one would be sneaking out of the camp. Once she had finished she wandered over to the tent and crawled in cautiously, relieved to see Rebecca curled up to one side, seemingly asleep. She undressed quickly and positioned herself on the other side, sleep pulling her under the moment she lay down.

She woke the next morning with a start and looked around the empty tent in confusion. Quickly she pushed her sleeping bag off and unzipped the door, sighing with relief when she saw the other three sitting round the stove. She yawned and rubbed her face before stepping out into the clearing and waving sleepily at Claudia.

"Uh, Maya," her friend said quickly, gesturing up and down with a shake of her head.

Maya looked at her in confusion, only getting her meaning when she saw the amused smirk on Tom's face. She looked down at herself and shot him a glare before retreating into the tent to find a more suitable outfit than her underwear, smiling a little as an affronted "Ow!" reached her ears. Once she had dressed herself she wandered over to the stove and poured herself a coffee, chuckling as she noticed Tom rubbing the back of his head. She sat next to Rebecca, taking a moment to gauge her mood before she spoke. She was hunched over, staring into her coffee with her hands wrapped firmly around her mug and a frown on her face.

"How're you doing?"

"Just fine, thank you," Rebecca answered in a clipped tone. "Although I would be better if we could get going."

"Of course," she nodded as she drank her coffee. "Just give me five minutes. What time is it?"

"Six thirty." Claudia answered as she started packing up the stove. "I was about one minute from checking you were still alive."

"Your concern is overwhelming, Claud," she drawled.

"I know, it's exhausting being so nice," the redhead beamed.

"The back of my head would disagree," Tom muttered as he stood up.

"Well then you shouldn't be such a pervert, should you?"

"Dude, she was practically naked!"

"I'm sorry," Claudia said with a shake of her head, turning to face him with a dangerous smile on her face. "I must have misheard. Did you just call me 'dude'? Whilst trying to justify leering at my best friend?"

"Oh, shit," Maya muttered into her coffee. She knew this Claudia. This was a Claudia you didn't want to argue with.

"Ah, come on, ma...Claudia," he sighed, his shoulders dropping as he realised this wasn't going to end well. "You know that's not what I meant."

"Oh, really? Then what did you mean?"

"Okay," Rebecca sighed, turning to Maya as she stood up. "Maybe we should go pack up the tent so we can get going?"

"Yeah," she answered quietly, following her away from the arguing couple. "Good idea."

"And pretend that they are not about to have a huge fight over him ogling you." Rebecca added with a pained smile.

They had been walking for about eight hours, their pace slightly less frantic than yesterday due in part, Maya had no doubt, to Rebecca's slight hangover, much as she denied it. She wiped the back of her neck with a cloth and took a drink of water before offering the bottle to the brunette, smiling at her as she accepted it gratefully. Tom and Claudia were a few feet behind them, their fight having long since been resolved as Tom appeared to be quite the charmer when he wanted to be.

"How are you feeling today?" Maya asked as they walked.

"I told you, I'm fine," she muttered back. "You're acting like I was wasted."

"No, I didn't mean the hangover, I meant the, uh, other thing."

"Oh," Rebecca shot her a look. "You mean the 'unhinged' thing?"

"Yeah, sorry about that," she smiled ruefully and pulled off her hat. "But then you know I'm not the most tactful of people."

"I am vaguely aware of it, yes," Rebecca said with a roll of her eyes. "But to answer your question I am not now, nor have I ever been, feeling unhinged."

"Good to know," she laughed. "Any other feelings?"

Rebecca turned to her and gave her a strange look, holding it for a second before turning her eyes back to the path. "No. Just want to get to the next marker."

"Yeah, well we put a sizeable dent in those fifty miles yesterday," Maya said with a frown. Claudia had marked their position the previous night as best she could and it looked like they had covered around twenty five miles, twice as far as they had covered in any of the previous days and around ten miles more than Claudia had predicted for them when they had pegged this as a possible route. No wonder her legs were stiff.

"I would still rather we had done more."

"I know, but we have to pace ourselves, Rebecca," she sighed. "Who knows how much further we have to go? Even if we reach the second marker today there's no telling how far away the third one is."

"By the looks of the map the last one is right next to it."

"Yeah, but the 'map' is not to scale, and why even bother having a third marker if they're right next to each other?"

"I don't know, Maya," she huffed. "I thought that part was your job?"

"Then maybe you should let me do my job and listen to me," Maya snapped. "I'm out here to help you, Rebecca, but I can't do that if you're going to keep riding me."

"I'd say that's the last thing I'm likely to be doing at this point," she laughed drily.

"That's not funny and really not helpful," Maya huffed, pulling her machete out of her belt and taking her aggression out on some helpfully placed vines blocking their path.

For the next three hours they walked pretty much in silence, the rapid pace being driven by Maya this time as she attempted to stay a suitable distance in front of Rebecca and avoid further conversation. Why the hell did she have to say stuff like that? It wasn't helping anybody and they sure as shit didn't need anything else messing with their heads. Maya was really trying to keep her anger about everything that had happened under control, knowing that her and Rebecca sniping at each other would do nothing but make this situation extremely irritating and unpleasant for all concerned. She looked around in agitation, her paranoia from the previous day washing over her again, stronger this time. Suddenly she caught sight of something through the trees and stopped dead in her tracks, her hand on her machete, her eyes scanning the treeline as she searched for whatever it was that had caught her eye.

"What is it?" Rebecca asked as she caught up.

"Nothing," she muttered. "Just, uh...nothing."

"Are you sure?"

"Yeah," she nodded as she started forward again. "Just a monkey."

She moved on quickly, her eyes darting back to the opposite bank more often now. Had she seen something or was it just the atmosphere that had been building up over the last few days? At this stage she really couldn't tell but either way her defences were up. Her eyes had gone into Terminator mode, sweeping from side to side with unerring vigilance, analysing every sight and sound that she encountered like it meant life or death. Suddenly the forest in front of them began to thin out and the sound of running water caused her ears to prick up.

"Do you hear that?" Rebecca asked, grabbing hold of her elbow. "Is that the waterfall?"

"It sounds like...Rebecca, wait!" Maya reached out as she pushed past her and ran through the forest.

Quickly she took off after her. She had a bad feeling about this. After they had been running for about five minutes they reached the edge of the forest where the river abruptly shifted to the right and cut off their route, ending around thirty feet away in a glistening pool of water with a fifty foot waterfall pouring into it, the light sparkling off it in dazzling rays.

Rebecca was rapidly approaching the edge of it and threw down her bag, her face lit up with relief and excitement. Maya almost felt bad for her apprehension and as she drew near she slowed her pace, her sense of unease calmed slightly by the sounds of the waterfall and the beauty of the lake. She even smiled as she heard Rebecca's excited whoop and stared up at the top of the cascade, closing her eyes to feel the sun on her face as she walked. She heard Tom and Claudia laugh as they ran up behind her and allowed herself a brief moment to enjoy the scene, her eyes languidly following the flow down the cliff face to where it dropped into the pool.

And that was when she saw it.

She closed the gap between herself and Rebecca in a heartbeat, clapping her hand over the shorter woman's mouth and whispering into her ear to be quiet as she slowly edged her backwards, her eyes scanning the area as her heart hammered in her chest. From the corner of her eye she saw Claudia take note of what was going on and stop Tom, pushing him back towards the treeline as well.

Chapter 31

Rebecca pulled her hand away as soon as the reached cover and wheeled around to face her. "What are you doing?"

"Maya, what's going on?" Claudia hissed as she and Tom joined them.

"Get back, quickly," she answered, her heart thudding in her chest. "There's somebody out there."

"Somebody?" Rebecca asked quietly, scanning the area as they retreated cautiously. "Like somebody we know?"

"I hope not," she muttered as she checked behind them. "I mean somebody like some body."

"As in dead?" Tom asked, his face paling slightly.

"Yes, Tom," she hissed. "As in dead."

They moved back in silence until they came to the rock face and walked along it towards the waterfall. Maya had seen there was a gap between the edge of the forest and the lake but she hoped it would be short enough that they could attempt to get across it without being seen as the other side was completely covered. Unfortunately as the trees started to thin out she saw that the gap was at least fifty feet and there was no way she was prepared to risk that.

"Shit," she swore. Now what?

"What's wrong?" Claudia asked, her voice shaky as she peered over her shoulder.

"We're too far to make a break for it," she answered, turning away and ripping her hat off, rubbing at her neck in irritation. "We're going have to wait till dark."

"What?" Rebecca said quickly. "No way, we can't wait."

"We have to, Rebecca, we can't risk it."

"My bag is out there!"

"Fuck the bag!" Maya said angrily.

"It has all my notes in it!" Rebecca snapped back. "If there is someone out there and they get hold of it they'll have everything they need to find the city and my parents!"

"How, exactly?" Maya said, throwing her hands up. "If we don't even know where we're going what makes you think they will?"

"Well I don't know, Maya," she answered with a tight smile. "Maybe they are smarter than you?"

"Maybe they are," Maya smiled back, squaring up to her as her temper flared. "Tell you what, you wait here till they show up and you can ask them to take over, and I can be on my way."

"Why don't you just do that anyway? I don't know why you didn't just go with your blonde bush pilot, that clearly would have been more pleasurable for you."

"It's funny," she said with a harsh laugh. "I've been asking myself the same question for the last four days."

"Oh, just pack it in, both of you!" Claudia said, her voice quietly angry as she pushed in between them. "You are behaving like teenagers and it needs to stop, right now!"

Maya bit back her anger and stepped away, slamming her fists into her thighs as she walked back over to where Tom was crouched at the edge of the forest alternately keeping watch and glancing over to where she and Rebecca had been fighting.

"We need a plan," Claudia hissed from behind her. "Rebecca is right, we need to get her bag back and we need to know what happened to that... person out there."

"He's dead, Claudia," she spat back. "What more do you need to know?"

"Oh, I don't know," the redhead snapped, her voice shaky. "What killed him, perhaps? So we know what we are up against? If you weren't so fucking angry with her you would be able to see that."

"Oh, great," Maya span back round to face her, blind rage contorting her face. "So you're on her side now?"

"I am on the side where we all get over this bullshit and stay alive!"

"Guys," Tom hissed. "Keep your voices down!"

"Oh, fuck," Maya swore, her blood running cold as she stared over Claudia's shoulder. "Where's Rebecca?"

Claudia turned to look behind her as Maya took off back the way they had come, the growing certainty that Rebecca had gone for the bag washing over her like a tidal wave. She ran back through the trees, cursing as she caught sight of the shorter woman just too late to stop her recklessly breaking through into the clearing and Maya could only drop to a crouch at the edge, her heart in her mouth.

"Come on, come on," she muttered, her hands clenched into fists as she scanned the forest opposite, her body like a tightly coiled spring as Rebecca crossed the space in a low run and grabbed her bag.

Maya heaved a sigh of relief which quickly caught in her throat when the brunette didn't immediately turn back but appeared to be looking for something. The body. It had to be. She couldn't let her see it, what if it was one of her parents? She closed her eyes and shook her head softly, thinking back to the fight that had brought on all this shit between them. It wasn't her call to make. Rebecca was a grown woman and if the body was one of her parents it wasn't her job to protect her from it. Nothing could protect her from it.

"Rebecca!" Maya said as loud as she dared. Slowly, she turned to look at her, her face set in an angry glare. Quickly Maya pointed over to the waterfall where the body lay, knowing that the sooner Rebecca found it the sooner she would get back to cover. She snapped her head in the direction Maya was pointing and quickly made her way over to it, staying low again and dropping to a crouch with a hand over her face as she reached it.

Maya made her way along the tree line in the same direction, her eyes constantly searching to catch any movement out there, totally aware that there was little she could do if anything happened. Run out there and risk getting killed herself? Take off in the opposite direction and leave Rebecca for dead? At this stage she was mad enough that the second option was the most appealing but she knew in her heart that she couldn't leave her.

Finally Rebecca seemed to have had enough CSI and ran back towards her, slinging her bag over her shoulder awkwardly as she went. She broke through the treeline and straightened up into a walk, barely looking at Maya as she headed back to the others.

"What the fuck are you doing?" Maya spat at her, seething with rage as she caught up. "Are you trying to get yourself killed?"

"Of course not," she hissed back. "If there was someone out there they would have made their move when we first got here, and we need..."

"And you're willing to bet your life on that? Tom's life?"

"Don't be so dramatic," Rebecca scoffed. "I'm fine aren't I?"

"Don't walk away from me, Rebecca," she said angrily. "We're not done here."

"I really don't see what the problem is!" Rebecca snapped, turning back to her and throwing her hands up. "I was just trying…"

"That is the fucking problem! The fact that you can't see the danger you're putting us all in with every stupid decision you make because you won't stop and think for a second!"

"We don't have time to stop, Maya! We're running out of time! They're running out of time, and if you don't want to help me then I suggest you leave."

"I am trying to help you," she said, her hands shaking with anger as she approached her. "But tell me how the fuck I'm supposed to help you when you won't listen to me and pull shit like that?"

"We needed to know more about that body, I saw the opportunity and I took it," Rebecca shot back, holding her ground with a furious expression on her face. "Stop talking to me like I'm some stupid kid!"

"Then stop fucking acting like one!"

"I am not acting that way at all, I am just trying to work my way through an incredibly difficult situation surrounded by people who hate me! I think I am handling the potential murder of my parents quite well under the circumstances. I mean, you won't talk to me unless it's to yell at me, I have Claudia looking at me like I'm some kind of devil woman and whispering with you about how awful I am…"

"Don't fucking flatter yourself, Rebecca," she spat. "I have more important things to discuss with her than you, in case you hadn't noticed, and the reason she looks at you that way is because you lied to us, so get over yourself and stop behaving like a brat. I am not going to let you use me as your goddamn punching bag. We're trapped in a fucking nightmare and I need you to get your head out of your ass and work with me so we don't all die out here, alright?"

With that Maya turned and marched back to the others, desperately trying to calm herself down as she went. Claudia was right, they really needed to get over this and work together if they stood any chance of making it out of here. Claudia and Tom looked up, anger and relief clearly visible on their faces.

"What the fuck, Becca?" Tom whispered, marching to meet her. "You could have gotten yourself killed!"

"Will everyone just calm down?" Rebecca sighed, throwing her bag on the ground as she sat down with her back against the rock. "Yes, there is a body out there but we haven't actually seen anyone else yet and I thought we should use that advantage while we still had it."

"Oh, well great then," he spat, throwing his hands up. "That would have been a real comfort to us all had you been shot in the head."

"Tom," Claudia said softly, running her hand up and down his arm. "She's okay, let's just deal with it later, okay?"

"Thank you, Claudia," Rebecca smiled.

"Please don't thank me," she said through gritted teeth. "What you did was mind numbingly fucking stupid and if you ever put us in that situation again I will bury you, do you understand?"

Rebecca flinched under the weight of her glare and swallowed slightly as she nodded, pulling her bag towards her self consciously.

"Alright," Maya sighed, dropping down next to Rebecca. "I love a good smackdown but we have slightly more important things to do. Tell us about the body."

"Ah," Rebecca shook her head and cleared her throat, glancing cautiously at Claudia before continuing. "It was a black male, fairly young, mid twenties to early thirties probably, shot in the head, close range. I tried to see if he had any ID but there was nothing obvious and I didn't feel like...rummaging."

"Were there any other injuries?" Maya asked as Claudia turned away, a hand over her mouth and a queasy look on her face.

"Nothing obvious."

"No bite marks?"

"Maya!" Claudia cried in disgust, looking like she might vomit at any second.

"If he had been out there since yesterday something would have been feeding off him by now," she explained quickly. "So if not then he died fairly recently and we need to be cautious."

"No signs of anything feeding on him," Rebecca confirmed.

"And the smell?"

"Oh, God," Claudia muttered, walking away from them quickly.

"There was kind of one, I guess. A little unpleasant. Like drains?"

"Nothing like metallic?" Maya asked to be sure.

"No," Rebecca frowned. "Why?"

"It means the blood has congealed," Tom said with a look at Maya. "It would take longer in this heat though."

"But it would start to smell bad much quicker once it did," she mused. "Not much to go off."

"A couple of hours maybe?" he shrugged. "I guess we'd have heard it if it had happened right before we got here."

"And we know it's not one of my parents," Rebecca said softly.

Maya nodded gently, watching her for a second before looking out towards the waterfall. "So, what do we think about that?"

Claudia followed her gaze as she walked back towards them, a frown on her face as she reached down for her bag and pulled out the photographs. "Obviously we need to look around and see what we can find. Are you still adamant that we can't go now?"

"Yes," she said firmly.

"Not to start another argument but I really don't see why," Rebecca said, her hands out in front of her placatingly. "We've kind of established that he was killed at least a few hours ago and obviously by someone ahead of us. Why would they still be around?"

"Lots of reasons," Maya replied as calmly as she could. "First off, we don't know who did it. Assuming that it was the group we heard about then yes, most likely they've moved on, but what if they haven't found what they were looking for? They were supposed to be about a week ahead of us. What if they come back?"

"True, but that could be the case even if we wait till dark."

"Fair point," she conceded. "But I still feel we would have more cover in the dark. We have the advantage that we know about them and will be on guard. They don't know about us."

"We hope they don't," Rebecca pointed out.

"Okay," she shrugged. "But also we don't know that it was them. We are right in the heart of the territory Felipe warned us about when we had planned to head out this way on our initial route. He told us there was a tribe that didn't welcome outsiders. A dead body seems like the definition of unwelcoming to me."

"Yeah, but the guy was shot. If this tribe is as closed off as they say, surely they would have used…"

"God, please don't say poison darts," Maya sighed, dropping her head into her hands with a shake.

"I was going to say other means, probably arrows," she shot back. "But I still think darts are more likely than guns for a tribe with little to no contact with the outside world, don't you?"

"Yes, but really I have no idea, that's kind of the point," she said tiredly. "Either way, and even if they didn't kill that guy they could still be following us and they could still go after us."

"But hasn't that been the case for the last two days?"

"Yes, and I have felt eyes on us the last two days!"

"Really?" Claudia said. "Why didn't you say anything?"

"Because," Maya sighed, dropping her head back against the wall. "I thought I was being paranoid."

"Maybe you were," Rebecca said with a shrug.

Maya cut her eyes at her but held her tongue. They needed to stay civil so they could get through this and Rebecca may even be right. Sure, she thought that maybe she had seen something but that could just be the atmosphere, stress and exertion messing with her mind.

"Maybe not," Claudia said quietly, causing all eyes to fix on her. "There is a third option. If Elaine's team is tracking the other group they should be around here somewhere?"

"But wouldn't they have made contact?" Tom asked.

"Not if they are anything like Elaine," Maya scoffed. "That would just slow them down. They'd probably just be irritated that we were messing up the tracks they were following."

"So we have no idea," Rebecca said with a bored sigh. "And we're wasting time."

"Oh, I'm sorry if our discussion about how best to remain alive is annoying you, Rebecca," Claudia replied angrily. "Would you mind ever so much if we perhaps came up with some sort of idea as to what we are looking for before we rush out to scratch our arses and stare in bewilderment slap bang in the crosshairs of angry natives and psychotic gunmen?"

Rebecca opened her mouth to say something but obviously thought better of it when she saw the furious glint in the redhead's eye. She held up her hands for them to continue then folded her arms and leaned back.

"Okay," Claudia nodded as she opened her bag and pulled out her notes. "So all we really have are the pictures from the cave. Do we get anything from them?"

"Not much," Maya sighed. "Only that the steps look close to the waterfall but there's nothing obvious."

"So what about the petroglyphs? We didn't know it at the time but they held the key to the stones."

"That's a good point," she said thoughtfully, taking some of the pictures off of her. "So the pawprints pointed the way here, maybe something at the end of their trail on the rock?"

"Pawprints?" Tom asked.

"They mean the constellation," Rebecca replied, looking at Maya with a raised eyebrow. "Right?"

"Yeah, right," Maya nodded, still focussed on the pictures. "Pleiades, comet, portent."

"So maybe the stones are the last mark in the trail?" Tom said, pulling out his laptop and studying his own set of pictures.

"I'm not sure it's that simple," she muttered, resting her chin on her hand with a frown. "Why would the stones be in the trail if nothing else was?"

"Wasn't it?"

"No, look," Maya moved over to him and pointed at his screen. "The caves, see? They are on a totally separate rock and I don't see anything on the first one that…"

"Maya," Claudia cut in quickly. "The caves."

"Yeah?" Maya said with a curious frown. She had seen this look in her eyes before, like she suspected something exciting but didn't want to get anyone's hopes up.

"Do you remember when we were trying to find them," she said as she pulled out her camera and flicked through the pictures quickly. "You know, you went to pee and found…"

"Yeah, yeah, Claudia," Maya muttered. "You have a point here?"

"Yes, of course!" Claudia said with a roll of her eyes, holding up her camera for her to see. "This. Remember? You thought it was about the caves?"

"What's that?" Rebecca asked, leaning forward to look. "Where did you see that?"

"In the forest by the petroglyphs," Maya said slowly as she took the camera and stared at the picture from the forest. "Jesus, I forgot all about it once we found the cave."

"Do you remember what you said?"" Claudia said excitedly. "The guy on the water, the mountain behind it, the trail leading off it?"

"Yeah, so?"

"God, do you really not remember this?" Claudia said in exasperation. "You were annoyed with me because you thought it was depicting the lake. Remember? 'It's obviously the lake, Claudia. It's round! And there's foliage and shit around it!'"

"I do not talk like that."

"You really do, but that's not the point," she tutted. "Round. Surrounded by foliage. And the man in the boat. Or what you thought could be someone walking through an area that was usually filled with water. Maybe walking through water? Like a waterfall?"

"Oh, fuck," Maya breathed. "Fuck, Claudia…"

Maya stood up and walked towards the edge of the forest, alternating her gaze between the waterfall, the pool in front of it, the forest around it and the picture of the rock on the camera screen.

"Do you think I'm right?" Claudia whispered from behind her. "I think I'm right."

"I think you're right."

"Um, I hate to put a downer on things," Rebecca said cautiously. "But how can there be stone steps behind the waterfall? It's not like it's an archway. It has to flow from a river up there which means there's a large expanse of ground up top, not a drop and another incline behind."

Maya looked back at Claudia, realising immediately that Rebecca was right. The two of them walked back to the wall with slightly stooped shoulders and sat down, Maya flicking back through the pictures as she tried to refocus her mind.

"Unless the steps are inside, of course," Rebecca added thoughtfully.

"Yeah, right," Tom chuckled. "Maybe the whole city is inside. Like Moria. That would explain why no one's ever found it."

The three women exchanged glances as Tom's words hung in the air. "How would they light it, though?" Claudia asked.

"Uh, guys," he said with a frown. "I was joking."

"Well, the Egyptians used complicated mirror systems to get light inside the pyramids," Rebecca supplied as she reached into her bag.

"Yeah, but they didn't live in the pyramids," Maya said, looking back to the waterfall and then at the rock behind them. "Is it big enough, though?"

"Are we seriously considering this?" Tom asked incredulously.

"Well, we don't know what happens behind the waterfall," Claudia said, totally ignoring Tom's contributions. "It could be a series of caves in there that eventually lead up to higher ground. On the map does the ground get higher?"

"It does," Rebecca answered holding it up. "See? It rises by about sixty feet over the next couple of miles, so it could…"

"Guys!" Tom said loudly, standing up in annoyance. "I was joking. No way would the Inca build an underground city. They worshipped the sun, right? They built their lives around seasons. How the fuck would they do that underground? You're reaching."

"He's right," Maya said after a moment. "But I still think there's merit in the theory that the steps are hidden inside."

"So?" Rebecca asked carefully. "We go and look?"

"I still really don't want to risk it in daylight," Maya sighed. "I think we get some rest for the next couple of hours and go as soon as it's dark. If we're right it won't make any difference when we're inside."

"I agree," Claudia said. "We should get some food then each of us try and get some sleep whilst one of us keeps watch."

"Tom?" Rebecca asked after a moment, the tension in the group palpable.

"I'm sorry, Bec," he sighed. "I'm with them."

"Fine," she said tightly. "I'll take first watch."

"Uh, no offence," Maya sighed. "But I don't think any of us would be able to sleep with you on watch."

"Brutally honest as ever," she said after huffing out an irritated laugh. "Fine, wake me up when we're ready to go."

"Get some food first," Tom said as he pulled out the supplies.

"No thanks, I'm not hungry," she muttered as she lay down and rested her head on her bag.

Maya looked down at her with a frown as she retrieved her own food. She felt like they were in a really strong position even though their idea was just that right now, an idea, one that could be completely wrong, and she wasn't prepared to risk that dash out into the open when all they would likely find behind that waterfall was solid rock. Still, she could understand Rebecca's frustration. She was desperate to catch up with the people she believed had her parents and that desperation was blinding her from any potential dangers. Maya felt sure that if it was her mother out there she would not only be blind to danger, she would actively not care about it.

She could only hope she was never in the same position.

Chapter 32

By the time the sun dropped out of sight the four of them were wide awake and ready to go, none of them having particularly slept and the anticipation of what they were about to do ramping up the adrenaline coursing through their veins. Maya kept glancing up at the sky waiting for just the right moment to make the move, Rebecca's restless fidgeting beside her slowly but surely making her own senses twitch.

Just as dusk began in earnest she stood up and moved towards the edge of the forest, beckoning to the others to follow as she pulled her backpack on.

"We're going now?" Claudia asked as she joined her. "I thought we were waiting for dark?"

"With the moon shining on us we'd be just as exposed as in the day. This kind of half light will make movement more difficult to spot." Maya took one last look out at the other side of the clearing and sucked in a breath. "Alright, I'll go first. If anything happens…"

"I'm not just going to run off and leave you, Maya, so don't even suggest it," Claudia said firmly.

"Actually I was going to say you better come and help me or I will haunt you forever," she smirked. "And you know I would be the most obnoxious ghost."

"I'm coming with you," Rebecca said, moving to stand next to her. "I don't believe there's anyone out there but two targets will split their focus if there is and it will be easier to protect each other if we're close."

"Alright," Maya nodded. "Claud, Tom, keep out of sight until we make it to the waterfall. If there's nothing there there's no point in all four of us risking it."

Tom nodded, a grim look on his face, whilst Claudia seemed affronted but shrugged in agreement anyway. Maya resisted the urge to hug her friend, knowing that the uncharacteristic gesture would give away how nervous she was, and set off towards the waterfall. She kept low, moving fast and keeping close to the wall, feeling oddly comforted by Rebecca's presence. Of course, she also remembered the last time she and Rebecca had been in a potentially life or death situation and that they had both almost died. The thought was not a reassuring one.

As she ran she kept one eye on the trees for movement, the feeling of being watched still present although hopefully that was just because of the vigil Claudia and Tom were keeping. Her gaze flicked to the body as they passed it and she wondered who he was? The other group's guide, maybe? Had he served his purpose and been disposed of or had he tried to run?

After what felt like four years they finally made it to the waterfall and spotted a ledge jutting out along the edge of the pool behind the curtain of water. She quickly moved onto it, almost losing her footing as it was slick with algae. Rebecca caught her arm and held her up as she struggled to regain her balance, looking down in the dim light to see where to step in order to find traction.

"Thanks," she said, looking back over her shoulder as she found a secure path.

"No problem," Rebecca smiled back. "Glad I finally got to return the favour."

"I think I'd prefer it if you didn't have to," Maya said ruefully before inching forward, keeping her eyes on the ground as she reached behind her for the flashlight she had clipped to her bag. "I think there's something back here. Can you wait there? One of us needs to be able to see Tom and Claudia, make sure nothing happens."

Rebecca frowned but nodded, looking back out to where their friends were waiting as Maya clicked the light to its lowest setting and moved further on. The ledge turned into a shallow cavern, about ten feet deep and fifteen feet high, almost like a mini stage with the waterfall as the curtain. She shone the beam around it slowly, looking for any kind of markings or breaks in the wall.

"Anything?" Rebecca asked, just loud enough to be heard over the roar of the water.

"No," she answered, her voice thick with disappointment, swinging the beam back the other way. "It's just…wait."

"What?"

Maya moved forward to inspect what she hoped was not a trick of the light. There seemed to be a shadow in the middle of the wall and as she got closer she saw that there was. The section of wall on their side of the cave was about a foot and a half further forward than the one on the far side and as she reached it she saw that there was a hole in the rock that joined the two.

"I think there's a passage here," she called back. "Give me a second."

"Maya, wait," Rebecca called angrily. "Let's get them over here and we'll all go."

"Just let me check it really is something first."

"Maya!"

She ignored her and pushed through the gap in the rock. It was a tight fit and she wondered if Tom would be able to get through. After a few metres it began to open up a little but it was pitch black and even though she turned the beam up to its fullest she could barely see more than five feet in front as the trail wound about so much. She had been following the passage for about five minutes when abruptly it opened up into a large cavern, once again absolutely no light present except for the one she held in her hand, and no signs of life. The stillness in the place made her extremely uneasy, like being locked in a church at night, and she had to force herself to shine the light around the walls and see if there was another exit before returning to her friends. Finally she found it, about three quarters of the way around, leading off to the left. She sighed in relief and pushed back through the tunnel, squeezing back out into the first cavern to see an extremely pissed off Rebecca.

"So it's okay for you to act like a reckless jackass, just not me?"

"What?" Maya asked with a frown. "That wasn't reckless, I was just making sure it went somewhere and it did."

"Right," she smiled. "And what would have happened it led to a hole in the ground like the last tiny passage we went down?"

"Well it didn't."

"Well that's okay then," Rebecca said, folding her arms across her chest. "And if I tell Claudia what you just did I'm sure she'll agree."

Maya's frown deepened as she considered this and she shifted awkwardly as she looked out through the water. "Well maybe we just don't tell her."

"That's what I thought," she smirked, moving back over to the entrance to gesture for the other two to come over.

They crossed the gap quickly, Claudia scowling as she carefully made her way along the ledge into the cave. "What took so long? I was really starting to freak out."

"We found a passage," Rebecca replied. "But Maya just wanted to be certain there was nothing in here that we had missed."

"And?"

"No, nothing," Maya said with a quick glance at Rebecca. "So I guess we try the tunnel."

Rebecca led the way as they set off through the small opening together, Tom struggling initially and ending up with a number of scrapes across his shoulders and bumping his head more than once, although since he was barely more than an inch taller than Maya she put this down to clumsiness more than size. They piled out into the large cavern with a collective sigh of relief.

"I really hope we don't have to come back this way," Tom muttered as he dusted himself off and put his bag back on. "I am really claustrophobic."

"Good to know," Maya chuckled. "Let's just hope it doesn't get tighter or we might have to leave you down here, Tex."

"That's not funny," he said quickly. "Seriously. That's not funny."

Maya laughed harder and marked the entrance with chalk before heading over to the next passage, flashing her beam around the cavern as she went to make sure there weren't any markings she might have missed. She felt much calmer now the others were here, the space less oppressive than when she had been alone. She pulled her lighter out of her pocket and lit the flame, holding it in front of the opening and frowning when it didn't flicker at all.

"What do you think?" Claudia asked.

"It's either a dead end or we are a long way from the exit," she answered quietly. "Best not tell your boyfriend. Panic is the quickest way to get stuck in one of these things."

She went through the gap, frowning slightly as she turned sideways to fit through and called back to make sure Tom followed her. The last thing they needed was for him to go last and get stuck. At least if he were in the middle they could help him. Thankfully, like the first tunnel it got slightly wider a few feet in, still much tighter than Tom would be happy with, she was sure, but unlikely to trap him. She stayed as far ahead of him as she could so as to give him as much warning as possible if the situation changed.

This passage was far longer than the first and Maya was starting to get a bit twitchy herself as the floor began to slope away sharply in front of her. She aimed the beam down to make sure there were no fissures; the last thing any of them needed at this stage was a broken leg. She glanced back at Tom, his face streaked with sweat and dirt, a look of fear clearly visible even in the small amount of light hitting him from Rebecca's torch at the back of the group.

"Could be worse, Tex," she said as the moved slowly forward. "There could be water up to your thighs and some creature trying to pull you under."

"Fuck, Maya," he spat through clenched teeth. "Why the fuck would you say that?"

"Come on," she laughed. "Remember? 'Shut down all the garbage mashers on the detention level!'"

Tom looked at her in confusion until it dawned on him and he smiled at her before his face dropped. "Wait? Why would I be the one getting pulled under? I'm not Luke. I'm Han."

"Uh uh, no way," she shook her head vehemently. "I'm obviously Han. You're the farm boy."

"I am not a farm boy," he shot back indignantly. "And just because you dress like Indiana Jones doesn't give you automatic dibs on all Harrison Ford roles."

"Hey!" Maya protested, gesturing as best she could in the enclosed space at her white tank top and grey shorts. "How am I dressed like Indiana Jones?"

"Well, maybe you just have on the fedora today but when you and Becca came back from the caves…"

"That was Claudia's fault," she muttered, shining the beam back up along the never ending tunnel. "I had to borrow her clothes cos mine got wet. Come to think of it, she gave me this hat. Claud, do you have a secret Indiana Jones fetish you never told me about?"

"What?"

"She says you gave her the fedora," he laughed. "Sounds like bullshit to me."

"No, it's true," Claudia confirmed. "I did initially buy it for myself but, as usual, it looked better on her. On me it was more Freddy Kruger. Not really the look I was going for."

"You'll have to show me later," Tom laughed. "But whatever, no way am I Luke."

"Luke?"

"Yeah, Maya thinks I'm Luke and she's Han. As if."

"Which would make me Chewbacca?" Claudia pointed out. "Cheers, Maya."

"Who am I then?" Rebecca asked from the back.

"Princess Leia," Tom and Claudia answered in unison, chuckling to themselves.

"Great," Maya muttered.

"Well, there was that moment, remember Maya?" Rebecca called to her. "When you were on top of me in the caves…"

"Hey, look. The end of the tunnel!" Maya interrupted loudly, never having been so grateful to see anything in her life. Although, at this stage had the tunnel ended in a Sarlacc pit she would have been happy to see it.

They piled out into the chamber and stretched themselves as they looked around, Maya and Rebecca searching the walls for an exit and finding three. Maya marked the way they had come in and checked the first possible route with her lighter, again the flame not flickering at all. She moved on to the next and got the same result, so approached the final one with held breath, knowing that if there was no air moving through this one they would be blind. She held the lighter up and sighed with relief as the flame gave the slightest twitch.

"Looks like this one," she said, stowing the lighter in her pocket and holding her bag in front of her as she started down the passage.

They followed the tunnel in silence, their way relatively easy and short compared to the last one, and arrived at another cavern, smaller and with only one exit. They took it and carried on, following the route through so many passages and small chambers that Maya was beginning to get deja vu when they finally arrived in a space so large the light from their flashlights barely reached the ceiling.

"Wow," Tom breathed as he wandered around it, running his hand over the surface. "It's huge."

"No shit, Sherlock," Maya muttered as she walked over to the exit, the opening to this one much larger than the others as well, at least six feet wide by ten tall.

"And these marks in the rock," he said, beckoning for Rebecca to come closer with the light. "Look, they're almost like tool marks. Like…"

"Like a quarry," Rebecca said thoughtfully as she ran her hand over them.

Maya dropped down on one knee and shone the light on the floor with a frown. "I think you might be right."

"Why?" Rebecca asked as they came over to her. "What is it?"

"Gouges in the floor," she pointed. "Like something heavy was dragged through here? Repeatedly I would guess."

"Turn off your torches," Claudia said.

"Why?" Maya asked as she did so.

"Just a thought," she shrugged. "If this was a quarry we could be fairly close to the end."

Rebecca clicked off the light and they waited in the darkness for their eyes to adjust, temporarily blind in the utter black. After a few moments Maya held her hand out in front of her and was relieved to see that she could just about make it out.

"Well," she muttered. "It's not exactly floodlights but it's a start."

"And of course it's the middle of the night," Rebecca mused. "So we could be as little as thirty feet away."

"Obviously," Maya replied easily, glad the dark was hiding the look of irritation her face had adopted as she realised she had overlooked that. "But the breeze would be stronger. I'd say we have at least one more cave to go through."

She stood up and clicked the light back on, heading down the tunnel with renewed purpose, the rest of the group appearing far more relaxed as they pressed on. Maya turned the beam down as they approached the next cavern just in case Rebecca was right and they were about to reach the end of the cave system. She didn't know how long they had been down here but she was suddenly exhausted and the air around her felt oppressive. For the first time it occurred to her that they had no idea how deep they were, or what kind of air they were breathing. The only change in level she remembered was the sharp descent during the Star Wars conversation but after that she had been so intent on finding a way out she couldn't recall if their path had taken them back up. For all she knew they were a hundred feet underground and would have to climb out of here. Her head started to swim a little, a sweep of irrational fear chilling her blood, her hand gripping on to the handle of the flashlight in an effort to keep the beam steady as images of canaries dead in their cages flashed through her mind and she struggled to breathe.

Rebecca and Tom passed her as her pace began to slow and she rubbed at her face as she pulled off her hat and sucked in a couple of ragged breaths as discreetly as she could. Her eyes started to blur and she rubbed at them furiously as unbidden her inner jukebox kicked in with the guitar solo from the end of Freebird and her heart started pounding, her lower jaw shaking like she had just taken a double hit of MDMA. She stopped dead in her tracks as she tried desperately to pull herself together, squeezing her eyes shut and letting out a shaky breath. Slowly she became aware of someone next to her and opened her eyes to see Claudia standing there, staring up the tunnel thoughtfully.

"You never bought me a new chair," she said quietly.

"What?" Maya managed, her voice shaky, her whole body trembling.

"That time in Belgium when you were drunk and set the campsite on fire while I was in the loo," Claudia replied calmly, turning to look at her. "My chair got destroyed. You said you would buy me a new one. You never did."

Maya stared at her in confusion, her brain frantically trying to process what she was saying. Slowly it started to come through. They had been driving across Europe and had stopped at a campsite in the Ardennes. She had managed to get herself ridiculously drunk somehow and Claudia had been really irritated with her so, when Claudia went off to find a toilet Maya had decided to do something nice and cook dinner. Unfortunately the camping stove had exploded and started spitting out fire on all of their stuff. In her drunken state she didn't know what to do except pick up the stove and run away with it. Realising too late that it was not a good idea to be holding a burning piece of metal she had thrown it down into an open space and turned back to see Claudia's camping chair on fire. She had run back and kicked it over, searching around for some water to throw on it, finally being helped by some people from the next pitch.

She laughed suddenly as she remembered turning back to the burning stove and seeing Claudia walking towards her, a look of pure rage on her face as some random man was trying to extinguish the flames.

"You were so mad at me," she said eventually, her grip on the flashlight easing slightly.

"I don't think I have ever been so angry with anyone," Claudia admitted with a smile.

"'I've been gone five minutes!'" Maya said, her impression of her friend uncanny. "'Five minutes!'"

"And yet you had managed to reign complete destruction down on our campsite," she chuckled. "God knows what would have happened if I'd been gone longer."

"You didn't speak to me for hours."

"You're lucky I didn't just leave you there," she laughed, throwing her arm around her shoulder as they walked after the others. "Drunkie."

"Yeah, I guess I am," Maya smiled, her heart finally settling down. She sighed and put her arm round her friend's waist with a grateful smile. "Thanks, Claud."

"Feel better?"

"Yeah, I don't know what that was but I am officially not a fan."

"Well, I'm glad you're done with it then, because I really need a wee."

"Great," Maya muttered. "Now so do I. What time is it?"

Claudia released her and looked at her watch. "Three thirty."

"Jesus, we've been down here almost seven hours."

"No wonder I'm so bloody tired," she yawned.

"Come on, let's catch them up."

They picked up the pace and caught up with the other two just as they reached the next cavern. Rebecca turned off her flashlight and looked back at them with a smile on her face.

"There's light ahead," she said.

Maya turned off her light and walked into the space, relief washing over her as she saw moonlight from an opening up ahead. Or at least she hoped it was moonlight. She approached it with caution, moving a little faster as she felt a soft breeze on her face, her eyes widening as she turned the corner and saw the start of some steep stone steps.

"We found them," she breathed.

"Thank God," Rebecca laughed as she pushed past her and started to climb.

"Wait, Rebecca," she said as she caught her hand.

"Why?" she replied angrily, yanking her arm free. "Haven't we waited long enough? What can you possibly want to wait for this time?"

"It's three thirty in the morning!" Maya said in exasperation. "We haven't slept in almost a day, we've been walking around in the dark for hours and you've hardly eaten. We don't know what's waiting for us at the top of those stairs, it could be anything!"

"You're right, it could be anything," she shot back. "It could be the murdered corpses of my parents and every second we spend debating what it could be the more likely that outcome becomes!"

"And what are you going to do if they're not dead?" Maya said with a step towards her. "How are you going to help them if you can barely stand?"

"I don't know," she said with a broken expression. "I'll figure something out, but I can't just sit here, Maya, I need to do something!"

"I know you do," Maya said softly, reaching out to take her hand and bring her back. "And we will, but we need to rest first."

"She's right, Becca," Tom agreed. "Just a couple of hours, okay? We'll set off at first light."

"At the waterfall you said you didn't want to travel in the day," Rebecca said, her face a mask of tiredness, confusion and sadness. "I just don't understand why we can't go now."

"Because we'll be exposed walking up these steps regardless of whether it's day or night," Maya said as she drew her back in. "We're all exhausted and you look like you might fall down at any second, or burst into tears."

Maya's eyes went wide as Rebecca's face fell and she did just that, putting her hand up to her face and turning her back on them as her shoulders shook. She turned and looked at Claudia and Tom with an alarmed expression and rolled her eyes as Claudia made a shooing gesture with her hand and pulled Tom back into the cave.

"Help me!" Maya mouthed at them as they retreated, putting her hands on her hips as she received frantic shaking of heads from both of them as the darkness swallowed them.

She turned back to Rebecca's sobbing form and frowned as she analysed the situation. She was terrible with people who were upset, always had been. Her default response was to get them drunk or offer sarcastic comments, neither of which seemed applicable in this situation. She took a deep breath and stepped forward, raising her hand and pausing awkwardly with it hovering just above the weeping woman's shoulder, willing herself to be rescued from this situation. Finally she resigned herself to the inevitable and gently placed her hand on Rebecca's back.

"I'm sorry," Rebecca said shakily. "I hate people who do this. I just can't seem to stop."

"It's not your fault," she mumbled. "This is shit."

"Yeah," she coughed, letting out a wet laugh. "That's one way to put it."

"Jesus," Maya muttered, pulling her hand away and putting it back on her hip. "I'm awful at this, I'm sorry."

"Don't worry," she laughed again, drawing her fingers under her eyes to try and clear the tears that were still falling. "I'm not exactly the best at public breakdowns myself."

"What's public?" Maya gestured to the empty space. "There's just you and me. Feel free to break down all you like. Just don't expect me to be able to help. My coping mechanisms aren't exactly suited for down here."

"Oh yeah?" Rebecca looked at her questioningly. "Dare I ask what your coping mechanisms are?"

"The usual," she smiled with a shrug.

"Sex, drugs and rock n roll?"

"Something like that."

"Figures," Rebecca said with a sad smile, finally succeeding in stopping the tears. "I really am sorry. I've been trying so hard to keep it together and obviously I haven't been doing a very good job."

"Hey," she said gently, reaching out to rub her arm. "There's nothing to be sorry for. Well, except for the running out into the open field with the corpse in it. That was pretty stupid."

Rebecca stepped forward with a soft laugh and wrapped her arms around her waist, laying her head on her shoulder with a sigh. Maya stood there for a moment, her eyes wide with alarm and her hands held stiffly out in front of her. She took a breath and eventually returned the embrace, shaking her head at herself as she slowly started to rub Rebecca's back, feeling herself getting sucked back in with every passing second and part of her not caring.

"Thank you," Rebecca whispered into her shoulder.

"S'okay," she said, mentally chastising herself. No, it wasn't okay. This was not okay. Danger, Will Robinson!

Her suspicions were confirmed seconds later when Rebecca looked up into her eyes, her gaze dropping to her lips as she leaned forward and kissed her cautiously. Everything in her was screaming at her to pull back but she couldn't make herself do it and as Rebecca's lips began to move more insistently against her own she found herself returning the kiss, their bodies melting into each other like the last three days had never happened. Like she hadn't lied about everything.

"Stop," she said, gently pushing her away and taking a deep breath to pull herself together. "I can't do this again, Rebecca, I just can't."

"I'm sorry," Rebecca said, dropping her eyes to the floor as she took a step back. "God, I'm sorry, I just...you just...it just felt really good to be close to you again."

"Yeah, but…" she pinched the bridge of her nose and forced herself to turn away and walk over to her bag. "We should get some sleep."

She crouched down and pulled out her sleeping bag, laying it out and crawling inside it before any argument could be made, her whole body humming.

"Okay," Rebecca said after a few moments. She picked up her own bag and followed her, setting up her own sleeping area right next to her and lying down. "Good night, Maya."

"Good night," she said, watching as she turned away from her. Her eyes grew heavy again and within a few moments she was sound asleep.

When she woke up Rebecca was gone.

Chapter 33

Maya jumped up off the floor and grabbed her flashlight, switching it on quickly and shining it around the chamber in the vain hope that Rebecca had just moved in the night, but all she saw was Claudia and Tom's stuff about halfway down the cave, their slumbering forms a little further on. She ran to the steps, a litany of Spanish curses rolling off her tongue as she stared up them in the early morning light. Seeing nothing she went back inside and ran down to her friend, a new spate of profanity spewing forth when she saw that Claudia was alone.

"Claudia!" Maya yelled, shaking her roughly. "Wake up! Get your shit together quickly, they're gone!"

"What?" Claudia mumbled, her eyes bleary as she stared up at her friend in a sleepy daze. "How are you here?"

"What? Claudia, wake up! Come on?"

"Maya?"

"No, the fucking Wicked Witch of the West," she huffed, rolling her eyes. "Get up, Claudia! We need to get after them!"

Finally Claudia seemed to realise what was going on. She looked down at Tom's empty sleeping bag with a frown, then glanced over at his back pack. "They're gone? But Tom's stuff is still here?"

"Yeah, I see that but Rebecca's things are gone and unless Tom got over his claustrophobia overnight and wandered back into the caves, he's gone too," she said, picking up his bag and heading back over to her own stuff. "We need to leave. Now."

Within thirty seconds they were out of the cave and moving up the steps, Maya taking two at a time and Claudia trying to slow her down and keep up at the same time.

"Are you sure they're gone?" Claudia called, her breathing heavy and her face a mask of uncertainty. "What if they both just went back into the caves to cook breakfast and didn't want to wake us?"

"Do you seriously think Rebecca would have waited for breakfast?" Maya called back. "You saw how upset she was that we didn't leave as soon as we found the steps."

"But why would Tom leave his stuff?"

"I don't know," she admitted, squashing down the top of his bag so she could see over it as she was wearing in on her front. "Maybe he saw her trying to sneak off and went after her, didn't have time to grab it. Or maybe just because his bag is ridiculously heavy."

"Maybe," Claudia said uncertainly. "Maya, we should slow down a bit. We don't know what's up here."

"I know but there's a long way to go before we get to the top," she said as she gazed up. "We'll be more careful as we get closer."

"Fuck me," the redhead sighed a few minutes later. "This is like the winding stairs. If there is a dark pass up here with loads of cobwebs I'm not going."

Maya couldn't help but smile despite the situation, but still she pushed on, ignoring the burning in her legs as she forced herself to make up as much ground as she could. God knows what time Rebecca had left but it could have been pretty much as soon as Maya fell asleep, which would give her almost a three hour head start.

"Maya," Claudia croaked out about fifteen minutes in. "I can't keep this pace up. I'm sorry."

"Shit," she swore softly, slowing up and looking back at her friend. She was bright red, sweat pouring out of her, her breathing laboured. "It's okay. We'll just...I don't know, take it easy for a bit and pick it up again, alright?"

Claudia nodded and struggled on, passing Maya as she stopped to let her friend take the lead and dictate the pace. Maya followed in silence, mentally cursing herself for having been so stupid to think that Rebecca would just wait. She wouldn't have if the roles were reversed, she would have done exactly the same thing without a moment's hesitation. She looked around as they climbed higher. The steps were steep, almost like on a Mayan temple, but winding around in line with the natural curve of the slope which reminded her of the steps up to Huayna Picchu. They were clearly carved from the final chambers they had walked through and she marvelled at the skill and time it would have taken to build them, especially without any kind of metal or blasting material. It made her wonder what they would find at the top.

Suddenly it dawned on her that this could be the day they found Paititi and she was struck with an odd sense of fear. What would happen to it once it was discovered? This was so much bigger than anything she had searched for before. Usually Elaine sent them out to retrieve an object, they brought it back and it was sold to a museum or a private collector. This, though, this was huge. And she wasn't talking spatially, although potentially it was, and certainly not something they could uproot and bring home, this was the last refuge of the Inca Empire. People had been searching for it for hundreds of years, and the interest in Machu Picchu would be dwarfed by it.

"Do you think we should try and get a signal?" Claudia asked, her breathing almost back to normal. "I really think we need to get our coordinates to Elaine."

"I agree, but not yet," she said. "Let's keep going for a bit, get as high as we can while the temperature is bearable."

Claudia gave her a worried look but nodded, picking up the pace slightly which Maya was grateful for. She looked up again, no end to the climb in sight which wasn't really surprising but annoyed her nonetheless. Up and up they climbed, the trees closing in on either side, occasionally a stray root breaking through the stone and forcing them to slow as they clambered over it. Maya kept looking ahead, hoping against hope that they would spot Rebecca and Tom ahead of them and she could vent some of her frustration yelling at them.

After about half an hour Claudia stopped suddenly, bending over with her hands on her knees, pulling in deep breaths, her legs shaking.

"Claudia," she said gently, putting her hand on her back and forcing her to sit down as she pulled her backpack off her. "Sit down, okay? You need food."

"I'm sorry," she said shakily. "I can't...my head is, uh, and my legs feel…"

"It's alright, just...here, drink this," Maya pulled a bottle of water out of her bag and poured some liquid glucose into it, shaking it up before handing it over. As Claudia drank from it she went through her bag and found a couple of chocolate bars, handing one over to her friend and eating the other herself.

As she waited for Claudia to recover her strength she pulled out her phone and switched it back on, desperately hoping they were high enough to get a signal and staring at it as though it had personally offended her when it stayed resolutely out of range. She sighed and slipped it into her back pocket, looking Claudia over as she did so. Her friend was sitting with her head in her hands, her elbows resting on her knees and looking as miserable as Maya had ever seen her.

"You okay?"

"Fine," she muttered. "Just annoyed at myself for being such a Fag Ash Lil I can't even walk up a bloody flight of stairs without practically dying."

"Don't be stupid," Maya laughed. "It's hardly a flight of stairs, Claudia. It's a fucking stairway to heaven and we're climbing it like we have hellhounds on our heels."

"You use the most ridiculous analogies when you are trying to make people feel better," she chuckled, pushing herself to her feet. "But thank you."

"That wasn't that bad, was it?" Maya frowned as she fell into step next to her.

"It made you sound a little bit like Dean Winchester."

"Who's that?"

"Oh my God," she said, putting her hand on her heart in mock horror. "Did I just make a pop culture reference you didn't get? Yay! I win."

"You do not!" Maya said, deeply affronted. "One reference does not mean you win."

"I don't know, Maya," she sighed. "It's a pretty big show. I think you might be losing your edge."

"Hey, I've been busy, alright?"

"It's been on for ten years."

"What?" Maya frowned. "What show is it? He must be a minor character cause I…"

"Ssh!" Claudia said suddenly, holding her hand out to stop her from moving forward. "Did you hear that?"

Maya stood stock still, her ears straining to hear and her eyes wide as she tried to spot movement. Together they dropped to the floor, after a moment moving slowly up the steps in a crouch until they reached the corner. Maya gestured with her hand for Claudia to stay back, inching forward and holding her breath as she peered up the steps. They ended about ten feet ahead, the forest opening out slightly and piles of rocks scattered about, some of them resembling walls that had crumbled away over time. She stayed low and quiet as she crept forward, her eyes scanning frantically for any signs of life as she went. She stopped as she heard a noise behind her and glanced back to see Claudia following her. Maya rolled her eyes and pressed her finger to her lips, her eyes going wide and her head snapping back around as she heard movement in the clearing.

She held her position but dropped flat against the steps, pulling her hat off and grabbing hold of her pendant as she strained to see where the sound had come from. She really hoped it was Rebecca and Tom out there but the pessimistic part of her knew that it wasn't. When no further sounds came she cautiously pushed forwards, her heart hammering in her chest and all her senses on high alert, adrenalin coursing through her veins. She reached the top step and paused, searching for anything that moved, and after a minute or two of silence pushed herself into a crouch and darted across the clearing to the first pile of stones.

When she had made sure that the area was clear she looked behind her and gestured for Claudia to follow. Her friend nodded once and rushed to join her, keeping low, her wide eyes sweeping from side to side. Once she was safe Maya shuffled over to the edge of the rocks and looked out at the space in front of her. It looked like it had once been a small settlement. There were maybe five or six dilapidated structures which could have been buildings, a few walls still standing here and there but mainly just piles of rock. It seemed unlikely to her that this place was built by the Inca, their ruins were usually much more intact, but maybe this had been a temporary shelter, a dwelling for the people who were working on the steps and not meant to last. Either way, the place provided a lot of cover, both for them and whoever it was that was out there.

She took a deep breath and straightened her legs, keeping her back bent and her head low as she moved across the next gap soundlessly. She figured if they stayed to the right they could make it around to the far side of the ruins and maybe get a better look. Perhaps the noises they had heard were just an animal? Or maybe it was Tom and Rebecca, pausing for a break after they made it to the top? She hoped so, she didn't know what Tom had in his bag but it was heavy as hell and her right shoulder was killing her. Plus she really wanted to slap Rebecca. Although not really. But that was a confusing internal debate for a less stressful time.

She reached the next cover and turned back to signal Claudia, her eyes going wide as she saw someone approaching through the forest behind her, his arm raised as he…

"Hey!" Maya yelled, jumping up from behind her cover and drawing his attention just as he got within striking distance. There was a high pitched pop and she ducked back down quickly, her heart thundering in her chest as she lost her footing and fell backwards. Suddenly Claudia appeared around the rocks, her face a mask of terror and she snatched at her hand as she scrambled to her feet, the pair of them sprinting for the next building, staying as low as they could whilst maintaining their pace.

As they reached the next bit of cover they heard another shot ring out and Maya glanced back to see a puff of dust clouding the air behind them, almost losing her footing as Claudia dragged her on. They ran blindly out into a confusing mass of rock and stone, jumping over small piles and vaulting over low walls as they tried to get out of sight. Eventually they rounded a corner and dropped down, their breaths shaky, Maya's whole body tense. She looked up to the sky and tried to calm her breathing, conscious of Claudia crouched next to her trying to do the same. After a second she took a deep breath and held it in as she peeked around the corner. She could see no sign of the person or people pursuing them and that scared her more than if she could. Pulling back she turned to Claudia and grabbed her hand, trying to smile reassuringly as she saw the fear in her friend's eyes, not at all convinced she had achieved the look she was going for.

"Okay," she whispered as she pulled Tom's bag off her front and set it down. "There's no sign of them so I'm going to try for that ridge over there. Follow me as soon as you see it's safe."

"Are you taking the piss?" Claudia hissed back incredulously. "There are people shooting at us, Maya! With guns!"

"I know that, Claud, but our friends are out there!" Maya answered, gesturing to the ruins behind her. "We can't just leave them and we can't stay here."

Claudia glared at her angrily for a second before huffing out a breath and dropping her shoulders with a quick nod. Maya nodded back and squeezed her hand before chancing another look out into the clearing. After a second she snapped her head back as she heard rustling behind her and saw Claudia pulling Tom's cast iron skillet out of the backpack.

"What the fuck are you doing?" she hissed.

"I'm not going out there without a weapon."

"They're not fucking cartoon characters, Claudia!" Maya whispered angrily. "These people are trying to kill us and your plan is to hit them with a frying pan?"

"Better than your plan of running across an open field and hoping you don't get shot!"

"Well Jesus Christ, what do you expect me to do?" she hissed back, trying desperately to keep her voice down, her anger and fear at the situation bubbling over. "If we stay here they'll find us, Claudia, and the longer we leave the others the more likely it is they will find them, assuming they haven't already."

The next few moments passed in a blur - a snap of wood, a sharp intake of breath, a shadow passing over them and a flash of red hair before a shot rang out and Maya was knocked to the side, forcing herself into a roll and popping back up as the man ran towards her. She dropped into a crouch and whipped her leg around as he fired again, taking his feet out as she felt a flash of pain across her cheek. He fell to the floor with a satisfying crunch and she jumped on top of him, punching him repeatedly in the face until he stopped moving, blood gushing from a gash above his eye and bubbling out of his mouth with each shallow, unconscious breath he took.

Maya stared down at his bloodied face, her breath ragged as she sat astride him, bile rising in her throat, her hands screaming pain through her as the adrenalin subsided and she realised what she had done. She stood up quickly, her bruised hands raking through her hair as she backed away, her head shaking from side to side as her vision blurred. Suddenly there was a groan from her right and she whipped her head around to see Claudia lying on the ground against the wall.

"Claud!" Maya cried, rushing over to her. "Claudia? Are you shot?"

"Fuck," she muttered. "My head feels like I got run over by a truck."

Claudia struggled to sit up, reaching to her forehead where a large, angry red bruise was already forming, her left eye starting to swell shut. Maya reached for Tom's bag and pulled out the water and one of his shirts, soaking it through and pressing it gently to Claudia's face, causing her to hiss.

"What the fuck happened?" Maya asked as she scanned her friend's body for injury. "How are you not shot?"

"I don't know," she slurred. "I just remember turning, seeing the gun and…"

Slowly she turned her good eye to look down at her left side and picked up the skillet, barking out a laugh as she held it up for Maya to see. The bullet was lodged in the front of it, dead centre.

"That'll teach you to mock my methods," she laughed. "We'd probably both be dead if it weren't for my cartoon defence."

"Jesus," Maya breathed, sitting down quickly and rubbing at her eyes. "Fuck, Claudia, I guess breaking my back dragging that thing up here was worth it."

"Oh, well, thank you very much," she huffed. "That thing just saved my life and 'you guess' it was worth it?"

Maya pulled her hands away from her face and threw her arms around her friend's neck. "You know what I meant, idiot!"

"Alright, I know," she said quickly, dropping her hand gently on her back. "Maya, are you okay?"

"Of course I'm not okay!" Maya said as she pulled away. "You almost fucking died!"

"I know, but I didn't," Claudia replied softly. "I have a face like the Elephant Man but I'm okay."

Maya laughed and took a deep breath as she tried to get it together. "Okay," she sniffed. "Where's the tent?"

"Uh, I don't think this is the best place to set up camp," she said cautiously. "I'm sure he wasn't alone."

"Obviously, but we need to tie him up before he wakes up," Maya answered pulling the tent out of the bag and cutting off the guide ropes with her knife before looking over at him guiltily. "If he wakes up."

"Hey," Claudia said, dropping the cloth and taking her friend's face in her hands. "He was trying to kill us, do you understand? You didn't do anything wrong."

"Look at him, Claud," she said, nausea building up in her again. "I did that."

"Yes, and it's a pathetic effort," she smirked. "He'd look a lot worse if I hadn't knocked myself out with a frying pan."

Maya laughed weakly and hugged her again. "Whatever. Help me tie him up."

Claudia winced slightly and wobbled as she got to her feet, but together they made short work of binding his hands and feet, ripping off part of his shirt to stuff in his mouth once they had dragged him somewhere out of sight. Maya stood up and looked around, spotting a relatively intact building on the other side of the clearing and together they pulled the unconscious man towards it. Finally they made it and dragged him over to the corner, collapsing next to him as their exertions took their toll.

"Alright," Maya said after a few minutes. "I'll go out and get some branches to cover him with, just in case."

She stood up to head out but the room went dark as a shadow filled the doorway. She looked up to see a huge man standing there, his expression furious. Maya sucked in a deep breath as she took a step back, her arms stretched out to protect her friend, her eyes shifting between her and the man as he raised his arm and a shot rang out.

Chapter 34

Maya was confused. She smelt blood in the air, the acrid stench of smoke, but she felt no pain. She heard a thud and briefly wondered if she had fallen down. If she couldn't feel a bullet wound, surely falling to the ground without being aware of it was not beyond the realms of possibility. Suddenly she realised her eyes were clenched shut and she opened them slowly, briefly amazed to find that she was still standing before her legs gave way and she fell to her knees, inches away from the man with the gun who was now lying on the ground with blood leaking from his head.

She lurched to the side and threw up on the floor, her stomach spasming uncontrollably as she brought up its meagre contents. She heard someone approaching and on instinct grabbed the gun from the dead man's hand, backing up against the wall and pointing it at the doorway, milliseconds from pulling the trigger when she recognised that it was Tom, staggering to lean on the door frame, his hand clutched to his side.

"Are you alright?" he asked, his breath laboured, sweat pouring from his face.

"Tom!" Claudia said shakily from the back of the room. "God, what happened?"

"I saw you dragging that guy over here and then this guy came after you and…" he slumped down the frame and sat. "Fuck, I really thought I was too late."

"I mean what happened to you?" Claudia said, walking shakily over to him and inspecting his wound. "Christ, Maya, he's bleeding really badly. Maya. Maya?"

"What?" Maya looked up at her, her mind flitting around all over the place.

"Tom," she said with a worried expression. "He's been shot. Can you help us, please?"

"Uh, yeah," she replied absently. Suddenly she realised she was still holding the gun in her raised hand and set it down gently on the floor next to her, staring at as if it were a rattlesnake. She shook her head quickly and stood up, taking a deep breath as she made her way to the door, reaching down to take Tom's hand. "Can you stand?"

"I think I'm good," he winced as he grabbed the offered arm and stood.

They moved him over to the opposite corner from the unconscious would be assassin and Maya pulled up his blood stained t shirt to see the damage. He hissed as it pulled at his skin and banged his head back against the wall as he clenched his fist.

"Okay, two holes," she said. "That's a good thing. Unless you were shot from the front and the back. That's just careless."

"Just once," he said through gritted teeth. "It was enough. Trust me."

"I do," she smiled, realising weirdly that she meant it. "I'm going to go grab the bag, get you cleaned up."

"Are you serious?" Claudia hissed. "What if there are more of them out there?"

"Then they will find us anyway," she said with a sigh. "And I'd rather we had the means to patch ourselves up."

"Fine," Claudia huffed, reaching for Tom's gun. "Can I borrow this?"

"Do you know how to use it?" he asked with a frown.

"After a fashion," she shrugged.

"What does that mean?"

"It means she and I were addicted to House of the Dead at university," Maya sighed with a roll of her eyes. "Just don't mistake me for a zombie, okay?"

"How could I?" Claudia smirked. "Even with that ever so attractive slash across your face?"

Maya raised her hand to her cheek in confusion and winced as she touched her fingers to where the bullet had grazed her. "Fuck," she frowned. "I forgot."

"Well, a lot has happened since then," Claudia sighed with a shrug. "We all nearly died for one."

"British people are weird," Tom said, looking at her in amazement.

"Ssh," Claudia said as she shuffled over to the door. "Maya is about to risk her life to get you some water and I am going to pretend I know how to cover her based on my experience of arcade games."

"Thanks, Claud," Maya said with a roll of her eyes, flexing her shoulders as she stood and made her way over. "That's really reassuring."

"You're welcome," she answered, standing and pulling her into a hug before whispering in her ear. "Don't get dead."

"I won't," she whispered back, squeezing her tightly.

She pulled away and scanned the area before dropping into a crouch and making her way back to where they had left the bags, ducking behind cover and checking carefully before moving on. She really didn't want to die. Her mamá would be so pissed at her if she did, she could just hear the angry words now. She had to stop behind a wall and compose herself as the ridiculous nature of that thought washed over her and threatened to send her into a fit of hysterical laughter. It was only the idea of Claudia watching and becoming enraged at her inappropriately timed bout of giggles that forced her to calm down and focus on what she was doing.

Cautiously she looked around before making the final sprint to where their stuff lay discarded and quickly began hooking the bags onto herself as best she could. Her eyes landed on the gun and, after a moment's hesitation she picked it up and tucked it into the back of her belt. As she stood to head back she spotted the broken skillet and picked it up with a smile, turning quickly and heading back the way she had come, arriving at the hut with a relieved sigh.

"Okay," she said as she approached Tom, pulling out the water and a small bottle of antiseptic that she could happily drink right now. "This is going to hurt, I'm not going to lie."

"Appreciate the honesty," he said, holding up his shirt and gripping onto the bag, his face set.

Maya nodded and poured the water over the entry wound to clear away the blood, wiping at it with yet another of her shirts before dousing it with antiseptic. Quickly she repeated the process on his back and then got Claudia to help hold him up as she padded him up with gauze and wrapped a tight bandage around his waist.

"There you go, Tex," she smiled. "Patched."

"Thanks," he grimaced. "Still feels like I have hot rocks in my stomach."

"Hot rocks?" Maya smirked. "Lost a lot of shirts to them."

"What?"

"Never mind," she shook her head, all amusing thoughts leaving her mind as she addressed the elephant in the room, or absent from the room as it were. "So, where's Rebecca?"

Tom looked up at her, swallowing thickly as his eyes met hers. "I'm sorry, Maya."

"Is she dead?" she asked, a lump forming in her throat as her heart dropped into her stomach.

"I don't know," he said. "I don't think so but they took her. I tried to protect her but they shot me and I...she pushed me out of the way, that's how I survived I think, but I…"

"It's okay," she said, her tone clipped. "Where did they take her?"

"I don't know," he said, covering his eyes with his hand. "I hit my head when I went down and got knocked out. When I woke up I heard gunshots and I followed thinking it was her but it was you guys and...I don't know where they took her."

"Or even if they took her," Maya said, getting to her feet and pacing across the floor.

"No, they took her," he said. "When they found us they said they had been waiting for her. Something about a book she had."

"A book?" Maya turned to him. "What book?"

"I don't know!"

"She did say something about notes in her bag," Claudia pointed out. "Maybe she knows something we don't?"

Maya resumed her pacing, her mind buzzing with this new information. All this time Rebecca had had information that could have helped them? Why hadn't she shared it? Maybe she had, she realised. She always seemed to be around to offer them random bits of information when they were stumped. But no, not always. Not at the stones. Not at the waterfall. What was this book, then?

"Alright," she said. "Okay, I'm going to see what I can find."

"What?" Claudia said, standing up to face her. "No. Not happening."

"We can't just sit here, Claudia," she sighed, dropping down to pat down the dead guy, see if he was carrying any kind of communication device. She smiled as her fingers found a rectangular object in his back pocket. She pulled it out and stared at it blankly. "What's this?"

"GPS," Tom and Claudia said in unison.

"Here," Claudia grabbed it with a sigh and looked it over briefly before switching it on. "Okay, so, this shows you where we are and that blob is, presumably, where they are."

"Alright," she smiled. "I'll go there then."

"Maya, don't you think that's a little easy?"

"What's easy?" Maya snapped. "They left two guys out here to kill us! They obviously weren't expecting us to kill them. Christ, we weren't even armed. Wait," she turned to Tom with narrowed eyes. "Where did you get that gun?"

"Uh, it's, I…uh…"

"Oh, for fuck's sake, Tom," Claudia huffed. "He brought it with him."

"What?" Maya yelled.

"How did you know?" Tom asked incredulously.

"For God's sake," she said with a roll of her eyes. "I've slept next to you almost every night we've been out here and I can tell the difference between a gun and a hard on."

"Alright, whatever," Maya huffed. "Just look after each other and contact Elaine. If these guys can contact each other we must be able to reach her."

"There is no way I am letting you go out there alone," she said, standing in the doorway to block her path. "Think about this rationally, Maya. Two people have tried to kill us in the last ten minutes. How many more are going to be waiting for you out there?"

"I know," she said quickly. "I'm not expecting to just waltz through."

"And what if it's a trap, did you ever think about that?" Claudia asked, her hands on her hips, a quick shake of her head. "I'm coming with you."

"For Christ's sake, Claudia," Maya said quietly. "He has been shot and can barely stand. He saved our lives. You have to stay with him."

"I am well aware of all that, Maya," she snapped, looking over her shoulder at Tom. "And thank you by the way. For the life saving."

"No problem," he replied, looking slightly bewildered.

"But I am not letting you leave here without me," Claudia said, folding her arms across her chest.

"Claudia," Maya sighed, squeezing the bridge of her nose. "The guy you have been sleeping with is sitting there, bleeding to death…"

"Hey," Tom said, chuckling nervously. "What?"

"He'll be fine," Claudia scoffed, waving her hand at him. "The sooner we find these guys the sooner we'll finish this and we can get him the help he needs."

"Uh, I am right here…"

"We are not going to finish anything by ourselves, Claudia," Maya spat. "The absolute best we can hope for is to get Rebecca back and get the fuck out of here, but if we can get Elaine's team here we might have a chance. Tom might have a chance."

"Again, I am right here…"

"Ssh, Tom, save your strength," Claudia said irritatedly, waving her hand again.

"Look, Claud," Maya sighed. "I get that you're scared. I'm fucking terrified. But I'm faster and less obvious alone and I don't need to be watching out for you. You have a dented face and most likely a severe concussion. What happens if they come at us when you're in a dizzy spell like you were out there? And I know you've just made staying here really awkward for yourself by acting like you don't give a fuck about him but I know that's bullshit, I've seen the two of you together and it's nauseating how happy you are. So right now I really need you to stay here, help him, check in with Elaine and get us some goddamn backup, alright?"

Claudia stayed silent, her arms wrapped around herself as she stared at the floor, a deep frown on her face.

"I'll be fine," Maya said softly, running a hand up her arm.

"Oh, for fuck's sake, Maya!" Claudia said, throwing her hands up in the air as a stray tear ran down her face. "You could have said literally anything but that and I would be less worried!"

"Claudia," she smiled, putting both hands on her friend's shoulders. "Trust me. Please. I'll be fine."

"Okay," Claudia said after a pause, wiping angrily at her face before pulling her into a hug. "But if you say 'I'll be right back' I promise I will knock you out so you can't go."

Maya made her way quickly towards where the green blob was glowing on the small screen. She kept herself out of sight as much as she could, conscious of the fact that although she knew where she was going she had absolutely no idea about what stood between her and her final destination. She shook her head angrily, annoyed at herself for thinking that phrase and at the people who made that series of films for distorting its meaning forever.

She dropped down behind a wall, pressing her back up against it and staring up at the sky, forcing herself to breathe and focus. She really wished Claudia were here but she knew she had made the right decision leaving her behind. They needed back up and they needed it now. They were archaeologists, for fucks sake. Like boring ones who read old, musty books and excavated sites with trowels and brushes, not ones who went scuba diving and got involved in gun battles. Lara Croft she was not.

She sighed and studied the GPS. It looked like they were a little over a mile away and the green blob hadn't moved since she had set out, a good indication that that was their camp, as she had hoped. She forced herself up and peered over the wall to try and work out the best possible route and then ran forward as quickly as she dared, glancing all about her and straining her ears for the slightest noise. When she reached the next cover she slid in behind it and swore slightly as something jabbed her in the back. She felt behind her and realised that it was the gun she had tucked in her belt earlier and she pulled it out, testing the weight in her hand as she stared down at it. Hopefully she wouldn't have to use it because she had never fired a gun before, never so much as held one before today, and she really wasn't sure she could do it. With a shake of her head she tucked it back into her belt and tried to focus her mind on finding Rebecca.

Fucking Rebecca. She couldn't believe she had gotten herself kidnapped. It was just unbelievable. And here she was, running around the goddamn rainforest like some kind of crazy person, prepared to do just about anything to save her and being made to confront all sorts of feelings about why that was exactly. Not that she would leave anyone to die if she could help it, of course, but running blindly towards where the bad guys were without any sort of confirmation that help was on its way...that was next level stuff, and it was forcing her to accept that her feelings for Rebecca were next level, much as she had tried to push them away. It just wasn't fair. She had fought for so long to keep herself out of any kind of emotional entanglement so of course she would find herself having feelings for someone at the worst possible time, in the worst possible place, and of course the fucking bitch would land herself in a life or death situation and pull Maya down with her. That was just the way her life seemed to go.

Fifteen minutes later she was almost there and still she had seen no sign of anyone. The whole thing made her feel extremely uneasy. Why would they have sent two guys out alone and why would noone have come to look for them when they didn't check in? She stared down at the GPS in her hand. The camp looked to be about three hundred feet away, through a dense thicket that she could see just ahead, and still nothing. There were only two marks on the screen, the large green blob which she assumed was the camp, and the small blue one which represented her position. How did these guys communicate? How did they know where the other members of their team were? She turned the device over in her hand and looked for any other buttons that could change the information on the screen. She sighed as she found nothing and jabbed her finger at the screen in frustration.

She pushed it back into her pocket and stood up to check her path. They must have some other way of communicating with each other, the dead guy must have had something else on him that she had missed. She slammed her hand down on the wall in front of her in frustration. Dammit. Why had she not taken a few minutes to check? What if they were trying to contact him now and his lack of response brought the whole group of them down on Tom and Claudia? Although surely if the blob indicating him was moving with her since she had this useless fucking tracker then…

Maya's eyes went wide as she realised what a complete idiot she had been. She was trying to sneak up on a group of people using the fucking tracking device of one of their dead colleagues. That was how they tracked each other, using the signal from the stupid piece of plastic she had in her pocket. Most likely, whatever the big green blob was showed the position of all the other people wandering around and they would see that whoever had this one was heading back towards them. That meant if they had been trying to contact him and he wasn't answering they would likely know that he probably wasn't the one moving around out here.

"Charamanbiche," she swore softly, placing the box down next to her and taking a breath as she steeled herself. Better put some distance between herself and the damn thing, for all the good it would do as they had most likely been watching her for the last half hour. She stood up quickly and broke across the open ground towards the thicket, not bothering to stay low any more. She hadn't seen anyone since Tom had arrived and she was starting to feel like that wasn't an accident. If they knew she was coming she had better get on with it and if they didn't, well, she had no time to lose. She pushed into the thicket, her heart pounding in her chest as she tried to stay calm and think things through. If they did know she was coming then she needed to do something unexpected, but what?

She forced herself to slow down as she swept the sharp branches aside, ignoring the scratches across her face, arms and chest, and looked around herself for some kind of sign. How the fuck could she possibly know what to do that would be unexpected when she didn't know who these people were, what they wanted or even if they knew she existed? She stopped and put her hands on her hips, checking each direction blindly before taking off to the right, walking quickly for a few minutes then turning forty five degrees and marching that way for a while, letting the forest dictate her direction.

Suddenly she heard voices ahead and slammed herself up against a tree, her heart hammering in her chest as she peered around it. Two men with rifles were standing in a clearing ten feet away, laughing and joking as they smoked, a man lying at their feet bound and gagged.

Felipe.

How the hell had he got here? She pulled herself back behind her cover and took a few deep breaths as she tried to work out what to do. She had to help him but how? She could try and shoot the two men but she was hardly a crack shot and the sound of gunfire would likely bring the whole group down on her. She looked down at her feet and bent to pick up a rock, making sure the men's backs were turned before she threw the rock as far as she could off to their left.

Their heads snapped in the direction of the noise it made as soon as it landed and they pointed their rifles in front of them as they headed off to investigate. Maya raised her eyebrows in surprise. She had honestly not expected that to work, but she took full advantage of their stupidity and moved quickly over to Felipe's prone body, praying that he was still alive. As she reached him she pulled the knife from her belt and cut through the ropes binding his hands and feet.

"Felipe!" she hissed, smiling slightly as his eyes opened slowly and he looked up at her in confusion. "Can you stand? We need to move."

"Maya?" he said with a frown. "What are you doing here?"

"I could ask you the same thing," she chuckled. "Now come on, let's get out of here."

He got groggily to his feet as Maya looked over to where the two guards had disappeared, frowning slightly when she couldn't see them. She gestured to Felipe and they ran deeper into the forest, a small wisp of smoke rising into the sky in the distance.

"Are you okay?" she asked when they were far enough away.

"I think so, a little confused maybe," he answered quietly. "They hit me in the back of my head."

"Yeah, the seem like a real friendly bunch of guys," she muttered. "They have Rebecca."

"They have Rebecca?" Felipe repeated. "What about Claudia?"

Maya held her finger to her lips and gestured for him to wait as she heard a noise ahead. He stopped where he was, watching her with wide eyes as she gestured for him to get behind a tree while she inched forward, staying as low to the ground as she could, her eyes scanning for the source of the noise. Suddenly she caught a blur of movement from her left and whipped her hands in front of her just in time to block the kick aimed at her ribs.

She fell backwards and landed painfully, just managing to recover and roll out of the way as the boot slammed down right where her stomach would have been, forcing herself up and back just as her assailant cocked his rifle.

"Stop," he said calmly. "Get your hands up."

Maya slowly started to raise her hands, her breath held as she watched Felipe creep up behind him and smack him in the back of the head with a piece of wood. The man let out a confused grunt and fell the floor, his rifle clattering down next to him but thankfully not going off.

"Pick that up," she said to Felipe as she pointed at the rifle. "Please, I know it's a lot to ask but I need your help."

"Shouldn't we call someone?" he said, his brow furrowed in concern. "Of course I will help you, Maya, but we are not exactly experts in this area."

"I know that, but what choice do we have?" she asked, cursing in fear as something vibrated against her backside. As she realised it was just her phone she reached to her pocket and pulled it out, realising that she finally had reception and that Claudia had messaged her. Without reading it she dialled Claudia's number and walked a little further on, looking around carefully for any other signs of life.

"Thank God," Claudia said as she picked up on the first ring. "Are you okay?"

"I'm okay," she whispered. "How are you guys doing?"

"We're fine, we've moved to higher ground and…"

"Good, cos I figure that GPS unit works both ways."

"Yes, yes," Claudia interrupted. "We gave Elaine the details and her team have patched into it and they know where to go so get yourself out of there."

"Really?"

"For God's sake, Maya, did you not read the message I sent you?"

"I just figured it was easier to call," she hissed back, glancing back at where Felipe was searching the fallen man's pockets. "Don't get pissy with me, Claud, I'm kind of in an intense situation here."

"Well, obviously." Claudia huffed.

"So, you want me to hang up and read the message or do you just want to tell me?"

"Don't be a smart arse," she snapped. "Elaine's team are about thirty minutes out…"

"Rebecca might not have that long!" she hissed, turning to look at the smoke rising over what she assumed was their camp.

"She'll be okay, Maya, as long as you stay away," Claudia said, concern heavy in her voice.

"What are you talking about?"

"It's you he wants, not the Bronsteins. You and Zuazola's journal. Rebecca is just bait."

"What?" Maya said, her voice rising a little. "Why?"

"I don't know, presumably because he knows how you feel about her?"

Maya stopped still, her blood running cold and her scalp tingling as she turned back towards Felipe as calmly as she could. He had pulled the

GPS out of the man's pocket and was turning it over in his hands, his brows furrowed in confusion.

"Who?" Maya asked as quietly as she could.

"Felipe."

Chapter 35

Maya stared over at him, forcing her face into a smile as he looked up at her and showed her the box, shrugging his shoulders as if he didn't know what it was.

"Maya?" Claudia's voice sounded in her ear. "Maya are you still there?"

"Yeah, sure," she said, clearing her throat when her voice cracked. "I'll call you back when I find it."

"Fuck," Claudia replied, her fear echoing through the phone. "Oh fuck, Maya, please tell me he's not with you."

"Uh huh, take care."

"Maya, do not hang up on me," she pleaded. "Just, fuck, please get away from him. Maya?"

"Love you too," she said quietly as she disconnected. She stared down at the phone in her hand, opened up Claudia's message and deleted it before switching the phone off and pushing it into her pocket. She forced herself to stay calm as she moved towards him. "What is it?"

"I am not sure," Felipe said, staring at the box with a frown. "Maybe some sort of tracking device?"

"We should probably leave it there, then," she said, desperately trying to keep her voice normal. "And definitely get away from him before someone comes looking."

"You are right, of course," he said, quickly pushing the box back into the man's pocket and stepping away. "Who were you talking to?"

"Claudia," Maya said as she walked away, once again scanning the forest in front of her but now far more concerned about the man behind.

"She is okay?" he asked, his voice sounding genuinely concerned. Damn, he was good.

"She's injured but okay," she replied.

"That is good," he sighed. "Maybe we should return to her? Use your equipment to summon help?"

"Unfortunately all our equipment got damaged," she lied. "We, er, had an incident with a waterfall."

"Oh," he frowned as he fell into step next to her, the rifle slung casually on his shoulder. "But you have your phones, no?"

"Well, obviously," Maya laughed nervously. "But who are we going to call out here?"

"Anyone you wanted to, Maya. Isn't that the point of a telephone?" Felipe said quietly as he stopped and slipped the gun off his shoulder. "Perhaps you should give it to me."

Maya broke into a run, darting through the trees as she circled away from the camp, branches and vines smacking into her from all angles as she pushed on. Slowly she regained a measure of control and remembered the route she had taken to get here, her body switching to autopilot as she followed it back, her brain fully focussed on ignoring the fact that Felipe was chasing her, she had no idea what she was going to do and that she had pretty much just left Rebecca for dead.

Suddenly a man stepped out from behind a tree directly in front of her and held out his arm. She ran face first into it, her head stopping as the rest of her body span comically into the air, pain blossoming out from her nose as she hit the ground with a clatter, all her breath shooting out of her in a blast and leaving her spread eagled and winded on the floor, a stream of blood coursing down her throat. She heard the telltale click of a gun being cocked and stared up in a daze as he appeared over her, the barrel aimed directly at her face.

"Get up," he said menacingly.

"You're going to have to give me a minute," she croaked. "I'm kind of having a situation here."

"I said get up," he snapped, kicking her in the leg.

Maya tried to sigh but only succeeded in choking on her own blood so she rolled over quickly to spit it out on the ground, her body protesting violently at the sudden movement. She groaned and touched her nose gingerly, sending a flash of blinding pain through her brain and confirming it was broken in one fell swoop.

"I said get up, bitch!" the man said, kicking harshly at her legs as he yanked the gun from her belt and threw it away. "I won't ask you again."

Maya glared up at him as she got to her feet. "Mama bicho," she hissed, her voice almost a whisper as white hot rage washed over her and wiped out the pain.

"Whatever, bitch," he sneered. "Get your hands up."

Maya folded her arms and looked around the area as though she didn't have a care in the world.

"Man," he chuckled harshly. "You really have a death wish, don't you. Alright, I'll give you to the count of three."

"Can you count that high?" Maya asked with a bored look.

"Don't fuck with me, bitch," he snarled, stepping closer and brandishing the gun. "Get your fucking hands up!"

"You know, I generally cooperate better with people who are a little more varied in their misogynistic pronouns," she said as she slowly clasped her hands behind her head.

"Right," he smiled as he pulled her knife from her belt roughly and ran it across her face, his fetid breath causing her lip to curl up. "I get it. You want to play? We can play."

"Dude, your breath is so bad I can smell it through my busted nose," she said with a gag as she looked around for a way out of this. "Seriously. What are you eating out here? You should really see a doctor."

"You think you're funny?" he whispered as he pressed the blade into the skin of her neck and ran it down her throat, dropping his gaze as he moved it lower, putting his gun back in its holster and sliding his hand over her breast. "Let's see how much you laugh when I cut into these babies, huh?"

"What do you think you are doing?" Felipe said as he appeared behind him, the rifle once again slung casually over his shoulder.

"Nothing, man," he smiled nervously as he turned to greet him. "No harm in having a little fun, right?"

Maya used the distraction to wrap her arm around his neck and grab his gun, pulling him in front of her body as she took the safety off and pressed the muzzle into his temple.

"Drop the knife," she hissed in his ear, her eyes locked on Felipe's.

"Shit," he whispered, his body tense as he shuffled on his feet and threw the knife out into the clearing. "Take it easy, alright? It was a joke."

"Drop the gun or I'll blow your dickless friends face off." Maya shouted.

"Don't be stupid, Maya," Felipe sighed. "You are far more important than he is. Now, where is the book?"

"What book?" Maya asked, shifting nervously behind her human shield.

"The book you stole from Fortín Solano."

"I don't know what you're talking about. Now drop your fucking gun or I will shoot him."

Felipe gave a bored sigh and reached behind him, quickly whipping out a handgun and shooting the man in the face. The force and shock of the impact knocked Maya off her feet and she slammed into the tree behind her and she fell to the ground, the dead man on top of her, his brains all over her face. She lay there gasping for air until the revulsion and fear kicked in and she shoved him off, searching around for her weapon before realising she was too late.

She was lifted off the ground by two men who had appeared from nowhere and dragged through the forest, her mind reeling as she tried to process what had just happened. This could not be happening to her. That's all there was to it. Clearly it was all just some horrific, extremely vivid nightmare that she just really, seriously needed to wake up from. Anytime now.

She looked up to see they were approaching a small camp, one half taken up by tents and the other housing three small stone buildings, two of them a few feet apart and one set off slightly by itself. She tried to pull free as they walked through it, her mind going back to the conversation where Claudia had told her the Bronsteins would be okay if she stayed away. Of course, by that stage she was already too late.

"Felipe," she sputtered, her mouth and throat dry. "Wait. Just...I'll take you to the book, alright?"

"Maya," he tutted, shaking his head sadly as he approached her and held up her phone. "I don't need your help to find it now I have this. You have obviously left it with Claudia. All I have to do is call her and tell her I will kill you unless she brings the book."

"She won't answer. She knows I am with you."

"I doubt that is true," he shrugged. "In either case we know where she is. You told me yourself she is injured which means you would have left her with the bodies of the men I sent to capture you. Obviously I should have sent more."

"Obviously, so don't underestimate me again," Maya said, willing herself to stand up straight. "I'm saying I'll help you, just let the others go."

"My men are almost at the steps. We will have the book soon enough. I don't need your help with that."

"Great," she laughed. "What's so important about the damn book anyway? We're here, aren't we? And Zuazola was hardly a literary genius."

"You expect me to stand here and give you some grand exposition like the villain in a poorly constructed crime novel?" Felipe said cheerfully.

"If the cap fits," she shrugged.

Felipe laughed loudly and gestured for her captor to march her into the building. Relief washed over her as she saw Rebecca sitting in the corner, an angry looking bruise on her face but seemingly alright. Her parents sat near to her, looking tired and weak but still alive which was more than Maya had believed possible.

As soon as she got through the door her guard shoved her roughly, her feet catching on a stone which tripped her and she landed heavily, her arms striking the bench Rebecca was sitting on as she tried to protect her face, pain blinding her as her broken nose bounced off them. She bit down on her lip so as stop herself shouting out and carefully pulled herself up, Rebecca reaching out to help her. She gave her a pained smile as she sat down and rubbed at her bruised arms.

"Please try not to cause anymore trouble, Ms Rodriguez," Felipe said from the door. "I would hate to have to shoot you before we reach the end of our journey."

"And people say I'm a bad liar," she muttered.

Felipe laughed again and walked off, leaving the four of them alone in the room. Rebecca pulled her into a hug and kissed her carefully, her eyes shining as she leaned back to inspect her face, using her shirt sleeve to start to wipe the blood off .

"I'm so sorry," she said quietly. "Are you alright?"

"Just peachy," Maya huffed tiredly. "How are you guys doing?"

"About the same," she nodded. "I should have listened to you, Maya, I know that, I should have waited and I feel…"

"There's no point in worrying about that now," she sighed. "If we're going to play the blame game I should have listened to you when you said you didn't trust him."

"It's not the same," Rebecca said, biting at her lip as she tried to control herself. "I was reckless and you're here because of me. Tom is probably dead because of me. Claudia…"

"Rebecca," Maya said quietly, putting her hands on her shoulders and waiting til she looked up at her. "I'm here. You're here. The reasons why don't matter, we just need to find a way out of it, alright? So I need you to focus and help me, okay?"

Rebecca nodded and clenched her jaw. "You're right."

Maya looked up as the guard outside the door walked a little way out into the clearing to talk to his friend and she quickly pulled Rebecca into a hug, pressing her lips up to her ear and speaking as quietly as possible. "Tom and Claudia are okay. Elaine has a team on the way. Just hold on."

Rebecca let out a sigh of relief and squeezed her tightly before sitting back and wiping at her eyes.

"Do you know why he wants the book?" Maya asked, looking back to the door.

"Because it's part of a set," Rebecca's father said as he rubbed his head. "We have the other one. Well, had. It's a journal written by a man named Jesus Manuelo. He was a compatriot of Zuazola's and together they stumbled upon information that pointed to a trail that would lead them to the lost city of the Inca. They fought at some stage and went their separate ways shortly before the attack on Fortín Solano."

"So why does he need them now?" she asked. "And how is he even here? How are you here?"

"We were kidnapped in Puerto Caballo, right after we found the caves," Daniella sighed. "They told us they were watching Rebecca and would have her killed unless we led them to the city. They had us locked away for months researching where the trail started, all the while showing us pictures to prove they were still watching her."

"About a month ago we came across some old records which seemed to show a stone circle in the middle of the Amazon which we thought was odd," David took over as Rebecca squeezed her mother's hand. "Stone circles are pretty much unique to Britain so we looked further into the area the records referred to, cross referencing them with the painting from the cave and it seemed like there could be something here. They brought us, we found the stones, and by that stage Felipe had Rebecca here so we had no choice but to keep going."

"I don't understand why Felipe was with us anyway," Maya interrupted with a frown. "Why wasn't he guiding you?"

"Because he isn't a guide," Rebecca said. "All his credentials are fake, really he works for Amaric. They've been following me since New York."

Maya nodded once as she took this in. "So the man at the waterfall…"

"Was our guide," David confirmed. "When you managed to get away from Felipe he flew up to our camp at the waterfall. He was not pleased that we were still trying to work it out. So he killed our guide in front of us as an incentive and told us Rebecca would be next. We went into the waterfall in sheer desperation at that point, and stumbled on the cave system by accident. He sent a few of his men with us and they contacted him with the coordinates when we reached the top of the steps so that the rest of them could get dropped off with their kit."

"But if they killed him just before you set off…" Maya said, her brain working through the timeline. "It took us around seven hours to get through the caves, another hour to get up the steps, which means…"

"They were watching us when we got to the waterfall," Rebecca sighed.

"When we got here and there was no city Felipe became enraged and decided we were holding something back. He showed us footage of a gun trained on Rebecca in front of the waterfall," Daniella said, clearing her throat and rubbing her hands together before continuing. "He demanded that we give him any information that we hadn't before or he would give the kill order. That was when we told him about Zuazola's journal. I'm so sorry, Maya."

"Sorry?" she frowned. "Why?"

"Well because that's why you're here," she said sadly. "He knew who you were and that you must have gone to Puerto Caballo to retrieve the book. And now you are his prisoner."

"Fuck that," Maya scoffed. "If you hadn't told them how long do you think the rest of us would have lasted after they killed Rebecca?"

"Good point," David shrugged.

"We've both been on the trail for months, though," she said. "Why does he think this will help now?"

"Because the information in the books gave us the starting point, the petroglyphs, but Felipe believes that together they also show us how to get to the end."

"How?" Maya asked as she summoned up the pages of the book in her head.

"There is a pattern in the back cover of the book," he said. "Felipe thinks…"

"Felipe thinks that you two," Felipe said, gesturing at Maya and Rebecca as he suddenly reappeared. "Need to join me outside."

Maya shot a quick look at Rebecca, her jaw clenching as she stood. She squared her shoulders and walked over to the door as nonchalantly as she could. "Why? We having a party?"

He chuckled as she pushed past him, standing aside to let Rebecca out with a wave of his hand. "That would strongly depend on your definition. I would like you to meet Alfonse."

The three of them walked out into the clearing where a mountain of a man was waiting for them. Maya smirked as she looked him up and down. "Definitely not my definition."

With a speed that didn't seem possible for a man of his size, Alfonse's fist shot out and connected with her gut so forcefully she felt like she would snap in half. She dropped to her knees, her mouth falling open as her cry of pain caught in her throat. She heard Rebecca yelling from behind her and looked back, gasping for air, her eyes watering, to see Felipe grab Rebecca by the hair and pull her against him, whipping the gun out of his belt to press against her temple. Maya lunged forward but he slammed the heel of his boot into her left temple and she fell to the floor, the back of her head smacking off the ground and the world going dark as his voice seemed to echo around her brain.

"It would seem that your friend is not where you left her," he hissed from a hundred miles away. "Your things are still there but the book is gone. Tell me where she is or I will shoot your girlfriend in her pretty little head."

Chapter 36

Maya clenched her eyes shut and tried desperately to make sense of where she was. There was noise, so much noise, and it sounded like words but she couldn't understand them. It was dark but she could tell it was really light, although she did have her eyes shut so that kind of made sense, and she was freezing but her skin was prickled with heat and sweat.

"Get the fuck off me!"

Okay, that she understood. Well, the words, anyway. Not the context. Where the hell was she? Slowly she forced herself to open her eyes and focus on the swaying shape in front of her. And it all came rushing back.

"Wait, Felipe," she slurred, holding her hand out as she tried to sit up. "Just...wait."

"You have ten seconds, Maya," he said calmly.

"Just give me a…"

"Nine."

"I can't…" she shook her head, wincing as it felt like a bag of marbles had been dropped into it. "I don't…"

"Eight."

"Stop counting!" Maya shouted, sitting up fully now, adrenalin taking back over. "I don't know what you want me to do!"

"It appears your friend has taken the book," Felipe said as he cocked the gun. "Why would she do that?"

"I don't…"

"Six."

"Fuck!" Maya ran her hands through her hair and thought desperately. "I don't know why she would have taken it and I don't…"

"Five." he said calmly, his voice soft but drowning out those shouting in the background and making her head spin.

"Jesus, Felipe, stop counting and talk to me!"

"Four."

"Rebecca…" Maya looked up at her, her heart pounding.

"Three."

"Don't," Rebecca mouthed, her face set.

"Two."

"Stop!" Maya yelled, pushing herself shakily into a crouch. "Just stop, I'll try and find her, just give me…"

"One."

"Wait!" Claudia's voice rang out across the clearing. Maya turned and saw her standing at the edge of the building, still close enough to dive for cover, her gun trained on Felipe. Her heart sank as she saw her. They were going to kill her for sure. "I'm here! I have it. Just let her go and I'll bring it, okay?"

"Claudia!" Felipe smiled brightly and shoved Rebecca to Alfonse, casually putting the safety back on his gun and reholstering it. "Thank you for joining us finally. Bring me the book please?"

Maya collapsed back onto the ground and turned to watch her friend's cautious approach, fear for her washing over her like a bucket of ice water. She wasn't sure how much more of this she could take before she passed out or died from stress. What the fuck were they going to do now? Claudia walked over to her, producing the journal at the last moment and holding it out, her gun still pointed at Felipe.

Felipe sighed heavily and shook his head. "You have just given up your position to stop me from killing your friend," he said. "Do you really think shooting me now will stop any of my men from shooting all three of you?"

"No," Claudia shrugged as she handed him the book. "I just wanted to give myself a fighting chance."

"Admirable," he nodded, taking the book and motioning for the gun. "But ultimately foolish."

He walked away from them and over to the third building, going inside and returning moments later with a second book almost identical to theirs but in better condition. He walked over to the fire and spoke to one of the guards who immediately started fiddling with a cannister. After a moment Felipe turned and looked at them, almost as if he had forgotten they were there.

"Won't you join me?" he asked, gesturing to the space around the fire. "This is a fairly significant moment, I'm sure you will agree."

Alfonse shoved Rebecca over towards him and Claudia glanced down at Maya with a shrug. Maya shrugged back and reached up for a hand to help her up, wincing and grunting as she tried to protect the parts of her that were hurting then giving up as she realised she was about forty hands too short.

"You fucking bellend," Claudia hissed. "I've been worried sick about you. How dare you just hang up on me like that?"

"What else was I supposed to do?" Maya sighed.

"Well not end the conversation by telling me you love me for starters," she huffed. "You might as well have just said 'right, I'm probably about to die. Nice knowing you!'"

"Claudia, please," she breathed. "I'm kind of having a bad day here. Can you save the outrage for later?"

"Sorry," she sighed. "I don't think I'm dealing with the stress in a particularly helpful way. This is a very difficult situation."

"You think?"

"And look at the state of you," Claudia said with a frown. "Your nose looks like a squashed slug and your right eye is completely fucked."

"Like yours is any better," Maya said, genuinely affronted now. "We can't walk next to each other when they start to heal and get all yellow. We'll look like Flotsam and Jetsam."

"Who?"

"From the Little Mermaid," she said, her brow wrinkling as she wondered if she was making this up. "You know? Ursula's...pets? I don't know, the two eel things that put their eyes together so she can see."

"I have no idea what you're talking about and since when are you into Disney films?"

"It was one of my favourite films as a kid," she scowled as she sat down. "And don't judge me, Claudia, I'm hanging on by a thread here."

Claudia stayed silent as she sat next to her but rubbed her shoulder reassuringly. Maya let out a grateful sigh and turned her attention to the awkward gathering. She and Claudia were sitting on one side of Felipe, Rebecca and her parents on the other. Their guards were no longer holding onto them but weren't far away and two more had appeared to stand behind Maya and Claudia. The man who had been fiddling with the canister was now wandering around them with containers full of liquid. When he handed Maya hers she took a large gulp of it, assuming it was water and almost choked as it burned down her throat, gagging as pure vodka hit her stomach.

"Fuck," she gasped.

"Something to relax you," Felipe smiled at her as though he hadn't kicked her in the face moments earlier.

"Don't count on it," she coughed. "Vodka gives me rage."

"Alright, let's begin shall we?" he said cheerfully. "Thanks to your combined efforts we have made excellent progress in finding the lost city of the Inca. However, we have now reached an impasse. End of the line. There are no more clues to be had after the steps, and yet here we sit, in a ruin not even close to the size or craftsmanship of Vitcos, let alone Vilcabamba. And so I reviewed the journal of Manuelo and came back to this code on the final page. I suspected there would be a corresponding one in Zuazola's and I was right."

Felipe flipped open the final page of their journal, a page Maya had barely glanced at after the text ran out as it was so faded she thought it was a watermark, and held it up next to Manuelo's. The pattern on each page skirted on and off the edge, every time it left one book it linked up perfectly to the other and the pattern resembled the body of a snake. Maya sucked in a breath and shook her head as she let it out softly.

"Would you like a closer look?" Felipe asked.

She frowned across at him and nodded in surprise. He passed her the books with a smile and watched as she held them together and studied the pattern. She stared down at the books as the wheels in her mind started turning, trying to find meaning in the jumble of black squares on the pages. A set of three on one side, two a little higher up, a line of them at the edge of the page, a void followed by a dark mass. There were no markers to give context and she stared at the pattern in despair, her brain starting to hurt as she felt the expectation of the group settle on her. She closed her eyes and let out a ragged breath, the blood pounding in her ears as she felt every injury she had sustained since they had reached the top of the stairs. She remembered the fear she had felt as they fled through the ruins, the certainty that she was going to die as she cowered in the hut with Claudia. The hut. One of three.

Suddenly her mind cleared and she held her breath, visualising the ruins as she slowly opened her eyes and stared down at the pages again. She felt her pulse quicken as the pattern took form and she forced herself to stay calm so as not to give anything away.

She studied the pages for a few more minutes, considering her plan carefully as she stared off at the thick tree line between the two buildings in front of her, watching the sun shining over the mountain in the distance, noticing how the forest stayed even between the two points, each tree seemingly summoned to a uniform height. She sighed as she looked at Claudia studying the pattern over her shoulder. After a moment or two Claudia looked up at her with a shrug, freezing mid gesture as she saw the look in her eyes. Maya raised her eyebrows questioningly as recognition settled on Claudia's face and she received the smallest of nods in return. She looked down at the books once more, hoping against hope that she was right as she tipped her drink over them and flung them into the heart of the fire.

"No!" Felipe roared, jumping up and trying to reach the burning books, fury flashing in his eyes as he turned to Maya. He started barking orders at the guards and Maya was grabbed roughly about the throat and dragged backwards as several of the men tried to stamp out the fire and get to the journals. Maya's victory was short lived as a seemingly endless succession of kicks and punches were rained down on her. Finally it ended and she lay there curled in a ball, her breath ragged, her mind reeling with what she had just done and if it would be worth it.

"You stupid little bitch!" Felipe spat at her as he stood over her and cocked his gun. "I will shoot you in the stomach and leave you out here to die a slow and painful death for that."

"You could," she coughed, spitting out a trail of blood. "But then you'll never know how to get there."

"What makes you think I don't already?" he hissed, leaning down and jamming the gun into her cheek.

"If you did you'd never have given me the books."

Felipe blinked at her a couple of times as her statement registered with him, his face splitting into a smile as he lowered the gun and stood up. "You are right, of course," he nodded. "And you have placed me in an unfortunate position."

"I don't see how," she shrugged. "Let my friends go and I'll take you to the city. Sounds fairly simple to me."

"I am afraid I can't do that," he said with a shake of his head. "Imagine how it will look to my employer when news of this discovery breaks and your friends come forward to ruin his triumph with tales of murder and kidnap?"

"Then you'll just have to kill us all and hope you stumble across it," Maya said, forcing her voice to take on a bored tone as she pulled her right arm up against her body, feeling it gingerly as she tried to work out if it was fractured.

"I don't think you quite understand, Ms Rodriguez," Felipe said, his voice lowering as he dropped into a crouch and locked eyes with her. "You will all die either way, even your friends in Boca. The only decision you have is whether you want your friends to die quickly or agonisingly slowly."

Maya swallowed thickly, the glint in his eye leaving her with no doubt that he meant every word. "What about if we all promise really hard?" she said, determined not to let him see she was scared. She reached out her left hand and extended her little finger. "Pinky swear?"

"Let's start with Claudia, shall we?" Felipe gestured behind himself. "Marco, give the redhead a haircut, please."

Marco immediately grabbed Claudia's hair and yanked her head back. He pulled out a knife and brought it quickly round to the front of her head, pressing it into her skin just under the hairline.

"Stop!" Maya yelled, attempting to jump up but being held down by Felipe. "I swear to God if you hurt her you will get nothing from me and I will die trying to kill you!"

"Wait, Marco," Felipe drawled. "Are you ready to tell me where to go then?"

"I was born ready for that," she muttered, looking over at Claudia with a frown as a thin trickle of blood ran down the centre of her face.

"What?"

"I'll show you where it is," she said. "I won't tell you."

"Marco," he sighed.

"Just stop with the threats, Felipe, okay?" Maya snapped, holding her hands up in frustration and wincing as pain shot up her right arm. "We both know that the minute you hurt one of them I will tell you nothing, so just cut to the chase, grab whatever you need and let's go."

Felipe eyed her thoughtfully for a moment as he weighed up her argument. "Alright," he agreed. "But just you. The rest stay here."

"No way," she said firmly. "I have seen what your boys are like when you're not around. Not a chance."

He turned and looked around the group, Maya following his gaze. Claudia's eyes were blazing with anger, the blood trickling down her face had run across her right eyelid and gave her a crazy look, like Sissy Spacek at the end of Carrie. Rebecca was watching calmly, her face devoid of all expression which, to Maya's mind, was scarier than Claudia's fury any day.

"Fine," he said finally. "But I must insist that the elder Bronsteins stay here. They are weak and will slow us down."

"Well then blame the guy who has been holding them hostage and starving them to death," she said with a shrug. "If we leave them here you'll have them killed the minute we're gone. We go together or not at all."

"You drive a hard bargain," he sighed. "Fine."

Felipe stood up and barked orders at his men who quickly gathered up the necessary equipment and moved to leave the camp, pushing her now gagged and bound friends in front of them as Felipe pulled Maya roughly to her feet and motioned with his gun for her to move. She glared at him and then up at the sky as she limped forward. Where in God's name were Elaine's team? They had better hurry the hell up or there would be no one left for them to rescue.

"Which way are we going?" Felipe asked her as they walked to the front of the group.

"This way," she muttered, pointing in between the two buildings and leading them along the path.

"How far?"

"I don't know exactly. It's not like they put an inches to miles conversion chart at the bottom."

"Roughly then," he said. "In your opinion?"

"I don't know, Felipe," she sighed. "Maybe two miles? Maybe ten?"

"I am starting to get the feeling you are lying to me, Maya," he said, pulling a knife from his belt and inspecting it casually. "I dislike being lied to."

"That makes two of us."

"But the difference is if you are lying to me people are going to start suffering a great deal of physical pain."

"As opposed to just getting shot in the head?"

"I will give you two hours to show me that you know what you are doing," he smiled. "Then one of your friends will pay the price."

Maya turned to look at him. There was no point in arguing, she knew that, and if her theory was right she wouldn't need to so she just let it go. She figured that the six squares on the snake's tail were the ruins where she and Claudia had first been attacked, the three on the start of its body Felipe's camp. After that there was a blank space which she assumed was this trail they were on, and then it was just the thick black line which she hoped represented the jungle ahead. If she was wrong they were as good as dead. She looked up at the sky again, willing the helicopter to appear and get them the hell out of here. If Elaine's team didn't get here in the next twenty minutes they would probably be too late.

Maya slowed and looked around for any sign of movement, the difference this time being that she desperately hoped there would be some, but she saw nothing. She sighed and stopped in front of a thick patch of forest, staring into it as she wondered if she was right and/or if this was where she would die. Everything hurt and she was starting to have trouble breathing.

"Why have you stopped?" Felipe asked her.

"This is it."

"What do you mean?"

"This is where we need to go," she said, gesturing at the forest.

Felipe turned and looked at it. The trees were so thick here it looked almost impenetrable and he looked back at her suspiciously, smiling as he shook his head.

"Do you take me for a fool, Maya?"

"No, Felipe," she said, returning his smile as she cradled her damaged arm. "I take you for a lot of things, but not a fool."

"Do you really expect me to believe that the entrance to the lost city of the Inca is through here?" Felipe spat. "How would they have transported the material to build it?"

"I have no idea," she sighed. "It's not like I was around at the time. How did they get the rocks up the side of the mountain to build Machu Picchu?"

He thought about this for a second and then waved three of the men forward, instructing them to start cutting. "If you are lying to me…"

"Yeah, yeah, I know," she rubbed the back of her neck, praying that this could all just stop. "Pain, torture, death. I get it."

"I hope you do," he replied quietly, stepping right up to her. "Don't test me, Maya. You do not want to see what I am capable of."

She narrowed her eyes and held her ground, really wishing she could hurt this prick. "I have your boot mark on my face, Felipe," she shot back, her voice dangerously low. "I think I have an idea."

He laughed and folded his arms, fixing her with an amused expression. "On second thought, I believe you. Or at least I believe that you think this is the place. You are by far the worst liar I have ever met. Your, ah, friend here," he gestured at Rebecca. "Is far more skilled. Had I not already known exactly why you were all here she may have fooled even me."

"Is there a point to this?" Maya asked. "Or is this share time part of your torture routine?"

"I was just thinking how frustrating it must be," he chuckled. "For someone with such a problem with trust to be so incapable of spotting when they are being lied to. It made it very easy to create tension in your group."

"Oh really?" she scoffed. "That was part of your plan, was it?"

"Of course," Felipe shrugged. "From when I first met you I saw that you were fighting, and that your way of dealing with conflict was to ignore it, whereas hers was to push for reaction. When we set out and you were together again I decided to give you information about her parents, knowing that you would not tell her but when confronted you would be unable to lie which would cause you to fight again. All too easy."

"Well, bravo, Puppet Master," she sneered. "But I'm confused as to exactly where us ditching you figured in your plan?"

"Yes, that was unexpected, I will admit," he nodded. "But, as I was listening to yourself and Claudia discuss your route in the tent I knew it would not be long until our paths crossed again. A shame, though. I felt that you trusted me at that point and would start to explain to me how you had worked it out. Things would have been a lot easier if you had."

"Yeah, and we'd probably all be dead by now."

"True," he admitted.

"So I call that a score for my 'problem with trust'."

"Oh, Maya," Felipe laughed. "I had heard such wonderful things about you as well. Imagine my disappointment when I discovered you were nothing but a damaged little girl with a big mouth."

"Yeah, that must have been devastating," she smiled. "Thankfully all I know about you is that you are Martin Amaric's lap dog, so I am perfectly satisfied."

Something dark and dangerous flashed across his eyes and it took everything she had not to flinch as her blood ran cold. He leaned in closer and whispered in her ear. "I am going to enjoy breaking you before you die."

"Patrão!" a voice shouted from the forest. "Há algo aqui atrás!"

Felipe snapped his eyes towards the trees and back at Maya with a cruel smirk. "Let's go."

He dragged her towards the newly cut path, pulling on her damaged arm with a sneer. She bit down on her lip hard enough to draw blood and her eyes swam in and out of focus as she tried to fight back the pain.

"Felipe," Alfonse called after them. "What about the rest?"

"Kill them," he replied without looking back. "Slowly."

Maya threw her full weight against him, pain screaming up her arm and rattling her skull like a pinball machine, white heat flashing across her eyes as she tried to scramble back towards her friends. She cried out as her head was yanked back, Felipe having managed to grab hold of her hair as she had made her escape, and she was dragged across the floor, her feet scrabbling to find purchase. She succeeded and shoved herself backwards, slamming into him again and knocking them both to the floor.

Felipe let out a volley of curses and wrapped his arm around her throat, choking her as he dragged her back to her feet, twisting her broken arm behind her back to force her into submission. She tried to pull herself away from him, bile rising up her throat as the bones in her arm ground against each other.

"If you would stop struggling this would go far easier for both of us," he hissed in her ear.

"Right," she gritted out as he loosened his grip slightly in an effort to make her walk. "Just a nice easy stroll through the woods while my friends are being murdered."

Felipe gave a low laugh and shoved her onward down the path his men had hacked through the trees as a shot rang out behind them. Maya slammed her eyes shut, all the fight going out of her as she tried not to think about what that meant, the laughter assaulting her ears growing louder with every second. They arrived at the end of the dense part of the forest and he paused as the ground dropped away, the trees in front of them reaching the same height as the ones on their level but rooted far below on the valley floor, a clear path between their trunks in which several stone buildings had been erected, their formation a clear S shape. In the distance, its base just visible from their position, was a much larger building, and glinting through the trees a large red jewel shone at its peak.

"It is beautiful," he breathed as he shoved her to the ground and walked past her, stepping towards the edge and staring out over the valley. After a moment he looked over his shoulder and smiled at her. "A shame your friends did not live to see this, no?"

Maya felt a rage like she had never felt before burning through her veins, her face shaking and her lip curling as she pushed herself up and ran at him, throwing herself at him with a yell. He sidestepped her with a laugh and punched her broken arm, laughing uproariously as she fell to the ground, pulling his gun on her as she tried to get back up and jamming it into her face. She lay there, staring up at him, seething with anger, pushing her face up towards the gun, recognising nothing but the sound of gunfire.

Gunfire which had not stopped. The first shot had been followed by another, and another, so many in fact that Maya briefly wondered if someone had lit some firecrackers. Felipe seemed to realise at the same time and a look of confusion fell over his face as he turned to stare back the way they had come. In a flash Maya knocked the gun out of his hand and slammed her leg up into his crotch, feeling a surge of satisfaction as he fell to the ground with a muted cry of pain. She rolled over and reached for his gun, feeling a crack in her ribs as he kicked her sharply and got to his feet, his face contorted with pain and anger. She scrambled to reach the weapon before he did and flipped onto her back to point it at him, cursing as she pulled the trigger and realised the safety was still on.

He sneered and came at her fast, her fingers shaking as she tried to find the catch, and then he was on her, kicking and punching as he towered over her. With all her remaining strength she swung out her leg and connected with his feet, her blow taking him by surprise and dropping him at an awkward angle. As soon as he was down he rolled over to try and pin her but she pushed up with her hips and the momentum flipped him over, his legs landing at the edge of the cliff and his haste to get back up causing the weak ground to give way.

With a startled yell he grabbed out for anything he could to hold himself up, clutching at Maya's left wrist with a wild look in his eye. Instinctively she grabbed onto him, his weight dragging her to the edge of the precipice. They stared into each other's eyes as the reality of the situation began to sink in, and Felipe's face dropped into a resigned smirk.

"It seems, once again," he panted, sweat running down his face as his other hand grabbed for the edge. "That you have put me in an unfortunate situation, Maya."

"Yeah, well," she answered through clenched teeth. "If you turn around you'll have an incredible last view."

"You will not drop me," he said, the tiniest hint of uncertainty in his voice betraying him. "It is not your way."

"Is that what you think?" Maya sneered at him.

"Yes, that is what I think. Listen to what's going on out there. That is not my men, there are too many weapons. Clearly someone has come to your aid, so you will pull me up and hand me over to them," he said as he tried to cling onto the crumbling ledge. "You are not a murderer, Maya."

Maya stared down at him, his smug voice reminding her all too clearly of what he had put them all through. Slowly she released her grip on his arm, feeling oddly calm as he looked up at her with panic in his eyes. "You have no idea what I'm capable of. If you did you wouldn't have ordered the murder of people I care about."

"Don't do this, Maya," he said, desperate now, his feet scrabbling for purchase on the cliff face as his hands began to lose their grip. "You won't be able to live with this."

"I'll be fine," she whispered, clenching her hand into a fist and yanking her arm out of his grasp.

She felt no emotion as his eyes went wide and he started to fall, his mouth opening to let out a scream that seemed to start like a mistimed backing track, and she watched as he disappeared into the trees below, the sound ending abruptly and leaving her hollow. She sat and stared down, her mouth suddenly dry and her breath causing her neck muscles to stutter. Slowly, she lifted her eyes and found herself looking at the blood red ruby on top of the temple, thinking about how excited Claudia would be to see it.

Claudia.

Maya jumped up and ran back along the path, grabbing the discarded gun from the floor as she went, everything in her hoping that the prolonged gunfire was from Elaine's team and that they had got there in time. She skidded to a halt as Alfonse stepped out of the forest in front of her, time slowing down as she raised her weapon at the same time as he did, white hot pain spreading across her chest as he staggered backwards and fell to the floor. She dropped to her knees, the pain in her right arm not seeming so bad as she pressed it against her chest. She looked down in confusion, cold fear rushing through her as she saw the bloom of red spreading across her top.

"Shit," she swore softly, her left hand trembling and dropping the gun on the floor as she realised what was happening.

"Maya!"

She looked up and saw Claudia running out of the trees followed by a bunch of guys in black combat suits holding guns. "Claudia?" she said with a small laugh as everything started to go black. "I think I fucked up."

Chapter 37

Maya woke with a start and tried to sit up, confusion swirling through her brain as she couldn't, her eyes rolling in her head as she tried to focus on her surroundings. Slowly she became aware of white walls, the low whirr and quiet beeping of machinery, a strong smell of antiseptic thinly masking the underlying odour of blood and sickness. She raised her left hand and saw wires snaking out of it, her other arm held in place by a cast. She tried to swallow but her tongue was stuck to the roof of her mouth.

She blinked her eyes a couple more times to try and focus and eventually made out Claudia's sleeping form in a chair by the window. She did not look comfortable. Maya dropped her head back onto the pillow, a tiredness unlike anything she had ever known washing over her and dragging her back down.

When she opened her eyes again the light in the room had changed, darker and hazy now, and there was a weight on her legs. She looked down to see brown hair splayed across the bed, Rebecca's hand resting on her own. She tried to swallow again and couldn't, her body tensing with the effort. The movement woke Rebecca and she looked up at her with sleepy eyes.

"Hey, you're awake," she said, a smile splitting her face as she sat up quickly and moved out of her chair to be closer to her. "How do you feel?"

Maya opened her mouth to respond but only managed a croak and a hiss as the effort cracked her dry lips. Rebecca reached behind the curtain and opened a bottle of water, putting a straw in it before holding it up so Maya could drink. She sucked on it gratefully, her stomach clenching and protesting as the liquid hit it, and she coughed and spluttered as she fought not to bring it back up. Pain shot through her shoulder and she gritted her teeth as stars exploded behind her eyes.

"Easy," Rebecca said softly, her cool hand brushing the hair from her forehead and calming her down. "Just take it easy."

She kept her eyes shut and waited for the pain to die back down, the heaviness settling over her again as much as she tried to fight it.

"How long?" she managed to croak out.

"Two days," she heard Rebecca answer just before she went back under.

The next time she woke up it was to the quiet murmur of voices and she groggily looked about as she tried to identify their source.

"Hey, Tex," she slurred as she made out Claudia and Tom standing by the door. A vague memory stirred. Had she been dreaming about him? "You have a hole in your stomach."

"Yes I do," he said with a smile as Claudia rushed over to the bed and gave her a careful hug. "And you have one in your chest."

"Shit, really?" she said, trying to look down in confusion. "Lucky I don't have a heart."

"Hey," Claudia said softly. "How are you feeling?"

"Peachy," Maya murmured, her head lolling as she tried to focus on her friend. "Floaty."

"That'll be all the drugs they've got you on, then," she smiled as she squeezed her hand. "Do you need anything?"

"Lots of things." she said. Or maybe she didn't. She didn't know. She didn't care. She lay her head down and went back to sleep.

Maya groaned and tried to shift her position. She felt stiff and all wrong, like nothing was where it was meant to be.

"Finally," a voice said from beside her. "I thought I was going to have to slap you."

She opened an eye cautiously, frowning in confusion as she tried to work out what she was seeing. "Elaine?"

"Do try and focus, Maya, I don't have all day to spend on idle chatter," the woman said as she reached behind her for some water. "Drink some of this."

Maya eyed her warily as she took a sip of the water, something telling her not to drink too much. "What are you doing here?" she asked as she lay back down.

"I would have thought that was obvious," Elaine replied tersely. "You were idiotic enough to get yourself almost killed as you made one of the most important discoveries of the last hundred years, so I have been forced to come out here and make sure our interests are taken care of."

"Sorry," she muttered, closing her eyes and willing herself to go back to sleep. Sadly it would appear that that part of her recovery was over. Perfect timing.

"Don't be ridiculous, Maya," the other woman said softly, her tone causing Maya to open her eyes again in surprise. "I'm just glad you're okay."

"What?"

Elaine tutted and moved towards the door. "I see your brush with death has not improved your ability to read people. I will be back tomorrow. Hopefully you will have regained some of your faculties by then."

With that she was gone, leaving Maya alone in the room and wondering just exactly how many drugs they had her on. Instead, she started to remember what had happened, the things she had seen and done over the last few weeks. The fort, the petroglyphs, the lake and caves, the trek through the jungle, the stones, the waterfall, the city. Felipe. Felipe's face as he fell. As she let him fall.

She slammed her eyes shut and pushed her head back into the pillow, her throat working as she tried to force down the bile that was trying to come up, images assaulting the backs of her eyelids as she tried to push them away. A falling body, a broken face, a giant of a man dropping to his knees. She started to shake, her breath caught in her throat as it all came back too quickly, too much, and she heard a noise, a keening sound, which after a while she realised was coming from her own mouth.

"Hey, hey, ssh, it's okay," she heard Claudia say, a hand reaching behind her head to help her sit up slightly, a plastic bowl in front of her to catch the bile as it spewed out of her.

She lay back down and squeezed her eyes shut, her nausea receding a bit as Claudia held onto her hand and sat next to her, her strong, silent presence keeping her grounded.

"I fucked up, Claud," she managed after a few minutes, abject misery swirling around her, tears leaking out from behind her eyelids against her will.

"No, I fucked up," Claudia replied gently. "I should never have left Elaine in here alone. I might have known you would choose that exact moment to wake up. I'm sure you did it just to piss me off."

Maya huffed out a wet laugh at this, her friend's inappropriate humour cracking a small ray of light into her darkness. "Yeah, well you know me," she muttered. "I live to piss you off."

"That's right," Claudia smiled at her. "And just you remember that next time you decide to run full pelt at a maniac with a gun."

"Well, it's not like I knew he was there," she protested. "I was just trying to get back to you guys."

Claudia sighed and squeezed her hand. "Fine. I will let it go for now but later we are going to have a proper discussion on the art of self preservation. Honestly, Maya, look at the state of you. Your mother is going to have a shit fit."

"Jesus," Maya said, trying to sit up. "You didn't tell her, did you?"

"No," she answered with a sad shake of her head. "Honestly, that first night I really should have but I...well, I couldn't really…"

"I'm sorry, Claud," she said softly, tugging on her friend's hand.

"So you should be, you bastard," Claudia said, clearing her throat as she ran her fingers under her eyes. "You promised me you wouldn't die. You know how much it annoys me when I have to worry about you."

"Well I kept my promise didn't I?"

"Only just," she said quietly before shaking her head and forcing a smile onto her face. "So, Rebecca is on her way back and she is really excited to show you the pictures. Do you feel up for it?"

"Sure," she said, attempting to shrug as best she could with her broken body and new realisation of how close she had been to dying. "Pictures?"

"You know," Claudia said with a frown. "Of the city. We figured it will be at least a week til you get to see it yourself so…"

"Right," she cut her off, looking down at her broken arm. "They won't let me out for a week?"

"Well, maybe before that, they do seem to be quite impressed with your recovery so far," Claudia shrugged. "But I think it would be a good idea if you got some rest first."

"Yeah, I guess you're right," she sighed. "How's everyone else?"

"Tom is doing okay. He went back out with Rebecca today, it's the first time he's been so…"

"He didn't go with you?"

"No, I, er, well I didn't want to leave," she said as she went behind the curtain to get some water. "You know, it wouldn't be the same without you there trying to act all nonchalant but really looking like a kid at Christmas."

"Shut up," Maya laughed as she took the drink with her good hand. "You should have gone. After everything we've been through, I can't believe you just sat here. It's kind of a big deal, Claud."

"Yes, well, I was more interested in whether or not my best friend was going to wake up," Claudia snapped, pushing her hair out of her face and folding her arms. "And it will still be there when you are able to go with me."

"Claudia…" Maya started, not really sure how to apologise for almost dying.

"Anyway, Phil, Candace and Vanessa are fine, thankfully," she continued quickly. "They came to see you a few days ago, but obviously you were asleep. They have been out at the site with Rebecca's parents most of the time."

"That's good. I'm glad everyone's okay."

"Well, not everyone," Claudia frowned.

"What do you mean?"

"Madalena, Rebecca's contact," she sighed. "When she didn't turn up for the meeting Vanessa went looking for her."

"Vanessa?"

"Yes," Claudia smiled ruefully. "She is the one who got most of the information and fed it back to Elaine. At any rate, Madelena had found a potential lead for Rebecca, went to follow it up and never came back. Unfortunately for her that lead was Felipe. Needless to say he didn't like the questions she was asking and he killed her the morning we set off."

"Fuck," Maya said softly. "Rebecca must have taken that hard."

"She did," she nodded. "She obviously feels responsible. Anyway, Vanessa followed her trail, somehow without attracting attention, and found the link between Felipe and Amaric. After we spoke to Elaine at the stones she contacted Candace, who was by this point frantic because she hadn't heard from Rebecca to tell her all this, and by the time I managed to contact Elaine after Tom was shot she had put it all together and told me to get you out. Unfortunately by then it was too late."

"Yeah," Maya sighed, dropping her head back onto the pillow as the images started flashing through her mind again.

"Are you okay?"

"Yeah," she nodded. "I am a little tired, actually."

"Oh," she said with a slight frown. "Okay. Do you want me to stay?"

"Why? You want to watch me sleep?" Maya smirked. "Pervert."

"Oh, good, the bitch is back," she huffed as she squeezed her hand again and stood up. "Definitely on the mend then. Honestly, I am going to start calling you Wolverine from now on."

"Great, there's an attractive nickname," she laughed as she rolled her eyes. "I'll see you later, okay?"

"Of course," Claudia smiled from the doorway. "Get some sleep."

Maya nodded and smiled back. She felt bad lying to her friend but she really needed some space to think. She sighed and shifted in the bed, her whole body sore and stiff from her injuries and lying in the bed for the last...however many days she had been unconscious. And there was just so much to sort through, so many things that she never thought she would have to deal with. It was all too much. She decided to start with the easy stuff. Elaine was here. That was unexpected. She wondered what it meant? They had found Paititi. She allowed herself a smile as she focussed on that piece of information, but the smile was tinged with the feeling of unease that had followed her around for the last week. What happened now?

The door opened quietly and Maya looked over to see Rebecca stepping into the room carefully. Her eyes went wide as she saw Maya was awake and she stopped awkwardly half in half out.

"Shit, sorry," she whispered. "I thought you would be asleep."

"Well I'm not so why are you whispering?" Maya laughed softly.

"I..." Rebecca's brow wrinkled in confusion as her shoulders dropped. "I don't know. Sorry."

"Stop saying sorry and come in," she said in amusement.

Rebecca smiled at her and closed the door before walking over to the bed. "How are you feeling?"

"Like I lost a fight with an angry freight train," she shrugged. "How are you?"

"Good," she nodded, tucking her hair behind her ears. "Better. I just..."

"What?" Maya said when Rebecca stayed silent.

"I'm just..." she took a breath and breathed it out slowly before looking up at her. "I'm so sorry, Maya, I never meant..."

"Rebecca," she interrupted gently. "Don't. Please. Felipe played us. We never stood a chance."

"But if I had just listened to you…"

"Yeah, and if I had just listened to you I would never have fallen for it," Maya sighed. "I was so blinded by my anger with you that it never occurred to me you were right about him."

"Well maybe if I'd been honest with you from the start," she said, her eyes trained on her own hands, feet shifting uncomfortably on the floor.

"Yeah, but you weren't," she shrugged. "And I understand why, honestly I do, but it doesn't change anything. What's done is done. Felipe saw where we were vulnerable and he exploited that."

"What do you mean?" Rebecca asked with a frown.

"Why do you think he told us about the other group?" she asked. "They were his men. What did he have to gain by letting us know they were out there?"

"I don't know. I guess I never thought about it."

"He picked up on the tension between us back in Boca do Acre and figured he could play us against each other," Maya sighed. "When we got out there he saw that we were closer so he fed us this bullshit story about his farmer friend spotting a second group, drip feeding me the information and acting like he didn't trust me to distract me from the fact I didn't trust him, knowing that when I told you you would freak out about your parents and probably take it out on me."

"Which I did," she said, dropping her head again.

Maya said nothing. Really what was there to say? When all was said and done they had put themselves in that position by allowing their own shit to cloud their judgement. She was just grateful the price had not been steeper. At least not for them.

"So," she said, clearing her throat to break the tension. "You have pictures to show me?"

"Ah, yeah," Rebecca said, shaking her head quickly and smiling as she swung her bag onto the bed and pulled out her camera. "It's so beautiful, Maya. I can't wait for you to see it in person."

"Yeah," she said, forcing a smile onto her face.

Rebecca turned on the screen and allowed Maya to flick through the pictures, giving her a running commentary as each new image loaded. The sequence started with a shot from above, and Maya shifted uncomfortably as she recognised the angle. She flicked to the next shot quickly, the houses getting larger and more ornate with each image, all of them paling in comparison to the temple. From ground level it was truly breathtaking, its wide base building to a point, a finely crafted doorway in the centre and there, sat on top like the eye they had seen in the caves, a blood red ruby at least five feet in diameter, set in a beautifully carved piece of stone, shining like the eye of a serpent. It was absolutely incredible. How in the hell had a besieged race, on the run from an enemy that had utterly destroyed them, half a world away from home, managed to create something so astoundingly beautiful? Maya felt herself welling up and choked the emotion back down, blaming her pain medication for the uncharacteristic display.

"Are you okay?" Rebecca asked with a concerned frown.

"Yeah, sorry, it's just," she leaned back and huffed out a breath. "It's just a little overwhelming, you know?"

"I know," she answered, perching carefully on the edge of the bed and running a hand gently over Maya's leg. "Especially for you."

"Oh yeah?" Maya said, staring down at her with a frown. "How's that?"

"It seems like your mind never stops working," she smiled. "Even now, seeing all this properly for the first time, I bet only about half of your brain is just enjoying what we have fought so hard to find, while the other half is wondering what will happen next and thinking of all the ways it could go wrong."

Maya laughed softly and looked down at the camera, wondering once again how it was this woman seemed to be able to read her like a book. "Good guess."

"It's not a guess, Maya," she said, playing nervously with her fingers, a frown on her face. "There's a reason you and I got off to a bad start, remember? Because of my parents. Because of the coverage they get. And now we're all here and we've found this. So tell me, what's on your mind?"

"It's just…" Maya started, turning the camera round so she could see the picture of the entrance to the temple. "I mean look at it, Rebecca. It's perfect."

"Yes it is."

"And part of that perfection is the fact that it's so untouched and I just feel…" she sighed and looked down at the picture with a shake of her head. "I know we can't unfind it. I just wish we could protect it."

"It's not ours to protect, Maya."

"Then whose is it?"

"I don't know," Rebecca said gently. "Someone with a lot more authority and knowledge than us."

"What, like the government?" Maya scoffed. "You've seen what they're doing to the rainforest here, the fact that they cut down huge areas of it for profit is what led us to the idea this could be here in the first place. When they find out they've been sitting on something bigger than Machu Picchu this whole time they'll cut a highway through here and turn it into a goddamn theme park."

"Of course they won't! There's no highway been built to Machu Picchu."

"No, but there is a railway line and a fucking luxury hotel. Tours are now limited for fear of damaging the area, but not enough and way too late if you ask me, and still people come. And Machu Picchu is not in the middle of the fucking rainforest!"

"I don't really know what to say," Rebecca said after a moment.

"I don't either," she sighed as she flicked to the next picture and realised this was the only way she would ever see it.

"I think you should talk to Elaine," Rebecca said cautiously. "Maybe the fact that we found it will give us some say in how it is handled?"

"Unlikely, seeing as we were never officially supposed to be out here," she said sadly. "Besides governments aren't really fond of outsiders telling them how to run their business. Especially not 'Americanos'".

"Well, then work with us to spread awareness. With the media coverage…"

"No," Maya said sharply. "I am not going to get caught up in some media circus. That's your world, not mine."

"Right," she said slowly. "I am so pleased you've learned so much about me in our time together."

"Jesus, that's not…" Maya stared up at the ceiling and took a breath to organise her thoughts. "Look, I just meant that I'm not a Hiram Bingham, and I'm definitely not like your parents. I leave all that stuff to Elaine. I'm just an archaeologist. Following leads, solving riddles, finding things, that's what I love. Can't you understand that?"

"Of course I can, Maya," she smiled. "That energy and passion you have, that's what I love about you. That's what everyone loves about you, even the ones who think you're a bitch."

"Great," she said with a tight smile.

"Kind of puts a dent in our whole Han/Leia dynamic if you feel that way," Rebecca said sadly, drawing her hands up into her lap. "You think I'm in it for the money? The fame?"

Maya took a deep breath as she tried to reconcile the woman before her with the things she had heard and seen. "I just...this? What happens next? I want no part of it."

"You want no part of this?" Rebecca asked, her expression guarded. "Does that include me?"

Maya stared at the camera, barely seeing the golden throne framed on the screen, her mind working furiously to answer that question, the same way it had been for the last two weeks. As usual she couldn't come up with the words to explain her conflict, so she just sat there, the tension between them growing with each passing second.

"Okay then," Rebecca said quietly. "Well then I guess...I'm just gonna, um…"

She turned and walked towards the door, hugging her arms around herself as she went.

"Rebecca," Maya called after her, her head pounding with unspoken words and the stress of everything that had happened. Rebecca stopped and turned back towards her, her eyes bright. "I'm sorry. I just...this whole thing has been...well, you know how it's been. You were there."

Rebecca smiled and took a small step back towards her. "I was."

"And I don't what happens next," she sighed. "I mean, I really have no idea. But, maybe if you, you know, want to call when you get home. Maybe we could talk."

"Okay," Rebecca said, her eyes on the floor. "Okay." She looked up at her with a small smile, swallowed quickly and bit on her bottom lip then nodded once and turned to walk out, leaving Maya lying there alone, staring down at the images of a place she would never step foot in.

"Everything alright?" Claudia asked softly from the door a few minutes later.

"Fine," she muttered, earning a disbelieving murmur from her friend.

Eventually Claudia let out a deep sigh and walked over to the bed, leaning against it as she turned to look at Maya.

"You're not going back there, are you?"

"No," Maya nodded sadly. "As soon as they let me out I'm going home. If I make enough of a fuss I'm hoping it'll be tomorrow."

"I think that's a little ambitious, Maya, even for you," Claudia smiled.

"Well, whatever but it better be soon," she huffed as she closed her eyes and lay back on the pillows. "Come see me on your way home?"

"Please," she scoffed. "As if I'd stay here without you? Besides, your mother would kill me if you arrived home in this state without me to explain that it was entirely your own fault."

"I don't think she'll take much convincing," Maya said with a roll of her eyes. "I was just planning on avoiding her for the next six to seven months till I'm all healed up. Or hopefully all healed up."

"Well you can't do that!" Claudia said firmly, whacking her playfully in the leg. "Once she's had the opportunity to yell at you for a few days and make you feel infinitely worse than you already do, she'll start cooking for you and it'll all be worth it."

"Yeah, for you," she huffed. "You just want her rum cake."

"I can't deny it," her friend admitted with a shrug. "It has been way too long since I have had any and it's my favourite thing in all the land."

"Which land?"

"All the lands."

"And what about Tom?" Maya asked curiously. "After you left him in the woods to die…"

"I did not leave him in the woods to die," Claudia scoffed. "He was quite safe after we hacked into their feed. Unless, you know, he'd had to run anywhere. Your field bandage was good but not quite enough to hold if he'd had to move suddenly. At any rate, he's clearly not too upset with me as he has asked to meet up once we get back to New York."

"Right, so I have a housemate for a while, huh?"

"Of course," she smiled. "Or I can look after your apartment whilst you stay at your mother's and get better."

"Oh, I see," Maya smiled at her and turned back to the camera to take a last look at the place they had almost given their lives to find.

The last shot was taken from outside the temple again, just as the sun hit the jewel above it and it gave off a deep, blood red glow, the colour of it richer than anything Maya had ever seen. As she lowered her gaze to the doorway the pillars on the steps seemed to fall inside the lines of the open doors and made her feel like she was looking at the bared fangs of a snake, the glow of the ruby warning her it was ready to pounce.

She pulled on her pendant and switched off the camera, staring out the window as she wondered what would become of it. After a moment Claudia patted her leg with a sigh and she looked up at her friend with a smile.

"Are you okay?" Claudia said quietly.

"I'm fine, Claud," Maya smiled, releasing her pendant and taking hold of her friend's hand. "I'm just fine."

Acknowledgements

To my family, especially my crazy parents, for helping me to turn into the kind of person who could write this - take that as you will!

To my friends for putting up with me and my one track mind for the last nine months, in addition to just generally putting up with me for the rest of the time you have known me…

To my army of proofreaders/ego strokers - Arti, Jackie, Jake, June, Lisa, Ophélia, Rix (#mayasbiggestfanalready), Shan (yamate), Stef… you are all legends.

To Dan, Rob and Gregory for containing my crazy when it threatened to take over the world.

To Jorge, Nicole and Fran for the random 3am messages like "How offended would you be if I said..(insert nonsensical Spanish/Portuguese swearing here)?"

To Pinar for getting me to see.

To Cynthia and Margaret. Miss you.

And finally to my Claudias - Marianne, Faye and Sacha. I don't know how you do it but I am eternally grateful that you do.